BOILERMAKER

By

David C. Brown

Book two of a modern man's adventures after fate has casted him into a parallel world of Civil War era technology, slavery, drugs, and competing colonial empires.

International Standard Book Nr: 978-0-9997994-0-6
1 2 3 4 5 6 7 8 9 0

Cover: Mark R. Hayes
Edit: Molly S. Brown
www.DavidCBrownAuthor.com
BISAC code FIC028010

Previously Published Works:
Concrete Girl
Serendipity Hollow
Gap Hollow
Sandlick Hollow
The Trashman's Daughter
Donnelly's War
Caroom's Raid
Nitro Wild

♠ Scott Depot, WV ♠

Boilermaker

Chapter 1

The ghastly medieval scene had Rex Knight wondering where he finds his optimism that a normal life is possible on this alien world. The heads of two men, jammed onto wooden stakes, bracketed the primitive dirt track cut through the massive virgin forest along Jarrell River. The buzz from a cloud of flies, yellow jackets, and hornets attracted to the rotten flesh and the occasional swish of a horse's tail the only sounds. He wondered if the others were having his difficulty of not staring at the fly-covered eyeball that dangled by its optic nerve from the head on the left. He knew those men. They had been part of a group of coal miners he had lectured on the importance of keeping black slate from contaminating the coal they sold to steamboats.

"I had them prospecting for a cleaner coal seam," Tom Jarrell, their employer, said. "They had left Smithtown a week ago to explore Jarrell River's unnamed southern fork. The area is uninhabited, except for a few Wapiti and Clovis families farming the river bottomland. No one expected this."

The people gathered on the trail in front of the appalling display—Jenny Jarrell, Tom Jarrell, Larry Hopkins, Lou Jarrell, and John Balers – were all Wapitis. They were veterans of the just-concluded war that had stopped Donnelly's slave raids on the Wapiti tribes. The men had served under Rex during the war. Jenny was

Larry's friend, Tom's niece, and a rescued slave. Larry Hopkins was the youngest veteran in the group, not yet eighteen, but he was a proven leader of men in battles. His advice had once saved Rex and the Wapitis from stumbling into an ambush. John Balers was another freed slave, about Rex's age of twenty-eight years, and a timber man and ex-sniper.

"Who would do this?" Jenny asked. She seemed sad, more curious, than alarmed. "I thought the war was over."

"I don't think anyone local murdered them," Rex said. "They would attempt to hide the deed, not flaunt it. I figure the prospectors were killed by strangers, probably Cinnabar's bandits."

"Or some of Donnelly's mercenaries," Tom said. The timber man was still irritated that some of the mercenaries had escaped. "They were good men, they didn't deserve this."

Amen to that, Rex thought, thinking of Earth. His modern world had vanished, gone without a moment's warning. It was the strangest thing. On that fateful day, he had been surveying, staking out the driveway to reach a new house site on a ridge overlooking Charleston. The complication was laying out the new drive to bypass a large sandstone boulder the property owner wanted left undisturbed. He was beside the rock when the cold blackness struck.

The boulder was still there when he regained consciousness. It looked the same. The topography of the ridge and valley looked the same. Only the city had vanished. Now, a forest of massive old oak and chestnut trees blanketed the ridge and river valley. He had no idea on what had occurred. Judging by the scorched twisted remains of his Topcon total station, that he had survived was the wonder. Later he had learned the inhabitants called the Earth like planet Erden.

Rex, endeavoring to understand how he had ended up in the alien world, had wondered if time travel might account for his experience after learning that the outpouring of melt water from glaciers fed the mighty Erie River. Similar conditions had occurred in the beginning of Earth's Holocene geological epoch. However, this world's stage of development, guns, colonial empires and steam engines, didn't resemble Earth's at the end of the last ice age. Then flint spear points and caves with wood fires were the advance technology.

The Wapiti language could support either explanation. It was a lingua franca of English and German, languages from Earth, and the indigenous Clovis language. Regardless, the presence of the non-human Ichneumons had convinced Rex that he was in an alternate universe, not back in an earlier Earth period. The Wapiti language meant other Earthlings in the past had been teleported and survived.

"We'll find the bastards responsible," Tom said, breaking the silence.

Similar in age to Rex, he was the patriarch of the large Jarrell clan. His father and two uncles had died a year ago, during an ambush by Donnelly's raiders. The Jarrells were timber men who were branching into coal mining. Tom and his brother, Lou, were formidable fighters.

"I reckon the party responsible for your cousins' deaths intended this gruesome display as a warning not to enter the Jarrell River's southern area." Rex added. Tom and Lou nodded.

If that was the murderer's purpose, a warning not to trespass, it was a futile effort, Rex thought. He had been around the group long enough to suspect that they all shared his aspirational and materialistic outlook. Their attitude was that the exploitation of the land's resources was their God-given opportunity for a better life, and threats wouldn't stop them.

"Well, sitting here won't accomplish anything," the older Jarrell brother said. "We'll need a posse to hunt down their murderers and avenge their deaths."

3

The fearsome Wapiti warrior's comment wasn't an idle threat. Though Tom's focus, like that of his younger brother Lou, was on their new coal mine, Rex was confident the brothers would never allow this affront to go unanswered.

"Mercenaries want to be paid, and with Donnelly dead, I can't think of anyone who would pay them to kill two prospectors," Larry said. "I have to agree, it was a warning to keep out. Cinnabar's warriors are the probable culprits, not wanting any interference with their slave raids. There are a lot of them, so a posse would be best."

"I have to go to Rainelle and finish some leftover war business," Rex said. "It'll take a couple of days. Some of you remember Jeb Piney. He's from the small Clovis community in the upper end of Jarrell River. We're going to hike into the backside of the watershed and visit his home. They might know the killers."

Jeb was another slave Donnelly's men captured eight years ago and whom the Wapitis had freed. His wife had escaped capture that day, and he wanted to returned home and learn her fate.

"Their families need told," Jenny said. She and Larry were side by side on their horses. Rex figured they would have been holding hands, except for the presence of her uncle.

"Lou and I will deal with the severed heads and tell their families," Tom said. "I'd like you, Jenny, to tell your mother and then the Smiths about what we found. And before you ask, no, you're not going with the posse. You're leaving for college."

Jenny Jarrell was an articulate girl, not yet sixteen, and she harbored strong opinions. Rex had wondered how she'd handle the strict, no-nonsense environment at Roanoke's Jesuit College.

Probably not well, Rex thought, because she was pushing the limit of acceptable Wapiti female apparel in her bright scarlet pants with the cut-off legs and a sleeveless blouse. On Earth, no one would bat an eye at Jenny's short shorts, one of the fashion world's better ideas. Here on Erden most non-Wapiti adults considered the exposure of bare legs by a proper woman to be a radical flaunting of Prussian social customs.

"Quit being such a nag, Uncle. I know I'm headed to Roanoke. I have to testify in the Prussian court." She blessed her skeptical uncle with a winsome smile.

"Rex, Larry raises a good point, though I agree that if anyone knows the killers' identity, it's Piney's gang. Just don't drop your guard around them." Tom said. "Look, we all respect you. Will you lead?" The group nodded in agreement with his request.

"That trip will take a week, ten days, what do you want us doing in the meantime?" Lou asked.

"Find out who would be willing to serve on a posse," Rex said. He had hoped the fighting was finished and he could concentrate on his new coal brokering business, finalize his land grant, and even look for a wife. He added, "And mine more coal. We all have bills to pay."

"You think the summons involves the boiler patent?" A worried Herr Dunlap asked Amy Caroom. She was waiting for the groom to saddle her horse. They both worked for Orleans Boatworks, part of Purnell Industries. As the name suggested, her employer built boats, both side-wheel and sternwheeler steamboats.

"I think that hullabaloo is behind us."

She also thought the summons to the palace worrisome. Benjamin Purnell seldom interacted with his bastard daughter.

"Maybe he decided to send you back to Heidelberg."

"To be so lucky," she said. Smiling, she remembered that order. Hard to believe it had been three years ago. At that meeting, he had stunned her with his command for her to attend Heidelberg University and learn chemistry.

The university life and class work had agreed with her. Amy's photographic memory and mathematical talent had enabled

5

her to learn everything that the Prussian university offered its engineering undergraduates. The Heidelberg professors had pleaded with her to stay and pursue an advanced degree. Steam was the new technology and the university was aggressive in seeking new instructors knowledgeable in the field. They wanted her experience in boiler design and steam engines. The school even offered to pay her while she completed her doctorate in steam thermodynamics.

Purnell had other plans for her. She had resisted his summons to return to Orleans, until the ultimatum. If she didn't return, he'd send her mother's head. She knew all too well that no one should ever ignore the monster's threats. She went back to Orleans.

Now, a year later, Amy was about to again meet her father. At the last moment, she had decided to bring her latest project to show him. While the hostler finished saddling the horse, she searched through the stable's dusty collection of empty feedbags for a small bag to carry it in. Her boss recognized the device.

"Is that safe?" Dunlap asked.

"Sure. I'm working on the new waterproof explosive. You're the one who told me he wants a black powder replacement. The device is just a convenient way to show him the power of the explosive."

The bottle of acid that she had swiped from the university's lab had sufficient nitric acid to make a half-kilo of picric acid. The boatyard lathe operator had helped her fabricate an iron cylinder in which to pack the picric acid. Her chemistry professor had made her aware that picric acid corroded certain metals and could form unstable explosive compounds, but figured she was safe since she had fabricated the bomb this morning. It contained a quarter-kilogram charge of fresh picric acid. A fellow Heidelberg student whom she had helped with his chemistry report had given her several of the Prussian army's new snap style grenade detonators. She used one to complete the device.

"Well, I hope it impresses him," Dunlap said. "I need your calculations on the size and number of tubes, not back in jail."

Foolish her, she had thought her father would have been proud of the boiler. Then again, her mother had warned Amy never to count on the familial connection to protect her when dealing with Benjamin Purnell. The jail sojourn had cured her of that foolishness. Amy's goal was her manumission from the monster.

"I'll try not to irritate him." The comments got Amy thinking about the patent uproar as she waited for the horse.

Nine months earlier, Dunlap, manager of the boat yard at the Orleans seaport, had asked Amy to work on a new boiler design.

"Do you have any thoughts on how to increase steam pressure? Safely, I'm not interested in boiler explosions."

Dunlap's request pleased her. As a little girl, she had played in the fire tube boiler shells and among the machines awaiting fabrication in the boatyard. How those workers turned pieces of iron into machines that used fire and water to move large boats had fascinated her. Now, thanks to Heidelberg University, she understood heat energy and thermodynamics.

"I do," Amy had said. "Instead of a tank to boil the water in, I want to pump the water through pipes in the firebox. A small diameter pipe would be much stronger than a tank. I think my new style boiler could safely triple the steam pressure, or even more."

"Seriously, three times?" Her boss had asked.

She had elaborated on her idea and he thought the design workable. Dunlap had then set about selling their boss on letting them make a proto type of the boiler for the Ichneumon steamboat the boatyard was building. Her father went along with the request, because if the new boiler didn't hold up or work effectively, it was the Ichneumon navy's problem.

Ichneumons were a non-human race who practiced a bizarre murderous religion of living sacrifices. Their empire ruled the southern continent and had spread north and entered the Erie River about fifty years ago and constructed a series of forts to support their traders. The locals called them 'blue bloods', not because they were upper-class aristocrats, but because their blood was blue like a crustacean's. They were good customers of the Orleans Boatworks.

The hostler had finished and Amy checked his work. Satisfied, she mounted the horse and headed for the back pathway to the ridge. She had always enjoyed horseback riding and the back path offered a beautiful ride to the large white mansion on the ridge overlooking Orleans and the bay. Her father used it for his office. The tall columns and covered, brick-paved driveway that looped through the front entrance lent an imposing aspect to the home. The local people referred to it as "the palace."

The two guards at the front door were aloof strangers, both Ichneumons. Amy, curious about the new guards, explained her purpose to them. The older guard told her to go to the first floor office. They'd see to the care of the boatyard horse.

Her father was fatter than ever, at least a hundred and fifty kilograms. The office smelled of tobacco smoke and onions. With a quick glance around the office, she spotted a large tray piled with dirty dishes and the remains of a roasted chicken. It was on the floor near the window. Though her mother had claimed Purnell was Amy's father, he had denied it in their past interactions, and she wondered about the validly of her mother's belief. She sure couldn't detect any resemblance between her and this squat, amoral man.

"Have a seat, girl. You made quite an impression on your Prussian professors. They recently asked the Myrtle Territory governor to contact Herr Caroom and request that he reconsider allowing his daughter to return and finish her PhD studies." He smiled at her surprise.

Could it be? She would love to go back for her doctorate.

"I told the governor that Herr Caroom would never consider the request," he said. Her disappointment must have shown, for he laughed. She should have realized the cruel man was just tormenting her.

"I'm not surprised. I had heard he was a sorry misogynist."

The smiling benign persona was gone, replaced by the tyrant she knew well. He studied her for another long and silent moment. Why hadn't she kept quiet?

"When I realized you were a freak, I should have sold you to Tyler Reed. However, Dunlap convinced me that you might be of use, so I decided to let the Prussians educate you. Now I'm giving you an opportunity to prove Dunlap correct."

"The boilers didn't convince you?"

She had a bad feeling about the direction of the now hostile conversation and remained standing in front of the desk, holding the burlap feed bag.

"Focke Wulf claims you stole their design."

She should just listen, but couldn't allow that lie to stand unchallenged. "Dunlap knows better, ask him whose design it is. What else could those Focke Wulf engineers tell their boss? You think they could admit a woman, forget the slave part, is capable of designing a boiler?"

"No, but they would believe you're capable of seducing one of their engineers and stealing the boiler design. Now pay attention. Chief Cinnabar's cocaine conversion is not producing, at least not as it should. He claims it's my chemicals and maybe the cannibal is right. I want you to go with Wright, find the problem, and fix it."

That talk scared her. No one ever talked about cocaine production in Orleans, even though everyone thought Purnell ran a cocaine-processing lab.

"Go to his stockade, the one in the wilderness?"

9

"You prefer six months in Reed's Sailor Hotel as a prostitute?" She blanched. "No. I didn't think so. And if you run off to the Wapitis, remember your sister and mother will still be here. Now figure out what you'll need to process several hundred tons of winter-sloe nuts and tell Wright."

The hostility and threats had Amy wondering if her tormenter planned to leave her with that animal, Cinnabar, after she corrected the problem. A problem she figured more due to cocaine abuse by the operators than the chemicals.

"Isn't he making the paste?" she asked. Amy knew the process to extract the alkaloids in the winter-sloe nuts wasn't difficult. The process started with crushing the nut and adding water, lye, and kerosene. Then the mixture is agitated periodically while it ferments for several weeks. Laborers then collect the kerosene, oils, and waxes that accumulate on the mixture's surface. A small amount of sulfuric acid separates the winter-sloe nut's oils and waxes from the kerosene. The workers saved the recovered kerosene for use in the next batch of crushed nuts.

To precipitate the cocaine paste, a gray sludge, from the acidic solution remaining after separating out the kerosene, workers add lime. They then dry the sludge and place it in barrels for shipment. Amy wasn't familiar with the process that the Orleans lab used to process the gray sludge into white cocaine, and had no interest in learning. She thought wasting a valuable nut to make a poison was a shame. Roasting the nut converted the alkaloids into a mild stimulant, similar to caffeine, and made the nut a tasty and nourishing food. However, she knew better than to complain.

"That's right, nothing challenging, so you shouldn't need long to figure out the problem. Wright will provide any necessary motivation required to keep those savages' attention focused on processing the nuts."

"What I want is a future, hope, freedom," Amy said. She wanted to learn if her dream of earning a manumission had any possibility.

"You're a slave. I can't treat you different from the other slaves." Purnell's attention was on opening a large ledger: apparently, he considered their business was finished. Hers wasn't.

"I will not go on as a slave. I'm your daughter. I want your manumission. Don't you have some feeling for me?"

She was treading on dangerous ground and he might sell her to one of Reed's whorehouses. He slammed the ledger shut.

"You're the daughter of a slave, of a prostitute, of a witch according to some people. You are not my daughter! Your mother is mistaken. Look at you, you're darker and a head taller than me. She needs to stop spreading those lies."

"So what," Amy said. "Mom's taller than you."

His face was red, but he paused and studied her while lighting a small, black, twisted cigar. After a cloud of noxious smoke to verify the vile thing was alight, Purnell added, "You want free, pay me twenty thousand D-marks and I'll issue a manumission."

"Twenty thousand D-marks? You can't be serious," Amy said, though on reflection, she hoped he might be.

"I don't joke about money. Any number of plantation owners would pay me that amount to have a courtesan that looked like you." Her father watched her for a moment before adding. "I can see you know that's correct. Look, agree to finish those designs for Dunlap and get Cinnabar's operation back on track and I'll set you up in business in Port Delta with a machine shop. It would give you a chance to make some money on the side. But you have to quit telling people that you're some bastard of mine. Until you pay for the manumission, you're my slave, period."

11

She was more apt to fly to the moon, than ever accumulate twenty thousand D-marks. But she wanted his unequivocal commitment to the deal.

"Unless I pay you twenty thousand?"

"Talk about not being serious," her father said. After a bark of a laugh and a cloud of smoke, he added, "Yes, that's my offer, pay me twenty thousand D-marks, girl, and I'll free you."

"You would sell me a lathe and milling machine, bankroll me?" She didn't believe him. He had probably just thought up the scheme, along with allowing her to purchase her manumission, to give her false hope. "Why would you do that?"

"I figure it would be cheaper than Dunlap's work and the competition would keep him on his toes. I'll give those old machines to you if you do those boilers, and don't fight me on the patent."

Dare she hope his offer was real? She could hope, but Amy's passport back home from the wilderness was to demonstrate her future usefulness.

"I have a new waterproof explosive that I'm working on and I wanted to demonstrate it."

Purnell's reaction to her announcement surprised her. He snapped, "Where is it?"

Not sure why he seemed so alarmed, Amy carefully pulled the black, beer-mug-size iron cylinder out of the burlap bag to show him.

"My god, a bomb," her father whispered. He dropped out of his chair to use the desk as a shield, sending the chair crashing into the wall, while yelling for a guard. The older guard who had let her inside ran into the room, looking for the threat, spotted the contraption, and knocked her to the floor while snatching the cylinder from her.

"Take it outside," Purnell ordered from behind his desk.

"Don't pull the pin!"

The guard was using the ring on the detonator's safety pin as a carrying handle as he ran out of the office into the hallway.

"My men aren't stupid, he knows enough not to light the fuse." He grumbled, as he regained his feet from his hasty dive behind the desk and flopped back in the chair. He appeared embarrassed.

"That's what I wanted to show you, a match isn't needed."

A loud explosion from the area of the front driveway shook the office, and something bounced off the office window. It left a blue streak, an aghast Amy saw.

Mazie Keeney couldn't ignore the note, and had sent word to her granddaughter, Indira that they needed to talk. Expecting her granddaughter in a few minutes, the elderly widow finished the tea in the kitchen. She had just placed several of Indira's favor cookies on the tray when the front door opened. Her youngest granddaughter had arrived. She greeted her from the kitchen and then watched the lanky teenager stop by the hallway mirror to examine the scar, a severe cut across her beautiful face. A slash she received while defending her tribe's day nursery during the last of Donnelly's horrifying raids along Hopkins River.

"Looks like it's healing well," Mazie said, carrying a tray into the front room. To her relief, she could see in the mirror that Indira had flashed her old smile.

"Doctor Freda has been looking after it. It no longer aches. Mom needs to buy a mirror, our old one was smashed."

After a last look, she turned and said, "Cookies, just what I need. What did you want to see me about?" she asked while hugging her and lifting a cookie off the tray.

That sounded like her confident granddaughter of old. Indira had inherited her mother's slenderness and beauty, along with her father's assertiveness. Setting the tray down, she held her granddaughter at arm's length and examined the scar. The deep knife slash had cut from Indira's right ear across her cheek and ended below her nose at the upper lip. It was an ugly scar. Donnelly's men had denied her any medical help, and they had held her in the filthy Hinton stockade as a slave. They had planned to trade her and the other captured women to Cinnabar for additional warriors.

"Well it gives you a formidable appearance. How are you doing otherwise?"

"Okay, as long as I don't think of Billy and Jane. Everyone is nice to me. Mom's worried I'll become embittered."

Mazie knew she was referring to the two- and three-year-old children that Donnelly's raiders had murdered along with the four babies at the nursery.

"Well, our warriors avenged those children. Every Donnelly man involved in that raid is dead."

"They were magnificent, especially Rex, Larry, and Imus." Before her grandmother could respond, she added. "I know it was a team effort, but as far as I'm concerned, and I know Mom agrees, we're alive because of Rex Knight."

"I believe we all agree on that. Which is why I wanted to see you. I've been handling church matters since your grandfather passed away two years ago. The Prussian Holy Church seems to be in no hurry to appoint a new priest. Instead, the bishop asked me to handle the necessary rites and correspondence until a new priest arrived. Well, three days ago, I received a letter from Jesuit Wilhelm."

Indira had just started to reach for the last maple sugar cookie and stopped. "Isn't he that odd priest who's always asking about strangers?"

"Yes, that's him. He had heard there was a Rex Knight who claimed to be from America living among the Wapitis."

"That is what he told me," Indira said. She looked worried. "Why would Jesuit Wilhelm mention that?"

14

"Jesuit Wilhelm is searching for a false prophet. It would seem the terms 'America' or 'American' implies the person is from another world."

"I can't believe the church believes such nonsense. Don't they burn those people to death?"

Both Mazie and her granddaughter knew the Royal Prussian Church considered anyone claiming to be from another world crazy or a devil and a threat to their dogma. The church calls such unfortunate souls false prophets and pays a handsome reward for their capture. Jesuit Wilhelm's responsibility was to investigate reports of weird strangers and interrogate them. If the Jesuit thought the person a possible false prophet, he had them arrested and shipped to Berlin, where the church, after further interrogation, burned the ones deemed devils.

"Believe it, girl. You're the one who told people he was from America. Wilhelm is a dangerous man and not to be taken lightly. And we both know Rex was vague at first about where he was from, though I always figured it was because he was a deserter from the Prussian army."

"You're serious." Indira paused and looked away for a moment, then turned back. "I don't know where that term America came from. It wasn't from me. Rex told me he was from a Mercia settlement on the ice sheet. That's all I know. Obvious someone must have misheard me." Her granddaughter's face was a study in guiltless perplexity.

"Mercia? Some of our ancestors were from there. Salt miners, and if I'm not mistaken, also involved in the salted fish trade." She studied her granddaughter. "If you just made that up, I'm impressed, but I'm not asking. If Jesuit Wilhelm asks, and he will, give him the same explanation. Thanks for clearing that up, because I like the man. I'll get word to Rex so he knows where he's from."

Indira laughed and grabbed the last cookie.

David C. Brown

Chapter 2

For the prior two hot and muggy late August days, Rex, Jeb, and Hokee had traveled up the gnat-and-snake-infested hollows to reach the high ridge that he had known on Earth as Kayford Mountain. *This place might be another world, but those damn gnats were just as bad*, Rex thought as they neared the ridge crest. On Earth, the ridge had been the location of the West Virginia Boone-Raleigh County boundary. On this alien world, it was just another unnamed ridge in the vast, trackless virgin hardwood forest of massive oaks and American chestnut trees. Jeb had claimed the wilderness stretched to the south for hundreds of kilometers.

The ridge crest also marked the beginning boundary of Rex's land grant from the Wapiti tribes. If this world was the twin of Earth, and so far, that appeared to be the case, then the land grant contained immense amounts of coal. Whether the coal would ever benefit him remained to be determined. Wood was the current fuel of this world, though Rex was confident the developing steam age would change that. The isolated location was a daunting barrier to ever developing the coal in his lifetime.

"What's bothering the squirrels?" Jeb asked quietly. "Hokee?"

Rex realized those annoying rodents had stopped their chattering. His domesticated wolf was off to their left looking across the small ravine and ignoring the treetops.

"How do these berries look to you?" Rex asked. He had stopped by a winter-sloe tree and picked a couple of berries to cut open. One purpose of the trip was to assess the quality of the winter-sloe berry crop, and unlike him, Jeb had some experience with the winter-sloe nut. "Think those nuts will be ready for harvest by October?"

The nut contained a valuable alkaloid. Harvesting those nuts offered Rex his best chance of paying the new land taxes that were due by January. Until those taxes were paid, it wasn't his land, and the nut crop harvest wouldn't happen if his workers felt unsafe. Gauging the danger of trying to harvest the nuts was his main reason for the trip.

"October, maybe, for sure by November those nuts will be prime," Jake said. He spit out the nut he had bitten and suddenly looked across the ravine, "You smell that?"

They heard voices, and located the source. Two Clovis hunters had emerged from the laurel thicket carrying several dead squirrels. The man laughed about something the woman said as they reached the camp. They were around thirty. Both wore brown leather sock caps, unadorned leather pants, and multi-pocketed vests decorated with the colorful beadwork that the Clovis people favored in warm weather. The man's cap had a large turkey feather as an ornament. They appeared to be in good health, lean, and vigorous. Three gunshots and a blood-curdling yell shattered the peaceful scene.

Tattooed warriors rose from the rocks about thirty meters from the camp. The biggest warrior charged at the stunned woman, who stood staring at the man crumpled on the ground. The attackers, shirtless Clovis warriors streaked with red paint and wearing dark

18

leather pants, had older percussion-cap muskets. The other two were reloading. A shot from Jeb sent the charging warrior tumbling into the camp and drew fire from the other two warriors.

Dropping his telescope, Rex grabbed Fritz's bolt-action rifle and shot both of the bandits still near the rocks. The woman had recovered and stabbed the wounded warrior trying to stand by the campfire. Hokee arrived a second later and pinned the marauder while Rex jogged across the ravine to check on the squirrel hunter and his attackers. Two of the attackers were dead. The head wound that the squirrel hunter had suffered was a terrible one. Though the woman was on her knees beside him, talking to him, Rex knew no one could survive such a devastating wound. The man would soon be dead.

Adding to the chaotic scene, the horse had gotten the wolf's scent. The terrified animal started rearing and pulling at its tether, a several-meters-long hemp rope tied to an exposed moss-covered root in the brook's bank. The rope held, causing the horse to lose its footing and roll into the creek.

Before worrying about the horse, Rex needed to stop the bleeding from Jeb's leg. The wound needed a pressure bandage and Rex wadded his felt hat to use as one. He had never liked that hat and, besides, he reckoned using it as a throwaway bandage was better than using his only extra shirt. Tied tightly in place with a hemp rope tourniquet, the felt hat stopped the bleeding.

Jeb yelled across the ravine after standing with Rex's help. "Are you Ellie? I'm Jeb Piney. Is he your husband?"

Ellie stopped her keening and after a moment of silence answered, "Yes . . . ." She must have noticed her horse's distress, for she ran to the terrified animal.

The act of standing hadn't loosened the rope tourniquet on Jeb's thigh. "You're lucky, partner. A little higher and you could forget having kids." He then helped Jeb cross the ravine to the camp while Ellie calmed the horse. They both studied the dead warrior by the fire.

"Look at that red tattoo. He's from Cinnabar's Panther tribe."

Rex had a better look, so he'd recognize the tattoo in the future. Ellie had settled the horse and joined them by the fire.

"Ellie, I'm sorry about your husband," Jeb said. "Was he one of the Cenci boys?"

The dead hunter was her husband, and his death had left four young children without a father. Those tattooed freaks hadn't been aware of Jeb and Rex across the ravine when they decided to murdered her husband. They hadn't tried to capture the man alive and hold him as a slave. Instead, they had murdered him without warning. Their only interest was to grab his woman, whom they undoubtedly planned to rape and abuse. The bastards wouldn't have given a second thought to their evil whim destroying a family and causing four orphaned kids.

On a more personal note, his land grant would had little value as long as Cinnabar warriors roamed it.

In response to Jeb's questions, Ellie told him his wife had disappeared on the same day he had. The community had assumed the raiders had captured or killed both of them.

"We need to clear out before more of those painted fiends show," Rex said, watching the surviving marauder struggle with his bonds. He was confident the knots would hold.

"There's no way I can ride or walk that far. And the prisoner needs to be questioned," Jeb said. The man was looking gray as he checked his leg. "Hell of a way to treat your hat."

"Ellie, you have any suggestions?" Rex asked. "I know you're grieving your husband, but I'm a stranger to your village and Jeb needs assistance. I hate to ask it of you, but could you go and get help?"

"If I left now," Ellie said, "riding the packhorse, I can be back before dark with men to help."

"Good, I'll cobble together an A-frame drag for Jeb while you're gone. Bring a horse big enough to pull one. If Luke and Nat are still around, tell them I need help with a prisoner." They were Clovis trackers that he knew who lived in Ellie's village.

Chief Cinnabar's war party had captured Richard Wilhelm, the magus that the chief remembered from his childhood. He was some type of high priest that supposedly hunted aliens. The nonsense that those Prussian priests believed amazed the chief.

The warriors had swept up, along with the priest, a farm family from near where Panther Creek joins the Erie River. They blindfolded the priest before the war party arriving near the stockade. The tribe didn't need the Jesuits as enemies, but they couldn't allow a stranger to see their operation and then let the man leave. The priest was cooperating, trying hard to be friendly, even though Cinnabar knew the man was scared.

"You were only a meter high the last time I visited your father. What's it been, twenty-five years?" Jesuit Wilhelm asked as a slave served the stew. The priest was dressed in black leather knee boots and black coveralls, and wore one of those wide-brimmed, black hats the Jesuits favored. He had a full, neatly trimmed gray beard and thinning hair.

"I was headed to Hinton to learn how the Wapitis beat James Donnelly's force and destroyed his stockade when I received, ah, Qua's invitation to visit your stockade."

"That's no mystery," the chief said. "The Ichneumons double-crossed my friend, James. They used Len Ruffner's men, with some help from the Prussians, to kill him." He figured there was no need to enlighten the priest to the fact that his brother had been there with a hundred warriors, or that only thirty of them had survived.

"General Mehta told me the Wapitis killed Donnelly and routed the Ichneumon army from the stone fort. They even killed General Meringa," the priest said. "General Mehta is now the commander of the Ichneumon army at Hickory Ridge. I figured that if anyone knew the Hinton story, he'd know."

"You doubt me?" Cinnabar said, peeved. "You Jesuits are always acting as if no one but you knows what's happening. The Wapitis are a bunch of old women, quick to run after the first shot. If the Ichneumons got whipped, it was by Prussians dressed like Wapitis."

The chief wondered what the strange man's reaction would be if he learned the meat in the stew he was picking at was one of the farmers. Fleas had Chief Cinnabar annoyed, and the Jesuit's tales of Wapiti victories weren't helping his mood or appetite.

"Who are you spying for, the Wapitis, Prussians, or the Ichneumon?"

"Spying?" Jesuit Wilhelm asked. "I serve God and the order. Your men brought me here. I wasn't trying to sneak in."

The priest had a sip of wine. "Is this a local grape? It's quite good."

The chief thought the vinegary wine smelled like goat piss, which led to his second thought: was the priest mocking them? Did the Jesuit lack proper respect for Cinnabar's tribe? Maybe the smug fool needed a lesson. Feeling mean, the chief snapped his finger to get the guards' attention.

"Bring those Clovis children in." Then he addressed his guest. "Jesuit, I think religion is a fantasy and there is no God."

"No," Wilhelm said. "God made this world."

Three large Cinnabar warriors rushed out of the room and moments later returned dragging three grubby children into the room, a girl around six years old and two slightly older boys. The terrorized, crying children were members of the family captured with Jesuit Wilhelm.

"Cut the smaller boy's head off."

His order startled the Jesuit whose head snapped around. The priest stared openmouthed at him, but turned in time to see the gush of blood from the boy's throat.

"Oh God, please have mercy. Don't kill those kids."

The warrior murdering the boy was strong and experienced in beheading people. The young boy's neck easily parted, and the man set the bloody head on the table in front of the horrified priest and the other children.

Cinnabar's mood improved when he saw that his brother and audience were smiling at the priest's shocked expression, the fleas forgotten.

"Can your God reattach the head, save the boy? Go ahead, pray, I'll give you a minute to beseech that all powerful God you claim to represent."

A mute Jesuit Wilhelm just stared at the boy's head and the blood seeping across the table. After a moment, witnessing no sign of divine intervention, the chief motioned for his men to finish. The girl's crying and screaming was starting to irritate him. The grinning guards' knives silenced the other two wailing children.

The priest vomited. Wiping his mouth, he cried, "Why?"

"Why? Well for one thing, we'll be hungry again tomorrow. Besides, kids aren't as tough as the man we just had." The room rang with laughter as the Jesuit fainted.

The Haggard brothers, Nat and Luke, and the horses arrived about three hours before sunset to help Rex move Jeb. Ellie had stayed home to comfort her children.

"Nat, I want you to stay behind to interrogate the wounded Panther. Luke, you'll help me take Jeb and the body of Ellie's husband off the mountain."

The trip was downhill and uneventful. They buried Ellie's husband in the family plot on a knoll by Jarrell River that evening. His death had left Ellie with four young children, three of them daughters, age three to ten, and an infant son. She asked Jeb to stay with her until he recovered.

The sun had set by the time Nat returned. He asked Rex to go for a walk along Jarrell River. The Clovis hunter had a small, clear glass bottle with a cork stopper. It contained a local corn whiskey. Between nips from the bottle, the hunter told him about questioning the warrior.

"That bastard and his two dead pals were part of two groups sent north from Cinnabar's stockade near Panther Creek," Nat said.

Rex knew from Chief Smith's earlier information that the cannibal's stockade was near what, on Earth, would be the Tug Fork of Big Sandy. In this world, they referred to Big Sandy as Panther Creek.

Nat had another sip from the bottle. "They were locating Clovis and Wapiti farms for the main force to raid."

"For what, slaves," Rex asked. From what he'd seen of the remote farms, the families that ran them barely eked out a living.

"Anything that Panther Creek scum isn't fussy. Slaves, goats, horses," Nat said. Out came the cork and another quick sip, then as the hunter corked the bottle he added, "They were expecting about fifty warriors to arrive before the harvest starts. That's their real target. The Wapitis they expect to be in the area collecting nuts."

Rex nodded in agreement. "So where's their camp?"

"They're operating out of a temporary camp in the upper end of South Fork."

"I don't understand why they were scaring their intended victims by sticking heads on stakes along trails. Didn't you just say that Cinnabar wants to catch people to sell for slaves? Where's the sense in alarming them with those gruesome displays?"

"I hadn't thought about it; didn't ask. Maybe it's their way of marking land. They're all crazy. Or they were just having fun." After a nip of the moonshine, the hunter concluded his report, "Anyways, that one won't be bothering us again."

Being involved with torture troubled Rex's self-respect, but he refused to be a hypocrite and look down on Nat. Thinking about the fate of Ellie's husband and the coal prospectors, along with the realization that the information was essential, helped mollify any ethical turmoil.

"Well we know they're not here on a social visit."

With night, mosquitoes had replaced the gnats and Rex, tired, decided to accept Ellie's offer of the screened hammock on her back porch. Waiting for sleep to take him, he considered ways to harvest his winter-sole nut crop.

Salt Furnace dock was a welcome sight. Rex arranged for a hot tub of water at the recently constructed boarding house. The lady who had run the boarding house in Smithtown, Helen, was now running this one. She welcomed him and Hokee. After a hot bath and a change of clothes, he headed over to the stockade to locate Chief Smith. He left Hokee chewing on a meaty deer leg bone, a gift from Helen.

"What do you know about Cinnabar? The folks living in upper Jarrell River think he's a cannibal."

"I've never met the man," Chief Smith said. "I'd heard he supplies most of Purnell's nuts. Until he joined Donnelly in his attacks on Salt Furnace and the raids up Hopkins River, I'd thought

25

the tales about Cinnabar's savagery were figments of overwrought imaginations."

"You're a busy man, but hear me out. The man's a problem."

The elderly lady who guarded his office door opened it to check whether the chief was ready for the next group. The chief held up a hand and said, "Give me another minute."

"His men tried to kill me last week. According to the one we questioned, Cinnabar plans to attack the workers collecting the winter-sloe crop, and sell them for slaves."

"Well then, deal with him, I don't care how."

"Is the council okay with that?"

"That crop has to be collected. We all need the money. You have the property tax due in January. I have a government payroll, or more correctly, the council has one. Take Larry Hopkins, I'll give him some blank arrest warrants along with one for Chief Cinnabar's arrest for murder. Larry's work will wait."

"Arrest warrants, out in that wilderness?" Rex asked, sure the man was joking.

"I don't want you getting in a shootout with some Myrtle Territory sheriff that Purnell sends to protect Cinnabar," Chief Smith said. "The arrest warrants give you legal cover to arrest that animal and anyone who tries to interfere. Don't make the mistake of thinking Benjamin Purnell is another James Donnelly."

Rex wasn't sure what the chief meant by that comment. He couldn't imagine a more cruel and vicious man than Donnelly. He was going to ask the chief to elaborate, but the chief instead got up from the table, signaling their meeting was over.

"I'm sorry to rush you, but I have to meet the Johnson delegation. The fools are pushing for an independent country under Ichneumon protection. Deal with the Cinnabar threat and keep me posted." Chief Smith walked Rex to the office door. "Oh, if anyone asks, you're from Mercia, and you've never heard of a place called America." He left a puzzled Rex in the hallway.

While shaving the next morning, Rex thought about his lack of capital to launch the winter-sloe nut business. It seemed a more intractable problem than dealing with Cinnabar's homicidal warriors. Time was against him. The winter-sloe harvest would start in less than a month. On the trip off Kayford Mountain, he had passed a few winter-sloe trees already dropping their plum shaped berries. Once a berry landed on the ground, it became vulnerable to rot and consumption by wildlife.

The opportunity to earn his property tax payment, due in January, by harvesting the winter-sloe nuts would be over within two months. However, until he eliminated the Cinnabar menace, the Wapiti women and children would never consider entering his remote land to gather the crop. Last night Rex had discussed his problems with the only reputable businessman west of the mountains with whom he was acquainted, Herr Simpson.

"I'm trying to decide how to pay the workers," Rex said. "Do you have any suggestions?"

"I might," Simpson said. "Tell me about the nut business."

"The pending deal between the Wapiti Council and Atlantic Tobacco calls for bagged, roasted, and salted winter-sloe nuts."

"Packaged in small paper bags, individual servings?"

Rex nodded. "The nut supplier and processor, that's me, will receive a quarter of the proposed retail price for the bag. The tobacco company plans to charge ten D-marks for a twenty-five gram serving." He had a sip of whiskey while the distiller considered those numbers.

"If I have the math right," Simpson said, "That's four hundred D-marks per kilo of nuts. I had no idea the nut was that valuable."

"Well, that's retail." Rex had a couple of wadded paper nut bags in his pocket. He fished them out and put them on the table after smoothing out the creases. "Give you an idea of what I have in mind."

"I can see where the nut business ought to be profitable if you can gather the raw, unprocessed nuts for a reasonable price per kilo." Simpson blew in the end of the paper bag to open it and then examined the printing. "Neat size, ought to sell."

"There are likely many costs I'm unaware of in turning the raw nut into a bagged, roasted nut. Nevertheless, the first step is collecting the nuts. How would you suggest I pay the picker?"

"Pay by weight or volume. Most of the pickers, who will be women, will want to earn at least a hundred D-marks a day. It is grueling work," Herr Simpson said as he opened the second bottle of whiskey. Helen had gone to bed.

"I agree. Picking fruit off those thorn-laden trees and from the ground on steep hillsides will be hard," Rex said. He didn't mention his worry about Cinnabar attacking the pickers.

"I've heard it's tiresome. Depending on the winter-sloe grove, a worker might collect seventy-five to a hundred kilograms of nuts per day. So they're going to want at least one D-mark per kilo for the nuts."

"I could live with that. A bigger concern is how to separate the hull of the fruit from the two inner nuts. Scott had told me that the practice is to crack open the winter-sloe hull by hand. That seems a tedious and labor-intensive process. Any idea how many kilos of nuts a person can crack open in a day?"

"No solid numbers," the whiskey man said, "but I've heard a woman might take three days to shell the nuts she collected in one day. So what's that, maybe twenty-five or thirty kilos a day?" Simpson laughed. "You need a nut shelling machine. A device, to the best of my knowledge, that doesn't exist."

"Thanks," Rex said. "Have any extra empty buildings? Processing the nuts will require a building for storing the collected fruit and keeping the shelling and cleaning equipment. I've been told mold ruins the nuts."

"You'll need that and another building. A secure and dry place to store the clean winter-sloe nuts until you can sell them. I'm going to bed, see you tomorrow." He corked the whiskey bottle after checking that Rex didn't want his mug topped off and left for his room, carrying the bottle.

More whiskey wasn't what Rex needed. His mind was already hazy. Instead, he needed to decide on a plan. Just talking about the various obstacles he faced to launch his nut business gave him a headache. Perhaps he should move on, try a different part of this new world. Get involved in building the railroad. He did know how to lay out construction work. But that would just be a job. In Wapiti land, he had an opportunity to gain control of a vast track of land, be someone important, and even guide the development to minimize the destruction of the environment.

Rex sat at the kitchen table, with Hokee sprawled under it and reviewed his financial position. It amounted to about seven thousand D-marks, his share of the war booty. It would be enough money to hire half dozen workers to collect some of the nut crop on his lands, but not enough to set up a processing operation. Selling the dirty, unshelled nuts to the council buyers would only secure him a fraction of the crop's value. To have a chance of getting a fair cut of that money, Rex had to have a clean, shelled, unbroken nut to sell to the roaster-bagger.

That still left the issue of how to finance an expedition to eliminate the Cinnabar menace, so he could harvest the nuts. That undertaking required serious money. Someone had to furnish the posse's supplies and pay the men, though Rex expected the Jarrell brothers, because of their desire to avenge their cousins' death, wouldn't expect wages. Weary, Rex went to bed still undecided on whether to stay in Wapiti land.

Hokee dashed out of the bedroom as the housekeeper yelled up the stairs that Rex had a visitor. Rex wiped off the remaining shaving soap, splashed some water on his face, and went to greet his caller. Feldwebel Hans Melas, one of Fritz's bodyguards, was in the kitchen hugging Helen when Rex arrived. Hokee was sniffing cautiously at several wooden crates by the kitchen's rear door.

"Hi, your pals, Tara, Franciscka, and Fritz, sent you some gifts," Melas said, still holding Helen who didn't seem to mind one bit.

Rex knew the chief's daughter, Tara Smith, had traveled with the two Prussians, Franciscka Weidman and Hauptmann Fritz Caprivi to Roanoke. Tara was after her attorney's license and permission to represent the Wapiti Nation before the Prussian Empire and Guderian Territorial courts.

"I wonder if she'll return as Tara Caprivi," Helen said. "Open the box, I want see what Tara sent you." She handed him a hammer and kept the pry bar. "I'll bet it's not cooking pots."

"I would hope not." He watched as Helen stabbed the sharp end of the bar between two of the nailed wooden planks that formed the top of the long box.

"Easy there, don't damage the contents," Rex said as he helped her pry up the planks to open the two long wooden crates.

The crates contained twelve new Mauser bolt-action, magazine-fed rifles packed in dry cedar wood shavings. Two of the rifles even had sniper scopes, and all had full cleaning kits with containers of oil and solvents.

"They're beautiful," Rex said, "and chambered for the 11.6 x 65mm round; there's a small fortune here." He handed one of the scoped rifles to Helen. After she worked the bolt to verify the chamber was empty, Helen put the rifle to her shoulder and aimed out the kitchen door.

"No wonder the Prussians rule the world, the bolt action is smooth, the scope is great," Helen said.

Melas nodded in agreement, as Rex opened the third crate. It contained letters, ten iron balls that had to be this world's version of hand grenades, and fifty boxes of ammunition. Each box held twenty new 11.6 x 65mm cartridges. He opened the letter addressed to him.

Herr Knight:

Franciscka and I thought you might find the enclosed rifles helpful when dealing with Cinnabar. The grenades are a new Prussian invention that replaces the old cumbersome match fuse with a neat mechanical delay fuse. The grenades are quite powerful and they may prove useful.

Franciscka and Tara have sent letters to Chief Smith explaining the opposition growing in Guderian Territory to the emperor's granting the Wapitis a new territory. The territorial issues are too complex to address in this short and unsecured message, but eliminating the Cinnabar threat would help demonstrate to the emperor and opponents that the Wapitis are capable of policing a territory.

I have also enclosed a special license that allows you to buy and import Prussian firearms, explosives, and ammo. Use Herr Jacobs in Roanoke for your contact to various arm dealers. He'll charge you ten percent of the gross, but it's still a great savings, for example a new Krupp rolling block rifle, which you're familiar with, sells in Guderian Territory for 1200 D-marks, with this license you can buy the rifle for around 500 D-marks, depending on shipping. The Mauser bolt actions are not yet available for sale. It will probably be another year before the Army releases any of the new rifles for sale.

As a favor, I would like you to allow Feldwebel Melas to tag along on your raid against Cinnabar. Yes, he's sort of a spy, but unless the Wapitis foolishly vote to seek independence, we're all on the same side. Plus he's an impressive marksman.
Hauptmann Fritz Caprivi

Rex studied the Prussian sergeant, whom he had met a couple of months ago at Hinton. The blue-eyed, blond-haired man had a no-nonsense demeanor and was a few years older than Rex was. Hans, maybe in his early thirties and strongly built, was a few inches shy of six feet, and around two hundred pounds, or as Rex remembered his vow to think only in metric, one hundred and eighty centimeters and ninety kilograms.

"Fritz said I should allow you to accompany us on our expedition."

"He thought I might help keep you from getting lost in southern forest. I even know how to use a compass and have one in my bag."

"That's very thoughtful of your boss. I'm always stumbling into trouble and could use a good point man in our column."

"Thanks, it's always exciting to be the person who triggers an ambush. Who wants to get old? Where should I store these weapons?" Hans asked.

Rex had Hans put the crates in his room and told the Prussian to be ready to leave in three days. Fritz's gift had solved the payment issue for the posse. Those repeating rifles were worth more than gold. Each man who went with him would receive one of those new bolt-action rifles for payment.

Chapter 3

The last three days had been a living hell for Jesuit Wilhelm. Cinnabar's warriors had beaten him unconscious with sticks after they murdered the farmers' children in the meeting hall. The following morning Cinnabar's men had tied his hands behind his back and blindfolded him. Then several warriors riding on horses marched and dragged him along forest trails, stopping at night and securing him to a tree. He lost count of how many times he tripped and fell. On the second day, his captives removed the blindfold.

The priest recognized the spot. It was the place where they had stopped and blindfolded him before completing the march to the stockade. Looking ahead, he saw the path that followed Panther Creek to its confluence with the Erie River. Hope surged. Could they be planning to release him?

Without warning, a volley of rifle fire erupted, and the Cinnabar warrior holding the priest's fetter fell from his horse. Two of Cinnabar's warriors managed to survive the initial volley. They raced back up the trail, nearly trampling him in the process of turning their horses on the narrow riverbank path. Wilhelm watched several Ichneumon soldiers emerge from the brush along the trail. They were fierce looking men in black coveralls with the Ichneumon gold double-headed snake emblem sewn on the right shoulder and the red patch with crossed swords under a skull on the left shoulder. More

Ichneumon soldiers on horses rode up the trail. Wilhelm recognized the officer on the lead horse. He was Captain Maqbool.

Ichneumon army officers had little use for priests of the Holy Prussian Church, considering them spies for Emperor Schnabel and Prussian interests. Still, Jesuit Wilhelm and the captain knew each other. They had met in General Mehta's office at Hickory Ridge. At that meeting, the general had told the captain to allow Wilhelm safe passage through Ichneumon territory.

"Why are you with these animals?" the captain asked.

Since the man was holding the other end of the rope tied around Wilhelm's neck, even an Ichneumon should be able to grasp why and guess that he wasn't there on his own accord. Then again, it was a poor time to be sarcastic.

"They captured me at the Panther Creek wharf while I was visiting with a local farm family." Knowing that this captain wasn't the brightest soul, he added, "I was their prisoner."

"Well you're fortunate we happened along. Come with us. I need information on Cinnabar's stockade," the captain said.

The soldiers brought him back to the Ichneumon camp at the confluence of the Panther Creek and Erie River. There, the priest discovered the Ichneumon captain had commandeered one of the surviving Clovis farmer's huts as his quarters.

"You reek, priest," the Ichneumon leader said. He then ordered one of the soldiers, "Tell those two camp slaves to bathe him and find him something to wear."

The priest noticed they were Clovis women slaves as they used freezing river water to wash him. The cold bath was agony, exposure of his genitals to females a blasphemy, but it was worth the distress to be clean. A set of clean and dry army coveralls made Wilhelm presentable.

A guard had instructed him to join the captain in the hut where they shared a meal. The captain was incredulous of his claim that the Cinnabar tribe practiced cannibalism.

"Well I'd suggest if you're ever a guest of that animal, avoid the meat dishes," the priest said.

"As far as I'm concerned, these savages can kill and eat each other all they wish. However, we need the Clovis farmers' food and don't want bandits like this Cinnabar fellow stirring them up. General Mehta doesn't want the farmers to think they need the Prussians to protect them from the local thugs. Where's the animal's lair?"

"It's not hard to find," the priest said. "Their stronghold is about a hundred kilometers up the trail from where you saved me. You'll smell the place before you see it."

The Ichneumon captain then asked a number of questions about the stronghold, which, because of the blindfold, the priest couldn't answer.

"I can tell you I saw at least fifty warriors in Cinnabar's hall," he said. "So don't try attacking without getting more reinforcements."

The caution irritated the captain. "I scarcely consider those illiterate savages a match for Ichneumon soldiers." Their discussion then turned to the source of the illegal cocaine. "Have you encountered any signs of the Clovis using the winter-sloe nut to make cocaine? Could this Cinnabar be making cocaine?"

"I saw little of the stronghold," the Jesuit said. "But I'd be amazed if that gang of swine could manage something complicated like the cocaine conversion process. The Prussian Empire is also interested in stopping the illegal drug sales, so if I hear any information, I'll pass it on to General Mehta."

Cinnabar's scout camp in the upper end of South Branch, near the eastern boundary of the Jarrell River watershed, was a primitive affair. Rex studied the camp through his scope. Two crude huts provided the camp's lone protection from the weather. The structures squatted at the base of a low cliff formed by the gray sandstone outcropping. The hut's walls were made of mismatched rough logs, the door an uncured buffalo pelt judging from the cloud of flies buzzing around it. The roofs were made of various animal skins draped over and supported by tree limbs laid across the log walls.

The four captives looked miserable and abused in their iron collars and heavy chains bolted to the rock face. The chains appeared about three meters in length, which allowed the prisoner enough slack to lie on the ground. They had no protection from the weather. All the prisoners were Clovis men.

Seven red-painted, tattooed men were in the camp. Four men sat on logs around a fire pit, two men were standing by a rope corral, studying the five, thin, swayback horses inside the roped area. One man was tormenting a prisoner by poking him with a spear. That the camp had not bothered to post guards, even after three of the warriors hadn't returned, spoke volumes about the Cinnabar scouts' contempt toward their Clovis prey.

The nine Wapiti men waiting with Rex along the west edge of the clearing would change that attitude. He considered the group a posse because of the council's arrest warrants, even though they were in lawless territory and the men worked for him. After a final check everyone had a target, he shot the man tormenting the prisoner to signal the attack. Cinnabar's other warriors were dead before Rex could work the bolt to chamber a second shot.

"Hans, post the perimeter guards," Rex said. Addressing the group, he added. "Make sure your spent brass is recovered for reloading, we're not rich like the Prussian army." Hans ignored his tease about the Prussian army never collecting spent brass cartridges at battle sites for reloading.

Larry and Tom Jarrell went with him to inspect the chained and trembling prisoners.

"Can you believe that," Tom said. "That bastard was an Ichneumon." The warrior with the spear lay in a pool of bright blue blood.

"Make a quick check, see if there're other Ichneumons. I'm not interested in encountering an Ichneumon army platoon." While Larry checked the other bodies, Rex wondered at the significance of finding an Ichneumon man among Cinnabar's raiders.

"The rest are human," Larry yelled. "Don't you figure Cinnabar probably hires any fugitive that shows up at his stockade?"

"I doubt he's much concerned about their backgrounds."

The lack of jubilation by the filthy and hungry prisoners at their rescue surprised them. One thing was clear to Rex as he sorted through the posse's collection of slave collar keys to find one that worked on the Cinnabar collars, the prisoners were terrified of their rescuers.

"Sam Welsh, is that you?" Tom asked as he walked up. Rex recognized the name of the missing hunter from Jeb Piney's village.

"Is that really you, Tom? When did you join Donnelly's crew?" Sam asked.

"Don't insult me. Besides, Donnelly is dead. Is that why they're so fearful?" Tom said pointing to other men chained beside Sam.

"We thought it was a Donnelly raid. They only know the old Mountain Clovis language, they can't understand you."

"I gather you do speak the lingo?" Rex asked. He nodded. "Well, tell them we're friends, Wapitis."

Speaking a different language, Sam quickly corrected the prisoners' misunderstanding. However, the posses' collar keys didn't fit the prisoners' collars, and the chained men started fussing and questioning Sam, who could only tell them to remain calm.

37

"Here, try this key," Larry said, pausing to clean blue blood off the key. "I found it on the dead Ichneumon."

The key worked. Freed, Sam told them that the other three men were from a small tribe eking out a primitive existence in the upper end of the watershed that Rex knew as Pond Fork.

"Their pantry is empty," Lou yelled, emerging from the far hut after riffling through the camp supplies. "Just two partial sacks of corn meal infested with weevils and the remains of a half rotten deer leg quarter."

"Toss the deer meat to Hokee and start a pot of mush," Rex yelled back. Appearing dubious, Lou nodded and disappeared back into the hut.

The older prisoner whom the Ichneumon had been torturing with the spear was Chief Akanji. The man had a number of small puncture wounds oozing blood but seemed unbothered by them. Sam acted as Rex and the chief's interpreter.

"He says your concern should be the hundred warriors who were expected three days ago with new supplies." The empty pantry was starting to make sense. "The chief says the warriors might arrive at any moment?"

Rex couldn't resist looking around the clearing. Cinnabar would come from the south. He glanced in that direction, though he knew the virgin forest of massive trees blocked the view. The forest could hide an army from observation until they entered the clearing. The chief then told them the warriors traveled on horses and used a mix of percussion cap and flintlock muskets along with bows for weapons. He also thought a few of the warriors had modern Krupp rifles.

"The chief thanks you for freeing them. He says you need to run, there'll be too many of them to fight," Sam said. "The chief said if you give them the guards' muskets, they'll find Cinnabar's men and alert you."

None of the Wapitis had wanted the dead raiders' muskets. "Tell him not to do that, but his men are welcome to take what they want." They were gone in minutes after stripping the corpses of shot, powder, knives, bows, arrows and the muskets.

"This gang is more destitute than we are," Tom said. "The Ichneumon did have a gold five hundred D-mark coin, and the rest of them had one hundred and fourteen D-marks among them."

Rex told him to inform the men and then hold it for their later division of spoils. The three ex-prisoners had passed on the offer of corn meal mush. A wise choice, Rex decided, as he tasted the hot mush.

"Why the odd taste?" Larry asked, inspecting a spoon of the yellow corn meal.

"Beats me, I picked the weevils out, before cooking it, at least the big ones."

Hokee, though, seemed quite satisfied with his meal of aged venison.

So far, the trip along the coast and then up the Erie River had been pleasant. Amy even had her own room on the Orleans Queen, a fast, shallow-water sternwheeler that had been in Orleans for repairs. The trip offered her an unhurried opportunity to evaluate the performance of her new superheater design.

Purnell's sternwheeler had the low-pressure fire tube boiler found on riverboats. In an effort to improve the boiler's efficiency, Amy had added an extra coil of pipes in the firebox exhaust. Its purpose was to capture part of the wasted heat discharged up the smoke stack. The extra heating boosted the steam's thermal energy and decreased the likelihood of condensate accumulating inside the engine cylinder and damaging the piston. Her superheater accomplished that with very little increase in the boiler's firewood consumption. The boiler's performance had pleased her and the crew.

The trip so far had been like a vacation, and she dreaded the coming two-to-three day trip up Panther Creek on horseback. The trip would offer no chance for privacy or baths. She even ran the risk of being someone's dinner, if she believed the wild tales circulating among the boat's crew.

The other worry was discovery of the boat's illicit cargo. The barrels of kerosene and lye, the captain could explain as trade goods, but the three barrels of concentrated sulfuric acid were another story. If the Ichneumon soldiers searched the boat and discovered the barrels of acid, they would know the cargo's intended use was cocaine processing, an illegal act. What was the greater threat, being arrested by the Ichneumons or traveling up Panther Creek? She couldn't decide if she hoped the Ichneumons discovered their cargo or not.

Herr Wright, a confident and capable middle-aged man, had told her not to worry. Amy had wondered why he'd work for a criminal like Purnell, who seemed to prefer sociopaths like Herr Wu and the Reed brothers.

The final stop before their destination would be at Hickory Ridge where the Ichneumons had a stone fort staffed with no-nonsense army inspectors. Those inspectors had them worried.

"Amy, when we arrive tomorrow at Hickory Ridge, I need a favor. Entertain the Ichneumon officer who boards the boat. Keep him occupied while I load the coal for the boilers."

The wharf area was a busy place when the Orleans Queen arrived at mid-morning. The Clovis Belle was at the upstream wharf. Amy and Wright watched the activity from the boat's upper walkway. The larger and older Clovis Belle was unloading cargo of sawed lumber and bolts of undyed cotton cloth at the neighboring wharf.

"I'll do what I can, but remember they may think I'm a Wapiti, and not care for me." She had little use for Ichneumon officers and none for their disgusting practice of human sacrifices.

"Amy, you're a beautiful woman, they'll visit. Keep it light. Let them feel they're dealing with a scatter-brained woman."

"The skipper of that sternwheeler, Captain Dalporto, knows me. He'll wonder why one of Purnell's slaves is so far from home."

Herr Wright suggested she tell the skipper, if he asked that, she was along to analyze the boiler performance. That was true.

"Won't that be at odds with your scatter-brained woman suggestions?"

"You're smart, handle it," the Prussian mercenary said, tired of her excuses. He left to organize the coal loading.

Amy didn't have to wait long for the visitors. Within a few minutes of docking, Captain Dalporto and General Mehta paid a visit. Captain Hube met the visitors at the north gangway. She could hear their greetings and learned they wanted to see the boat's new superheater.

Captain Hube looked around, spotted her leaning over the upper walkway handrail, and yelled, "Amy, come here."

The Orleans Queen officer had been respectful toward her, though Amy had heard he told others that he thought she was a witch. That nonsense didn't bother her. She knew the captain was new to steam powered ships and still a bit mystified by the process. One of her Orleans neighbors, a seaman who worked in the boiler room, had told her that Hube suspected magic was involved. For sure, the captain made no secret that he was in awe that he could now command a boat to travel against the wind and current.

"Fraulein Caroom is Herr Dunlap's engineer; she designed the superheater."

The Ichneumon general was studying her while Captain Dalporto enthusiastically greeted her. She wondered what the general thought of a woman engineer. Amy had heard that Ichneumons disapproved of educating their women.

"Focke-Wulf tried to steal her boiler design and is fighting Purnell's patent claim in Berlin," Captain Dalporto told his audience.

"Are you a slave?" The general asked. She nodded yes.

The question had cast a shadow over the group's enthusiasm. Amy figured every one of them knew slavery was evil.

"The Wapiti territory starts a couple of hundred kilometers up the Erie," the general said. "They'd welcome you." Maybe this Ichneumon wasn't such a beast Amy thought.

"General, what are you suggesting to her? Herr Purnell would be in General Bezdek's office in a flash, demanding your head for encouraging his prized slave to escape."

"If I'm that fat toad's prize slave, I feel sorry for any slave out of his favor," she blurted.

The Ichneumon commander laughed.

"Forgive me, Amy. I can't afford to offend your owner." At least the captain had the decency to appear embarrassed, and Amy now wished she hadn't spoken. Word was sure to reach Purnell.

The Ichneumon general had a point. Contrary to all the stories she had heard in Orleans about the Wapitis being passive savages, she knew they had sent the Ichneumon and Donnelly's slavers fleeing and sunk two of her owner's largest steamboats. Why anyone ever thought them a passive people puzzled her. It was accepted wisdom among the Orleans workforce that all Wapiti women carried knives and knew how to defend themselves.

Her mother, an attractive slave from the tribe of tall people who inhabited the gulf islands, had told her not to worry about the threats. "If the chance to escape presents itself on the trip, take it," her mother had said.

Boilermaker

Amy didn't share her mother's belief in Purnell's benevolence. Besides, she was a city girl and had no plans of seeking asylum in the some uncivilized territory of knife-brandishing women.

General Mehta had one more year before he could retire. Two months ago, he'd thought his career finished and his son, Major Mehta, doomed, when that fool General Meringa lost Fort River Point and Prince Cherukuru to the Wapitis. None of that disaster was his son's fault, but Emperor Ratakonda believed it was better to execute several innocent officers than to overlook one guilty officer. He thanked his lucky stars for Colonel Paget.

The Wapitis had demanded the return of all their abducted women, or they promised to hang the Ichneumon prince. Rex Knight, the Wapitis' military leader, had offered Colonel Paget a deal. If the Ichneumon colonel helped locate and safely extract their women from Ichneumon controlled territories, the Wapitis would ransom the prince to Colonel Paget. General Mehta had fully cooperated with the two men, figuring he had nothing to lose.

Five Wapiti women had been on the last Purnell boat to leave River Point before the attack. Miracle of miracles, the Wapitis had located and recovered the missing women at Bone Swamp saline works. Perhaps even more amazing, the savages had kept their word and released the prince unharmed. Then again, perhaps it wasn't so amazing, considering the two million D-mark ransom that changed hands.

Of course, nothing ever seemed to go according to plan. The Wapitis had gone ahead and freed all the saline works' slaves. That action had his commanding officer General Bezdek in an uproar. He expected Purnell's slave hunting teams to arrive any day to try to recapture the escaped slaves. Hopefully, that rash action didn't trigger another war.

General Mehta had a new curse. General Bezdek's bootlicker, Colonel Xavier had arrived last night on the other small Ichneumon army steamboat. The sister to the one Prince Cherukuru had lost in the recent hostilities with the Wapitis. On leaving the Clovis Belle and that intriguing female engineer, he joined the colonel for a late breakfast. In an effort to impress their Port Delta visitor, the general had instructed his orderly to place a table in his office and used a white linen tablecloth, the fort's silver, and the best dinnerware to set their places.

"I'm to make you aware that Emperor Ratakonda expects the illegal cocaine source to be located and destroyed," the colonel said.

The emperor might as well wish for gold to fall from the sky, Mehta thought. "Let's order first, then business."

He had worked up an appetite on his visit to the docks and wanted to eat before listening to Bezdek's nonsense. They settled themselves at the table and ordered ham, eggs, and at the General Mehta's suggestion, the colonel tried the local corn bread and honey. Their food arrived. For a few minutes, the only sounds were those of eating.

"I suspect a few Wapitis are using the winter-sloe nut to make cocaine," he said to open the topic. He'd finished his breakfast and decided to discover if headquarters had any comprehension of how vast the southern wilderness was. "I have nothing concrete to support the hunch, nor any idea how much cocaine is involved. Then there is the issue of what force would be available to stop the Wapiti bootleggers, if they are the source. We're talking about ten thousand square kilometers of wilderness."

"I'm not here to tell you how to do your duty, but General Bezdek expects results," Colonel Xavier said. *The man knew how to avoid responsibility,* Mehta thought.

"Well then, you'll be pleased to learn that I sent Captain Maqbool with a recon force into Panther Creek. His orders are to end

Cinnabar's raids and investigate his connection to bootleg cocaine."

"The captain is a good man, he's my brother-in-law. Has he made contact?" the colonel said. Mehta had forgotten the family connection.

"Not yet. It's a wild place and pigeons have a tough time escaping the hawks. Have you heard the rumors that Benjamin Purnell is the source of the cocaine? That he operates a large winter-sloe nut conversion to cocaine operation in the Cinnabar's wilderness?"

"Sure, there're always rumors in Port Delta. I even asked General Bezdek if those rumors might be true. 'No' was his response. They were just that, rumors, and probably instigated by the Wapitis to divert attention from their bootleg operations." The colonel then reached for another piece of cornbread. "Please pass the honey, this cornbread is good."

It was common knowledge there was no lost love between Purnell and the Wapitis. And the Wapitis harvest most of the winter-sloe nuts, so it would seem reasonable they would do the cocaine conversion themselves, and eliminate the middleman so to speak. So, General Mehta was inclined to agree that those wily Wapiti bootleggers had started the rumors about Purnell.

Still, the businessman was an oily character with fingers in everything, including slavery. That got Mehta thinking about Fraulein Caroom. For the last several years, stories of Purnell owning a genius slave with a knack for engineering had made the rounds on the river. General Meringa, during his stop on his ill-fated trip to the River Fort, had told him of the gossip in Berlin about an Orleans slave girl who had attended classes at Heidelberg University and won all the honors. Could they be the same person? No one had mentioned that she was beautiful.

Rex had the posse set the scout camp in order. His men had thrown the bodies of the slain men in the huts to get them out of sight and started a campfire. They removed saddles from the posse horses and put them the corral with the scouts' swayback nags. The saddles displayed on the corral's top rail. The arriving warriors would think the horses were part of the scouts' plunder and ought to help divert the arriving warriors' attention from the Wapitis waiting in ambush above the huts.

The night was crystal clear, the stars bright. Rex wondered if they were the same stars that he had watched from Earth, or if they were alternate stars, just as this planet was an alternate Earth. They looked the same, and the moon appeared identical to Earth's moon. Hokee's barely audible growl snapped his thoughts back to the present. Silent men on horses were entering the clearing. Dawn was several hours away. Cinnabar's force obviously didn't share the Wapitis aversion to night travel.

The clearing around the huts filled up with men and horses, though a number of riders had stopped at the edge of the clearing. Several warriors dismounted. The thirty or so mounted warriors waited quietly for the three dismounted men to enter the hut.

A sudden yell and five shots rang out from inside the hut, then silence. The mounted warriors outside the hut yelled several questions about the shots. Receiving no response, two more of Cinnabar's men rushed toward the hut. More shots and one of the warriors fell back out the hut's door. His partner, who hadn't reached the open door staggered off toward the corral, before collapsing.

Hans had obviously survived the first assault. His action triggered a volley of fire into the hut from the still mounted riders. The Cinnabar warriors, their attention focused on the hut, crowded their mounts closer for better shots.

The success of Rex's strategy depended on the new Mauser bolt-action rifles with their built-in five round magazines. The nine

Wapiti men lying along the top of the cliff and waiting for his signal were all excellent marksmen and capable of firing five aimed shots in less than a half minute.

Rex wanted the rest of Cinnabar's warriors to leave the protection of the forest, so he held fire. The darkness, flashes, and smoke were rapidly interfering with his vision, and the hail of lead balls was ripping Hans' hut to shreds. Rex was afraid to wait any longer and shot one of the undecided men standing by the forest edge. A storm of bullets erupted from along the cliff top.

Reloading the rifle's magazine with five cartridges required more time than Rex needed to fire five aimed shots and empty the magazine. The Cinnabar warriors, at least the ones who were still alive, were riding madly for the forest. Several of the riders reached the safety of the trees before Rex had finished reloading. The backs of the fleeing warriors still in the clearing presented perfect targets in the moonlight.

Only about a dozen of Cinnabar's warriors survived the frantic dash back to the trees. A quick voice check showed only one Wapiti casualty. Tom's neighbor had caught a musket ball in the forehead. The man was dead. Horses without riders were wandering about, but Rex figured the animals wouldn't go far.

"Pass the word that I want the men to remain on the cliff until dawn."

Hans soon joined Rex. "It got a bit hot, I was beginning to worry other Cinnabar men had surprised you," while petting Hokee. "Are we going after them?"

"If the men are willing, I want to." Rex said. The black gunpowder they were using made a mess in the rifles. He started cleaning his rifle barrel and then paused to add. "Every time I clean a firearm, I wonder why a smart Prussian hasn't discovered how to make smokeless gunpowder."

"Never heard of such a thing," Hans said while borrowing Rex's short cleaning rod to clean his revolver's cylinder and barrel.

It was light enough to see.

"Tom, Lou, the three of us and Hokee are going to make a swing through the woods on foot. See if any of these tattooed animals still have an interest in fighting. Hans, Larry, watch for my signal. I'll wave when I'm sure there're no snipers waiting in the woods, then I want you to check the bodies scattered across the clearing and round up the horses."

Something had caused the hut to start burning by the time Rex and the Jarrell brothers finished their sweep through the woods. The burning hut added a plume of foul-smelling smoke over the camp.

"Look at this," Lou said. The Wapiti warrior was back near the edge of the woods.

Rex was still a good fifty meters into the forest, where he had found the last body, when Lou called out. He rejoined Lou, who had made the grisly discovery of Chief Akanji's head. It had been stuck on the end of a spear and dropped by one of the fleeing Cinnabar men.

Did the chief disregard his warning, or did Cinnabar's men ambush the chief? Then again, what difference did it make? "Add it to the pyre." That discovery settled Rex's mind on who had murdered the prospectors.

Stray bullets had killed several of the horses, but the posse managed to recover twenty-four healthy animals. The deal Rex had worked out with the posse members included splitting half the booty captured from Cinnabar's operation with him, since he'd financed the posse. The men would split the other half, and horses counted.

"Tom, you take charge of collecting the spoils while the men build the pyre."

The men collected thirty-two bodies and stacked them on a large pyre. Five other Cinnabar warriors had serious wounds.

"They won't live out the day," Tom said, adding, "They'll be dead shortly, let them suffer."

The only survivor was a young Clovis, not much older then fourteen. He was a trembling wreck with a nasty scalp wound.

"Who's paying the chief to murder Wapitis?" Rex asked. He planned to ask Chief Cinnabar directly when he caught up with the homicidal monster. Cecile, terrified, didn't know why the Ichneumons were there, and Rex believed him. "Cecile, you're going to show us the way to Cinnabar's home, right?"

"Hans, do you have your compass?" He did, and Rex broke the news to the posse members that they would use Hans's compass to hike south straight across the ridges and valleys. The riders would lead their horses when crossing the steep areas. In three days, or less, they should be above Cinnabar's stockade at the headwaters of Panther Creek, and with luck, they would arrive ahead of the survivors from the battle at the scout camp.

"Why south? How do you know that's where Cinnabar's men are going?" Larry asked. Hans also looked curious.

Well the truth wouldn't do. Rex said, "Jeb's neighbor, Herr Cenci, told me where Cinnabar's stockade was located. Now no more questions, we've got a tough hike ahead of us."

"Tough? Do you have any idea how steep those ridges are? I've never heard of trying to go in a straight line across those mountains," Tom said. Some of the men joined Tom in grumbling.

"Any of you softies prefer being the forward guard and risk stumbling into an ambush along the trail?" Rex asked. "No, I thought not. By going cross country with Hokee in the lead, we greatly reduce the danger of triggering an ambush."

"I have to agree. Getting off the trail is an excellent idea. I'll be the column's rear guard and help motivate the stragglers. I've had enough of this stinking camp."

"Then form up. We move out in five minutes," Rex said, while verifying his sense of south agreed with Hans's compass.

The lack of inhabitants encountered surprised Rex. In two days of crossing one forested ridge after another, they had only encountered two overgrown and abandoned farms. The land was empty of people and teeming with wildlife. The first night Lou Jarrell had shot a deer and everyone ate his fill, including Hokee. Since then, Rex had imposed several bans: no shooting, no fires, and no loud talking. Tom wanted to know why.

"We're about to cross into the Panther Creek watershed," Rex said. "I prefer not to inadvertently alert any Cinnabar hunting parties to our presence and lose the element of surprise."

"What about the survivors and pigeons? Surely Cinnabar knows about the battle and about us," Tom said. They had gathered at the ridge crest taking a short break before plunging down another steep valley.

"I suspect you're right, Tom," Rex said. "But Cinnabar will be expecting us to come down the trail, chasing the survivors, not appear on the ridges above his stockade."

"Or Cinnabar figures that the Wapitis were satisfied with winning that battle and went home with the captured horses," Hans, said. "Isn't that how the Wapitis used to do things?" Even Tom had to agree.

Larry Hopkins appeared to have established a certain rapport with their prisoner, Cecile, and after the short rest at mid-day, he asked Larry to walk with him and pass on what he had learned.

"Cecile is illiterate, never been out of these hills, thought Wapitis were vicious savages that preyed on the Panther tribe, and believed that the Ichneumons were their savior."

"I suppose we have the Ichneumons to thank for that nonsense. Did Cecile know why the farms are abandoned?"

"Slinks are a problem, according to him, but Wapitis murder most of the farmers to steal the winter-sloe crop."

"What's a slink?"

"It's a giant flightless bird, but I've never seen one. It's too far north for them. The snow gets deep in these mountains, and they'd never handled the long winters. They're even more nocturnal and secretive than the panthers," Larry said.

"I don't understand, what's a slink have to do with the abandoned farms?"

"Supposedly, slinks prefer human flesh to deer," Larry said. "I figure Cecile's just repeating nonsense he's heard. The panther is the real danger to someone wondering alone in these hills at night."

Bears would be Rex's concern, not birds.

"Oh, and the rumor is, the creatures have azure blood."

"Azure? Larry, are you working on your vocabulary to woo college-bound Jenny?" Larry blushed, but didn't comment as they looked for an easier path around the rock outcropping that blocked their descent to the ravine.

Curious about the stolen winter-sloe nut remark, Rex asked, "Did Cecile say if Cinnabar harvests the winter-sloe? Or who the guy is and his connection to the Ichneumons?"

"Cinnabar is the chief and none of Cecile's acquaintances has ever met him. They only see him at a distance. The foremen are the ones people like Cecile deal with daily. Until the disaster at the scout camp, he had been trying to impress the Prussian who handles the horses that he was worthy of being one of the porters who would transport the winter-sloe nut south this winter. Now he's a pariah. Cinnabar executes any warrior who surrenders."

"The boy is a Clovis, right? Who are his coworkers?"

"His family was murdered by Wapiti raiders when he was a two-year-old, or at least that's what he believes. Cinnabar's men took him in and raised him. All the people in their camp are survivors from Wapiti raids and smallpox. They all work for Cinnabar. Cecile also claimed that Wapitis have taken most of the neighborhood children. He even asked me what we did with them."

"Never heard of that nonsense, have you?" Larry hadn't. "Cinnabar is running a slave operation," Rex said. "He's just another James Donnelly. The only difference is that unlike Donnelly, who was a Prussian, I'll bet Cinnabar is an Ichneumon."

Hokee, off to the left, was sniffing a large snake coiled beside a rock outcropping. It was one of those yellow colored diamond back timber rattlers. The wolf didn't need snake bitten.

"Hokee, get back here," Rex yelled. In a more normal voice, as Hokee trotted back to him, he asked Larry, "Did he say how many men are in the camp?"

"Cecile's not into counting. Five is about his limit, but he said a lot of the warriors and foremen went on the scout camp raid."

The gnats were extra active by the small creek they were crossing. Rex checked the compass.

"We're drifting to the west and need to cut up that ridge to our left. Get away from the damn gnats," he said, stopping to get a drink. Along with the other men, Rex was drinking a great deal of un-boiled creek and spring water to stay hydrated in the humid heat. He hoped parasites like giardia hadn't polluted this world's water. They didn't need diarrhea.

"Do you think we're ahead of them?" Larry asked.

"If Cinnabar's men followed the river valley trails, we're a day ahead if they stop for a night, otherwise it'll be a close race as to who arrives first. Ask your pal what trail they'll take into Welch. Ah, I meant Cinnabar's stockade."

Larry dropped back to confer with their prisoner. Rex started watching for winter-sloe trees as they neared the top of the ridge. The cross-country trip had provided Rex with an opportunity to evaluate the trees. They grew best under large oaks and did okay under the American chestnut trees. He was surprised to learn the winter-sloe didn't grow well under other species of trees and fared poorly in clearings.

The other quirk of the winter-sloe was the narrow elevation zone the trees favored. Rex estimated the winter-sloe zone at hundred meters in elevation. The trees also preferred the north-facing ridges. Like most hardwood trees, the winter-sloe grew on the south facing slopes, but not near as well as on the wetter, cooler, north slopes. So, though the winter-sloe grew throughout the mountains, there weren't very many of them. By chance, the trees Rex passed were loaded with berries and ready for harvest.

Firewood cutters had denuded hillsides across the valley and the slope below the ridge Rex stood on. The treeless valley meant that the posse had arrived at Cinnabar's stockade. The fort and camp layout was a primitive affair, scattered across the floodplains at the confluence of the creeks that formed Panther Creek.

In the stockade, two log structures faced each other. The barracks and warehouse were about thirty meters by ten meters, with wood shake roofs. A thirty-meter-wide open lot separated them. A forge and stable area anchored the hillside end of the enclosed area.

"It's similar to Hinton, except for that cut stone building. Look at the terracotta tile roof. Cinnabar didn't build that."

Tom had joined him on the western ridge crest. They studied the stockade and settlement, trying to decide the best approach to attack the garrison.

"Donnelly had better walls at the Hinton stockade," Tom said.

An oval-shaped earth berm, varying from three to four meters in height, surrounded the entire area. Logs laid horizontally along the berm's top edge formed a modest retaining wall on the top inside of the berm and created a crude parapet for defenders to shelter behind during an attack.

"Anyone could walk over that wall," Tom said. "Hell, I could ride a horse across it."

"Sure not much activity," Rex said. A few women and children moved between the warehouses as they watched. Two guards armed with muskets leaned against the main gate looking bored.

About twenty small huts, some not much better constructed than the two at the scout camp, were scattered along the creek above the waterwheel impoundment. Two more of the log warehouses, with several large stone chimneys protruding through their roofs, were located outside the earth berm and beside a waterwheel and dam arrangement on Panther Creek. Those buildings by the waterwheel had the appearance of a rudimentary manufacturing operation.

Several horses waited at a rail in front of the waterwheel building. Four men were busy in the clearing below the dam. They appeared to be constructing a large fire by stacking alternate layers of logs and thin slabs of a local marlstone.

"A few are working. It looks like they're making lime."

"I'm inclined to agree. Those remains of bonfires scattered around the clearing suggest it's a limestone roasting operation." Rex was familiar with the method once used by his grandfather back on Earth to make lime. "I'd like to know why. Is the lime for agriculture?"   "Sure, what else could they used it for? Did you catch that?"

He figured Tom was referring to the faint, foul odor occasionally detected when the wind came from the settlement. He initially thought he had smelled himself.

"The place must have had a rank odor for us to smell it up here," Rex said.

Across Panther Creek from the bonfire activity, waterwheel, and millpond was a settlement of weathered and ramshackle cabins. The place had a hardscrabble appearance. Scattered among the shacks were numerous garden plots. Several small barns, with hog pens attached, bordered the east side of the settlement. A large field with several horses, enclosed by a ring of log stakes, was located below the settlement. The long narrow building along the hillside of the fenced field was a large stable.

The top of the millpond's earth dam functioned as the main access between the stockade and settlement, with a simple bridge providing passage across the waterwheel's stone raceway. The bridge was fashioned from logs laid across the stone ditch and decked with rough-cut wood planks.

Larry brought Cecile to the overlook. The boy had never been to one of the ridge tops and thought the view of his home amazing. The Wapitis thought the man's lack of travel astonishing.

"Qua must be out on a raid," their prisoner volunteered. Rex asked why their prisoner thought that. "When we left, there were many horses," he said, while pointing at the settlement's corral with the few horses.

"Who is Qua?" Rex asked, glancing behind them. Hearing about missing enemy forces made him uneasy.

"He's Cinnabar's brother. Qua wasn't with us."

The number of horses Cinnabar's warriors had was a surprise. The posse had twenty-four of them that they had recovered at the scout camp. He knew about twenty more horses were with the raid survivors the posse was planning to ambush. And though counting was an alien concept to Cecile, Larry and Rex concluded from quizzing their prisoner that the size of Qua's war party was around twenty warriors, which meant at least another twenty horses.

Rex was no farmer, but the valley surrounding the stockade didn't appear to him to have near enough pastures, fodder, and grain fields to feed that many horses and the people who rode them. Between the stockade and the village, a couple of hundred people appeared to call the place home. The lack farmland might explain why most of Cinnabar's horses were such sorry-looking nags. They were starving.

The Wapitis held a second war council behind the crest of the ridge that overlooked the stockade. The posse knew it had the same weakness as Donnelly's stockade at Hinton, nearby higher terrain surrounding it. Several of the Wapitis wanted to start shooting at the stockade and Cinnabar's men.

"I agree we can pick off the defenders on the fort's walls. But I don't know Cinnabar's strength in the stockade, or Qua's. Don't forget, after the first shot, surprise is gone." Rex paused to allow comments, but the men remained silent. He then explained the need for caution. "Wherever Qua went, he'll return here when his task is completed. The man could be gone for a day or a week. We don't need him ambushing our rear while we are attacking the fort. Plus remember, there are the survivors from the scout camp headed this way."

"What do you reckon? There're thirty or forty men between the two groups?" Tom asked.

"That would be a good guess, if it was just Cinnabar. But the Ichneumon involvement worries me, and we don't know what's to the south of here. Is it all wilderness for another six hundred kilometers?"

No one answered him.

Rex added, "And what's down Panther Creek? The Ichneumon garrison at Hickory Ridge isn't that far from where this creek hits the Erie River. There are nine of us and we're a long ways from help. I don't want to stumble into a company of their troopers."

"Are you thinking we should set up an ambush on the river trail a few kilometers below the fort where there was a good escape route in case things went bad?" Tom asked. "It would allow us to chew up the survivors from the scout camp in relative safety. Keep them from reinforcing the fort or trapping us."

"Yes, but the lack of activity in the stockade intrigues me. Maybe a reconnaissance tonight would be a profitable use of our time."

David C. Brown

Chapter 4

Chief Qua was waiting irritably, along with his dozen warriors, at the camp about twenty kilometers below their stronghold. They were at the intersection of the side trail from the Jarrell River headwaters with the main Panther Creek trail to the Erie River. He had sent the two surviving warriors from the Jesuit's escort ahead to locate the Ichneumon soldiers who had attacked them, while he waited for Captain Gupta.

Earlier, Qua's brother under the influence of too much cocaine and whiskey, had flown into a rage on learning of the unprovoked Ichneumon attack.

"I want those soldiers killed. They had no call for attacking our men," Cinnabar said, pausing to take a lungful of smoke. The smell had told Qua it was tobacco, not the crazy weed.

"They're probably already back at Hickory Ridge with the priest. We need to deal with the Clovis."

"Probably back at Hickory Ridge . . .? They're coming here. Don't you get it? Under no circumstances can we chance the Ichneumons learning the purpose of our operation. Go kill those soldiers, now, before they arrive," Qua's drug-crazed brother screamed at him.

Chief Qua attempted to reason with his brother.

"My hesitation is because most of our warriors went with Captain Gupta to round up Clovis slaves for the harvest. There're only about twenty fit warriors left, if I take another dozen warriors to deal with the Ichneumons, there're only eight men left to guard you and the stronghold."

He realized his brother's attention was toward the kitchen. He paused in his explanation and turned to learn what had his brother's interest. A pig, who had allowed that muddy pig in the hall? It was under the guards' table scavenging food scraps.

"You're worrying about nothing," Cinnabar said rejoining the conversation. "Who other than the Ichneumons could attack here, the Clovis? You're fearful of them?"

His brother shook his head at that. Then, to his alarm, Cinnabar had leaned forward and selected one of the flintlock muskets stacked by his chair.

"Do you remember if this musket is loaded?"

"How would I know?" Qua said. He wished his drug-addled brother wouldn't fool with that musket, and wondered if he had forgotten the pigeon message from two days ago. "What about the message? Something occurred at the scout camp. Maybe it's payback from the Wapitis for helping Donnelly."

"The man is dead. The Prussians turned on him for siding with the Ichneumon. That's why I don't want the Prussians thinking the Ichneumon control us. Best way to accomplish that is for you to go kill those soldiers. Show them who controls Panther Creek. Besides, I figure some panicky underling of Gupta wrote that message."

"You can't seriously believe that. Why wouldn't he have sent a new message?"

"Maybe the pigeons got killed. Maybe Gupta didn't know about the message. You think that fool handling the pigeons is going to tell his boss that he panicked. One thing is for sure, farmers didn't rout my warriors." Qua did agree with his brother on that point.

"So get organized and run those blue-bloods out of Panther Creek, and then we'll deal with the farmers," Cinnabar said and then aimed the musket at the pig and shot.

The explosion was deafening in the confined space. The lead ball ricocheted off the stone floor behind the pig and slammed into a wood keg by the head table. The startled animal tore out of the hall, squealing, as Qua watched a small stream of wine begin to drain from the keg onto the table. He idly wondered if the musket ball had gone clear through the oak keg, but never checked.

At the time, Qua hadn't considered the vinegary wine a loss. Now, waiting on the trail, a mug of that wine would have tasted good. The first of the slave-raid force survivors entered the clearing. The pigeon message hadn't exaggerated the beating that Captain Gupta's force had suffered. Watching the first survivors stagger into camp, Qua wished he had been more forceful in opposing the Jarrell River raid. His brother's love of cocaine had eliminated whatever residue of sense he might have once had. Until this ill-advised venture, their operation had all the able bodies needed to start the winter-sloe harvest and cocaine conversion process. There had been no need to tear off on another slave raid.

Now Qua realized, and he suspected even Cinnabar had to know, the crop's harvest was in jeopardy. The winter-sloe berries were starting to drop. The lazy Clovis slaves would require motivation to gather the crop before it rotted. Surely, his brother realized that. Yet here he was, about to send their remaining experienced warriors off on another unproductive raid that might precipitate a war with the garrison at Hickory Run.

Rex lacked the information he needed to decide the next move. The stronghold below them appeared nearly abandoned. They had seen only three guards that afternoon patrolling the walls and gates. The horse corrals held only a few horses. Since the posse had arrived on the ridge above the fort around noon, no riders had come or gone on the trail along Panther Creek. None of the survivors from the scout slave camp had appeared. Where were Cinnabar's warriors? Was the seemingly abandoned fort just bait for a trap?

The Jarrell brothers and Rex decided to sneak into the village after dark for a reconnaissance. Larry would assume command if they failed to return. In the meantime, he told the posse members to get comfortable, but make no fires.

The warehouses by the waterwheel were unlocked, and based on Hokee's behavior, unoccupied. First, they examined the ash piles the men had been working around on the bank downstream from the waterwheel area. Two piles were still smoldering, but the men and horses were gone. They had been burning marl to make lime.

Tom and Lou left him by the warehouse. They planned to circle around to the rear of the fort. The brothers would enter the stockade by simply crawling up the earth berm and squeezing through the openings between the stakes of the palisade.

Rex and Hokee entered the warehouse through the door near the waterwheel raceway. It was no great surprise to learn the water wheel drove a large stone grinding wheel, but what it had been grinding was a surprise. Based on the residue on the sandstone grinder wheel, the mill had been grinding unshelled winter-sloe nuts when last used.

A dozen large low-wall wood vats and tanks cluttered the rest of the floor space. They were empty and, in the darkness, the vats appeared clean. A number of long-handled wood paddles were propped against the walls near the vats. The other warehouse had two large tables supporting sand beds that obviously served as filters.

The purpose of this layout appeared to be for making cocaine paste from the winter-sloe. This was probably the source of the bootleg cocaine. Thinking of the limestone burning, he wondered if the winter-sloe-to-cocaine conversion required lime. Both warehouses had a faint odor that reminded Rex of kerosene, probably another part of the process. Tom whistled for him from the warehouse door.

The arrival of the slave-raid leader, Captain Gupta, snapped Qua's thoughts back to the here and now. The captain, a fugitive from the Ichneumon army, was in a bad way from two bullet wounds. Gupta was a tough soldier. In spite of his wounds, he had managed to ride away from the battle and remain in his saddle.

"The Prussians ambushed us."

"That's all we need, the Prussian army in Panther Creek." Prussians learning about their operation could potentially be a bigger threat to them than anything the Ichneumons might do. He made a quick count. "Only fifteen men, what the hell happened? Thirty of my warriors are missing. Shit, so are a bunch of horses."

"I saved ten of our horses, but I had to leave the others. A special force unit ambushed us," the captain said. "What did you do to piss off the Prussians?"

"What would Prussia's best soldiers be doing in that god-forsaken wilderness?" Qua asked. The captain was obviously trying to cover up his incompetence by inventing superior forces.

"How would I know? But they had the new rapid firing rifles, the ones that aren't for sale. Those were Prussian troopers."

"Bolt-action rifles, you're sure?"

"Well, I never saw the damn things," the wounded man said. "But there would be five quick shots, then a pause, like they were reloading it, then another five rapid shots, so yeah, I'm sure. It wasn't some single shot rolling block rifle, too fast."

"Are these Prussians pursuing you?" Qua doubted there were Prussian soldiers involved, but someone had kicked their ass.

"We set two different ambushes and no one ever showed, so I don't think they're in pursuit. After all, we gave them a good lick," the captain said. "Is it safe to return to the fort?"

He was referring to Cinnabar's propensity to have warriors who disappointed him executed. Qua had always thought his brother's policy counterproductive. However, with an Ichneumon patrol and possibly a Prussian army unit headed toward them, dissention in their ranks might prove fatal. The quickest way to settle down those skittish survivors from the botched slave camp raid would be to blame their failure on their captain's poor leadership. He shot the man.

"That Ichneumon bastard sold you out to the Prussians." He said pointing at Gupta's twitching body on the ground. "Now check your weapons, we have some Ichneumon soldiers to run out of our land."

Qua's force numbered thirty men. He only needed half that number to deal with the patrol, and he had considered sending some of the survivors back to the fort to strengthen the guard force.

The Clovis man who normally operated the waterwheel said, "The men asked me to speak. They feared meeting your brother without you to explain Gupta's treachery. Take us with you on the raid. We want to help."

The man had a legitimate concern. After a moment, reckoning it was always better to have too many warriors, than not enough, he said, "Get to work digging the Captain's grave." He pointed at the two men he knew were poor shots, but strong laborers. "Then take those extra ten horses back to the corral and wait on me. The rest of you, saddle up."

The trail along the Panther River was the only trail from the Erie River into Cinnabar's stronghold. Qua's force rode cautiously northwest looking for the two warriors he had sent earlier to find the Ichneumon patrol.

Rex and the Jarrell brothers, standing behind the waterwheel warehouse, considered their options. Sunrise was several hours away. Beetles humming in the background, and the flashes from hundreds of fireflies, contributed to the peacefulness of the warm, clear night.

"All but three of the warriors are in the stone building drinking," Tom said, pausing to look around the warehouse corner and across to the stockade gate, "The gate guards are still missing."

"They're in the guard shed snorting some white powder," Lou added, "Probably cocaine. Everyone else is watching two naked young girls sing and dance in the meeting hall."

Earlier, Rex had heard the faint sound of drums and had feared the guards had discovered the Jarrells, until he heard the faint shrill female voice chanting some indistinct ballad. Now only the beetles were singing.

"The place is essentially undefended. The three of us could take the stronghold now," Tom Jarrell said. "What's in there?" He pointed at the warehouse.

"I'm not sure. I suspect it's where they process the nut into cocaine. Listen, my concern is being trapped in this pigsty if the missing warriors return."

"Have to agree, that berm is a joke as a wall to keep people out, not to mention all the high ground around the place," Tom said. "Be a great place, though, to ambush the returning heroes."

Looking around at the lack of cover outside the stockade berm, Rex had to agree. "Then why wait for morning? We should take the place now. You two agree?" They did. "Lou, go collect the men. No horses, no talking. Make sure the men understand. Tom and I will wait by the footbridge across the millpond raceway and intercept any early kitchen workers."

Chief Qua was pleased. The two survivors from the Jesuit's escort had done well. They had located the patrol's camp avoiding detection. It was beside Panther Creek, about halfway between the stronghold and the Erie River. Though the Ichneumon commander had posted two guards, one at each end of the camp, Qua's warriors had killed them without alerting the camp. His men needed a few minutes to finish infiltrating the camp of sleeping soldiers.

Just as Qua was prepared to shout the war cry and trigger the attack, the fifteen horses in the rope corral by the creek started fussing. He held his war cry, hoping the animals would settled down before their noise alerted the sleeping camp. His warriors were nearly in position. Suddenly, the horses started neighing loudly, and before he could act, a monstrous form tore through the sleeping camp and grabbed one of the horses. Pandemonium erupted, terrorized horses running through the dark camp trampling Cinnabar warriors and Ichneumon soldiers, panicked men shooting at anything that moved, and injured men screaming.

The Cinnabar warriors only had four Krupp rolling block rifles. The other warriors had muskets and hatchets. All the Ichneumon soldiers had versions of the Krupp rolling-block rifles. Three of the Ichneumons who had jumped to their feet first had five shot revolvers and knew how to use them. Qua realized they were in trouble.

Chief Qua smashed his hatchet in the head of the Ichneumon soldier. Then, screaming his war cry, he pivoted to smash the head of the other soldier a couple of meters away, when a rifle bullet smashed into his right leg. The bullet dropped him in a wave of agony. His second victim's scream had attracted one of the pistol-firing Ichneumons, who shot Qua twice.

Within a minute, the warriors realized their chief was dead and that the surviving Ichneumon soldiers had rallied around their officers. The tattooed men broke contact and fled up the trail for their horses.

Captain Maqbool had to yell several times.

"Stop shooting! They're gone! You're shooting blind! Find the camp guards!" the captain said. If those guards were alive, they wouldn't be for long. God bless that bear, he thought, otherwise those savages would have massacred them.

"Where's that worthless slink?" Maqbool yelled. "Some guard animal it proved to be." One of the troopers pointed toward the riverbank where the slink was feeding on a corpse.

The fifteen-man patrol now had eleven soldiers, though two of the men had wounds that were sufficiently serious to prevent them from joining the pursuit. A dozen of the savages who had attacked were dead, their bodies were scattered about the camp. One of the dead savages appeared to be a chief and probably accounted for the sudden retreat of their attackers.

"The upstream guard had his throat slit," Sergeant Moor said returning from up the trail. "We haven't located the other guard," the sergeant added, and then asked, "What woke us?"

"A bear, it was after a horse. My slink got one of the savages, but made no noise to alert us. I need a guard wolf, something that knows to howl and bark."

"A bear did that?"

Maqbool wondered if the sergeant was forgetting his place, questioning an officer. They were both looking at a mangled horse lying by the edge of Panther Creek, near where the slink was eating something.

"Those are the tracks of a short-face bear," the captain answered. He decided not to correct the sergeant. "I figure the gunfire scared it off. Form up the patrol. We're going to teach those savages why they shouldn't attack Ichneumon troopers."

"That's not one of the savages! It's the other guard," the sergeant said. "Lord, did that monstrosity kill one of our own?"

The captain jogged over and kicked the slink away from the man.

"No, his throat is slit. The bird just wanted the brain."

Maqbool considered shooting the creature as it crouched snarling at him, but he had put a small fortune into it. That plantation owner in Port Delta had wanted to buy it to hunt down runaway slaves. Maybe the fool still did, and at least then, he could recover his investment. Regardless, that could wait, the matter of Cinnabar needed addressed. He called the men together.

"There's a slight risk of rushing into an ambush, but I figured those undisciplined animals lacked the military training to set a rear guard blocking force. So we're pursuing those bastards, and I want to catch them before they reach shelter in the stockade. Then kill them!"

The men cheered his order, and after a moment, he added. "Leave the dead. We'll clean up on our return. Instead, find our horses."

The men scattered to round up the horses while the captain and first sergeant made sure the two wounded men could defend themselves until they returned.

"Get Sergeant Moor's revolver, then give his and yours to the wounded soldiers." Then, addressing the two wounded men, he said, "We're going after the bastards, but I should be back in a day. Use the revolvers for protection. Sergeant Moor is getting two water bags, a small bag of goat jerky, and several rock biscuits for you."

"Thank you, sir, we'll be fine. Kill those animals," the older wounded soldier said.

Less than half an hour after the attack, the Ichneumon soldiers were in pursuit of the savages. The captain's slink loped along behind them. Sunrise was still a couple of hours away.

The posse's assault was over in a few minutes, and the three outside guards and two of the drunks were dead. Cinnabar and three warriors in chains were huddled together on the stone floor in front of a massive wood chair that appeared to be a throne. Larry and the two men who had checked the kitchen in the rear of the hall returned with the horrifying news.

"My God, look in the kitchen," Larry yelled.

Rex looked where he pointed. A partially dismembered body hung from a meat hook. He thought of the two terrorized young Clovis girls they had found behind the throne. Had that monster intended to butcher them for a future meal?

Cinnabar had much to answer for, and Rex wanted to ensure nothing happened to the evil creature. To no one's surprise, the place had a dungeon of sorts. It was comprised of two circular pits about two meters in diameter and about five meters deep with an iron grate top. Judging from the water around the two skeletons in the bottom of the north pit, about a foot of water was in that cell.

"Tom, put the prisoners in the south pit." When the prisoners refused to move, Rex added, "Throw any prisoner that causes trouble in the wet pit. Or just shoot them." The captured warriors hurried into the dry cell.

"Put the chief in the room behind the throne. There's an iron eyebolt in the floor, chain him to it. Leave the door open, so you can keep an eye on him."

A quick search discovered another room that appeared to be Cinnabar's bedroom, his private quarters. There was an iron hook high in the wall in that room, as well. The presence of that hook in a bedroom added an aura of wickedness. How had this evil operation survived, was the whole tribe corrupt?

Answers would have to wait. Already the four kitchen workers had arrived. Rex turned them and the prisoners over to Larry, Cecile, and Sam Welsh who had just arrived with the posse's horses.

"Larry, if this doesn't work, put a bullet in Cinnabar's head before you run."

Next, the ambush to welcome the returning warriors needed to be set before sunrise. Posse members wore Prussian camouflage fatigues that looked nothing like Cinnabar's warriors' rags and skins. Tom and one of his cousins found enough semi-clean rags and skins to dress like the gate guards.

Joining Rex above the main gate, Larry said. "I found some fresh eggs and told the cook to scramble them. What she calls a biscuit is like no biscuit I've ever tasted. Anyway, the Clovis girls will bring the food out when it's ready. Are you ready for the tattooed freaks?"

"Well, since none of us knows what's coming up the trail, we might as well be positive. Yeah, we're ready." They both laughed.

The two rescued girls arrived shortly afterward with their breakfast. Scrambled eggs and the hot fresh "biscuit" lumps that Larry had warned him to expect. The food was in grimy wooden bowls, but they were too hungry to care.

Rex was able to put that dismembered girl out of his mind and tried a bite of the biscuit. "It's corn meal, and, maybe rye flour. At least it's not rock hard." He studied the bowl and added, "The cook needs a lesson in kitchen sanitation."

"The cook called it buckwheat," Larry said, finishing his biscuit. "You're right about sanitation. The cool morning has tempered the stench, but the hall is a pigsty. The whole place needs a thorough cleaning."

Several hours after daybreak, the sound of faint gunfire from down the trail put the posse on alert. Rex had the Wapiti flag, a white rectangle with gold trim on the edges and a large five-pointed green star in the center, ready to run up the unused flagpole over the stockade gate. He had all the doors in the hall, warehouse, barracks, and stable bolted, so that no one who entered the fort could escape out of the open yard. The gunfire implied that someone was chasing the Cinnabar survivors from the scout camp battle. Could the warriors have had a falling out amongst themselves? Based on the occasional shots, they would know shortly.

David C. Brown

Chapter 5

Only two Ichneumon soldiers, along with a beat-up older Prussian wearing Ichneumon coveralls and a Jesuit priest hat, were at the small dock where Panther Creek entered the Erie River to greet the Orleans Queen.

"Who might you be?" Wright had asked the man in the Jesuit's priest hat. Several bruises and scabs were visible on the man's face and hands. Amy, watching and listening from the steamboat's second floor walkway wondered if he was a prisoner.

"Richard Wilhelm. I need a ride to River Point. I'm on official church business. The Ichneumon soldiers rescued me from the Cinnabar tribe."

On hearing that, Amy decided it must have been that wild man, Cinnabar, not the troopers who had beaten the priest, just what she didn't need to hear.

"Official business, you don't look very official."

"Don't allow these rags to mislead you," the stranger said with authority in his voice. "The church has charged me with investigating false prophets and their enablers. That animal, Cinnabar, delayed my mission, and it's imperative I reach River Point to investigate rumors of a false prophet among the Wapitis. I caution you to remember, the church considers anyone who obstructs my investigation to be an enabler."

Amy thought the church's program of torturing and killing crazy people who claimed to be from another world barbaric. She wondered how her minder would deal with this religious zealot.

"Did you just come from Cinnabar's village?" He asked.

"Three days ago. And if you're thinking of going there, be careful. Cinnabar's men and the Ichneumon patrol have been trading gunfire. Everyone's on edge, quick to shoot."

The two soldiers, impatient, attempted to push by Wright, who was blocking the gangway. Amy suddenly realized that the crew was probably bringing up the chemicals from the lower storage room, and none of these people needed to see the acid barrels.

"Hold up, pal," Wright said. "Wait for the captain's permission to board his boat."

"Captain Maqbool wants the Orleans Queen to take the priest back to Hickory Ridge," the older Ichneumon sergeant said. "If he will, we'll leave and rejoin our patrol. Send word to the captain, or get out of my way." The trooper with the sergeant unslung his rifle.

"Please, just let him talk with the captain," the Jesuit said. "They need to get back with their patrol. The captain will need all his men when he arrests those savages for attacking his patrol."

Amy had thought the fact that none of Cinnabar's warriors and pack horses were waiting at the dock meant she could stay on board the Orleans Queen until the porters arrived. Wrong, with no warning, Wright shot dead the two Ichneumon soldiers and the stuttering Jesuit priest. He noted her horrified look.

"Remember this when I tell you to do something. Now get ready to travel, boots and coveralls. You won't need dresses or makeup where we're going," he said while nonchalantly reloading his Prussian revolver.

"Where . . . where are we going?" Amy felt queasy. He ignored her question, instead told Captain Hube, who had arrived to investigate the gunfire.

"Clean up this mess and dump the bodies out in the river. Then steam to River Point for more coal. I'll meet you back here in five days. We're going to go find out what happen to Cinnabar."

The "I'll meet you" part registered in her mind. Did he intend to leave her with those savages? She was a city girl who knew little about surviving in a wilderness. She didn't even have a knife.

Amy, Wright, and his muscular Prussian helper, Ivan, used the three horses belonging to the murdered soldiers to ride up the trail. She wondered if she'd ever see the Orleans Queen again.

As they progressed inland, she was vaguely aware that the land was lovely on this clear early fall day. Massive trees surrounded the trail along the valley and sparkling creek, except where farmers had cleared them for their fields. That the farms appeared abandoned didn't help lessen her sense of impending doom. In several hours of travel, they hadn't encountered a single person in the valley. Finally, mastering her dread, she asked.

"What's the plan? Without the chemicals Cinnabar can't process the winter-sloe."

Amy wanted to grasp why they were plunging into the wilderness, knowing that without the chemicals, they couldn't process the nuts. It would be nice, also, to learn where she fit in the scheme of things. "Why'd you bring me?"

"I need to find out why our man wasn't at the dock with the pack horses. I gather our boss didn't discuss this part with you. The plan is for me to deliver the chemicals and motivate the savages to harvest the nut crop. Your job is to organize the processing. Neither of us can return to Orleans until the forty barrels with the chemicals are full of cocaine paste."

That answer didn't satisfy her question of why he was dragging her along on this trip to find porters.

"I'm not being left with those savages?" There, she had voiced her real fear.

"Don't be ridiculous, you're too valuable to waste."

Amy didn't know whether to be pleased or alarmed, but she felt a bit calmer knowing the Prussians would be around for protection. Seeing her relief he added, "You're right to worry, the chief would consider someone like you a tasty treat." Ivan laughed at his boss's remark.

By now, she was starting to accept that savages, slinks, bears, and vicious snakes weren't lurking behind every clump of brush, ready to pounce on her. She liked the big bay that Ivan had told her to use. It was a friendly animal and she had always enjoyed horseback riding, Amy had just decided this trip might actually be interesting when she noticed four vultures circling ahead, past where the trail left the creek bank. She let out a squawk when suddenly noisy crows seemed to erupt from the brush along the trail.

"My god, is that a body!" Amy cried. Her fears roared back and she looked for Wright. He was thirty meters in front of her, Ivan about the same distance behind her.

Another look verified that it was a body, sprawled face-up in the grass beside the trail. The dead warrior in red war paint was a bloody mess. An animal had eaten most of the warrior's right thigh, and a determined crow or raven was pecking at the corpse's eyes. The bolting crows flying to nearby trees dragged her unwilling eyes to several other bodies lying in the clearing. A dead horse lay near the creek; its belly ripped open, fly-covered intestines spilling out on the ground. She vomited, soiling her right leg and boot.

Shots rang out, and Amy saw Ivan flop forward in the saddle. Terrified, she froze, not sure what to do. Ivan's horse galloped past her with a bleeding Ivan teetering in the saddle. He fell off after about fifty meters. The horse kept running. About then Herr Wright started firing his rifle and yelled, "Run Amy, run up the trail."

Thankfully, she was still in the saddle and no longer vomiting. The big bay needed no encouragement, and they raced up the trail out of sight. After a couple hundred meters, she encountered Ivan's horse eating grass. She felt lost about what to do and waited beside the other horse. She prayed Wright was okay. After a half hour of silence, Amy turned, and leading Ivan's horse, rode back to check on the Prussian.

"Can you believe the bad luck?" Wright asked. He was digging a grave in the sandy bottom by the stream. Ivan's body laid off to the side of the excavation effort.

"Two wounded Ichneumon soldiers panicked and started firing before even asking who we were." He paused in his digging to check her. "Are you okay, girl?"

"No wounds, but I want out of this evil place."

She felt like crying, a luxury she couldn't afford. Sadly, Amy knew the Ichneumon soldiers had made the correct decision in shooting first, even though it hadn't worked out. Wright would never have left them alive.

"Sorry, but the only way we're leaving is with the cocaine paste. Losing Ivan was a blow. Can you use a rifle?"

"I'm a slave. You know Purnell hangs slaves found with firearms. Even having a knife can get you whipped." Suddenly she was mad over the unfairness of slavery and the evil society that kept her a second-class citizen. It had even forced her against her will to enter this hateful wilderness.

"But I know the theory." Amy knew more than theory, thanks to her Prussian friend, Count Rudolf Habsburg, who, among other things, had taken her skeet shooting. Thoughts of the handsome Prussian aristocrat for a moment distracted her from the horrors surrounding her.

"Where's Ivan's rifle?" Wright pointed to the horse she had been leading. Embarrassed, she muttered, "Of course, where else."

She directed the horses to a patch of lush grass near the creek bank, dismounted, and yanked Ivan's rifle out of the scabbard. While the horses munched on the grass, she examined the weapon. Concentrating on how the rolling block breech worked, she nearly stepped on the body of an Ichneumon in the weeds as she walked towards the grave digging. A glance revealed the back of the man's skull was missing along with his brain. She panicked.

"A slink killed that man," Amy cried. She pointed toward the creek. Doubting the accuracy of her claim, Wright stopped digging and went to check the corpse.

"Damn, you're right. I'd hoped we were far enough north to be free of slinks. You'd best learn how to fire that rifle."

"Was it with the Ichneumon patrol?" Amy asked. She knew a slink was a carnivorous, nocturnal creature that looked like an enormous bird without wings. It killed its prey with a bite to the brainstem. The animal had several peculiarities: fear of fire, blue blood, and the ability to be domesticated.

"Well that's an Ichneumon soldier, so I wouldn't think it was with them. It must be a wild one. Focus on the rifle," he said, and returned to Ivan's grave.

Willing herself to relax, she concentrated on the Krupp rifle. She knew the basics of firearms, expanding gas from the burning gunpowder propelled the bullet, a piece of lead, out of the barrel. The rifle's sights allowed the shooter to align the barrel on a target. Gravity and wind affected a bullet's trajectory, complicating the shooter's job of where to aim the rifle in order for the bullet to hit the intended target.

Amy walked over to the gravesite, and Wright handed her three 11.6 x 65mm cartridges to use. He pointed out a tree about a hundred meters in the distance, and told her to aim at a dark spot on the bark. She did and fired, forgetting about the recoil. The gun nearly knocked her down and hurt her shoulder. Still, the bullet had hit just below the dark spot. She raised the aiming point ten centimeters and fired again. The bullet hit to the side of the spot because she had slightly jerked the trigger. Still, her shooting impressed Wright.

"You'll do. Switch horses or saddles and use Ivan's rifle and supplies. Clean the rifle, do you know how?" She nodded. "You might as well be like all the other women in this god-forsaken wilderness." After another minute, he freed and tossed her Ivan's boot knife and sheath.

Herr Wright went back to digging the grave. Amy studied the boot-knife sheath and tried it in her boot. It felt fine, and positioned the knife very handily. She left it in her right boot. She also liked the bay horse and her saddle. "You care if I just move the rifle scabbard and leave his saddle?"

"Suit yourself, just be damn sure it's tied tight and won't fall off if you have to gallop. In fact, take his entire ammo supply, or better, take his saddle bags."

The knots in the rawhide lacing that held the scabbard to Ivan's saddle proved unyielding, and in frustration, Amy used Ivan's razor sharp boot knife to cut the lacings. Lacking any new ties, she used the cut pieces to fasten the scabbard to her saddle. It wasn't near as neat as Ivan's arrangement, but it would hold her rifle.

She then cleaned out all Ivan's ammo, nearly a hundred rounds of the 11.6 x 65mm. How quickly she had grown used to being around dead men surprised and, to a degree, worried her. Twelve dead Cinnabar warriors and six dead Ichneumon soldiers were scattered across the clearing. One of the Ichneumon soldiers had a hatchet stuck in his skull.

"Amy, get that hatchet and unsaddle Ivan's horse and set the saddle by the trail. Put it there," he said, pointing at a boulder by the trail's edge.

"I don't want to touch that handle. It's bloody."

"It's a good hatchet, we may need it. Just stomp on the handle, it'll come loose."

After studying the corpse, she decided instead to kick the hatchet handle. Two kicks were required, and then she used her boot toe to shove the hatchet to the creek shore, where she cleaned it.

"It's got a nice balance," Amy said, taking several swings to help dry the war hatchet, before handing it to Wright.

The crows and vultures quietly watched them from the trees. Amy worried about her sanity. Rifling through dead men's pockets before an audience of menacing birds was starting to seemed sensible behavior.

The Wapiti posse's trap worked perfectly, except there were two hostile parties and a number of extra horses with Cinnabar's men. Nine frantic Cinnabar warriors raced through the gate into the stockade on lathering horses screaming for the guards to close the gate. Reining up their own lathering horse about a hundred meters from the fort were seven Ichneumon soldiers. A number of riderless horses were with them. They started shooting at Rex and the two posse members who were standing above the gate. One of the Ichneumon bullets hit the man beside Rex as they dropped behind the wall for shelter.

The immediate concern for the Wapitis was the Cinnabar warriors inside the fort walls who had realized their mistake and started shooting. The posse made short work of the trapped enemy while Rex shot two Ichneumon soldiers to scatter them. The wounded man had the job of running up the new flag, forcing Rex to crawl to the flagpole and raise the flag. The Ichneumon soldiers stopped shooting when they saw it raised.

Tom, who had been at the gate, ran up to Rex's position while his brother and two posse members started sorting the wounded

Cinnabar men from the dead and the milling horses. The Ichneumon soldiers had found shelter behind the warehouse by the creek.

"Where did those bastards come from?" Tom said. "Damn, they shot Jim."

"I figure from the Hickory Ridge garrison," Rex said. "But they're obviously no friends of Cinnabar. Help Lou first; make sure we have accounted for all those savages. Jim's hit bad and we can't tolerate losing any more men, so be careful. While you do that, I'll try to discover what those bastards want. Larry can help Jim."

"Who's in charge? I want a parley with the officer in charge." One of the soldiers yelled back asking who he was. "I'm Rex Knight. General Mehta at Hickory Ridge knows me. Who are you?"

"I'm Captain Maqbool. Everyone knows the commanding general at Hickory Ridge. Prove you're not with Cinnabar."

"It's a shame that Colonel Paget's not here, he knows me. I'm tired of shouting. I'm coming out to talk with you."

After making sure Larry was on the way to help Jim, Rex walked out the gate toward the warehouse. A moment later, an Ichneumon officer rode from around the warehouse on a lathered-up horse. Rex didn't waste time on preliminaries.

"We came here to stop Cinnabar's raids on our settlements. I have the chief in chains and will take him to Salt Furnace for the Wapiti council to deal with."

"Is that so? Then why'd you shoot my men?"

"I thought you were part of Cinnabar's men," Rex lied.

"Our mission is to stop the marauding," the Ichneumon captain said. "His warriors prey on the farmers along the Erie River, disrupting commerce. If you have him in chains, great, but this is Ichneumon territory and the chief will go with us."

What an asshole, Rex thought. That was not going to happen, but in the interest of peace, he said, "Come on, I'll show him to you."

The officer hesitated, then after a moment, dismounted and motioned to one of the soldiers.

"Sergeant Moor, come with me, after you have a man take my horse," the captain said. He then addressed Rex. "General Mehta is also interested in the source of illegal cocaine. Do you know anything about that?" The captain asked, while eyeing the growling Hokee who had run over to them.

Rex ignored the question and got a firm grip on Hokee. The wolf apparently didn't like the Ichneumon officer.

"Tom, would you take this mutt? I need to show Captain Maqbool our prisoner. Maybe he knows something about your cocaine. We don't."

The captain appeared unimpressed by the evidence of the Wapiti posse's lethal blow to the marauders and offered no comments. Undoubtedly, as an Ichneumon commissioned officer, he considered himself superior to mere humans, but Rex figured missing the credit of being the one who had ended Cinnabar's reign of terror probably accounted for the captain's disparaging attitude.

The young sergeant, who had come with the captain, was studying Larry's rifle, a Mauser bolt-action. The sergeant's rifle was an Ichneumon knockoff of a Krupp single-shot. The captain appeared to notice his sergeant's interest in Larry's rifle.

"Where did he get that rifle? Only a few Prussian special forces have those." Rex figured the fact that most of the posse members were wearing Prussian camouflage fatigues, sans the insignias, accounted for the captain's next question. "Or are you Prussian soldiers?"

"No, we're Wapitis who work in timber and coal mines. All my men have those rifles. Here's the chief," Rex said opening the cell door. "He's suffering drug withdrawal." The curled-up, sweat-covered man on the floor was shaking violently.

"What a rank odor," the captain said. "This place reeks, don't you guys ever clean?" He remained in the doorway and after a quick glance at the chief, he asked, "What drug?"

"I'm not sure, but alcohol for sure and maybe cocaine."

The captain stepped into the room for a better look and asked.

"Is he really a cannibal?" Rex nodded. Maqbool then asked, "What did you plan for him?"

"Turn him over to the Wapiti council if he behaves. Or hang him here if he acts up. Now, I want you leave. Your traders and army have caused the Wapitis a great deal of misery over the last few years, and my men harbor hard feelings toward the Ichneumons. Personally, I have respect for your commander, General Mehta, but you need to leave Wapiti territory."

"Wapiti territory, this is not Wapiti territory," the captain said. Larry was watching the sergeant and had his rifle ready.

"That's a Wapiti flag over the gate, and Panther Creek is now their territory until the Prussian Empire decides its status."

"Prussians? They have no say in Ichneumon territories, and I don't recognize Wapiti laws. Only Ichneumon law counts and my orders were to stop cocaine bootlegging and raids along the Erie. Hand over Cinnabar and I'll not have you arrested," the captain snarled, unsnapping his belt holster flap and reaching his revolver.

Rex's reflexes were stunningly quick, and his fist smashed into the Ichneumon's small nose. As the stunned captain dropped to his knees, Rex twisted the revolver out of his hand. The sergeant, despite Larry having the drop on him, brought his rifle up to shoot Rex. Larry, having no choice, shot the foolhardy but brave sergeant.

It was chaos. The sergeant was thrashing on the floor, holding his right hand, trying to stop the spraying blue blood. Cinnabar was licking at the blood splattered on his arm. The captain was on the floor cursing and screaming for a guard. Rex hit him again, knocking the fool out cold.

"Here, I'll use this for a tourniquet," Larry said, removing his belt. Pieces from the smashed rifle and bullet had ripped open the sergeant's right wrist and hand. The belt stopped the blood flow.

Several Ichneumon soldiers were waiting behind the warehouse for their captain to return. If their captain didn't come back soon, they would go searching for him. The Wapiti posse didn't need to be involved in another gunfight and risk losing more members. Rex also did not wish to kill the Ichneumon troopers waiting behind the warehouse. He just wanted them to leave. The sun would be down in another couple of hours, and the stockade needed secured before darkness complicated the effort.

Rex dumped a bucket of water on the captain to bring him around. Hatred radiated from the dripping Ichneumon.

"Take your wounded sergeant and leave." Rex doubted it would soothe the captain's animosity, still he said, "Tell the general that Cinnabar won't be a problem. Say that you helped the Wapitis eliminate the scourge. When I see General Mehta next, I'll confirm your story."

"I don't want that incompetent fool. He let a hick boy shoot him. Give me my revolver and I'll leave."

And be back with a company of Ichneumon soldiers, Rex thought as the captain bent over to retrieve his hat and then held out his hand for his revolver. The wounded Ichneumon sergeant looked stunned by his captain's remark.

"I'm not negotiating. Leave or become a prisoner," Rex said. He kept the revolver.

Herr Wright stopped at a clearing where another trail from the north joined the main trail along Panther Creek.

"Why'd we stop?" Amy asked. She was miserable. Her butt ached and she was filthy. She didn't wish to imagine how she'd smell and look after a week on the trail and wondered just how cold the creek water was.

"We're about twenty kilometers from Cinnabar's stockade. It'll be dark shortly. We'll stay here until morning. I don't want to arrive in the night. With that undisciplined bunch of savages, they're as apt to shoot as ask questions, especially after those Ichneumon soldiers chasing them."

Amy figured he was right. Earlier they had passed two more dead bodies, Cinnabar's men, not Ichneumons, in the grass beside the trail.

"They're not today's, probably casualties from an earlier skirmish." Wright said in response to her unasked question. "Not more than a couple of days ago. The slinks, bears and wolves haven't found them. The bodies are still intact."

Her minder might seem unconcerned. Not Amy. Discovering corpses scattered along a trail had kept her nerves on edge. Ivan's rifle and knives went everywhere with her. Orleans was starting to seem like paradise.

"Are we in a war zone?"

"If the Prussians seized Cinnabar's operation, there'll be a war. I think this is just some rambunctious Ichneumon captain chasing Cinnabar's warriors. He's after glory, but death is what he'll probably catch. After all, the cannibal has over a hundred warriors."

Wright dismounted and appeared to be looking for a place to build a fire. He probably was, as she was, worried about that slink. That and the reminder about cannibalism did nothing to settle her nerves. To stay occupied, she helped gather dead tree branches to build a small fire by the trail's edge so they could heat water for tea. He seemed satisfied to sit by the fire. Amy wasn't. She wanted her back protected from wild things sneaking up at night. Considering her limited options, a large sycamore tree about twenty meters from the fire seemed her safest choice for protection.

Amy wrapped Ivan's dark, dirty, wool blanket around her body and snuggled in tightly between two large roots and against the massive tree trunk. Her rifle was in her lap, loaded and ready. She was nibbling on a salty strip of leathery goat jerky in the dark and wishing for morning when several Ichneumon troopers arrived on horses.

A few hours of sleep did wonders for Rex's ability to think clearly. The settlement across Panther Creek from the stockade contained about a hundred people, mostly women and a few children. Cinnabar's warriors had murdered the men, or drafted them into their ranks and then had gotten them killed in raids and battles. The Wapiti posse, with help from the Ichneumon troopers, had killed or wounded most of the remaining warriors. The little community was leaderless.

Larry poked Rex, who had fallen asleep. "Boss, there's a delegation outside. They want to see you. What should I tell them?"

The delegation was half the settlement, fifty or more people, mostly women and elderly men. They crowded into the meeting hall in the stone building. The Jarrell brothers and Larry formed a guard force in the hall as Rex stood to address the quiet crowd. Public speaking wasn't his forte, but he was the logical one to address the group.

"My name is Rex Knight. Many of you have lost husbands and sons in the recent fighting. So also, have the Wapitis and peaceful Clovis. They have lost family members to Chief Cinnabar and his men's predations." Still undecided on the depth of evilness in this community, Rex paused and studied the group. They looked bewildered. Should he threaten or offer hope?

"That was yesterday. Today you have a choice. Join us as free people or leave. Wapitis do not allow slavery, nor cannibalism. Both crimes are punishable by hanging." The crowd seemed receptive, even to relax. Rex decided the place wasn't hopelessly evil and took charge of the settlement's affairs.

"Lou Jarrell will be the Wapiti representative," Rex said. The Jarrell brothers looked at each other and laughed. He gave them a moment to realize he wasn't joking, before adding, "In the next few days I want you to pick several people to represent your community who will deal with Herr Jarrell."

"Will the Wapitis hire us?" One of the several older women in a group near the front of the crowd asked. "We need work, food, winter's coming."

"You raise a good point. We all need to make a living. Other than a few kitchen jobs, there's little work in the stockade." Then Rex had an inspiration. "However, there is a bountiful winter-sloe crop in the hills that needs to be harvested."

The crowd quieted on that.

"I'm a coal broker." Sensing his audience didn't understand what a broker was or did, he elaborated. Pointing at the Jarrell brothers, he said. "I sell their coal and take a cut for my services. I think I can sell winter-sloe nuts. I'm going to set up a nut cleaning operation in the warehouse by the waterwheel and buy all the nuts you bring there."

Rex had only the vaguest idea of how he would process those nuts, but he sensed a great opportunity, and decided that the circumstances called for audacious action. One of the women, a crone beside the woman who'd asked about jobs, asked what he'd pay.

"I'm thinking one D-mark per kilogram."

That number had the room buzzing. Rex wondered: was the price too high or too low? Should he worry about the women burying him in nuts he couldn't pay for?

"The price is it for clean nuts?" the same gray-haired woman asked. The group in the hall hushed again to listen.

"No, that's for nuts in their shells," Rex said. "Clean nuts with no pulp attached to the shell." She smiled a toothless grin and he could tell the crowd liked that offer.

"Can we start collecting the nuts now?" a different gray-haired woman asked.

"I have to make some arrangements, but sure, go ahead and collect the nuts."

The crowd broke up, with people leaving the hall in enthusiastic groups and the Jarrell brothers looking at him as if he had lost his mind.

Herr Wright's greeting had surprised the troopers. Amy had seen plenty of Ichneumon army officers in Orleans and despite the darkness, recognized that the lead soldier was a captain.

"Identify yourself and state your business," the Ichneumon officer said. He sounded hostile. The troopers remained on their horses and watched Wright, who appeared relaxed to her.

"I'm Herr Wright. I'm on my way to Cinnabar's stronghold to arrange the purchase of winter-sloe nuts."

"You're too late," the captain said. "The Prussians, with our help, have arrested Cinnabar. There'll be no winter-sloe harvest this year."

One of the soldiers had dismounted and thrown some brush on the hot coals, causing the fire to flare. Amy could see there were only three soldiers with the captain, who was in a bedraggled state, even missing his sidearm. Usually Ichneumon officers pride themselves on their appearance. It probably accounted for his unfriendly attitude. But she welcomed his news. Bless the Prussians, she had thought. No Cinnabar, no reason for them to go on.

"Prussians? Are you sure?" Wright's question seemed to irritate the captain.

"They claimed to be Wapiti miners, but wore Prussian uniforms and had the newest Prussian rifles. So, yes, I'm sure they're Prussians. The bastards probably plan to seize Panther Creek, but General Mehta won't allow that land grab. I . . . ." The captain trailed off. Amy figured the captain realized he was talking too much to a stranger. "Are you a Prussian?"

"No, I work for Herr Purnell. I'm a nut buyer from Orleans. What happened to Cinnabar? Did the Prussians kill him?" Amy hoped so, as she listened to the men.

"He was alive when I last saw him," Captain Maqbool said. "The Prussian leader, he didn't wear any rank, said they'd probably turn him over to the Wapiti council. How'd you get here, a boat?" Wright nodded. "Did you meet my men with the priest? They should have been at the dock."

"They were, waiting for a boat."

"Why didn't they put the priest on your boat and come back with you?" The Ichneumon officer asked. Amy held her breath. Wright could hardly say why because he shot them down in cold blood.

"Err . . . the boat I got off was headed into Wapiti territory, and I guess being Ichneumon soldiers, they didn't want to go there."

"What nonsense, why'd they care where that damn priest went? Arrest this spy." He reached for his missing revolver and Wright shot him.

As the captain fell, he turned and shot the soldier mounted on the right horse. The left horseman, Amy realized, had surreptitiously pulled his rifle earlier. The rider had fired just as Wright shot the other mounted solider. The Ichneumon by the fire was unarmed and Wright shot him. He then shot the left horseman as he reloaded his rifle. The shot knocked the Ichneumon from the saddle. Her guardian then slumped to the ground near the fire beside the dead unarmed soldier.

David C. Brown

Utter silence settled on the clearing. She remained huddled by the tree, quietly convincing herself that she couldn't allow fear to paralyze her. If she wanted to escape this murderous wilderness alive, she needed to quit depending on other people. Take charge of her future.

The fire had died to a few embers by the time Amy resolved to get up and go from man to man to check for signs of life. A loud crunch stopped her. Looking for the source of the eerie sound, she caught sight of a large dark creature hunched over Wright's body. It had to be a bear, but then she spotted the beak. It was a slink eating Wright's corpse.

Some people claimed slinks could strike faster than a bullet. She knew that was nonsense, but this monster was about forty meters from her location and could be on her in a heartbeat. One section of her mind had screamed at her not to move or attract its attention, while another part shouted, "Kill it before it escapes." As far as Amy knew, she was the only other human for many kilometers, and humans were a slink's preferred prey.

There really had been no other choice. Amy had no illusions that her reflexes were especially quick or that they matched the slink's reaction time. To gain time, she slowly brought Ivan's rifle to her shoulder and aligned the gun sights on the creature. Then she awkwardly pulled the hammer back, maintaining the sights on the slink. A loud click announced the rifle was cocked and ready.

Light from the few embers reflected off the creature's two large eyes as it stopped eating and searched for the source of the click. She slowly squeezed the trigger. The gun flash briefly blinded her. As Amy worked the action to load a new cartridge and the shot's echo faded, her night vision returned. The slink was twisting around and grunting about ten meters from her. She realized that, even wounded, the monster had almost reached her. Amy shot the evil creature again.

They were all dead. She had soiled herself. She didn't care. She was alive. Standing by the dead slink and looking at the bodies, Amy realized she was alone in a wilderness. Instead of frightening her, the realization had a calming effect.

Puzzled by her lack of fear, she suddenly comprehended that the disaster offered a chance to be free of Benjamin Purnell. No one in Orleans need ever learn what happened to Herr Wright or Amy Caroom. People would probably assume that Cinnabar murdered and ate them, and that would eliminate any reason for Purnell to take vengeance against her mother and sister.

After throwing more logs on the fire and reloading Wright's revolver and Ivan's rifle, Amy stripped off her unmentionables and washed them and herself. Wet, cold, but clean, Amy found Herr Wright's small shovel and dug his grave. During the excavation, she decided the Prussians, who the Ichneumon captain had claimed were at Cinnabar's stockade, offered her best hope for safety. After she finished burying Wright's body, Amy rode up the trail to the stockade.

After the impromptu public meeting, Rex, Larry, and the Jarrell brothers headed to the kitchen. They were eating a breakfast of hardboiled eggs and several-day-old rye bread when one of the gate guards brought in a tall, slender young woman. She was dressed in filthy black coveralls, muddy black leather knee boots, and wore a belt with an empty pistol holster.

"She asked to talk with the Prussian commander," the Jarrell brothers' younger cousin said, smiling. He handed over a new style 9 x 19mm Walter revolver identical to the one Rex carried. "This is hers. I told her no guns in the hall."

Lou Jarrell turned to his brother Tom with a false whisper, "I told you he's a Prussian."

Hokee had been chewing on a deer's lower front leg bone beside the large fireplace. The animal got up and went over to sniff the woman who casually petted the wolf's head, while she watched him examining her revolver.

"This is an expensive gun," Rex said. He popped open the cylinder and dumped the five cartridges on the table. "Who are you? Where'd you come from?" He gave the Jarrell brothers a look that said 'behave.'

The female stranger was tall for a Wapiti, but had the race's characteristic angular cheek structure, high forehead, and dark hair. She had dark brown eyes, instead of the more typical green eyes of the Wapitis, and a light olive skin tone. Whatever her ancestry, under the mud and grime was a beautiful woman with an attractive physique.

"I'm a teacher. My name is Amy Dalporto. The Jesuits hired me to teach the children in the village, but there's no school in the village. The women said I needed to talk with the Prussian. Is that you?"

"A Jesuit teacher? How did you get here, I mean in the village?" Rex asked. "Who's your escort?"

"I wish I had a pet wolf, what is its name?" Amy asked while petting the wolf's head.

Tom answered, "Hokee."

"The Clovis Belle dropped me at the Panther Creek dock. I bought a horse and rode here. I'm not one of your delicate Prussian ladies." Her brash answer startled Rex.

The Jarrell brothers loved her insolent remark to his question and laughed loudly. Hokee liked the stranger, which surprised him. The wolf normally paid little attention to strangers after he had decided they didn't represent a threat.

"By yourself? Get serious," Rex said a bit harshly. He had a disturbing thought, could she be an Ichneumon, though he had heard, the Ichneumons never allowed their women to travel. He doubled checked her eyes, the pupil was round. Could she be a diversion for an attack, or a spy? "Jarrell, was there anyone else with her?"

"No sir, just her and a horse. It had an Ichneumon army brand," the guard said.

"You traveled up Panther Creek from the Erie River through a hundred kilometers of wilderness. Why didn't those Ichneumon troopers detain you?"

She was both stupid and incredibly lucky if that story was true. Or, more likely, she was lying about what really happened.

Rex didn't believe an asshole like that Captain Maqbool would pass up a chance to grab a lone, good-looking human woman, especially a Wapiti. The Ichneumons would claim she was a runaway slave. His remark had touched a nerve. The fräulein had lost a bit of her defiant air and he pushed the point.

"How did you convince the captain you're not a runaway slave? Or are you in their pay? Oh, excuse my manners, have a seat and some hardboiled eggs." Rex gestured to the table. "Lou, don't eat that, let the lady have the last piece of bread."

"She's no Ichneumon," Tom said. "She could be an island girl." He then reached across the table toward Rex. "Let me look at her revolver."

"Well, we could cut her, just to be sure," Lou said. That suggestion appeared to rattle the stranger's composure. Then Lou grinned to show he wasn't serious, before adding, "Aren't some of those southern island women witches, Tom?"

Lou's comments had the woman's attention. She studied the brothers for a moment, then laughed and said, "Witch? You had me going for a moment."

The woman sure appeared unconcerned. She acted as if she belonged here. He watched as she picked up the egg with the speckled brown shell and examined it. The other hardboiled egg had a bluish shell. Rex could imagine the wheels turning in that pretty head as he watched her trying to decide on some outrageous, but plausible story. The lady bought time by putting back the brown egg and picking up the bluish egg.

"They all taste the same. Please feel free to have both eggs," Rex said. "So how did you get by the captain?"

Finally, she selected the brown egg and as she cracked and peeled it, told her tale.

"I was fortunate. I had crossed the creek to a dense patch of hemlocks to--ah, attend to some business when they galloped by. There were four Ichneumon troopers in the group, and one wore the uniform of a captain. Can I have some hot tea?"

Amy pulled out a chair, sat down to join them at the table, and finish picking off pieces of the shell from the egg. She had apparently realized she had an ally in the Jarrell brothers, for she flashed them a winning smile. Rex heard Tom mutter,

"Damn, she's as good as Jenny in whipping up a yarn."

Whoever she was, she was quick and a cool customer. Rex didn't believe that too fortuitous tale for a moment, though it was certainly conceivable. He decided to press her.

"Did you kill them? Not that we care?"

After a momentary gasp, she said, "I am not a murderer."

The woman cook, Frau Benes, the crone that had asked him about the nut price and claimed to have never worked in Cinnabar's evil kitchen, had entered the room to listen. Frau Benes and the Jarrell brothers all looked first at him and then at Amy who had dropped her egg on the floor. The stranger was resilient. She retrieved her egg before Hokee could snatched it and finished peeling it.

"Hokee must be getting slow. Who is paying your salary to teach?" Could she possibly be telling the truth? No, Rex decided. The Jesuits would never be that irresponsible, to send a young woman alone into Cinnabar's lair.

"I suppose you," Amy said, "Since you killed Chief Cinnabar. The Jesuits aren't big on addressing those tiresome details. My salary is 1000 D-marks a month." She favored him with a lovely smile.

"Frau Benes, where is this school?" Rex asked. She was easy to look at, so he decided to play along.

"Cinnabar never allowed a school, that's why none of us can read or count. Please hire her. Our poor children need her. Bless Jesuit Wilhelm, he said he'd get us a teacher," Frau Benes said. She hugged Amy, who seemed to Rex to be greatly relieved. The Jarrell brothers were grinning at him, knowing the ladies were about to maneuvered him into providing a teacher and school.

"Did you say Jesuit Wilhelm was here?" Rex asked. Why would the false prophet hunter have been here? He learned from the cook that the Jesuit had been Chief Qua's prisoner and later released. "Where is he now?"

The cook didn't know, just that the Jesuit had left three days ago with several warriors.

"Amy, did you meet the Jesuit on the trail?"

A concerned look flashed across her face, and he suspected she knew something about the Jesuit even though she shook her head no. Rex didn't like her evasiveness but decided to wait until they were alone before interrogating her. He didn't want anyone knowing he was concerned about the Jesuit. Then Frau Benes offered to provide Amy a bed until she found her own place.

"May I have my revolver back?"

Rex thought, why not and nodded to Tom to hand it over. She then gathered the cartridges and reloaded her revolver's cylinder. Her trembling fingers told Rex she wasn't quite as unflappable as she acted.

"Am I on the payroll?" She asked.

"I suppose, but none of us has a pfennig to spare until the winter-sloe nut is harvested." He looked forward to learning her real story as well as the whereabouts of Jesuit Wilhelm.

"That fine with me," Amy said, "As long as I can eat here. Pay me when you can."

Chapter 6

The pronounced epicanthic folds at the inner corner of Edward Wu's dark brown eyes suggested considerable Mongol ancestry, though his manner and speech were that of a Prussian aristocrat. Benjamin Purnell knew that the thin, short man was a killer who prided himself on always completing the conditions of the agreed-upon contract. In return, the killer expected prompt payment from the client. Woe to the customer who reneged on Herr Wu's payment. Benjamin always prepaid the exact amount.

The two criminals were in Purnell's office in the white mansion that overlooked the Orleans harbor. They were drinking island rum with orange juice and discussing various business issues. Edward had just returned from New Hamburg, the capital of the Prussian's Guderian Territory, where he had met with the Royal Governor's Chief of Commerce, Stan Blankenship. The subject discussed had been Emperor Schnabel's threat to install martial law and military governors if the current administrations couldn't or wouldn't stop the illegal, or rather non-taxed, cocaine sales in the Prussian western territories of Guderian and Myrtle.

"Your pal, Governor Bullard, according to Stan, needs additional funds to ensure that Berlin's investigation into the source of the illegal cocaine remains ineffective," Wu said.

97

"And how does that blowhard expect to block Emperor Schnabel?"

"The governor plans to selectively enforce the antislavery laws in Guderian Territory and create a backlash against the emperor among the plantation owners. The cotton growers in Myrtle are especially worried. They fear they will be next. The plantation owners are Emperor Schnabel's key supporters in the territories. The governor figures that it will keep the emperor busy sorting out how to keep their support and still satisfy the reformers' demand that the territorial governments enforce the antislavery laws."

"How will that help protect the bootleg cocaine?"

"The governor is betting that emperor will not have the stomach to upset another group of his supporters, the law enforcement establishment, by replacing them with military policemen. Stan wants two hundred thousand D-marks to fund the ruse."

"The governor's scheme is rather pathetic, but it might delay things," Benjamin said. "I have another problem. Wright didn't meet the Orleans Queen. Cinnabar can't process the winter-sloe nuts without those chemicals."

"Stan told me the Wapitis were threatening to end Cinnabar's raids in Jarrell River. Could that be connected with Wright's disappearance?"

"Possibly, but Captain Hube told me the market chatter at Hickory Ridge was about the fate of their last army patrol sent up Panther Creek to stop Cinnabar's raids along the Erie River. They had gone missing. Another puzzle is the disappearance of Jesuit Wilhelm, who was traveling to Salt Furnace to check out reports of a false prophet among the Wapitis. He also stopped at Panther Creek."

"I can't believe the church worries about such nonsense," Wu said. He finished his rum drink and saw the banana bowl was empty.

"It is amazing that educated men believe in people from other worlds magically appearing, but they worry about witches too," Purnell said. "I figured it was worth the cost of a ticket to River Point for the Jesuit. Anything that causes those Wapitis grief is good for us. I just sent the Orleans Queen back with Amos Reed and several men. I'm hoping they'll find out what's happening in Panther Creek."

"I pity any Wapitis who encounter Amos after that Wapiti woman cut his brother's throat. What about your chemist, did she vanish?" Edward asked. "You have any more of those bananas?"

Purnell rang and told the servant who opened the office door to bring two plates of fruit and several bananas. "Amos did take his brother's death hard. To answer your unasked question, he knows the fräulein is off-limits until Cinnabar's problems are fixed."

"The other item is the Wapitis' petition for a separate territory," Wu said. "Chief Smith's daughter, a lawyer, is in Roanoke working with Prussian attorneys and the IRS to prepare the new territory request."

"People seriously think Emperor Schnabel would grant that. Allow a bunch of savages to control the coal fields and the Erie River, no way."

"Stan swears it's serious. And the inability to stop the illegal cocaine hasn't helped their argument for just extending the current Guderian territory boundary to the east bank of the Erie River."

"Then you need to go to Roanoke and convince the Wapitis that they're making a terrible mistake," Purnell said. "Take enough money to pay Blankenship and have some extra for other helpful people. Best take an extra hundred thousand gold D-marks. I want results. Len Ruffner has men and knows the Wapitis. Use him if you need heavy help."

A great opportunity had opened for Rex, if he could pull all the loose ends together. The ladies were proving very industrious, and the winter-sloe nuts were starting to accumulate in the village. The families were waiting for him to organize the warehouse to receive the crop and pay for it. Rex and Tom were in the warehouse inspecting the millstone drive train, trying to figure out a way to use it to power a nutcracker. The new teacher, Amy Dalporto, interrupted their meeting.

"Did you know that there are few children to teach?" she asked.

"No, I hadn't paid much attention." He was still trying to get a read on the teacher and learn what kind of person she was, other than a beautiful young woman.

"There are only eleven children between the ages of four and fourteen to teach. The village has over seventy families. There should be at least thirty or forty children. No one will talk about it. Was it disease, smallpox, what?"

She was apprehensive. Rex suspected she knew the answer, but not willing to say it.

"The night we stormed the place and captured the stockade, there was a partially dismembered young girl hanging from a meat hook in the kitchen."

Amy shook her head and looked faint.

"I believe Cinnabar and his men did eat some of the people that they captured on raids, but their own kids, I doubt it. Look at the place it's filthy. Their diet's horrible. Disease and ignorance of basic hygiene probably account for the lack of children. The question that perplexes me, though, is how ingrained is cannibalism in this settlement? Cinnabar didn't murder, cook, and eat those people all by himself."

"And I thought the Orleans Queen crew was teasing me about cannibals. Why haven't you hanged the monster?"

"I considered hanging him, but a skilled interrogator could learn a great deal from him about the illegal cocaine trade and the players involved." Then realizing what she had said, he added. "You said earlier that the Clovis Belle dropped you off at Panther Creek. Benjamin Purnell owns the Orleans Queen and he's our number one suspect. Are you involved in his cocaine bootlegging?"

He was almost certain after her Orleans Queen remark that she was involved with Purnell and her Jesuit teacher business, bull. How she responded would tell him a great deal about her character.

"Bootlegger? Who are you, a Prussian officer?"

"Does it really matter who I am?" Rex said. "For the record, I'm a Wapiti by way of the Northern Ice fields, son of a Wapiti slave and a cod fisherman. Now, answer my question."

A tense, unsmiling woman studied him for several heartbeats. After a sigh, she answered in a stronger voice. "I'm one of Benjamin Purnell's slaves. I'm trained as a chemist and an engineer." She glanced toward Tom and then continued.

"He sent me here to help Cinnabar's cocaine paste operation. Are you going to arrest me?" Amy's hand had gone to her revolver and Tom, from a distance of several meters, aimed his rifle at her and clicked off the bolt safety. Her earlier dismayed look was gone, replaced with a defiant glare.

"No damn gunplay, by either of you two." He had zero interest in harming her. He just wanted the truth.

Amy clasped her hands together and muttered, "Okay." She glanced at Tom who then lowered his rifle and clicked the bolt safety tab on.

"Thank you," Rex said. "No kidding, a slave? Well you're not one here."

"Purnell has a long memory and even longer reach. The only way I'll ever be free of that monster is if he thinks I'm dead, or, I purchase my manumission from him. Otherwise my mother will pay for my rebellion."

"Lord, this world is something else. What does emancipation from slavery cost in Orleans?" Rex had read about such things in the American south before the Civil War, but never dreamed he'd ever encounter it.

"His price is twenty thousand D-marks. He claims a plantation owner offered that. Tends to make one feel subhuman, being treated as chattel."

Tom had whistled on hearing the amount, and she had glared at him, before turning her attention back to Rex.

"Do you believe him? I mean if you paid him twenty thousand D-marks, he'd free you."

"Not if I'm testifying to the Prussians about his bootleg cocaine operation. He'd kill me."

"If the Prussians hanged him, it'd save you twenty thousand D-marks. No one is going to arrest you, though later I'd like you to consider telling the Chief's Council about this operation."

She shrugged okay.

"Did I heard you right, you're an engineer?" That got a smile and nod from her. "You know anything about nut crackers?"

Tom laughed and left them.

Eight members of the Wapiti posse had survived, and most of the men wanted to leave, except Lou Jarrell. A local Clovis woman had caught his eye and he'd agreed to stay and run the place. Rex should stay and organize the winter-sloe business, but he worried Captain Maqbool might return with a company of Ichneumon soldiers to take Cinnabar by force.

"Tom, plan on leaving in two days. We'll take Cinnabar to River Point," Rex said.

"I hope by way of the trail down Panther Creek, not across the mountains."

Since Rex was stuck in the stockade for a bit longer, the next morning he put several women to work cleaning Cinnabar's former quarters. The other night a large black spider had run across his face as he lay in the bed. He hated spiders. To aid a thorough cleaning, he helped the women move chests and boxes so they could clean under and behind the items.

When moving the bed platform, he had discovered a cut stone block that looked similar to the Ichneumon altar stone found at River Point. It even had the drain hole, for the victim's blood. Its presence removed any doubt in Rex's mind that his bed platform had once been an Ichneumon altar. A wood plug with a brass handle was stuck in the drain. Loud pounding on the bedroom door stopped his effort to pry the wood plug out of the hole.

"Boss, we need you, there are several serious looking Prussians in the stockade demanding to see Cinnabar," Larry said.

Rex tossed the sorry husk-stuffed mattress back over the platform, checked that his revolver was loaded, and grabbed the Mauser rifle.

Larry hadn't exaggerated, but he never did. Thugs, four of them sat on lathered horses. Two of the big Prussians held double-barrel breech-loading shotguns; the one in animal skins had an Ichneumon face and held a Krupp rolling block. The apparent leader of the group was another large Prussian in one of those light blue coats that Donnelly's men wore. He had two revolvers in shoulder holsters. They all wore the dark brim-style hats favored by slavers.

The posse members had remembered their training. The Wapitis had made no pretense of being friendly. They had positioned themselves around the stockade so each stranger had two armed posse members covering him from different, but not opposite, directions. In their effort to intimidate by riding into the stockade as a group, the thugs had placed themselves at a disadvantage. The Wapiti posse had them surrounded.

"I'm Amos Reed, sheriff from Myrtle Territory. I'm here to pick up a prisoner, Chief Cinnabar, and find Sheriff Wright."

"Are you now, a sheriff? Well it's a shame you had to come so far. The chief died during the attack by the Ichneumon troopers. There's no sheriff named Wright here."

"Where's his body? Who are you? And tell those foolish Wapitis to put down their rifles before they get hurt."

"We burned it," Rex said and pointed to the remains of the pyre on the hillside. The information seemed to cause uncertainly in the group of thugs.

"I'm also looking for Sheriff Wright's female slave, goes by Amy," the sheriff said. "Where is she?"

"You're the first strangers we've seen. Other than an Ichneumon army patrol that passed through a number of days ago. I'd suggest you check at Hickory Ridge for your friends. The Ichneumons have a bad habit of thinking every stranger is a spy and grabbing them."

Rex realized where he'd heard the name Reed before. He had been Purnell's notorious procurer. He knew a Wapiti woman had killed him during a rape. He couldn't resist checking to learn if this belligerent ass was his brother. "Did you have a brother named Tyler, a pimp for Purnell?"

The red face of the thugs' leader answered the question. Amos snarled, "We're going to search the place." He reached for his left revolver.

Rex, already holding a rifle, said, "Don't be a fool, sheriff."

Amos was and yanked out his revolver. The posse's first and only volley killed all of the thugs. The sheriff's horse received most of the pellets from the rear guard's shotgun blast, but several pellets still hit Rex.

One of the few teenage boys in the village, Lee, was helping Amy repair the waterwheel when he spotted the four riders and whispered the alarm. Lee was small and thin. The boy could fit in places among the gears that Amy couldn't. She looked out the mill house door and nearly fainted when she recognized that the lead rider was Amos Reed. Three of his hoodlums followed in a string behind him. The horses looked exhausted. Fortunately, Purnell's thug and procurer didn't notice her.

She should have warned Rex that Purnell would send other people to check on them when they didn't pick up the shipment of chemicals. Now it was too late and Amos Reed would kill them all. Sure enough, gunfire erupted in the stockade. Amy pulled her pistol and ran to the gate. Two frightened horses galloped out as she entered. Amos Reed was lying in the dirt along with his three riders. Two men were helping Rex to his feet.

The Wapiti leader was a big man. He towered over her as Amy ran up to him. "Are you alright?" she asked.

"No, some of those damn shotgun pellets hit me. The bastard knew you. He was looking for you and a Sheriff Wright. Larry, help Lou clean up this bloody mess. Throw the damn fools on the pyre." Rex crossly glanced at the Clovis women who had rushed into the stockade yard to watch. "You're being paid to clean." His reminder and scowl sent the women hurrying back to their work in the meeting hall.

Amy followed him meekly into his quarters. She realized that someone, probably one of Frau Benes' crones, had just cleaned the room. It smelled of vinegar.

"What do you want?" The big Prussian was clearly in no mood for any more of her omissions and evasions.

"I didn't tell you everything," Amy said.

"So I gather. Who is Sheriff Wright?"

"Before I get into that, let me clean those wounds. You do not need an infection."

Without waiting for agreement or more discussion, Amy unbuttoned Rex's fatigue blouse and located the pellet wounds, while taking in the magnificent male body in front of her. Judging by the sudden swelling, she wasn't the only one affected by their close proximity. She forced her focus back to the wounds, noticing that they had the potential to be life threatening if not properly cleaned.

The man was no stranger to bullet wounds. His right arm had a recently healed gash. Three of Tyler Reed's BB size lead pellets had entered Rex's massive right pectoral. The three entry wounds formed a triangular pattern about two centimeters across. No pellets were visible, nor had the wounds bled.

Amy knew that the trivial appearance of small deep puncture wounds often caused the patient to ignore them with fatal results. His wounds scared her. The pellets would have dragged fabric from his dirty fatigue into the wounds. She would need to remove it along with the pellets. Larry came in to check on them as she was resolving how to proceed.

"Larry, I need a candle, a clean cloth, and alcohol."

"Just what are you planning?" Rex asked.

"To remove the pellets, but outside, where I have better light."

She had Ivan's pocketknife, though she would have preferred one of the tiny scalpels used in the lab. Ivan's knife appeared almost new and was razor sharp. After Larry had the candle burning, he placed it on the stair tread, and she sterilized the knife blade by running it through the candle's flame. Next, she washed the pectoral surface with the gin, and then said.

"You ready?"

Rex nodded, while watching her. The lead pellets were about a centimeter deep. The pellets were deformed and had sharp edges, and they didn't want to pop out. She had to cut and dig each one out. The pain had to be terrible, but he said nothing. On the plus side, there was little fabric and the wounds bled profusely, which helped to clean the punctures. Her patient presented a frightful sight, with his chest dripping blood.

"I hope you know what you're doing, woman," Larry said.

"She does. Better that a puncture wound bleed than seal too quickly. Have the cook boil a cloth and let her know when it's ready. I don't want anyone but Amy handling the cloth," Rex said. "Let me have the bottle." He took a drink of gin.

"Not a lot of people understand about infection and microorganisms," Amy said. "Where did you learn?"

"Don't worry about that. Who is Sheriff Wright, no, better, where is he?"

He seemed weary and sat down on the hall's entrance steps in the warm sun.

Amy quietly told the big Prussian the rest of her story, including her real name and about the death of Captain Maqbool, his men, and the fearsome slink. She even told him about Herr Wright killing Jesuit Wilhelm at the river dock. She finished by repeating her fear that Purnell would kill her mother. To Amy's surprise, Rex seemed more relaxed and lost in thought after her disclosures. He was probably trying to decide if she had told the truth.

"I agree, best Amy Caroom stays dead," Rex said. "I suspected this place was involved in converting the winter-sloe nut to cocaine when I saw that grinding wheel and vats. Cinnabar's and your testimony will hang that bastard Purnell."

"Don't forget two things," Amy said. "A slave's testimony carries little weight in Prussian courts, and he has my mother."

"I'll not make light of the fact that in certain areas slavery is still tolerated, but here, you're a slave only if you want to be one. No

Wapiti recognizes slavery, and the Prussian Empire has outlawed the practice. There has to be a way to protect your family."

Lou waited at a respectful distance in the yard, clearly not wanting to eavesdrop on their private conversation, but also needing something from Rex.

"Amy, let's not tell anyone about this until we've had time to decide how best to use your information and protect your family. Go check on the dressing, I need to find out what Lou wants."

"Is she the Amy those guys were looking for?" Lou asked. He sat down on the stairs beside Rex, who was considering another shot of gin for the pain, but too many issues needed to be resolved to cloud his head.

"That's her. She's involved in some serious business that I'm not at liberty to talk about," Rex said. "All I'm going to say is that it's very important to the Wapitis' future that nothing happens to her or Cinnabar. When she finishes with this bandage, I want you, your brother, and Larry to meet me in my quarters." He spotted Amy approaching with the boiled cloths and a bowl. "Lou, find four Clovis willing to help guard this place and give them those rifles. Keep the shotguns." He pointed at the bodies.

The younger Jarrell brother asked if it was okay to use women as guards. Rex nodded and waved Lou off. The engineer had heard his remark about using women and looked perplexed.

"Women serving as guards," Amy asked.

"Sure, why not, most are better shots than men. As you can see, we're not exactly overrun with Wapitis and we need all the help we can find. Hell, you're living proof a woman can handle a rife."

Smiling and quiet, Amy dressed his shoulder. On her completion of the bandage, Rex said. "You've met a number of the Clovis women. I'd like you to ask them to spread the word that the Clovis families collecting the winter-sloe nuts need to store the nuts at their homes. Tell them it's only until I can return with a scale to weigh the crop."

"Sure, I'll do that. Keep this wound clean. In the morning I'll check it."

"Be ready to travel in the morning."

"Where are we going," she asked. The news appeared to make her nervous.

"River Point, I want to put Cinnabar some place safe and you need to speak with Chief Smith," Rex said. She appeared dubious as to the wisdom of that idea.

"What about my family?" Amy asked. "They're still in Orleans and under Purnell's thumb."

"Amy, consider this, what if Amos had seen you first? I'm sure Purnell sent those thugs to eliminate potential witnesses. Amos would have shot you and we would have been in the dark as to why. Once your story is out, killing you won't help Purnell. Then he'll need you alive to claim that the Wapitis forced you to tell lies."

"You're the only one who knows," Amy said. "If no one talks, he'll think I died with Wright."

"Everyone here heard Reed say he was looking for Purnell's female slave," Rex said. "He even called her Amy. You really think they haven't figured out you're that slave? The story always manages to surface. In the end, Purnell will keep your family alive to have leverage." Rex corked the gin bottle and handed it to Amy.

"Is the pain not bad?" Amy asked, examining the bottle. "You hardly touched the gin."

"I'll survive. Now back to Purnell learning your fate. I'd like to delay that. While we're on the river, it's important to keep your identity a secret from the crew. So try for a grimy androgynous appearance when you dress tomorrow. I don't want every man on the sternwheeler remembering a beautiful Wapiti maiden going to River Point. If you stink, that's even better."

A tentative Amy just shook her head in wonder at his last instruction. "You're serious?" He nodded. "Okay." Without further comments, she walked off toward the waterwheel with the bottle of gin.

Rex made his way back to Cinnabar's old quarters to check that stone altar, which might be a vault. He could hope. His men were waiting in the room.

"Tom, pry that plug out of the drain," Rex said. A cavity about the size of a loaf of bread was under the wood plug. There was another plug of mortar below the cavity to seal the drain. The space contained two leather pouches. The heavy pouch had three hundred and fifty-seven gold coins, each worth five hundred D-marks. The beautiful gold coins reminded Rex of American quarters in their size. The wealth on the table transfixed them.

"Well, what's in the other pouch," Larry finally asked. Rex dumped its contents out. There were pearls, small cut red stones that could be rubies or garnets, and a dozen small diamonds of various styles. The jewels appeared to have been from rings.

"As I recall, our deal was that we'd split the loot with you for financing the posse," Tom Jarrell said. "Then the posse members would split their half evenly." Larry and Lou nodded in agreement with Tom.

The men had been in the field going on a month, and their share of the booty would pay them well for their time. In Rex's case, it would provide the funds to pay the new Wapiti land tax. The value of the modern bolt-action rifle given to each posse member would have been enough to make the men think their time well spent. Tom agreed to see that the dead men's families received their shares and supervise the sale of the captured horses.

"Okay if I take the jewels to Herr Jacobs in Roanoke and ask him to sell them?" Rex asked. It was. "Tom, divide up the coins. In the morning we leave for River Point."

The two-day ride down the Panther Creek trail went without a hitch. However, the sight of several gnawed-on Ichneumon skeletons lying in the weeds along the trail reminded everyone of the recent woeful events in the valley. Amy had buried Herr Wright the night of the confrontation, but she hadn't buried any of the Ichneumons.

"In the interest of neighborly relations with the Hickory Ridge garrison, do you think we ought to bury them?" Larry asked. Rex wanted to get his prisoner, Chief Cinnabar, safely locked away in River Point.

"Okay, we'll do one grave. Sergeant Moor, you gather their name tags," Rex said. The sergeant's injuries prevented him from helping with the grave digging. The ground was a soft, sandy clay. The Wapitis quickly had a deep grave dug. Nothing had touched the slink carcass, except flies.

While the men gathered the Ichneumon troopers' remains and threw them in the grave, Rex walked over to inspect the slink carcass. It was a feathered, bird-like creature, and reminded him of the prehistoric terror birds he had seen in pictures. Hokee was sniffing at it. The slink was sprawled on its side and puffed from decay, making any determination of its size difficult. The creature was at least as tall as Rex was. It had a massive, heavy beak made to rip apart prey. It was like a super ostrich on steroids with lethal-looking talons and a massive eagle-like beak.

"God, I wouldn't want to encounter a live slink on a dark night," Rex said. He thought anyone who could keep his or her wits during an encounter with that creature was a tough character. Even dead, the thing gave him the willies. "Amy, you're evidently not one to panic."

Tom nodded his agreement. He had a stick and used it to pry open the eyelid. The slink's eye was huge. It was the size of a baseball, and that probably explained the creature's noted night vision. One of Amy's bullets had ripped a hole in its shoulder, but the leaked blood had congealed and turned black, so they couldn't verify whether the slink had the azure blood Larry had claimed.

"I was too terrified to panic," Amy said. "Come here, Hokee. Stay away from it, before it gives you some alien disease."

Sergeant Moor kept looking at Amy. Rex figured the young Ichneumon was having difficulty believing any woman could kill such a vicious creature, and in the dark no less.

"Are all Wapiti women like her?" the sergeant asked.

"God no, most of them look and smell better," Tom said.

Amy and the men laughed. The Ichneumon sergeant looked perplexed. Following Rex's instructions, she had dressed like a dirty vagrant and had the odor of a skunk. A blanket wrapped around her waist drastically changed her delightful young figure to that of a slatternly androgynous creature.

"Sergeant, you know our agreement. You can never talk about her or a woman who killed a slink," Rex said. That didn't stop the Wapitis from asking the Ichneumon sergeant about the strange animal.

"Captain Maqbool bought the slink in Port Delta. He wanted a guard animal when he learned his next assignment was to pacify Panther Creek," Sergeant Moor said.

"Are they easy to train?" Tom asked.

"I've heard they're not. The captain and his slink never bonded. I think the animal proved to be more trouble than useful," Sergeant Moor said.

Rex was delighted to learn that slinks were rare, difficult to train, and expensive. The only wild population of slinks was in the southern continent, though some escaped animals could conceivably be breeding in the lower Erie River basin. Rex had the slink dragged to the grave and thrown in. Then his men filled the hole.

Larry Hopkins and Tom Jarrell had Cinnabar shackled and blindfolded on a horse. They took turns leading the prisoner's horse. Rex didn't want a repeat of what had happened to the other prisoners. The three Cinnabar warriors captured with the chief had died from snakebites shortly after capture. Rex suspected that the Clovis women had dropped the rattlesnakes in the warriors' prison cell as the men were sleeping, probably retribution for killing children.

The next afternoon, Rex's group found the tiny Clovis hamlet at Panther Creek dock still abandoned. To his joy, the Clovis Belle came up the Erie River an hour after their arrival and someone on board saw them. The boat headed to the dock.

Amy didn't share his joy. She walked over to him on the dilapidated dock, from where he watched approaching boat to take charge of Rex's horse, Zack. The skunk smell emanating from her was fearsome; it made Rex's eyes water.

"Captain Dalporto knows me."

"The captain probably knows everyone along the river. He'll never recognize you. Your own mother wouldn't. Try to relax."

"Don't get over confident, you big oaf," Amy said. "That jolly old man is owned by Benjamin Purnell, and he'll pass on everything he learns. Like where you took Chief Cinnabar. In his black heart, Captain Dalporto is a slaver."

Rex knew Amy's characterization of the Clovis Belle's captain and his loyalties was correct, but still he couldn't help liking the old reprobate. Dalporto had a key part to play.

"Amy you have him pegged, but I have a plan that'll work if he doesn't discover who you are."

As Rex watched the Clovis Belle maneuver into the new wooden dock at River Point, he had a startling realization. In the past when things weren't going well or the smoke and bugs got to him, he'd wonder if there were any way to escape back to his comfortable

21th century life in the good old USA. Not once had he thought of his former life on Earth since meeting Amy. He was sure what to make of that.

The little paddle wheeler, Mischief, another prize taken from the Ichneumon Army, normally shared the dock, but it wasn't there. It was probably up river at Salt Furnace. Talk about boilers had him wondering what type of boiler the Mischief had. He knew the steamboat had a Focke-Wulf compound steam engine. As soon as the Clovis Belle cleared out and the Mischief arrived, he wanted Amy to inspect the boat's boiler.

Matt Brewer, commander of the River Point garrison, and his assistant, Andy Smith, were waiting at the dock. They were pleased to discover the posse members aboard the boat.

"Andy, I need a favor," Rex said. "That vagrant with the horses, see that she gets a hot bath and clean clothes." Andy and Matt looked a bit mystified by his request. "She's hiding from Captain Dalporto and Purnell's spies. I'll explain later."

Andy walked over to the big Wapiti trooper, Luther, at the dock and told him something that brought a laugh and a glance toward Rex. Luther went on the boat and cleared a path for Amy and the Jarrell cousins to lead the horses off the boat and into the fort.

"I have a present for you," Rex told Matt, and they went onboard to find Larry Hopkins and Chief Cinnabar.

Chapter 7

Amy was thankful she had listened to Rex, for Captain Dalporto inspected each horse as it disembarked. The captain hardly glanced at her, but must have smelled her, for he wrinkled his nose and waved for Zack and her to hurry off the boat. The big Wapiti guard did examine her, shook his head at something, and told her and the cousins to follow him.

Well-tended gardens covered most of the land around the fort. White flags with green five-point stars flew from each corner of the fort. No litter marred the grounds nor shoreline. The area inside the fort was clean, no manure piles were scattered across the fort. Amy knew that meant the fort must have a crew dedicated to cleaning up after the livestock and horse traffic. Looking around, she decided that the Wapitis ran a tight organization.

"You smell terrible," the Wapiti boy said. He had been loafing on a bench in front of the stable when she walked up with Rex's horse. "I'll take your horse," the grimy urchin said. "Wow, skunks smell better," he added, and reached for the reins, while he pinched his nose with his left hand.

"Billy, be polite," the beautiful woman who had come out of building across from the stable said as she walked up. "I'm Lily Hopkins, this imp's teacher. I arrange a hot bath and a change of clothes for you. Do you have lice?"

115

"I don't think so. Fleas, but no lice," Amy answered trying not to scratch while handing Zack's reins to the annoying stable boy.

"We're going in that door, it's my private quarter with a bath, but I don't want fleas. Inside the door stop and remove everything. Throw it outside, and then we'll get you cleaned up."

Amy was embarrassed. Did this woman think her an untidy, slovenly woman? "I'm not-" she began.

"I know. It was necessary to get by the captain. How hot do you like your water?"

The water was wonderful and after a good scrubbing, and several hot rinses, Amy felt clean. Lily handed her a large cotton towel and started searching for an outfit that Amy could wear. The two women were about the same age, size, and build. Amy asked about Rex Knight.

"Did he rescue you?" Lily asked. The question caught Amy by surprise, but after a moment of reflection, she decided he had and nodded yes.

"I'm not surprised," Lily continued. "He saved Tara and me, Indira, and, well, one might say he saved the Wapitis from the slavers, though he'd never take credit. He's a good man, but I think his eye is on the Prussian ice queen, Franciscka Weidman." The Wapiti woman knew how to deliver the important information, Amy thought, as she toweled off.

After the Clovis Belle embarked up the Erie River for Allegheny and Rex had completed the arrangements with Matt, he went to Lily Hopkins' place to check on Amy. Two beautiful women greeted him. Amy wore a short dress that confirmed his guess that she had a delightful set of legs to go with her fine derriere and wide shoulders. Her coloring was slightly darker than Lily's, and she had brown eyes, whereas the Hopkins' lady had green ones. They were having a meal of venison stew and corn bread when he arrived. Lily invited him to join them, and they made small talk.

"Amy, in the morning, say an hour before sunrise, meet me at the dock. I want you to check the boiler and engine in the Wapiti Mischief. Wear a pair of Lily's fatigues. We're going to visit Chief Smith, so he can hear your story and I can pay my taxes."

Harsh Malik, captain of the paddle wheeler, Mischief, was waiting on the boat with a pot of hot coffee when she arrived.

"Captain Malik, do you have an extra mug? I love coffee." Amy said. The captain nearly spilled the coffee pot as he gave her a hug.

"My god, it's Amy Caroom in person. How did you escape that tyrant?" the captain asked while holding her at arm's length to examine her. Rex emerged from the pilothouse. "Herr Knight, how did you know?" the captain asked. He appeared at a loss as to what Captain Malik thought he knew.

"Amy built this boiler. It's the original water tube boiler, the first," the captain said. "Come on, girl, check your handiwork. You'll see I've taken good care of her. I use rain water whenever I can."

"I thought you didn't talk with women," Amy said. The Ichneumon captain's friendliness was a surprise, after her experience with the officer in Orleans.

"Please, don't remind me. The Wapitis cured me of that foolishness."

"Maybe there is hope. You say you've taken good care of her. If that's so, what are those patches?" She pointed at firebox patches that looked suspiciously like repaired bullet holes.

"Ah, these crazy Wapitis are always sticking their noses in places where they're not welcome."

117

"I'm learning that," she agreed while inspecting the firebox. "My god, I count twenty-four holes . . . ." She feared to ask about casualties.

"Minor stuff, the boiler tubes are fine. It's a good design. I've run boiler pressures over three million pascals with no leaks."

"That's over four hundred psi . . . ah, is it safe?" Rex asked.

"Is it safe? Yes," she said while wondering what a psi was. She then turned her attention to the captain who showed her a steam gauge he had installed. Rex followed them as they inspected the engine cylinders and valves.

"That rod packing needs to be replaced. What is the engine's water consumption?" The captain named a number. "Ah, that's not excessive. Later take me through your boiler blow down procedures. I want to hear it run."

Amy helped the captain light the boiler and by then, Kyle Baler had arrived with their horses and rifles. He helped Amy finish shoveling coal into the boiler's firebox while Rex boarded the horses. Thanks her father and those misogynistic Ichneumons, she had never ridden on the boat, or had a chance to watch her boiler operate, and was anxious to see her handiwork operate.

"Captain Malik, check the boat, we'll have the steam pressure up shortly."

"You're not supposed to give the captain orders," Kyle said. Captain Malik laughed and went to check the paddle wheels and drive linkage.

"You finish," Amy said, putting up the coal-shovel. She went to find Rex. He was on the dock talking with Matt Brewer, three guards, and Cinnabar in chains.

Rex boarded a few minutes later and Captain Malik engaged the paddle wheels. A half dozen people watched the Mischief back away from the dock and then depart. Amy wondered if one of them worked for Purnell.

Chief Smith and John Hopkins were in the upper conference room of the new two-story wood frame office building near the Salt Furnace stockade, according to the elderly, prim, no-nonsense woman who served as Chief Smith's office manager. Fortunately, she liked Rex, and told him to go on in, the chief's other business could wait. Rex asked Amy to wait until he first talked with the council. Hokee would keep her company.

On shaking hands with John, Rex asked about Indira.

"My daughter is well," John said. "Fully recovered, and driving her mother to distraction. The girl has mastered the Krupp rifle. I finally gave in and promised to take her on the fall bear hunt."

"The bear won't have a chance. When does she go to Roanoke?" He asked and wondered if her father was correct about Indira having recovered from the murderous brutality she witness.

"Next fall," John said. "We're sending her a year early."

"With Indira following Jenny, the Jesuits may bar Wapiti females from their college," Chief Smith said, laughing. The chiefs were friends and had been through much together with Rex. He spent the better part of an hour telling them about the posse's adventures. They were very happy to hear about the early land tax payments, and Rex did not dwell, nor did they ask, on the source of the payment.

"Cinnabar is a nasty creature," Rex said. "But we need to keep him alive for he is the key to convincing Emperor Schnabel that the Wapitis had no involvement in the illegal cocaine that is flooding the territories. Amy Caroom, who is waiting downstairs, can testify that Benjamin Purnell sent her to Cinnabar to help improve his operation by upgrading the first step of the cocaine conversion process, the cocaine paste."

"You caught a couple of actual cocaine bootleggers?" Chief Hopkins asked. "One of them is a woman?"

119

"Amy is more of an informant," Rex said. "Don't plan on arresting her." That remark earned a glance between the two Chiefs.

"Is she pretty?" John asked. Rex shrugged as the chiefs exchanged smiles.

"I have never met Purnell, but based on his reputation, I figure you're right to worry, killing a hostile witness wouldn't trouble the man," Chief Smith said. "Tell Fraulein Caroom to come up, we'd like to make her acquaintance."

"An unusual name, Caroom, is there any connection to the boiler people?" Chief Smith asked. Amy explained the connection to the amazement of the two chiefs. Rex explained the need for keeping her real name secret and asked about their progress on a territory.

"Tara sent a letter," the chief said, after asking Amy if she'd like some tea. She didn't. "The letter explains my daughter's concern over Governor Bullard's campaign to convince the Prussian Emperor not to grant the Wapitis a new territory. The governor contends that since the Wapitis have not been able to protect themselves from bandits such as Cinnabar, or control bootleggers making illegal cocaine, granting the Wapitis their own territory would be a mistake." He handed the letter to Rex.

"Then we need to let the Prussians know Cinnabar is our prisoner and will be tried for cannibalism and banditry," Rex said. "Especially the IRS and Guderian newspapers need to be made aware. Invite everyone to the trial."

Amy's interest was on studying the broken end of the short sword on the table.

"Can you believe the gall of the New Hamburg gang of thieves?" John asked. "The governor fears a Wapiti territory would become a haven for bandits and contraband that could further damage the empire's peace and revenue. That thieving bastard even suggested it might prove a worse problem than the current illegal cocaine."

"Tara said the Emperor's biases make him predisposed to believe self-government might be beyond the savages', that is the Wapitis', innate abilities," the chief added.

"Not much we can do about that, but actions speak louder than words," Rex said. "Tara needs to let Franciscka know that the Wapitis have shut down Cinnabar's illegal cocaine operation."

Amy had looked up from examining the broken sword when he mentioned Franciscka. The chiefs and Rex then discussed how to get the information to Franciscka in Roanoke.

Edward Wu had to agree with Stan Blankenship, the railroad car was a genuine improvement over a horse drawn stagecoach. The speed of forty kilometers per hour was amazing, but the real pleasure was to have a hot meal served at a table while flying through the countryside. Leave it to his boss to know about railroads and manage to invest in one before most people had realized the steel rail's potential to change the world. Wu spent the ride collecting his thoughts and deciding on a course of action in Roanoke.

The essence of Blankenship and Governor Bullard's strategy to block the Wapitis' petition for a new western territory was to harp on the lawlessness in the tribal areas. It would help ignite Emperor Schnabel's known prejudices toward the territories' indigenous populations. Wu was well aware of the disdain Prussian aristocrats harbored for foreigners and the lower class. He believed the odds were long on the emperor granting the Wapitis their own territory and thought his boss's concerns overblown.

However, Purnell wanted to be certain. He had told Wu that Herr Simpson had requested a license to sell corn whiskey in the Prussian territories. Simpson's whiskey had Baron Hoess concerned that a new competitor with a new product might have an adverse impact on the baron's liquor business. Wu had used that knowledge to arrange a meeting with the baron's son, Rudolf, under the pretext of Purnell Industries having influence with Herr Simpson. Rudolf was one of the Guderian Territory Assistant Attorney Generals and the lawyer assigned by the AG to assist the Wapitis' lawyers.

The locomotive had developed mechanical problems about twenty kilometers from Roanoke. The resulting delay had caused Wu to miss the scheduled office visit with Rudolf Hoess. He had sent a note using one of the pigeons the train crew carried aboard to advise Roanoke of delays and mechanical problems. It was an expensive proposition, as the railroad charged him one hundred D-marks to send the message, which was twice the normal territorial rate for a pigeon.

Wu's note explained the delay and requested an evening meeting. Rudolf had left a note at the station. The attorney would be at the Roanoke Hotel that evening and was willing to meet with a friend of his father's partner.

The baron's son was in the bar drinking vodka when Wu arrived. He was impressed with the room's cleanliness. The waiter seated them at a corner table for some privacy. The white linen tablecloth seemed to glow, the silverware clean and shined, and the glassware spotless. He hoped the food was equally well prepared. He ordered a vodka, made the usual polite inquires, and then went to work.

"As I'm sure you appreciate, Herr Purnell has many interests. He hopes to make an offer for certain Donnelly properties the Wapitis may sell."

"I'd advise Herr Purnell to be sure any properties the tribes might offer for sale have valid titles and deeds recognized by Prussian courts," Rudolf said. "If the Wapiti land becomes a territory, then the courts will recognize their titles and deeds. If the land becomes part of the Guderian territory, those legal documents may not be recognized."

He flagged the waiter and ordered vodkas for both of them.

"That's an excellent point. Our understanding is that the Wapitis are asking for their own territory. Do you think the attorney working on the Wapiti petition would know the status of Donnelly's properties?" Wu asked, while ignoring the second vodka.

"She might. I know Len Ruffner has filed a lien on Donnelly's River Distillery equipment. Herr Simpson has filed a counter-claim, whether there's any validity to their allegations I can't say." He paused to wave to a middle-aged couple who had entered the crowded dinner room. They didn't acknowledge his greeting.

"Herr Kullman has a number of slaves. Hates me, but I'm always polite to the cruel bastard."

Wu was aware Rudolf was currently prosecuting a local plantation owner's son, Heinz Williams for having slaves. Blankenship had told him the case had polarized the territory. The plantation owners thought Rudolf a traitor to his class. The progressives thought the assistant attorney general a hero, and believed he should be the next attorney general.

"She? I wasn't aware Guderian Territory allowed females to practice law. What's her name?"

"Tara Smith. She has powerful friends in the Prussian IRS and army. My boss had to approve her license, and now there are several other well-connected daughters of plantation owners demanding the right to practice law in Guderian courts," Rudolf said draining the second vodka. "It's poor business allowing women in court. Everyone knows females can't control their emotions, but no one asked my opinion." He waved for refills.

Wu was starving, and he wished they'd order some food, but he didn't want to interfere with Rudolf getting drunk. His second vodka went into a crack in the floor when Rudolf stood to greet another dining room patron, an older woman who complimented him on fighting slavery.

"Who are her powerful friends?" Wu asked, when the woman left. Uncertainty made him nervous. He considered powerful a synonym for dangerous. A piano started playing near the center of the room, making conversation difficult. The young man banging away on the baby grand lacked talent, and the music irritated Wu.

"Franciscka Weidman and Major Caprivi," Rudolf answered. "They're the ones who forced me to arrest Heinz for buying those two girls. I thought I was finished in the AG's office until people started commenting on my bravery. Weird how things can turn out, now I'm a hero," Rudolf muttered and then remembered the question. "Caprivi is the Prussian officer who is credited with rallying the troops on the Volga River bridgehead. Emperor Schnabel personally pinned the Iron Cross on the major, and now the major is running around with the Smith girl."

"Isn't Caprivi one of the oldest of the Prussian aristocratic families? What do they think of their son's involvement with a half-breed woman?" Curiosity made Wu ask.

"I understand what you're asking, but the truth of the matter is that the Wapitis are becoming accepted as quality people in certain circles. I was raised a bigot, probably still one, but the Jarrell sisters, Tara Smith, and even you, Herr Wu, have made me realize one should never prejudge a person because of his skin color or ancestry."

Wu doubted the sincerity of that pronouncement. Instead of arguing, he said, "I don't understand the IRS interest. Aren't the Wapiti tribal areas lawless and the source of contraband, like the illegal cocaine?"

Rudolf wasn't proving as malleable as Purnell had implied. In his boss's opinion, the lawyer was the typical indolent rich man's son. Not especially bright or energetic, but not stupid either.

"Well for sure it's been a war zone for the past couple of years, but the Wapitis have beaten their oppressors." He said as he cut a small piece from his lamb chop and tasted it.

The chops looked overcooked to Wu, but the roasted rosemary chicken looked and smelled delicious. The ham slice he had ordered arrived with a baked sweet potato. The first bit of the ham was delicious, the sweet potato cooked just right, tender, juicy, and flavorful.

"Oppressors, I thought it was more the various tribes fighting?"

"Not as I understand, but I'm no expert," Rudolf said. Using his bare hands, he ripped a leg off the roasted chicken, dripping juice and fat on the linen tablecloth. "Oh, I received word just before I left my office that the Wapitis had captured the cannibal. That should end the raids and the area ought to settle down."

"Cannibal?" Wu lost his appetite. After a moment to collect himself, he asked, "Who are you referring to?"

"Chief Cinnabar, the madman from Panther Creek."

"Is he alive?"

"I believe so. There's talk of putting the chief on trial for cannibalism. I'm going to ask the AG to assign me to the prosecution team, could be my chance to become famous. It's sure to attract attention from Berlin and the emperor. First though, the IRS wants to interrogate the outlaw on his involvement with illegal cocaine."

Captain Dalporto had asked for a meeting. Benjamin Purnell had granted it. They waited for the servant to finish serving their hot coffee and slices of spice cake.

The captain was an independent boat owner who occasionally borrowed large sums of money from Purnell to finance cargos. Purnell's relationship with Captain Dalporto was that of a factor, the purchased cargo serving as the loan's collateral. In return, the captain passed on interesting rumors and bits of information that were not widely known. Purnell figured the captain had some new gossip.

"I picked up a party of Wapiti warriors at Panther Creek dock and dropped them at River Point. They had a prisoner, Chief Cinnabar," the captain said.

A chill went through Purnell. The term 'prisoner' meant that Cinnabar was alive, but he didn't want Dalporto knowing he had concerns. "Try the cake, it's delicious. I love the cream cheese frosting. Any sign of Herr Wright or Amos Reed. I asked them to check on the winter-sloe crop in Panther Creek."

"That's the other odd thing," Captain Dalporto said. "There was a wounded Ichneumon sergeant traveling with them. I had a chance to talk with him in private. The sergeant said their patrol had stopped a Prussian trader with a slave girl called Amy. The Ichneumon army captain believed the trader was a spy and arrested them. They had already arrested a Jesuit priest as a spy." The captain put his untouched cake back on the table.

"Those stupid Ichneumon savages, every stranger they meet, they claim is a spy. So where is Wright?"

"Herr Wright is dead, at least according to the Ichneumon sergeant, along with his female slave, Amy Caroom," Captain Dalporto said. "How could you do that?" The captain stood up.

"I don't know what business that is of yours," Purnell said. "But I needed someone who understood chemistry to sort out a problem. Did you see any bodies? How'd they die, did the Wapitis kill them? How do you know the Ichneumon was telling the truth?"

"How in the hell was I supposed to see bodies?" The captain said. "That animal, Reed, attacked the Ichneumon patrol and the fools managed to kill each other, even the priest. I can't believe you sent our best engineer to Cinnabar's cesspit. Your own daughter!"

"She was just another blow-by, not any daughter I ever claimed. I don't like your attitude."

"You were always resentful that a Clovis slave gave you a daughter who outshined those refined daughters from your patrician

126

wife. Comparing Amy to your aristocratic darlings is like comparing sunlight at high noon to a light from a stinking tallow candle." The captain said, throwing his napkin on the plate.

"She was a damn freak! Get out of my sight before I do something I'll regret."

"Aye, and if I was you, I'd be worrying about what Cinnabar's telling the Prussians." With that parting shot, Captain Dalporto stormed off, his piece of spice cake untouched.

Purnell knew his mistake had been allowing that girl to accept the Myrtle Territory scholarship to Heidelberg University. His wife was still out of sorts over that. The captain was right about Cinnabar being a problem. He told his office manager to find Bill Hickman.

Rex needed to decide. Return to Panther Creek and organize the winter-sloe harvest using Cinnabar's warehouse to clean and sort the nuts, or trust that operation to Lou Jarrell and escort Amy Caroom to Roanoke to testify about Purnell's involvement in the illegal cocaine trade.

The windfall from Cinnabar's treasure had enabled Rex to pay the yearly property tax due at the beginning of the year on his land grant. He'd asked the clerk how they had arrived at the staggering sum of ten thousand D-marks as his tax bill.

"Chief Smith said to use fifty thousand hectares. He didn't want to shortchange you," the teenage clerk said. He gave Rex a mischievous look and added, "The chief did say you could pay less, if you wanted less land."

Lord, he'd been thinking more along the lines of five thousand hectares. What an opportunity, but to keep it, he'd have to develop enough income from the property to pay the annual taxes. One could hardly expect to discover hidden gold hoards every year. He counted out twenty of his five-hundred D-mark gold coins and placed them on the desk in four neat stacks as the awed and silent clerk watched.

"I'll take a receipt, please."

Now that his land grant wasn't dependent on income from winter-sloe nuts sales, Rex felt he could delay returning to Panther Creek and take two weeks to escort Amy to Roanoke. The trip would allow him to see Herr Simpson and Herr Jacob about other matters. Larry Hopkins, who was hot to see Jenny Jarrell at the Jesuit College in Roanoke, offered to go with them to help. First, though, Rex wanted to pay a quick visit to Matt while Larry showed Amy the salt brine operation. The Mischief had Rex back at the stone fort dock before dark. He found Matt in the fort commander's office writing a letter to the council on his first interrogation of Chief Cinnabar.

"This guy is nuts. He stares off into space for hours. It's like there's no one home. You said we can't mark him, so I've been gentle, but he's still unresponsive most of the time."

"Were they making cocaine?"

The office tabby cat jumped off Matt's desk and into Rex's lap. It wanted petted.

"Cocaine paste was their product. They shipped it out in wood barrels to the Panther Creek dock where one of Purnell's boats would take it aboard. He didn't know where it went from there."

"How was he paid?" He had the cat purring. "I mean, who paid him?"

"Whoever the captain was on the boat that picked up the barrels, paid. Which doesn't tell you much. Let's go see the chief."

Rex and Matt walked down the stairs and through the rear hall to Cinnabar's cell. The tattooed monster hobbled to the cell door. Drug addiction had wasted what Rex reckoned had once been an impressively muscular body.

"Brought your Prussian master with you, I see." The monster addressed Matt but stared at Rex. "I'm not talking anymore until you give me a young girl."

"Chief, be nice unless you want a beating," Matt said. "Who sent the boat, supplies, and money for the paste?"

"Not until I get a girl," Cinnabar said and scuffled back to his cot.

"Commander Brewer, you were right," Rex said. Raising his voice, he added. "Skin him, whatever it takes to get your answers. But first I would suggest you castrate him to get his mind off girls." The gasp meant the animal had heard him. "I'm going to Roanoke and will be back in a week, ten days. It'd be useful if the prisoner's alive, but answers are more important, so, commander, do what you think necessary."

They then walked back to the office.

"I suspect he'll be more cooperative now. Cinnabar did tell me most of the gold coins were from James Donnelly who paid him to send a hundred warriors to help with the defense of Hinton after their defeat at Salt Furnace."

"That's where we figured it came from. Probably part of the Ichneumon payment to Donnelly," Rex said. He headed for the dock.

David C. Brown

Chapter8

Amy, Larry, and Rex had arrived the previous evening in Roanoke. The men with their horses had gone on to a boarding house they had used before. Amy stayed with Franciscka Weidman; the one Lily Hopkins had referred to as the Ice Queen. She didn't know if the "ice" part was fair, having just met her, but the "queen" part was.

The young Prussian IRS agent, who Amy figured was about her age, had an elliptical shaped face, vertical forehead, small straight nose, angular cheekbones and dark blue eyes. Franciscka was a beautiful woman. She had cut her light brown hair short. Her lightly tanned skin tone and complexion clear of blemishes meant she didn't fear the sun like Amy's half-sisters who flaunted their porcelain white skin as proof of their aristocratic pedigree.

In the past, the fact that her skin turned quite brown in the sun had never bothered her, but now as she had started to take an interest in men, she wondered if she should avoid the sun. Did Rex care about a woman's skin color? Amy knew she shouldn't, but her history of being a slave and a bastard still made her a bit defensive around quality people such as Fraulein Weidman.

Rex had told Franciscka that Amy was an engineer who had attended Heidelberg University. After getting over the surprise, Franciscka had warmed toward her.

"Amy, I'm impressed. That is a rare honor to win a territorial scholarship to Heidelberg. Was Rex pulling my leg? He said you were one of Purnell's slaves. I'd heard in the Myrtle territory that authorities frowned on teaching slaves to read."

"Regrettably you have heard right. My mother works at Purnell Industries boatyard in Orleans and one of the lathe operators taught us to read. I was always good with numbers. My mother and the engineers started using me to check their math and then, well, then one thing led to another."

"The emperor is a fool if he doesn't embrace the Wapitis," Franciscka said. "Tell me about Cinnabar's operation." Amy told her everything.

The next morning the two of them went to the Prussian IRS office. It was in a three-story, red brick building with glass windows on the second and third floors. On the street level, all the windows had heavy iron bars and wood shutters.

"Why the fortresses look?" Amy asked.

"For security and in case of riots," Franciscka said. Seeing her concern, she added, "Though no riots have ever occurred in Roanoke."

They were at the Roanoke IRS office so Franciscka's boss could meet Amy. The meeting was in the conference room on the third floor. Access was by steep narrow wooden stairs. She was surprised to discover that most of the third floor consisted of rooms for dusty junk and record storage. However, one of the storage rooms had remained empty except for a large wood plank table with benches. It was the room for sensitive meetings.

A fat and bald man sitting in the conference room cheerfully greeted them. Amy learned that he was the Roanoke IRS manager, Joachim 'Joe' Hansen, a sixty-year-old former military police officer.

"I've heard a great deal of good about you, Fraulein Caroom. It's a pleasure to meet you. I was about to have tea, or would you prefer coffee?" Joe asked while handing Franciscka a sealed Prussian Army dispatch envelope. "That message came in on the train last night but wasn't delivered until this morning."

From her work at the boatyard, Amy knew those types of envelopes were only used for serious and confidential messages. An ancient, hunched-over man served the tea. Her request for black tea had delighted Joe.

"Finally, another civilized person, Franciscka only drinks that awful coffee."

"My mother has fallen deathly ill and I've been requested to return home. The Archduke is sending his fast steamer to pick me up at New Hamburg, tomorrow. How can I make that? What about our project?"

Amy wondered how an accountant could rate such service. Franciscka obviously had high Prussian connections. She started to ask her if she knew the Archduke's son, Rudolf, than thought, better not.

"I'm sorry to hear that," Joe said. "We can get you to New Hamburg in time. The train's in town and scheduled to leave at noon. I'll send word for them to wait."

"I'm not packed. My cat, who'll look after her, and my horse?"

"I'll need Amy for several weeks. Can she stay at your place and look after your cat. The department will cover the rent and attend to the horse. On the train, you can write your report and give it to Herr Haines, and he'll get it safely back to me. The main thing is to get to Berlin. You know it must be serious for the Archduke to send his steamer."

Amy noticed that Herr Joe Hansen had another Prussian Army dispatch envelope in front of him, and she wondered if that was a copy of Franciscka's message or a different message from General Guderian.

"Do any of you know where Herr Knight might be found?" Joe asked.

"He had business at Jacobs and Jacobs and then with Tara Smith," Franciscka said. She turned to Amy. "I'll leave the key on the kitchen table. Take good care of Tabby." She said, and left to pack.

Amy, feeling a bit alone, was glad she had Wright's revolver in her satchel. Joe walked with her to the Jacobs store. The large hardware and farm supply store was her kind of place. They found Rex in the office with the proprietor, Bill Jacobs, drinking coffee. Joe broke up the meeting after introductions.

"I wanted a moment in private with Rex."

The owner got the hint and said, "I'll show Amy the clothes we stock for women."

She would have preferred to stay and hear what the manager wanted to discuss, but she desperately needed unmentionables, socks, coveralls, and a better pair of boots. "I don't have any money, Herr Jacobs," she whispered as they walked to the display area.

"Not a problem, young lady. I'll put it on Herr Knight's account."

Rex couldn't imagine what information Joe Hansen had to share with him that needed kept from the rest of their group.

"I'll get right to the point," Joe said after the door closed. "Franciscka's uncle, General Guderian, sent me a warning that the Ichneumon interests are actively working in New Hamburg and Berlin to sabotage the Wapitis' efforts to join the Prussian federation as a territory. She says you can be trusted."

Rex wasn't as sure about Hansen's sincerity toward the Wapitis' cause. The image Rex had of the manager was that of a spider, admittedly a friendly one, but still weaving webs to ensnare foes of the emperor.

"I can't say your news is a surprised. Along with the Ichneumons, I figured any number of Guderian Territory politicians are actively working to scuttle the idea of creating a new territory. What do you suggest?"

"Help me complete the investigation into the source of the illegal cocaine. Amy's information needs to be collaborated by Cinnabar's testimony. The emperor needs to be convinced the Wapitis aren't a tribe of bootleggers and that the source of the illegal cocaine is Benjamin Purnell."

"I have a good man interrogating the chief," Rex said. "I think the cannibal will cooperate. I also believe there will be an attempt to eliminate witnesses such as Cinnabar and Amy. Whether the Orleans trader cares about the Wapitis' territory issue, I'm not sure."

"Well, I'm sure Purnell prefers the tumult caused by the lawlessness in and surrounding the Erie valley, including the Wapiti tribal areas. It suits his criminal operations." The manager paused to check Jacobs's large pendulum clock in the room's corner and then continued, "You're right to worry about assassination. I harbor no doubt that Purnell knows where to hire competent assassins."

Rex expected nothing less. "Amy and Tara will be guarded."

"There's another concern. The church will want to satisfy themselves and the emperor that no false prophet is involved with the Wapitis' sudden military prowess and their request for a new territory. They don't want another York."

Rex wondered if the fear that flashed through his mind from Joe's comment showed. Fortunately, the manager had been adjusting his gold pocket watch's time to match Jacobs's clock, while delivering that dreadful news.

"I need a better watch." Joe said, looking at Rex after snapping the watch cover close. "This one seems to lose several minutes a day. Well, the train departs shortly, and I want to wish

Franciscka a speedy and safe trip. Oh, you do know that Amy has no money."

"Jacobs loves to charge my account, she'll be fine."

He followed Joe out of the office, thinking the invoice listing her purchases would be give him some insight to her interests. Then his thoughts returned to Joe's comments on the church's background check. He remembered Franciscka's explanation of the church's concern over people such as himself, but Rex wanted to hear Joe's opinion and said, "What I don't understand is the church's interest in crazy people, the false prophet nonsense."

"Oh, I can explain that," Joe said, pausing at the door. "Though the church discourages talk about the York rebellion, most people know the details. A little over two hundred years ago, York rebelled against Prussian rule. The uprising almost toppled the Schnabel dynasty. The rebel leader was a man called Joseph Warren, who, according to rumor, claimed to be from another world, a place called America. Since most of the Wapitis have York rebels as ancestors, it makes a certain sense for the church to check their leaders' backgrounds. You have nothing to worry about, unless you're a fugitive from the Prussian army."

Benjamin Purnell had bigger problems than the Wapitis getting a new Prussian territory to administrate. Seeing Amy Caroom walk out of the Roanoke IRS office had astonished Wu. Purnell had told him that he had sent the young woman to Cinnabar's remote fort. She was to whip the cocaine paste operation into shape. Afterwards, Sheriff Wright was to ensure she never returned to Orleans.

Those damn Wapitis had obviously captured her along with Cinnabar. After the way Purnell had treated her, Wu hated to think of the tales that she could tell. Joe Hansen would be a receptive audience. He wondered if that beautiful young Prussian woman in their group was Franciscka Weidman, the IRS agent working with Tara Smith.

The three people all exchanged hugs, then Joe and the Caroom girl, with two Prussian guards following, walked toward the train station. The Prussian woman went in the opposite direction, without guards, and Wu decided to follow her. After a fifteen-minute walk, the fine-looking lady entered one of those new style bungalows that were so popular in the neighborhoods around the Jesuit College. Two armed IRS guards arrived shortly afterward with a horse-drawn wagon.

When the guards started carrying bags to the wagon, Wu realized Weidman was packing. They appeared to be in a hurry, so he found a spot where he could observe the cottage unnoticed and leaned against a large hickory tree to wait. Only he and Purnell knew of the plan to murder the Wapiti lawyers, so something else was responsible for the Prussian woman's actions. He wondered if it involved Amy Caroom and Cinnabar. Once he dealt with the Wapiti lawyer, Tara Smith, he needed to deal with those two.

A half hour later, Weidman and the two IRS guards rode off in the wagon. The lady had several trunks, so she must be planning a long trip. To be sure, he followed the slow wagon on foot. He soon realized their destination was the train station, and she was leaving Roanoke. As a result, the Prussian woman was no longer his immediate concern.

While waiting in the growing crowd that had come to see off the train, Wu considered how best to locate the Wapiti attorney, then he had a lucky break. Two Prussian officers and a gorgeous Wapiti woman walked up to Fraulein Weidman. He thought Amy Caroom was exceptionally good looking, but that Wapiti woman talking to Fraulein Weidman was in a league all her own. The Prussian officer in the captain uniform talking with the women was big, but the other Prussian, not in uniform, was a monster. The man was at least a third of a meter taller than Wu and probably weighed fifty kilograms more, and all of it appeared to be muscle.

Friends, he wondered, or guards for the women who was seeing off Fraulein Weidman? Wu worked his way toward them through the crowd in an effort to catch their conversation. One of the Prussians addressed the Wapiti woman as Tara.

He had located his target and then noticed Herr Hansen had finished talking to the train conductor. Not wanting to chance the IRS manager or Amy recognizing him, Wu retreated. One advantage of not being tall was the ease of getting lost in a crowd.

After the train with Franciscka aboard had pulled out, Joe Hansen waved over the two IRS guards who had helped with her trunks and instructed them to help form a ring around Amy and Tara. Then they, along with Rex and Fritz, made a beeline for the IRS office and went to the third floor conference room.

"Amy, I'm not trying to upset you, but who would Purnell send to . . . ah, have you ever heard if he would have witnesses, ah harmed?" Rex asked.

"I don't know," Amy said. "He doesn't confer with his slaves. And you don't need to be afraid to say it, we're not going to faint on hearing an assassin is after us. But why would he be after me? I'm dead as far as Purnell knows. Plus he always has my family to threaten. Tara is the one that's in danger."

"Danger. Why, because of the territory request?" Joe asked.

The threat to Cinnabar had been Rex's concern, but he agreed that Amy had raised a valid concern. "Good point, Tara, how long before you can leave Roanoke?"

"I've completed the legal work that can be accomplished in Roanoke. The Wapitis and I thank you, Herr Hansen, for recommending Rudolf Hoess. He was a great help. My next destination is New Hamburg. If the Wapiti vote in two weeks favors becoming a territory, then I'll travel on to Berlin and officially present the Wapiti petition to Emperor Schnabel."

"I and three armed guards will travel with Fraulein Smith to provide protection," Fritz said. "If Rex and Larry protect Amy, then the ladies should be fine."

"I assume your father is aware of your plans," Rex said. Tara's scowl caused him remember the lady valued her independence, and add, "Because he's head of the council. That is the only reason I asked, and he needs to know your plans. And you need to know the results of the vote."

Joe wanted to know if there was any doubt of the vote not being in favor of a territory. "It's a secret vote," Tara said. "And remember, as recently as four months ago a Wapiti couldn't buy a rolling block rifle, so not everyone is pro-Prussian. Besides, the Ichneumons are pushing the Wapitis to vote for an independent country."

"Are the Wapitis foolish enough to listen to the Ichneumons?" Joe asked. Tara shook her head. Rex didn't share her certainty, thinking of Pete Chin.

"Well then, to business," Joe said. "Amy, I have Rudolf Hoess and a stenographer coming over to take your statement on Cinnabar's cocaine processing operation. To protect you, I'll seal it until Purnell is arrested."

"Do you trust Hoess?" Fritz asked. The only Prussian that Rex trusted completely was Franciscka, and she had left for Berlin. Though he figured, as long as the Wapitis sided with the Prussians, Fritz would remain an ally.

"Herr Hoess, I trust," Joe said. "I'm not at all comfortable with the trustworthiness of the Guderian Attorney General's office in New Hamburg. For that reason, Amy will be witness number twelve. Tomorrow she needs to disappear into the Wapiti tribal lands until the emperor orders Purnell's arrest."

"Where do you stand with Chief Cinnabar?" Fritz asked.

"Cinnabar is in a cell at Salt Furnace awaiting interrogation on the cocaine issue," Rex said. None of the Prussians needed to know the prisoner at the furnace was not Cinnabar.

"Numerous witnesses are ready to testify to Cinnabar's cannibalism and murdering of Clovis families. Those crimes are sufficient for the council to hang him. But additionally, the council desires to establish that the Wapiti tribes are not involved in the Guderian and Myrtle territories' illegal cocaine sales. To accomplish that, the council will cooperate with the Prussian IRS."

"His willing testimony that he converted winter-sloe to cocaine paste for Benjamin Purnell, along with Amy's testimony, would accomplish that," Joe said and started gathering his papers.

"The willing part is the problem," Rex said. "But I'm working on it. Before we all scatter, I have a few thoughts on identifying potential assassins. Criminals, such as Purnell, have people that they use to deal with troublesome employees. A hatchet man, if you will. Amy, who did Purnell use for his hatchet man?"

"Sheriff Wright, but he's dead. The Ichneumon soldiers killed him in Panther Creek," Amy answered. She had been setting beside Joe, but was now over by the table trying to get the last dregs of that hideous black tea from the conference room teapot. "He had some thugs like the Reed brothers, but as you well know, they're dead too."

"Must be dangerous working for the man," Fritz said. The comment lightened the tense atmosphere around the table.

"I doubt you'd be in a position to know, but do you have any idea who he used to deal with politicians?"

"Not really," Amy said. "Herr Wu did make a lot of trips east. He was someone important. The man was always coming and going to Purnell's office when he was in Orleans. It was a mystery around the boat yard what the guy did."

"Edward Wu? Was he a middle-aged small man with some Mongol ancestry?" Hansen asked. Amy nodded. "I know the man. If Purnell hired an assassin, Wu would know. He's Purnell and the cotton growers' bag man, though I can't prove it."

The AAG Rudolf Hoess and a young woman arrived to take Amy's statement. Rex, Fritz, and Tara went to the lobby. While waiting for Amy to finish her deposition, Rex and Fritz learned that Tara had changed her mind about traveling to New Hamburg, and instead she wanted to return to Salt Furnace.

"There's no point in going to New Hamburg until the vote results are known," Tara said. "I'll be of more use visiting the Johnson tribes. I need to counter Pete Chin's traitorous propaganda on the joys of independence and the Ichneumon's altruistic willingness to protect us from Prussian encroachment. My father should have hung the traitor. Will you help?"

"You know I will," Fritz said. "I didn't realize the vote for a territory was in danger. Governor Bullard would love that vote to be for independence. Don't people like Chief Chin realize the Prussian Empire will never allow the Ichneumon Empire to take control of the Erie River and the west?"

"Every society has fools," Tara said. "As to the Prussians never conceding control of the Erie River, they already have."

"How can you say that?" Fritz asked. The Prussian captain had been looking at the landscape paintings by local artists hanging in the hallway, but Tara again had his and Rex's full attention.

"Other than River Point, and maybe Allegheny, the Ichneumons control the entire river fort system," Tara said. "

Edward Wu followed the Wapiti women and their Prussian escort from the train yard until they entered the IRS office. Two of the Prussians carried double-barrel shotguns. The other Prussians had revolvers in shoulder rigs. All of them were alert to their surroundings. Probably he could have gotten close enough to kill the Smith woman, but it would have been a suicide mission. Now Rudolf Hoess and another woman had just entered the IRS office. It'd be interesting to know for sure their purpose, but he figured it involved a deposition, likely on Purnell's cocaine operation.

A couple of long hours later, the AAG and woman emerged and walked toward the courthouse. A few minutes later, an army coach pulled up and the Smith woman, a Prussian officer, and two guards climbed in and headed south, presumably to the army post.

Finally, Amy Caroom and the huge Prussian exited the IRS office and walked in the direction of Fraulein Weidman's cottage. It required no great insight to determine that the IRS would put her up in Weidman's empty abode. Wu had earlier noticed a narrow alley that intersected with the street on which Weidman's house was located. At the time, he thought the location might make a good point to ambush people walking along the sidewalk.

Wu would have time to get in position at the alley, since Fraulein Caroom was moving slowly and gawking about at the buildings. The Prussian guard with her was paying attention. It would be dangerous, but he decided to chance a shot. He hurried over a block, and then walked fast along the parallel street to the alley six blocks away. He was at the alley mouth and considering which door way would be best to wait in when a young Wapiti, or Prussian trooper, materialized behind him with a rifle.

"Mister, keep your hands where I can see them," the young man said.

Wu decided his challenger was a Wapiti trooper, though he wore Prussian camouflage fatigues. His uniform lacked the usual rank and unit insignia favored by the Prussians. Then the trooper turned and he saw the Wapiti green star emblem on the right shoulder. Wu had shoved his revolver in his belt before entering the alley and it was handy for a fast draw, but the trooper had the drop on him. He heard the click of the Wapiti's rifle safety release and suspected the young man wouldn't hesitate to shoot him.

The Prussian ban on selling modern weapons to savages was a travesty. The kid was threatening him with the army's most advanced rifle, a bolt-action Mauser. Wu wasn't sure that even with all his contacts he could obtain one.

"You have no right to threaten me. What are you, one of those Wapiti bootleggers? Guderian Territory doesn't allow your kind to own rifles."

The kid just smiled in response, then said, "Sir, keep those hands up while you explain why you're lurking in this alley."

"Be careful, you have the safety off. I'm not lurking. I was just passing through. Besides, I don't have to explain myself to you."

"Yeah, you do," the big Prussian yelled.

The man and Amy had arrived across the street from the alley and spotted him and the Wapiti trooper. The Prussian jogged across the street, while Amy waited. Her alarmed look meant she had recognized him. The Prussian had his revolver out, hammer back, and aimed at him.

"Is this Herr Wu?" the Prussian asked. Purnell's bastard daughter just stared at him for a moment before nodding. "Larry, take his weapons and tie his hands."

"This is outrageous, stopping a Prussian citizen and robbing him. Police, help!"

Suddenly he couldn't breathe. The monster had sucker-punched him in his gut. Hands stripped him of his pistol, billfold, money belt, and three knives. The big man grabbed his coat collar and marched him across the cobblestone street and into Weidman's house. Wu's struggling ripped his new sport coat collar, and he vowed these savages would pay for that and much more.

Joe Hansen wasn't happy to learn they had Edward Wu tied to a chair in Franciscka Weidman's house. Rex had known the IRS manager planned to meet AAG Hoess at the Roanoke Hotel for dinner and had found Joe waiting in the lobby.

"You can't kidnap Prussian citizens. What law did Wu break?"

"He's probably the assassin. Why else would he be waiting in that alley across from Franciscka's bungalow with a gun?" Rex said. They were attracting attention from the desk clerk and porters. "Let's step outside."

"You're probably correct. Wu was up to no good, but there's no proof. Many men carry a pistol or revolver in the territories. And with his connections in the governor's office, no sheriff is going to arrest him. They'll arrest you."

"Amy's beside herself worrying he'll tell Purnell she's still alive and then Purnell will hurt her family."

"So why bother me? Why didn't you just kill the guy?" Joe asked. "I doubt many people would mourn Herr Wu's death in a mugging gone wrong."

Rex had asked himself that very question, and hadn't resolved it to his satisfaction. True, he had no solid proof that Wu was an assassin. Then again, the guy worked for Purnell. Eliminate a witness to Purnell's illegal cocaine business did make sense, except Wu had no reason to know the girl wasn't still at Cinnabar's fort. So he didn't come to Roanoke looking for Amy. Rex had killed a number of men since arriving in this strange world, all of them in self-defense or in a war-related capacity. He didn't want to cross the line of killing for the purpose of convenience. That was murder, and he figured that was what would save Herr Wu's sorry ass.

"What about Amy's concerns?" He asked, spotting AAG Hoess coming up the street.

"Tell her too many people already know she has escaped Cinnabar for word not to get back to her father. He won't hurt her family because that's his leverage to stop her from testifying," Joe said. The AAG lawyer had stopped at the hotel entrance and waited on them to finish.

"Amy doesn't agree, but I think you're right. Wait a day, then check Franciscka's house for rats," Rex said. "And her cat, don't forget Tabby." Joe nodded okay.

Rex jogged back to the house. He first wanted to check that Larry had Wu under control and then asked Amy to come with him to Jacobs. The sullen prisoner now had a gag and blindfold. Larry and Amy had been counting gold five hundred D-mark coins on the kitchen table. Franciscka's cat was puffed up and perched on top of the kitchen dish cabinet, watching Hokee who was sleeping under the kitchen table. Amy had her boots off, and she was warming her bare feet on the wolf.

"Where did that come from?" Rex asked, pointing at the coins.

"Killer's money belt," Larry answered. "He has a hundred thousand D-marks. Who is that guy?"

"Trouble, other than that, I'm not sure. Amy get your boots, I need your opinion on an investment idea. Herr Jacobs invited me to meet Al Leslie at his office. If we hurry we can make it."

Hurrying along the darkened streets to a meeting at Jacobs's store, Amy was still getting her mind around the casual decisiveness of her friend and bodyguard. Herr Wu was a man that no one in Orleans would willingly harass. Not Rex and the Wapitis, they seemed unconcern with the man's threats. They had ignored the enraged man as they sorted through his property and counted his fortune in gold coins.

"Leslie and Jacobs are trying to raise money for a primitive telegraph line along the new railroad from New Hamburg and Roanoke. In a world that currently uses pigeons for fast communications, it should be a great success and a good investment with honest partners," Rex said. He slowed his pace when he saw her difficultly keeping up.

"What's a telegraph? A semaphore," Amy asked.

"That's a good way to look at it, except Leslie uses clickers instead of flags."

"I heard at the university that the Berlin railroad used electric impulses over a wire to send messages. I also heard it didn't work."

"Well I know it can. Do you know anything about electricity? Making magnets?"

Amy had studied battery theory, static electricity, and magnetic fields at the university. It was the frontier of science, and she wondered how a cod fisherman's son knew about it.

"Yes," she said. "I can make an electric current using zinc and copper. I've even made magnets using electric current. Why do you ask?"

She even knew about the very latest discovery. If you rotated a copper loop of wire between the poles of a magnet, an electric current appeared, though she had read that it was different from battery current. Amy was tempted to ask if he knew about that discovery, but Rex spoke first.

"Tonight I want you to ask questions. Afterward, tell me if Leslie knows enough science to be the inventor or if he stole the idea from someone or from the Berlin railroad," Rex said, as they stopped at the front entrance to Jacobs's store and waited for the proprietor to unlock the door.

"Not all inventions come from large companies. Nobodies can invent things."

"I know that. In fact, all inventions probably start from some individual's insight. But there're also plenty of people out there ready to steal a good idea, and that's what I'm after, your opinion on this guy. Is he even capable of dreaming up the idea he is peddling? Afterward, use my account to finish getting whatever clothes and supplies you need while I help with the ballots."

Rex handed her a folded paper, adding. "Leslie handed these out earlier to Jacobs and me. It's his proposed code for the wire."

The storeowner, Herr Jacobs, was friendly and made her feel welcomed. Al Leslie gave her a cursory acknowledgement and focused on the men. Walking through the store, Leslie asked about the difficulty of reaching Salt Furnace. Rex explained the two means available to reach the interior as the group seated themselves around a large, rectangular, oak table in the office.

Amy sat beside Rex and across from the inventor in the well-lit office. Two of those new kerosene mantle lamps she had read about accounted for the pleasant light. At a nod from Rex, Jacobs started.

"The word I hear, Al, is that the messages arrive garbled," Jacobs said.

Amy read the code paper while listening to his explanation.

"The problem is the ignorance of the railroad workers and management. They don't follow procedures," Al said. "The message requires the proper sequence of dots and dashes to identify the letters forming the message. For example, one dot followed by one dash is "A." One dash followed by a dot is the letter "N." The operators must be trained to pay attention at all times during transmission of a message or the message may be muddled."

"A weak current would cause the same trouble," Amy said. She had little use for people who blame the workers for their device's poor performance. "If the current isn't strong enough to fully energize the electromagnetic coil, an intended dash impulse might arrive sounding like a dot."

The man's flush suggested he hadn't liked her critique. She laid the paper with the code on the table and in an attempt to smooth ruffled feathers added.

"That's a neat code. Did you write it?"

"Who do you think wrote it? Who are you?" He turned before Amy had a chance to respond and addressed Rex. "If you want to bring your, ah, courtesan to this meeting, fine. But ask her to stay out of the discussion."

What an ass, she thought, looking to Rex for guidance. He shrugged his shoulders, which she interpreted as "do what you think best." That response by a certain class of men to discount the intelligence of a person because of her gender was all too common, and it irritated her. The jerk's remarks were just another manifestation of the bigotry she had encountered most of her life. Still she had a job to do, and heaping well-deserved scorn on the arrogant inventor tonight would accomplish nothing useful. Besides, the fact that Jacobs looked as irritated as she was over his remarks, cheered her.

"Herr Leslie, I do hope your grasp of science is better than your understanding of why I'm here." A little of her disdain for the bigot's behavior did slip out. "My name is Amy Caroom and I'm an engineer here to advise these gentlemen. Now answer my question, did you invent the code?"

The man appeared a bit bewildered and looked to Rex for guidance.

"I would strongly advise you to answer her questions," Herr Jacobs said. Rex nodded in agreement.

Leslie seemed momentary flustered by Jacobs's response, but turned his focus on her. "It's mine. I invented it, though I got the idea after seeing a magnetic coil used to ring a bell and remembering the Mongol smoke signals on the eastern front. Then once I knew a battery could be used to make two different sounds from a magnetic coil, it was easy to make up a new alphabet using dots and dashes."

"That was an inspired insight, building an alphabet with dots and dashes. So what is the problem on your Berlin wire?"

Leslie explained that the Berlin railroad's difficulty with line loss and faded signals had several causes. "I was forced to use an iron wire and that's the primary cause of the weak signals."

"An iron wire," Amy said.

"Why wouldn't you use copper wire, cost," Rex asked. He appeared as surprised as she was did that anyone would use an iron wire for a conductor.

"Well you're correct, copper is much better than iron, but you're not allowed to use copper for wire," Al said. "It's against the law." Seeing their puzzled looks, he explained that last year the Prussian Navy requested that all copper be reserved for copper sheeting to plate their wooden boat hulls.

"All the copper, are shipworms and marine weeds that big a problem?" Herr Jacobs asked. "I just ordered five hundred kilograms of copper roofing for Hayes's plantation. No one blocked that order."

"It's Berlin politics," Al Leslie said. The inventor appeared a bit more amiable now that the subject of the conversation had moved on from his invention defects to the behavior of venal politicians.

"Pigeon farms are a big business in Prussia," Leslie said. "You know that, Herr Jacobs. The government, army, and businesses use tens of thousands of pigeons for messages. The Berlin railroad uses several hundred birds a day, and each station has to have pigeons trained to fly to all the different stations. It's an industry, all that training and rearing of birds, the railroad even has hunters to control the hawks along the flight paths."

"All reasons why your wire is needed," Rex said.

"Safety was another alleged worry. The pigeon farmers' lobbyists harped on safety to our craven politicians. How could they allow greedy railroad management to save a few pfennigs by trusting passenger safety to sparks traveling along a wire? In short, my invention threatens the pigeon industry and their multitude of farmers who vote in the senate elections."

That litany of woes had left Amy shaking her head and mute.

After a moment Al added, "Stan Blankenship brought up the copper wire issue when I was in New Hamburg. According to the governor's man, certain ill-advised patriots in the Guderian legislature were talking about outlawing the use of copper in the territory in support of the navy. Herr Blankenship offered to put me in touch with a lobbyist who might be able to block the misguided effort. He thought the effort to stop the copper wire ban might require fifty thousand D-marks."

"Well Al, you've certainly gotten a crash course in Berlin and New Hamburg corruption. They're shameless," Herr Jacobs said. "I'll see if I can nip that nonsense in the bud. Besides, the Ichneumons would be happy to sell you copper."

The meeting broke up shortly after that. They learned Al Leslie had meetings scheduled with Herr Ruffner at Narrows and then with Herr Simpson and the council at Salt Furnace.

"Frau Caroom, please accept my apology for that mean and uncalled-for remark," Leslie said.

"Think nothing more about it."

She didn't want unnecessary animosity with the inventor, who was probably under considerable stress. Besides, glimpses of a solution to a high current battery design swirled just out of reach in her mind. Such a battery would make his invention work dependably if he also used the proper wire.

"Herr Jacobs, do you have ingots of copper and zinc?"

Hokee was living large. The wolf had caught and eaten his third gray squirrel that morning. Winter was in the air. The hardwood leaf colors were past their prime, and the leaves were carpeting the forest floor. Squirrels seemed to be busy everywhere that Rex looked, collecting acorns and nuts. In another couple of weeks the trees in the higher elevations would be bare, which served to remind him that the winter-sloe nuts were also falling. That realization kept Rex's focus on how to process the winter-sloe nuts that he knew were piling up at Panther Creek. He had asked Amy if she had any suggestions on a quick way to remove the hulls. However, Amy's thoughts were on Leslie's invention.

No wonder, Rex thought. Cracking open nuts wasn't near as exciting as building a new, lightning-fast message delivery system. The Prussian inventor had impressed both of them. After their meeting had ended, Al had given Amy a pamphlet that explained the dot-dash code and method of communication over a copper wire in detail. It was a handout to help bankers and potential financial backers understand his invention. Rex figured few of them bother to read it.

Herr Jacobs had readily supplied Amy with a couple of two-kilogram ingots of zinc and copper, along with a small container of copper sulfate from supplies the Jesuit College order. He also gave her three rolls of thin copper wire. One roll of wire had silk insulation and the other two rolls had lacquer insulation. From her smiles and hugs, you would have thought the storeowner had given her diamonds. Rex figured the cost of Herr Jacobs's gifts would manage to show up on his next billing invoice.

From his Earth life, Rex knew the invention was this world's form of a telegraph. Those thoughts caused him to remember Hansen's warning about the church sending an investigator to look for aliens. He needed to ditch everything that had arrived with him from Earth, even the Topcon scope and Ruger pistol.

Amy's questions made clear she thought the dot-dash line was an exciting new idea. Once she realized Rex had some knowledge of chemistry, she kept bouncing ideas off him for solving the weak battery problem.

"Those voltaic piles he's using for a current are okay, but the porous pot cell would work better as his battery."

"Never heard of that kind of battery," Rex said. "What is it, a lead acid battery?"

"No, it uses a copper cathode and zinc anode with a porous stone barrier to keep the solutions separated, but the pores get plugged, which weakens the current. I know how to fix that."

"Well, help me with the nut hulls and I'll set you up in a lab," Rex said. That earned him a smile and a lull in the questions and comments.

Amy had found in a Roanoke shop, a black felt hat with a large circular brim. The ugly hat looked like something a McCoy or Hatfield henchman would own. Thanks to Franciscka, Rex knew Amy wore the unattractive hat to keep the sun off her face and neck. The IRS agent had told Joe, who told him that Amy was worried about all the outdoor activity making her skin too dark.

Rex thought her skin and color looked fine and was tempted to tease her. She appeared to have little awareness of just how beautiful she was or appreciation for the awe her intelligence generated in those who dealt with her. However, he kept quiet on the sun-hat subject, that type of joking had a way of offending. Besides, he wanted Amy thinking about processing winter-sloe nuts, not about her skin color, or batteries.

They made the trip from Roanoke to Salt Furnace in three days and waited there for Tara, Fritz, and his Prussian guards to arrive. Tara's party had gone to the Narrows and rented boats for the trip down the Southern River to Salt Fork. Fritz had learned that a Prussian Army ocean-going sternwheeler planned to visit River Point after the territorial vote, ten days from now. They planned to hitch a ride on the Prussian steamboat for their passage to Berlin.

Edward Wu had expected a bullet in the head the morning his abductors had cleared out of the Weidman cottage. He didn't want to die. As he listened to the sounds of the Wapitis packing their belongings, he prayed for help. His thoughts formed and vanished as he searched in his memory for a deity he could appeal to for help. There was nothing. Wu realized that he believed in nothing. Then the Wapitis were gone. There were no final threats. His captors had ignored him.

The silence had initially been a relief. Now, on the start of the second day, he wondered if they had cruelly left him to die of thirst. The sounds of the front door opening set him to banging his chair against the wall to attract attention. There was more than one person, for a man commented on the stench. Wu was past embarrassment, he had crapped and pissed his pants, knew he stank, and would kill for water.

"Herr Wu, what are you doing here?" Joe Hansen asked. One of the two IRS guards had jerked the hood off and cut the gag.

"Water," Wu managed to gasp. As he drank two cups of water, he considered how to answer Hansen's question about the circumstances that had resulted in him tied up in an IRS investigator's private cottage. Had the Wapitis said anything to Hansen? Wu didn't understand why that big Prussian hadn't killed him.

"Some thieving Wapitis kidnapped and robbed me. Roanoke is getting lawless. I intend to speak with the governor." While talking, he stripped off his filthy clothes. His audience be damned, he needed to clean himself.

"Excuse me," Wu said. He then stepped into the shower. The cold shower was tough, though he liked the smell of the soap bar. On emerging from the shower, he learned that Hansen had sent one of the guards back to the office for a clean set of old army fatigues.

"I'm sympathetic to you taking a moment to eliminate the stench, but I'm still waiting for your explanation." The IRS manager was sitting in the bedroom chair petting a cat. A guard with a shotgun watched from the bedroom doorway. Wu's filthy clothes were missing. "Did they rob you of much money?"

"As you can see they stripped me of everything." He hoped that the guard hurried back, as being naked gave him an odd feeling of defensiveness, and decided there was no reason not to mention the gold. "I had a money belt with a hundred thousand D-marks." He said, while filled his cup with more delicious cold water from the bathroom sink.

"Really, a hundred thousand . . ., why would a man carry that kind of money," Joe asked.

The other guard returned with a ratty set of the old fashioned, gray-green fatigues and tossed them to Wu. "Once you get presentable come in the kitchen. And someone, open the window and air the place out."

Wu's boots were missing, so after quickly donning the ugly fatigues, he entered the kitchen barefooted. He saw his boots by the door. Then he saw the gold coins stacked on the table along with his pistol, knives, wallet, and empty money belt. Hansen was counting the coins.

"There's twenty of the five-hundred D-mark coins here. Hard to imagine a robber not taking all of your gold, so what's your game? Why are you in my assistant's private cottage?"

The bastards, Wu thought. They left those few coins to make him look the fool.

"I'm at a loss to explain. The thugs had me tied up and blindfolded for nearly three days. I have no idea why they didn't take the gold and kill me. How'd you find me?"

"A neighbor reported strange sounds from the house."

Wu seriously doubted the legitimacy of Hansen's explanation. More likely, he was conspiring with the big Prussian and that girl, though he also appeared perplexed.

"Herr Wu, I'm not in the mood for evasions and lies. Why are you in Roanoke?"

Wu had an inspiration. "I'm headed to Salt Furnace to buy winter-sloe nuts for Herr Purnell." He could tell his spontaneous explanation made sense to Hansen and he embellished it. "I had business in New Hamburg, and I wanted to ride the new railroad. So I came through Roanoke, planning to catch a Ruffner boat at Narrows for the trip to Salt Furnace. Otherwise I'd have taken Purnell's sternwheeler up the Erie to see the Wapitis."

With the blank ballots safely delivered to the council, Rex stopped at the Salt Furnace jail to check on Slim, the Cinnabar decoy. The jail was the large brick firebox of the currently idle furnace used to evaporate the brine. The guard's caution to him to be careful, verified the deception had worked. Everyone he encountered thought Slim was the cannibal and treated him as an insane and dangerous prisoner. Only Larry, Chief Smith, and Matt Brewer knew otherwise. After asking the guard to leave, Rex visited with the Clovis hunter.

"How much longer will I be locked up? The Erie goose hunt is about to start," the prisoner said.

"Slim, you're doing great as Cinnabar. No one has caught on to the deception. I need you to give it one more week. The people, who have reason to fear Cinnabar's testimony, now know that the Wapitis captured him alive. I expect an attempt on your life. It's a risk, but you did volunteer, and Larry will do everything to protect you. It is important. Capturing the assassin alive would further help prove who the bootlegger is. "

"Yeah, well I'm not too thrilled being a sitting duck in this cell. What if they overpower the guard?"

Rex agreed and handed the prisoner his new five-shot revolver.

Chief Smith, his daughter Tara, and the council were a hive of activity, with people coming and going with ballots and voting supplies to all the outlying areas. The goal was to give every adult in the proposed territory a chance to vote. As a result, the council asked Rex to take the ballots to Panther Creek and organize that area's voting. As he waited for the ballots, he again expressed to the chief his concern that Purnell would attempt to assassinate Cinnabar, Tara, and Amy to stop the IRS investigation into the source of the illegal cocaine.

"And you, Chief. I wouldn't be surprised if you're on the assassin's kill list," Rex said. "It would help throw the territorial petition vote into chaos."

"Could be, but Cinnabar and I are as safe as one can be today. My daughter has guards, and you can take Amy with you and guard her. Arduous duty, I'm sure." The chief smiled, and added. "Besides, didn't you need to check on Lou and the winter-sloe harvest?"

"I do, hard to tell what trouble he's stirred up in Panther Creek. Has the bagger arrived yet?" Rex had order a machine for bagging the roasted winter-sloe nuts, sight unseen, from Jacobs, who would ship it by riverboat to Salt Furnace.

"No, it hasn't arrived. Paul Moyer has agreed to run the bagging operation," Chief Smith said. *Not good news*, Rex thought.

"I need you to tell Matt that I'd like the stone fort ready for an inspection in a week. Admiral Scheer is visiting Port Delta in one of the new Prussian ironclad battleships. While there, he will use one of the smaller ocean-going sternwheelers accompanying the battleship to travel up the Erie River and visit Hickory Ridge and River Point. He's expected there the day after the vote, and I want to impress the admiral."

"The Ichneumon will welcome the Prussian navy?" Rex said.

"I've wondered the same thing. Regardless, it would be an ideal time for Cinnabar to confess and tell the admiral about Purnell's involvement in the illegal cocaine trade. Admiral Scheer could arrest Purnell on his return through Orleans and haul both of them back to Berlin for trial."

"I assume the gangster knows about the admiral's planned Erie River visit?" Rex said. The chief agreed that was likely, while opening desk drawers to look for something. "Then I would expect the man to make an all-out effort to eliminate those witnesses before then."

"I'm sure he wants to," Chief Smith said. "But he suffers from the same problem we all have, knowing what's going on in a timely fashion. How can Purnell even know for sure that Cinnabar's still alive, let alone where he's at?"

"Well, a lot of people in Roanoke know about Cinnabar's capture and that Amy is alive. I figure Purnell knows, or will shortly."

"I met Edward Wu during a trip two years ago to the market at the Erie River delta. He and Manuel Prado were buying winter-sloe nuts. I thought he was an accountant, hard to believe he's an assassin."

The chief pulled a short sword with a broken point out of the bottom desk drawer. It looked like that sword Amy had had found so interesting. He used it to pry the lid off one of the wooden boxes holding two thousand unmarked ballots.

"Well, I have no proof. If I had, Herr Wu wouldn't be an issue today. I'll head downriver in the morning. Let me have an extra pack of those ballots."

Rex was well aware that the Mischief's captain didn't like leaving the Southern River and traveling down the Erie River. Being an Ichneumon, Malik feared capture by Ichneumon troopers from the Hickory Ridge garrison. General Mehta, the commander, considered him a traitor.

"Look, I know it's risky, but Kyle's not available and we need to reach Panther Creek."

"Okay, I don't like it, but I'll do it," the captain said. "Just do me the favor of telling everyone to disembark the moment the Mischief docks."

"We'll be off before you can reverse the paddles. Tell Kyle to returning in a week to pick us up."

The next day, he, Amy Caroom, Hokee, and two skilled carpenters disembarked at Panther Creek, and a day later, they rode into Cinnabar's old stockade.

Lou Jarrell and Frau Benes's youngest daughter, Eva, greeted them. Though it was late and the travelers were tired, after a quick meal Lou had them go to the warehouse. The village people had filled one end of the warehouse by the waterwheel with winter-sloe nuts.

"Look at all the nuts!" Rex exclaimed. "They've been hard at work. Lou, the people who harvested the nuts were to keep the crop at their homes until I had a scale setup. How will we know who is owed what?"

"There're a couple thousand kilos of nuts in that pile," Amy said. She picked up two nuts in their hulls and cracked their shells against each other. "These are nicely filled out, prime nuts."

"I hope someone has an idea on how to clean them," Rex added, looking at Amy. Several of the village residents that had followed them into the warehouse, along with Lou, looked apprehensive on hearing his remark.

"But they filled their huts and needed more room," Lou said. "Eva and I used a simple beam scale with a rock to weight the nuts that each person brought in. All you need to do is weigh the rock and you'll know how many kilos each person brought. You did bring the money?"

Rex had thirty thousand D-marks in his saddlebags, mostly one, five, ten D-mark denomination paper bills. Amy had a small beam scale and weight set to determine the rock's weight. She also had found in the Roanoke store basement, and wheeled from Herr Jacobs, a stout bronze eccentric powered by a large hand crank. At Smithtown, she had found an iron plate and brought it along.

"In the morning, I need help to make a shaker table to clean the dried pulp and dirt off the nut," Amy said. "That piece of boiler plate, I'll use for the anvil in the nutshell cracker. Now let's get a good night's sleep: tomorrow will be a busy day." With those instructions, she left with Frau Benes.

Lou and Eva had taken over Cinnabar's old bedroom, so Rex and Hokee slept on the floor in the hall near the fireplace with the Smithtown carpenters. The hall was clean and smelled of pine.

The following morning, with Lou and Eva's help, Rex set about organizing the vote at the stockade entrance.

"You're aware the majority of the Panther Clovis can't read?" Lou asked.

"Yeah, I am, that's why I wanted your and Eva's help. I figure the whole concept of voting is new to them. Consequently, the villagers won't vote unless we make them."

Rex was sympathetic to the villagers' position, but it wouldn't serve the Wapitis or the Panther Creek community's interest in the long term, if they didn't help the Wapitis create their own territory by voting.

"Eva, start a rumor that only people who vote and have an ink stained finger can sell winter-sloe nuts at the warehouse," Rex said. "I'll mark several ballots in favor of the territory and post it around the polling station, as an example of how to vote."

Before evening, they had two hundred and eighty-nine marked ballots, along with the supporting inventory sheets with the inked thumbprints. All the votes, so far, were yes. His grandfather, Jeb, from Logan County would have approved of this voting method.

159

"From what I saw, I figure Amy will have clean nuts piling up in another day. The girl's a genius. But what do we do with the clean nuts?" Lou asked, as Eva showed an elderly couple how to ink their thumbs.

"The nuts can't get wet. Mold ruins them for roasting. I'm thinking of putting them in burlap bags; say forty or fifty kilo size, and using packhorses to move them to the river during good weather. Does anyone have an idea where I might buy the bags?"

"They sell burlap at Hickory Ridge, and we could make bags," Eva said.

The next afternoon Amy had the waterwheel running. Her crew had rearranged the millstone to roll the winter-sloe nut against the piece of iron plate. A wood hopper above the millstone fed the whole nut in the gap. By adjusting the gap between the large rotation millstone and the stationary anvil, the rotation of the millstone dragged and forced the nut through the gap and cracked its shell.

Collecting and then shaking the cracked nuts on the shaker table, which Amy had fabricated with her eccentric, finished the separation of the shell from the nut kernel. At that point, a person only had to pick out the few remaining shell fragments from the clean nuts falling off the shaker. It was tedious, but not strenuous work. The Panther Creek Nut Processing Company was ready for business, and they retired to the kitchen for a late snack.

"Amy, that nut-shelling operation actually works," Rex said. "That was brilliant engineering." Lou nodded in agreement.

"I agree. It was a neat idea you had. But there are still costs, people are needed to run it, and they'll expect to be paid," Lou said. "Instead of daily rates, how about paying the crew so much per one hundred kilo for cleaned and bagged nuts?"

"Keep in mind, that cobbled-together cracker will require constant attention and adjustment," Amy said. "The goal is a clean, whole nut to roast, not a paste of crushed nuts and shells."

"Who do you recommend to watch after the cracker?" Rex asked.

"Lee seems to have the knack. Put him in charge of the waterwheel and cracker. It'll take a half dozen or more people to run the place, so how would you propose the payment be split among the workers?"

"First, if everything worked, what can the plant clean in a day?"

"With no machinery breakdowns, I figure six hundred to eight hundred kilos per day of raw nuts."

"So maybe we could expect to average five hundred kilos of clean nut production?" Rex asked. Amy nodded. "Well then we could pay up to five laborers eighty D-marks per day along with a manager at a hundred D-marks per day, and still keep our cleaning cost around one D-mark per kilo of clean nuts."

"Okay, then what about me and Eva?" Lou asked.

"Here's my proposal, Lou. I'll . . .

Wu wasted a day in Roanoke verifying that his quarry was gone. At Narrows, he learned the Wapiti lawyer and her escort had taken three of Len Ruffner's fast boats to Salt Furnace two days ago. He had lost his chance to beat her to Salt Furnace and arrange an ambush along the trail. He needed an inspiration.

"Len, our boss is in serious trouble if Cinnabar starts talking to those Prussians in her escort," Wu said. He still worried that he had a foul odor, even after two hot baths. Now his stomach felt queasy. He shouldn't have eaten all that bacon after not eating for three days. "Len, would hot tea and a piece of dry toast be too much trouble?"

His host walked over, opened the door, and yelled down the stairway for hot tea and some toast and cookies. Len left the door open and returned to the massive wood table that served as his desk and asked.

"I haven't received any cocaine in the last month, is Benjamin hoarding his supply?"

"He didn't say anything, other than I'm to donate to the governor's reelection, so I'd say it's safe to assume our boss isn't getting out of the cocaine business. Any word on where the Wapitis have Cinnabar?"

"I've heard from several people that he is being kept in the old brine furnace. What's the plan? Free him or kill him?"

"Now what do you think?" Wu said. The trader could be a bit soft and Wu wasn't in the mood for dealing with sensitive feelings. "I plan to kill the fool. I'll need several good men. Well, not good, dependable, and not afraid of the Wapitis. My cover story is that I'm buying winter-sloe, so armed guards shouldn't cause much of a stir."

"You obviously haven't been in Wapiti country recently. They're all armed, and as the Ichneumons found out, know how to fight. So if your plan is to surprise some lonesome and sleepy guard and then shoot Cinnabar in his cell, forget it. I heard there're always a dozen soldiers camped around the furnace."

"Yes, I know they're not the passive savages you and Donnelly used to raid with impunity. That's why I've become a whiskey salesman. I want at least five empty Simpson whiskey barrels and five hundred kilos of black powder."

Rex had spread a white linen cloth on Chief Smith's polished maple desktop and then dumped a kilogram of the clean, raw winter-sloe nuts from Panther Creek on the desk. The chief poked and inspected the sample, but his body language was that of a man with other matters weighing on his mind than the subject of their current conversation. Paul Moyer, whom Rex didn't care for, was the chief's brother-in-law from the Moyer tribe north of Lewisburg. The thin, standoffish man was sitting beside the chief, biting one of the Panther Creek nuts.

"Paul's having trouble with Atlantic Tobacco," Chief Smith said. "They want the raw nuts delivered to their roasting and bagging operation at Port Delta."

"I thought the understanding with their lawyer, Rahul Malhotra, was that the Wapitis would roast and then bag the nuts in twenty-five gram portions. That Atlantic Tobacco would only market the bags. The Wapitis were to get a hundred D-marks per kilo of bagged nuts."

"Paul tells me, now they're offering to pay twenty per kilo for dry, mold-free, clean, raw nuts. And that's only after we deliver them to Port Delta," Chief Smith said.

"That is quite a cut from the hundred D-marks. Did you get the bagger working, Paul? I'd heard it wanted to tear the bags instead of sealing them."

"I'll sort it out. That bagger is a piece of junk. Jacobs ripped you off. It keeps jamming, but shelling the nut is our real holdup. I have twenty-five women cracking nuts. In fact, I was considering asking the company for an unshelled price."

Rex decided if the man didn't want help, he wouldn't offer it, but still he wondered about the jamming. He thought the Jacobs bagger with its clusters of polished bronze gears, hopper, chains, rollers, and levers was a sophisticated piece of machinery for this society. It even determined the proper amount of nuts for each bag as the hand crank was turned.

"Are you letting the shell fragments contaminate the nuts?" Rex asked. "Jacobs did caution that pieces of the shell could jam the machine."

"Look, pal, we're cleaning them the best we can. It's a poor design, too delicate for the real world."

Paul, red faced, was too quick with an excuse. The Moyer tribe had offered nothing but excuses when asked to help the other Wapiti tribes in the war with Donnelly's men.

"What will the Prussian IRS think about all our raw nuts going to Orleans?" Rex asked. "Of course, Purnell will love it. He can just go over to the Port Delta wharf and buy all the winter-sloe he needs to make his cocaine. No need to deal with insane killers like Cinnabar."

"That's my worry. Until the nut is roasted," Chief Smith said, "it can still be converted into cocaine. Can you roast them, Paul?" The chief glanced toward his office manager, who had opened the door. He told her, "We'll be done shortly. Just wait and I'll go with you."

"I don't have the oven set up yet," Paul said. "Besides the tobacco boys don't want the nut roasted until right before the bagging step. They say the nut goes stale and can get dirty."

Rex wondered what the jerk had been doing with his time. The council's nut processing operation sounded utterly unprepared for the current harvest. Chief Smith wasn't happy, but Rex figured with the end of the voting period only a few days away, he didn't want the Moyer tribe upset.

"It sounds to me like you were never in the position to fulfill the tobacco company's original contract." Rex didn't mind upsetting the pompous fool.

"If you think it so easy, take the bagger, I don't need the hassle."

"You know the saying. It's a damn poor craftsman who blames his tools."

Rex thought of Suzie Sweetwater. He hadn't seen the bossy woman since he put her in charge of the mess tent right after the Salt

Furnace battle. Between her and Amy, they probably could get the contraption to work. "Is the bagger here?"

"Yeah, it's down by the dock," Paul said.

"Who actually paid for it?"

"No one yet," Chief Smith said standing up.

"Herr Jacobs wanted thirty-eight hundred D-marks, but no one had the cash. So we offered fifteen hundred bags of roasted nuts in trade. Jacobs didn't want the bags he wanted cash. If you want it, agree to pay Jacobs for the piece of junk." Paul got up to join his father-in-law and then added, "I don't have the time to fool with it."

"Are you interested, Rex?" Chief Smith asked, standing by the open office door. "Otherwise, for this season, sell the nuts however you can. I can explain the problems to the Prussians."

"It'll help the Wapitis' standing with the emperor if we do our part to close down Purnell's illegal cocaine operation. I'm willing to set up the bagging operation if it makes financial sense. What's the council expecting?"

Rex stood up from the table. Why the chief was so antsy to end the meeting wasn't clear. This bagging business needed resolved and he would tag along with the chief if necessary.

"I was going to do it for nothing, to help the tribes that depend on the harvest for their livelihood," Paul said. He looked toward the chief, obviously expecting approval. Chief Smith pointedly ignored him and asked Rex what he had in mind.

"Best I can gather, that's what your help has been worth, Paul, nothing."

After giving the annoyed Paul a moment to respond, Rex added, "I'm not interested in another project, but if the council will settle for a fee of ten D-marks per kilo of bagged nuts sold to Atlantic Tobacco, I'll do it."

Amy was inspecting the stained white cotton fabric tent, which had leaked in the last rain, when Rex and Hokee arrived. Andy Smith had told her the five by ten meter rectangular tent was an old Ichneumon mess tent that one of the Jarrell brothers had come by in some past barter deal. Rex had bought the tent and set it up behind the brick forge used by the Smithtown boat yard. At the time, she thought the tent was part of the machine shop operation, a place for storing scrap iron.

Her deal with Rex had been a new lab in exchange for her help with the Panther Creek winter-sloe nut operation. A heavy wood table, an empty wooden rain barrel with a metal dipper, and a large black cast-iron cauldron were in the tent. Amy, on discovering this junk inside the tent, had been wondering if this was her promised lab. Rex cleared up her confusion.

"What do you think of the lab? I couldn't find any lab equipment. No glassware, no lab scale, no alcohol torch to heat samples, but Tom did find a couple of glass jars and a collection of miscellaneous candle stubs."

"That cauldron adds a special touch. Are you like Pete Chin who already thinks I'm a witch?" She had hoped for better from the big Prussian. "Why didn't you ask? The lab needs to be in a real building, a house with doors and locks. Do you want children around vats of boiling sulfuric acid, strangers stealing the copper and zinc? You can't have a lab without security," Amy shouted, sweeping her hand across the tent interior. Hokee stopped sniffing the table and vanished from the tent.

Rex appeared thoroughly upset at her tears and angry remarks. Well, the fact that the big oaf at least appeared upset, and he didn't attempt to justify his pathetic excuse of a lab, helped calm her. She despised people who took her for granted.

"Besides, I need a place to stay at night."

"You're right. You're correct. I never gave security a thought. You do need a place," He tried a tentative smile. "In other words, you need a house."

Amy wasn't finish being snappy with the lout.

"I'm not talking about some dainty cottage like your Prussian girlfriend has in Roanoke. I need room to manufacture prototypes, like batteries." What was she thinking, bringing Franciscka into their conversation?

"My girlfriend . . . Okay, okay, I'll get with Tom Jarrell and Andy. Tell them to build you a building. This location okay," he asked, indicated the tent area.

"No, it's to near the river and the boatyard foundry."

Actually, it wasn't a bad location and her annoyance evaporated. Besides, he had shared Wu's gold with her and Larry. Silly her, she had been hesitant about accepting her share until he reminded her it was Purnell's gold intended to financer mayhem and assassinations. Buying her manumission with the gangster's gold seemed only fair.

"I'll see that your money is well spent." She could handle those two, Tom and Andy, which meant she would be in charge of building the lab.

"The reason I stopped wasn't to get yelled at. I need your help on the bagger. Paul Moyer can't make it work. Will you help?"

"You know I will. Tom needs to leave the cauldron. I might make some hard white soap." She gave Rex a quick peck on his cheek.

They headed toward the dock and the waiting Mischief. Rex looked relived. Maybe he did like her. For sure, she was feeling more than friendship toward the cod fisherman, Newfoundlander, or whatever. He reminded her of Count Habsburg, at least in appearance, which casted serious doubt on Rex's claim of Wapiti blood. Regardless, so far, he had treated her like a younger sister, unlike the Count who had certainly known how to charm a woman.

Her love life was nonexistent, but she could hope and was becoming optimistic about her future. All the Wapitis she had met, including Andy's fearsome looking foreman and blacksmith, Imus, treated her with deference. For the first time since the university, she felt free, appreciated, and valued.

On the ride upriver to Salt Furnace, Amy told Rex about her battery plans and Imus's help.

"Imus, our boatyard blacksmith," Rex asked.

"Yes, I had him melt a piece of zinc. I'm working on a battery. To create a pattern for casting a zinc anode, I pressed my hand in clay to form a four-prong mold for the molten metal. The zinc melted easily, but he had trouble getting his wood burning forge hot enough to melt the copper. In the end, with help from some coal, he managed to melt it."

"Yeah, copper melts at twice as high a temperature as zinc. Tom needs to make some coke. A coke fire is hot enough to melt iron."

They were on the bow watching the river. Amy knew Rex was checking for signs of the black eel, though everyone had assured him the eels wouldn't return before winter.

"How do you know about melting points and coke? But then claim to know nothing about labs?"

Where Rex had acquired his knowledge puzzled her. She didn't want to annoy her friend and protector anymore today, but the fisherman's son claimed no advanced education, while in conversations, he appeared to know about and understand chemistry and electricity better than any of her Heidelberg University professors. How could she not be curious?

"The first thing an iceman learns is melting points. Have to watch that ice. The other stuff is just stray information I've heard from the traders buying the salted cod. Tell me about your battery," Rex said, while studying the river ahead of the boat. She didn't buy that claim, but she dropped the matter. She wanted his opinion on another issue.

"Those crude galvanic stacks of copper, brine soaked cloth, and zinc that Al Leslie uses for power are dangerous and unreliable. The battery I'm building has a copper cathode in the bottom of a glass jar. When I get back, I'll cover it with copper sulfate powder, and fill the jar with rainwater. The last step is placing the zinc anode just under the surface of the rainwater in the jar. When I connect the anode to the cathode, I should have a useful current. How can I prove the quality and quantity of the current to Leslie? Do you have any suggestions?"

"String a wire to the boatyard and see if the battery has enough power to activate a coil of wire around a nail," Rex said. "Make the nail magnetic."

"An electromagnet," Amy asked. "You know about those?" He hesitantly nodded. "I'd sure like to meet one of those cod buying prodigies," she said.

"Look at those," Rex said, pointing at the three wood buffalos in the clearing on the hillside.

She dropped the matter, but the thought *false prophet* crossed her mind. Another person she wanted to meet was Sally Atman. Lily Hopkins had told her about a Prussian trained teacher who had married a Clovis man from the Moyer tribe and ran a school in Lewisburg. The middle-aged woman knew how to make lightning bolts.

David C. Brown

Chapter 9

General Mehta had just finished his report to the army staff at Port Delta explaining Captain Maqbool's calamitous encounter with Cinnabar's bootleggers when the watch sent word he needed to check the river. The scene that greeted him on the river below the fort gave the old soldier pause. What it heralded wasn't auspicious for his chance of retiring gracefully at the year's end.

The HMS Hendrick, a dark gray ocean-going sternwheeler, and flying the red Imperial Prussian flag with the black iron cross, was maneuvering to dock. It was the first Prussian warship he had ever known to travel this far up the Erie River. The cannon muzzles protruding from the sternwheeler's turrets wore white canvas caps.

"Captain, sound the alarm, load and man the front cannons, but don't roll them forward. Have the corporal saddle my horse. I'm going to pay them a visit. Colonel, you know what to do if it turns hostile."

There had been rumors that a Prussian warship planned to travel up the Erie River, but nary a word from his commander, General Bezdek, nor the Ichneumon headquarters at Fort Delta. The fat weasel was probably partying in Orleans and didn't even know about the warship. Emperor Ratakonda needed to replace his useless brother-in-law before the Prussians woke up and seized Delta.

Without the fort at the river's delta, the Ichneumons couldn't control the Erie River.

With the fort secure, having no instructions and ample curiosity, the general had decided to go greet the ship's captain and invite him to dinner. Besides, the act would show the men that they shouldn't fear the Prussians.

The warship wasn't on a social visit. About fifty men from the ship's crew were shoveling and hauling coal into the boat. A number of them looked suspiciously like Prussian marines whose presence gave him some comfort that he hadn't overreacted by loading the front cannons. The captain of the sternwheeler and a young Prussian naval officer greeted him on the wharf.

"The coal bunkers are low and we only stopped to take aboard enough coal to reach River Point," the Prussian captain said. "We'll be gone shortly."

The Prussians were rightfully nervous. One volley from the fort's forty-eight cannons would destroy the HMS Hendrick. Fortunately, the two empires were not at war.

"Any chance I could grab a quick tour of your boat, captain?"

"Hello General Mehta, I'd heard you had your own command." An older, fit-looking Prussian General Staff officer spoke from the upper deck, interrupting the captain's chance to speak, then added, "Captain, remind the men that we're in a hurry."

Mehta recognized Admiral Scheer, whom he had first met thirty years ago in Berlin at a Bismarck Chemical lecture series on the proper use of large powder charges and shells with delayed fuses. An older, thin-faced, clean-shaven man wearing a plain black cassock and a black skufia with a small silver imperial cross attached, stood beside the admiral.

"General Mehta, this is Bishop Alexandra von Bingen," the admiral said. "He wanted to see the Erie valley and meet the Wapiti chiefs."

"Perhaps, Bishop Bingen, on your return trip you'll have time for a visit."

Mehta had little use for any priest, but at least the Holy Prussian Church didn't believe in those appalling sunrise sacrifices, though they did like to burn people alive. He wondered if the intervening years had tempered the admiral's racist views on the Clovis and Wapiti people, and of course the Ichneumon.

"Why, thank you, General," Bishop Bingen said. "I'd like that very much, and even a tour of your imposing fort."

"Admiral Scheer, did you irritate Emperor Schnabel? Last I heard you commanded fleets and had one of the Prussian Navy's two iron-clad battleships for your flagship."

"The Schlesien, yes, she's anchored off Delta with the rest of the fleet. I wanted to see firsthand if the Ichneumons were violating the Erie River neutrality treaty." Waving toward the row of cannon ports looming above the wharf, he added, "Appears that you are. Emperor Schnabel will be most upset at this unambiguous disregard of a long-standing treaty."

"The neutrality treaty, surely, you jest. Our great grandfathers quit worrying about that piece of history a century ago. Besides, for your information, that pile of rocks is owned by Orleans Salt Company. The company contracted with the army to supply security for the site. It's a police station to guard the market and wharfs."

"Yeah, right, what's up there, fifty cannons to hold the scofflaws and river pirates at bay?" The Prussian admiral thought for a moment, before he shrugged and added, "Well, emperors never ask our opinions and we do have to obey their orders. Are those cannons loaded?"

"You're not planning on paying for the coal?" General Mehta joked, while stepping to the wharf's edge to allow the elderly Clovis woman who taught math to crowd by with her class of a dozen excited children, ranging in age from six to nine years. "You should allow a tour," he added, then greeted the teacher who appeared fascinated by the warship.

"When I return, if you're interested, I'll open the ship to the public, let everyone see why the Prussian Navy rules the world's oceans." The young children with her cheered on hearing the tour offer.

"You wish," the general said, smiling. "However, let's not argue. Your offer is most considerate. I'm sure most of the residents would enjoy the tour. But I'm curious how any boat on a river hopes to prevail against forts. Even those untrained Wapitis sank two of Purnell's boats in one night."

"Yes, I know," the admiral said. "Major Caprivi was there and submitted a detailed after-action report. Surprise and Ichneumon hubris destroyed those boats, not Wapiti military potency."

"Let's be respectful. Hubris menaces all military organizations, and General Meringa did die fighting for Emperor Ratakonda. Your captain is waving. It appears your men have completed the coaling. There's a man you should try to meet while at River Point, Rex Knight."

"Why do you suggest that?" Bishop Bingen asked. "Is he different?"

Mehta was suddenly cautious, wondering if the grandfatherly-looking bishop could be a fanatic.

"Herr Knight is a Prussian, a coal dealer who seems to work well with the Wapitis and Ichneumons. I even heard the man is brokering winter-sloe nuts. He's a businessman, but what you might find of interest, the man is also an antislavery zealot."

"Major Caprivi mentioned a Herr Knight in his report," the admiral said to the bishop before turning back to Mehta. "I'll endeavor to make his acquaintance while there."

The captain, paying Sam McCoy with gold coins for the coal caught their attention, and after a moment the admiral added, "This is a fast boat, but it devours coal. I would like to send the Wapitis a message to advise them of our expected arrival time. Do you have pigeons that home back to River Point I could purchase?"

General Mehta couldn't think of any reason not to provide a couple of pigeons to the Prussians. "The coal dock office has pigeons. They're reasonable folks, I'm sure they would sell you a couple of their birds."

Some people just have the knack, Rex Knight thought, watching Amy Caroom set up the well-used, hand-powered candy bagger the Wapiti council had bought. *Correction, which he was buying.* Jacobs and Jacobs had acquired it from a defunct cough drop company in New Hamburg. The unit had bagged hard candy, primarily licorice and lemon cough drops. The machine had a rickety wood frame supported by six wooden legs that had to be perfectly level and anchored to ensure proper alignment of the moving parts. The contraption would have charmed Rube Goldberg.

Chief Smith and the nut sellers in the crowd of spectators watched quietly as Amy carefully threaded the roll of printed white bags through the numerous rollers and levers in preparation for bagging the batch of nuts that Suzie Sweetwater was cooling and salting by the oven.

"That's not the problem. When you turn the crank to advance the next bag, the paper binds up and tears the bag. She's wasting our time," Paul Moyer told the chief.

Rex, who was standing on the other side of the chief with Hans Melas and Helen, said, "Ten D-marks says she'll make it work. Want to bet I'm right, Paul?"

"She might get lucky for a few bags, but not the thousands we need."

Helen gave a derisive sniff, "Paul, you're such a whiner, at least she's trying."

Suzie dumped a bucket of the cooled, salted, roasted nuts in the bagger's hopper and Amy gently turned the crank. Several cranks were required to load the machine and the drag chain feeding the measuring cup that tipped a measure of nuts into the bag. The mechanism that dispersed a minuscule amount of glue to seal the bag apparently failed to work correctly. The bagger didn't seal the first twenty bags properly. Suzie handed those bags to the spectators, who munched on the treats, while she studied the glue dispenser.

"I told you it wouldn't work. The tobacco company won't buy bags that leak nuts."

Amy ignored Paul, cleaned the tiny orifice again, and tried another batch of bags. The first dozen sealed perfect, then the glue started skipping bags again.

"Leave the plug out of the glue tank. I think a vacuum is forming as the glue flows out of the tank," Rex said. Amy gave him a smile and removed the plug. The bagger quickly used up the nuts in the hopper. Eighty neatly filled and sealed bags of nuts landed on the table.

"Let's give Fraulein Caroom a round of applause. She just saved the Wapitis' winter-sloe sales," Chief Smith said. The crowd cheered her as she beamed with pleasure and waved Suzie Sweetwater and the cooks over to share the applause.

Rex looked around for Paul. Apparently, he had slipped away. In the process, he noticed another large Prussian man, whom he hadn't seen around Salt Furnace before, watching Amy. The man was probably just admiring a pretty woman, but he had the build favored by the Prussian army for their combat feldwebels and by criminals such as Purnell for their hired enforcers.

"Hans, know that guy leaning against the shelter's corner post?" Hans didn't, but Helen did.

"He's Billy Hickman," the rooming house manager said. "He's waiting for Ruffner's fast boat. Ruffner hired him to help take it back up the river to the Narrows. Seems a pleasant sort, been in camp for several days, even got yelled at for hanging around the furnace."

A stranger with an interest in the old furnace, Rex thought.

"Hans, you're looking for honest work, ask him if he thought Ruffner would hire you to help."

"An honest job, I thought I had one spying on you savages for the emperor."

"I stand corrected. However, you must admit Hickman has that ex-feldwebel look. My experience is that most of them are reprobates. I thought with you also being an ex-feldwebel, it might allow you to find out who he is and what his purpose might be. If it's dragging boats up the Southern River, I'll be most surprised."

Out of roasted nuts to bag, Amy walked over to them. "Any word from Al on when he'll be here?"

"End of next week, after the vote. In the meantime, we need to meet Tara and Fritz at River Point. A Prussian warship is due in, but I'd like to have some bagged nuts to hand out," Rex opened a canvas bag by his leg. "There's about five kilos of hard cherry and lemon candy drops in the bag. If you can adjust that contraption to bag the candy, we could hand it out to the kids. I'd like to take three or four hundred bags with us to pass out while we're passing out the nuts to their parents. I thought it might help get Panther Creek Nut Company's name out and about."

Amy had readjusted the measuring device to load five candy drops in a bag and left two of Suzie's crew working the bagger. She had a half hour and headed to the boarding house for one of its clean outhouses. She had just completed her spider check and lowered her pants when someone rattled the door.

"Amy, I know who you are, so listen carefully. Where is Herr Wright?"

A Purnell man, she stalled. "I don't know what you're talking about."

"People say you're smart. I never leave a witness alive, so figure out where that leaves you if I have to open this door to get my answer. Again, where is Wright?"

"The Ichneumons killed him in Panther Creek." She held her breath. Would he believe the truth? After several minutes of silence, she realized the man was gone.

Edward Wu hated river travel in Ruffner's crude open boats. Between dodging boulders and the cold spray of water over the boat's bow, it was impossible to relax on the trip. It was fast, though. The real question in Wu's mind was whether he should have allied with Sanita Chopra, a middle age Ichneumon man who Len Ruffner claimed answered directly to the Ichneumon Emperor. Chopra owned the only large amount of black powder in the territories not controlled by the Prussian military, twenty-five barrels at the Narrows magazine.

Three no-nonsense Ichneumon mercenaries guarded the kegs of gunpowder. The agent had no issue with selling several barrels of his black powder, if in turn Wu helped him slip the rest of the powder shipment past the Wapitis at Salt Furnace and River Point.

The reason Herr Chopra offered was the garrison at Hickory Ridge needed black powder due to the Prussian Navy blockading the Erie River at Delta. Wu had heard no rumors of pending hostility between the two empires, but he reckoned that whatever use the mysterious Ichneumon trader had planned for the explosives would likely create turmoil in the Wapitis' territory. That could only help him. Next, with the gunpowder issue settled, Wu asked Len Ruffner what detonators with delays he might have available.

178

The next day a wet, cold Wu and the convoy of open boats arrived at River Falls. An empty coal barge tied off to a large sycamore bobbed against the riverbank just below the falls. Several woodcutters waited beside a large stack of split firewood on the riverbank.

"Can those woodcutters be trusted?" Chopra asked. "They'll see the powder barrels."

Wu knew that the woodcutters, though mostly Wapitis, worked for Len Ruffner. "Give them a couple of liters of gin. Tell them it's a sample of the barrel contents. They're laborers. As long as those barrels don't leak, we'll be fine."

"Dead men don't talk either."

"On that you're wrong. Corpses can speak volumes. Are you planning to kill the Wapiti crew on the Mischief? Maybe you forgot it's picking up the firewood barge."

"We can hide the bodies. Tell anyone who asks, that they left for home."

"Too late, see the smoke."

The Mischief, hired by Ruffner to push the barge to River Point, came around the last river bend before the falls. The plan, as understood by Wu, was for the Clovis Belle to take the barge from River Point to Hickory Ridge.

The deception depended on the Wapitis believing Chopra's barrels contained cheap gin. Wu's part was to convince curious persons that the gin was payment for winter-sloe nuts and sawed timber. However, the garrisons at Salt Furnace and River Point might question the need for twenty-five barrels of gin on one buying trip down the Southern and Erie Rivers. Chopra and Ruffner had decided to bury most of the gunpowder barrels under the firewood. Out of sight, out of mind was their operating theory.

The three Ichneumon guards and the woodcutters quickly transferred all but two of the barrels to the barge. They then neatly stacked the firewood over the hundred-liter barrels. The men were careful to place Wu's two barrels of "gin" and duffle bags on top of the firewood.

"Looks fine, a typical load of firewood that won't merit a second look," Chopra said, and with two of his guards boarded his canoe and headed down the river. The older, taciturn guard stayed with the barge and Wu boarded the Mischief.

The people working at the Salt Furnace wharf were in a festive mood as they unloaded Wu's two barrels of gin and delivered his bags to the rooming house. He learned from the guard at the warehouse that the winter-sloe nut roasting and bagging operation had been successful. That explained the town's jovial atmosphere, since it would ensure a good price for their crop. Captain Balers from the Mischief joined Wu on the dock.

"Everyone seems in a festive mood," Wu said. He wondered if that might make his task easier.

"Wait until the vote for a Wapiti territory is announced. Then you'll see a serious celebration with lots of whiskey," the young boat captain said.

"What are you expecting? Doesn't voting on the territory question end tomorrow?"

"Yep, and it will be for joining the Prussian Empire as a new territory. I'm going over to check out that tent."

Wu looked where the captain indicated. Several women were cleaning an odd-looking contraption, while other women were handing out hot tea and cider to anyone with a cup or mug.

"See that pile of small white wax paper bags stacked on a table in the tent? Those bags contain salted, roasted winter-sloe nuts. They're going to make us rich," Captain Balers said. "Try some, they're free." Wu grabbed a couple of bags to try later.

Wu had six of the half-liter bottles of gin, two of which he gave to men working at the warehouse near the council's new office building, where he'd stowed his two barrels. Standing on the warehouse loading dock, he was trying to decide where to look for that Smith woman when Bill Hickman greeted him. He was glad to see Bill. Having a helper would make using a diversion more effective.

"Are you here on Purnell business?" Bill asked while looking around to make certain no one was nearby. Wu acknowledged that he was.

"Benjamin wants me to stop the chief's lies."

"I understand these savages are becoming a nuisance. I'm after Tara Smith. She's a lawyer, and supposedly, the brains behind the new territory request. Our boss wants it blocked. I missed connecting with her in Roanoke, but damn if I didn't see Caroom there. She's potentially as big a problem as Cinnabar on a witness stand."

Wu's coat had two large pockets stuffed with four bottles of gin. He gave Bill one of the bottles to lighten the load.

"Amy! Yeah, I guess she could be a problem. Well, you're in luck, she's here, working on the nut-bagging operation. If I'd known, I could have dealt with her an hour ago."

"There's no guessing, the girl knows all about the operation at Panther Creek. So where's that hot shot Wright been? He was supposed to keep her under control."

"Our comrade is dead, according to her. He was killed in Panther Creek by Ichneumon soldiers," Bill said. "Why are you acting so nervously?"

Wu realized that if the Caroom woman was here, then probably her big Prussian bodyguard was also.

"Does she know who you are, and that you're interested in Cinnabar?" He continued to scan the area for that big Prussian

181

bodyguard of hers. "There's a very dangerous Prussian with her, I'm not sure of their relationship, lover, hired guard, IRS agent, whatever, but you should be careful with him."

"I know who you mean, I saw him earlier. I've also found Cinnabar, but can't figure how to get at him. They have him locked in the old furnace jail cell under heavy guard." Bill popped the cork and sniffed the gin before taking a small sip. "I've been warned off from the furnace area, but you're new, and the guards won't say anything if you walk by. Go look and see if any thoughts come to mind for how to distract those guards long enough for me to enter and deal with the chief. I'll wait by the warehouse."

Rex and Larry were just finishing their late lunch of brown beans and cornbread, when a frightened Amy rushed into the boarding house kitchen looking for them. She related her terrifying experience while in the outhouse. Rex had to agree with her interpretation. Whoever the person was, he worked for Purnell, for how else could he know of Amy's connection to Wright?

"The only reason for one of Purnell's thugs being in Salt Furnace would be to find Cinnabar," Rex said. "You're obviously not the mystery man's target. Shooting someone through a flimsy wood door would have presented no problem, so that left Cinnabar, Tara, or the council as the target."

Rex still wasn't clear on Wu's purpose for tracking Amy and wondered if he remained a threat. He needed to get her to the safety of River Point immediately.

"Whoever he was, he was after Cinnabar and looking for help. I gather this Wright character was another of Purnell's killers?" Larry asked. She nodded in agreement and reached for a piece of Helen's delicious cornbread and the honey pot. Actions that Rex interpreted to mean her nerves were recovering from the shock.

"The heavy guard force at the furnace has him stymied, for the moment," Larry said.

"I think you're right. So what would you do in that case?" Rex asked. Amy looked eager to answer but waited on Larry's reply.

"Create a diversion to pull the guards away, like a fire." Larry answered. Amy nodded in agreement.

"Then you'd best caution the guards."

Rex and Amy found Hans at the stockade talking with the farrier. Amy related her story. The feldwebel concurred with their suspicions that the assassin would stage a diversion to draw the guards away from the furnace. They also learned he had lost track of that Prussian stranger and had not had an opportunity to check out the man's reason for being here.

Hans went looking for the stranger, while Rex and Amy hurried back to the rooming house for their bags and Hokee. They wanted to catch a ride down the river on the Mischief. He needed to deliver to Panther Creek the burlap that he had bought from Jacobs's supplies at the Salt Furnace warehouse.

After a quick pass by the furnace, Wu knew Bill Hickman was correct. To get inside the furnace to kill Cinnabar, he would need a diversion to draw away the guards. Wu had also learned during his stroll around the village that Tara Smith was at Chief Chin's village, campaigning against the chief's effort for a "no" vote on the petition to become a Prussian territory.

Bill's diversion was in Wu's power to grant. Even better, he had bought the expensive Ichneumon timer-delayed detonators, instead of the cheaper Prussian units from Ruffner. Essentially, the Ichneumon timer was an alarm clock that struck a percussion cap instead of a bell. The timer allowed a person to set the moment of detonation at any time within a twenty-four hour period. Prussian timers, though much safer to use, had fixed delay periods, usually five minutes or one hour. It used a glass capsule of strong acid that was broken to start the delay period. The leaking acid then ate through a wire that held back a powerful spring. When the wire parted, it released the spring and allowed the striker to hit a percussion cap.

"I'll need at least two hours to get in position," Bill said. They were leaning against the hitching post near the warehouse. "The lady at the rooming house told me the Chief's daughter and her Prussian guards went to Johnsonville."

"I know. The steamboat leaves in thirty minutes for River Point. I'll head after the Smith woman if you can handle Cinnabar and Amy."

"Cinnabar's the tough target. Amy's a piece of cake," Bill said. "But a good explosion in the warehouse ought to pull away his guards. Set it for two and half hours."

The sidewheeler needed that much time to embark and be down the river far enough that no one on the boat would hear the blast.

"Two hours, thirty minutes, it is," Wu said. They shook hands and went separate ways.

Ruffner's men had added an extra threaded side bunghole to some of the powder barrels. The added bunghole threads matched the threads on an Ichneumon detonator. The warehouse guard was no hindrance to Wu's plan. The man had apparently drunk the entire bottle of gin and was snoring in a chair, leaning against the loading dockside door. Satisfied he was alone; Wu removed the plugs and then, in their place, screwed in the two timers.

It was nerve-racking work, as the timer striker pawl was fragile and prone to sudden failures with catastrophic results for the sapper. The side location of the threaded barrel hole had the advantage of shielding the timer from curious eyes, but allowed the gunpowder to spill out when he removed the bung. The detonator was made of brass, and the barrel was oak, so there was no danger of a spark.

What he wasn't certain of was whether grains of the gunpowder caught between the threads posed any danger of detonation from being compressed. The proper method of inserting the detonator was to roll the barrel on its side, clean the threads and then screw the detonator into the hole. The tight space around the gin barrels precluded that option.

The steamboat blew its whistle. That meant departure was in a few minutes, but still he carefully and gently threaded the timers into the bungholes. Next, he wound the clock spring and set the time in each unit. Then he paused to watch the timers work for a minute to satisfy himself that everything was in order. After pulling the safety pins from the detonators, he threw a piece of canvas over the barrels and headed to the wharf. He waved to the half dozen boys playing in the sand pile beside the warehouse. They waved back as he hurried by to the wharf. Wu hoped Bill made sure the Caroom girl was dead before leaving Salt Furnace.

The growling was his first inkling that his day might become difficult. The Prussian's wolf, bedded down beside the two horses in the rear of the boat, watched him.

"Herr Wu, where did you come from," the big Prussian asked. The monster had pulled his revolver and pointed it at him. "I'll take your weapons until you disembark, and speaking of that, what's your business?"

Wu could scream in frustration, but he couldn't chance a delay, not with the warehouse only a hundred meters from the wharf. They needed to be gone before those timers went off.

"What is your name? Why do you keep threatening me?"

Chopra's guard had startled on seeing the revolver and reacted too late. The Mischief's captain, holding a short double-barrel shotgun, had stepped into the room.

"My name is Rex Knight. Kyle, cover that Ichneumon trooper while Amy disarms him."

"I'll kill that bitch if she touches me," the guard said as he laid his revolver on the floor.

"Knives too," the big Prussian said. The trooper gave the Caroom woman a nasty look, and she edged away from him and toward the Wapiti with the shotgun. The wolf had slipped into the room to stand by the woman. Wu wondered if the trooper appreciated how close death was. The man finally placed his belt knife by the gun. Another Wapiti entered the room, and the captain gave him the shotgun.

"We're still headed to River Point?" Captain Kyle asked. The big Prussian nodded, his attention remained on Chopra's guard and Wu.

"The boot knife, too. Now why are you here, Herr Wu?"

The jolt from the boat paddle linkage engagement gave him hope they were about to leave the wharf.

"Mister, you can go sit on the barge where we can keep an eye on you, or we can chain you to that eyebolt in the wall, your choice."

The guard flashed an evil smile and appeared pleased with the choice of riding on the firewood barge, for without another word, he turned to go. Wu didn't like that look, thought of those Ichneumon suicide warriors, and wondered if the guard might have a flint and steel on him. The Prussian must have sensed something off in the guard's behavior.

"On second thought, Kyle, chain him to the eye bolt. Amy, hold the shotgun," the big Prussian said.

It was a near thing. The trooper tensed and appeared to consider grabbing for the shotgun. The silent girl looked ready to pull the trigger. Then the crisis was over, the man chained to the eyebolt with a slave collar. Even better, the boat had cleared the dock area and was picking up speed down the river.

"You're trying my patience, Herr Wu. What is your purpose for visiting Wapiti territory?"

"I'm just a simple trader. I buy winter-sloe nuts for Herr Purnell." As the boat gained speed, his confidence returned. He could spin tales with the best. He also wondered if his gold was on the boat. "So why are you tormenting me?

"What'd your boss decide? To buy the nuts and do all the cocaine processing in Orleans, now that Cinnabar's operation is closed?"

"I'm not familiar with cocaine or this Cinnabar character, other than I've heard he's a cannibal. Fraulein Caroom, have you ever known me to be involved in anything illegal?"

"I have no idea what you do for that criminal," she answered, while handing back the boat's shotgun to the Wapiti trooper. Chopra's guard, squatted in the corner of the small room that offered protection from inclement weather, gave her a murderous look.

"How much are you paying for clean, shelled nuts?" the Prussian asked.

"It depends if the nuts are bagged and I get credit for the gold you stole. In clean dry fifty kilo burlap bags, I'll pay a hundred D-marks for a bag at a river location."

"That's no deal. That price wouldn't buy dirty unshelled nuts. Atlantic Tobacco is paying twenty a kilo plus providing the bag. Offer fifteen hundred a bag and I put you in contact with up to two hundred bags of nuts at the Panther Creek dock."

Wu saw the girl looked concerned over the offer and he wondered why she'd care, not that he had any plans of actually buying nuts.

"I might be interested in that amount of winter-sloe at a thousand D-marks a bag," he countered. "Since, so to speak, I've prepaid." He loved to haggle and started to relax.

"Actually I'm more interested in keeping Tara Smith alive."

Rex wanted to beat the Prussian sternwheeler to River Point, but stopped briefly at Johnson Village to confer with Fritz about the admiral's visit.

"Admiral Scheer belongs to the general staff group of officers who believed only the strong presence of the Prussian Army will keep the Ichneumon Empire out of the Erie River and prevent them from colonizing the vast unsettled western land."

"Hard to argue with that opinion," Rex said. Hokee was nosing a crate of brown rabbits on the wharf. "Hokee, get back here," he called. The wolf ignored him.

"The Scheer group of generals and admirals also think encouraging local militias and territorial armies is a mistake. They believe it might lead the territories to one day demanding their independence from the empire."

"I reckon how that event plays out would depend on how the empire treats the territories."

With a nut harvest to complete, Rex considered worrying about future geopolitical events a distraction from events he could influence, like Hokee's misbehavior. He walked over and pulled the wolf away from the case of trembling rabbits while his friend speculated about the navy visit.

"The main item the admiral's going to be interested in is the fort. It controls the Erie River. That's the prize the Wapitis have to offer the Prussian Empire," Fritz said. He was using a burlap bag of winter-sloe nuts on the dock for a seat. Hokee and the Prussian major eyed each other, and then the wolf flopped down beside Fritz as an elderly woman stormed onto the wharf, holding a broom.

"You keep your cur away from my rabbits!" she admonished Rex and Fritz. "You Prussians think the rules don't apply to you. A market is no place for a wolf, there're children here." Fritz appeared surprised. Hokee acted as if he was asleep.

"I'll see the animal behaves, madam," Rex said, fighting a smile. The grandmotherly woman wasn't amused.

"You do that, young man," the lady said. She looked Rex in the eye for a moment, apparently decided he was sincere, and then gave Hokee a last scowl and shake of her broom, before returning to her crates of chickens and rabbits.

Rex, Hokee, and Fritz, watched as the elderly woman walked off the dock.

"Your mutt has a lot of nerve, trying to hide beside me from the rabbit woman," Fritz said. "As for the admiral, be aware that he harbors a low opinion of non-Prussians. If he thinks the Wapiti garrison isn't capable of protecting the fort from an Ichneumon raid, I fear he might be tempted to seize it. He would justify his action as preventing a bunch of incompetent savages, who got lucky once, from losing a valuable security asset."

"Seems a sure way to start a war, no one needs that. Where's Tara?" He looked around, not seeing her near the wharf and market area, but he did catch the hostile glare of the rabbit woman toward Hokee.

"Hokee, quit dallying around. Get on the boat," Amy yelled.

Still the wolf stopped several times to look back and check on the woman and her crate of rabbits. The woman now held an ax. After a last look, Hokee hopped on the Mischief and nuzzled Amy's leg.

"Tara is working in the outlying areas around Johnson Village with its new chief, Steve Johnson. She wants to counter Pete Chin's influence. The Ichneumon pawn is pushing for a vote against forming a new Prussian territory."

David C. Brown

"Aye, Pete's a fool. I need to deliver my prisoners to River Point and make sure Matt is ready. I'll send the Mischief back for you and Tara."

They could hear Wu, chained with the seething Ichneumon trooper, demanding that Captain Malik release them. Malik was Mischief's senior captain and an Ichneumon who had switched allegiance to the Wapiti cause. He had been off for two days and was now taking over command from Kyle.

"Who's hollering?" Fritz asked.

"Some mystery man who works for Purnell, named Wu. I suspect he's an assassin after Tara and Amy. However, lacking any real proof, I'm keeping him locked up until I can send him down the Erie."

The other unresolved issue was who was to take delivery of the barge's cargo. The Ichneumon trooper wasn't talking, and Wu said a man named Chopra owned the firewood and barrels. No one claimed to know what the barrels contained, though Wu ventured he thought it was gin for trading along the Erie. That explanation sounded reasonable, and after Captain Bailer confirmed that Chopra existed and would be at River Point waiting for the barge, Rex quit worrying about the barge's cargo.

The Mischief arrived at the River Point wharf near sunset. Rex released the Ichneumon guard after he apologized for his earlier behavior and explained his job was guarding Chopra's barge of firewood and gin. Andy Smith was waiting on the dock with several Wapiti warriors. On learning of Rex's concerns, he ordered his men to escort the loudly protesting Wu to the fort's jail. The mystery man would wait in a cell for the arrival of the Delta steamer.

"I'll put his bags and weapons in Matt's office," Andy said. Amy looked relieved, and with Hokee tagging along, went to find Lily.

190

The Mischief left the unclaimed barge of firewood at the wharf for Chopra and headed back to Johnson Village to pick up Fritz and Tara. Rex wanted them at River Point in the morning to greet Admiral Scheer.

"When you do head back to Salt Furnace," Matt said, "Remind me to give you two crates of pigeons. Someone there left the coop open. A dozen pigeons arrived about an hour ago from the council with no messages." Rex nodded.

Andy had given Wu's wallet, with the gold coins to Rex, who in turn gave it to Matt. "Put this someplace secure."

"Cinnabar's talking," Matt said, as he put the wallet in the large iron safe inherited from the former Ichneumon fort commander. "He admitted to supplying Purnell with cocaine paste for several years. So what's next?"

"It'll depend on what kind of man Admiral Scheer proves to be. Fritz says he has a poor opinion of Clovis and Wapitis. Though I'm hopeful he'll act like a gentleman, his true condescending attitude toward us may creep out. Warn everyone not to respond in kind. How strong is the garrison force?"

"Thank you, glad you asked," Matt said.

"What's that supposed to mean?" Rex asked, a bit irritated by the remark.

"Andy and I wondered if you had gone soft on the Prussians. Our concern is how big of a force could be hidden on the boat. Captain Dalporto told me those ocean going sternwheelers are bigger, with a deeper hull, than riverboats like the Clovis Belle. He claims a couple hundred soldiers could hide below deck."

"First, no deep hull boat will make it past the sandbars below Panther Creek. So forget a second deck below the water line. Also, the HMS Hendrick carries iron cladding and armored turrets with twin heavy cannons in each, so room for soldiers is limited. Fritz figures thirty, maybe fifty tops, but he cautions that they'll be the very best troopers the Prussian Navy has."

"The simplest way to deal with the threat would be to sink the boat," Matt said.

"I trust you're joking."

Matt told the guard at the office door to enter. He had a pigeon message.

The two hundred kilos of black powder detonated on time, leveling the warehouse along with the attached messenger pigeon coop. Burning debris rained down across the settlement, starting several fires, the most serious of which were in the stockade's stables and the new council office. A dozen people working and loafing in the warehouse and dock area died instantly, including three of the boys at the sand pile.

A flying metal shard from one of the iron bands off the barrel of powder wounded Chief Smith in his arm. The fragment had torn through his office window like a bullet. Pieces of the warehouse, landing as far as the furnace cell, sent Cinnabar's guards scrambling for cover while they tried to make sense of what had just occurred. The billowing clouds of dark smoke and dust rolling through the village added to the apocalyptic appearance of the explosion.

"Did the stockade's magazine explode? Do you think that was the diversion you warned about?" the head guard asked.

Larry and a number of Wapiti troopers were in front of the furnace for the changing of the guards. They looked around the furnace neighborhood and saw nothing that resembled a hostile force.

"It has to be an accident," Larry said. "We need to help the injured and start putting out fires. Two of you stay at the jail entrance, just in case it was the assassin's handiwork."

"I'll stay," the senior guard said. "Joey, you too, just in case it's a diversion." Larry appreciated that offer from the senior man.

They both knew Joey was new to the guard force and needed close supervision.

Bill Hickman waited as the remaining guard force raced into the village. He had broken into a chicken coop about a hundred meters from the entrance to the furnace. The location offered him a clear shot at the two guards in front of the furnace. The approaching black cloud of dust and smoke had the guards' attention. His first shot dropped the left guard, an older man. The other guard, barely older than a boy, ran to the downed guard who said something that caused him to turn and race for the furnace entrance. Bill's second shot caught the young guard in his back and he collapsed before reaching the door. An open and unguarded jail beckoned, and he jogged to the entrance, pausing to shoot the older guard again.

The heavy wooden door that enclosed the furnace had a small-screened opening to see in the cell. Inside the brick firebox of the furnace, chains supplied an additional means of securing prisoners. The Wapitis had anchored one end of the chain to the brick wall with an eyebolt. They had then attached a key-locked iron collar to the other end of the several meter long chain.

Looking through the screen, Bill saw a large tattooed Clovis warrior wearing one of the collars. The prisoner had heard the explosion and shooting. He sat on a bed looking toward the door. He had a worried expression. Other than that prisoner, the cell was empty.

"Are you Chief Cinnabar? Herr Purnell sent me to free you."

Bill enjoyed giving his victims hope. It made more fun to see them wilt when they realized the truth. Still, he couldn't dally long, as he had to find that Caroom girl.

"Who are you?" the prisoner asked.

Bill had to shove his revolver in his belt to free his hands, in order to use the guard's key and open the heavy wooden cell door. As the door swung open, he saw that the prisoner's hand was under his pillow.

"Put your hands were I can see them." Those were the assassin's last words.

Chopra and his two guards had been approaching Johnson Village when the Mischief and the firewood barge left for River Point. They didn't stop at the village and instead kept paddling down river. The sun had set by the time they reached River Point. The Mischief had passed them an hour earlier on its way back up the river without the barge. They beach the canoe above the wharf where the Mischief had left the barge tied. The third guard that had stayed with the barge greeted and assured them the barge cargo was undisturbed.

Though tired, Chopra wanted to install the timers, but he hesitated. The acid wire detonator's delay period of twenty-four hours limited his options on when to install the device. The HMS Hendrick's arrival time wasn't that certain, it was expected around noon tomorrow, but it could be just as well sometime in the next couple of days.

He decided to wait and hope Wu showed up with one of those new Ichneumon clock timer detonators. He should have remembered it at River Falls. All that remained for him to accomplish the emperor's mission was to distract the Wapiti guards and insert the detonators. He had to laugh. It sounded so simple but there were many risks. The Wapitis and Prussian Navy guards would kill them without hesitation if discovered in the act of installing the detonators. But the successful detonation of twenty-three barrels of black powder on the opposite side of the wharf from the Prussian warship would demolish the warship, along with the Wapitis' hope for a territory.

Emperor Ratakonda had promised Chopra great rewards on the successful completion of his mission. However, the emperor had emphasized that success depended on the Prussian navy believing the

Wapitis had detonated the bomb. Nothing must point to Ichneumon involvement. Toward sunrise, one of the Ichneumon troopers woke him and whispered that someone was on the barge of firewood, a young boy.

The pigeon message was to advise the River Point garrison of the HMS Hendrick's plans for a high-speed run by the fort tomorrow at around noon. Later that same day, the sternwheeler would return to dock at the Southern River side wharf. Rex wondered if the Prussians were just putting on a show for the natives.

"Was it an excuse to sail out of sight upriver from the fort and disembark an assault force on the fort's side of the river before returning to dock? Or am I getting too suspicious. Amy said the HMS Hendrick has the latest Prussian fire tube boilers, the largest available. She worries about how safe they are."

Seeing Matt's pained look, Rex added, "Hey, that's the kind of things she talks about. Maybe the admiral just wants us to ask him why the Prussian boat is so fast, so he can promote the new boiler."

"I seriously doubt the admiral is interested in promoting boilers to savages," Matt said. They both laughed. "I'd like to send John Baler and most of the Owl fire team with Redfox's Clovis warriors to guard the possible landing sites. The question is what to do if the admiral attempts to land armed soldiers."

About fifty empty brass 11.6x65 cartridges were scattered across the wood table Matt used for a desk. Between pauses in their conversation and sips from a cup of black tea, the fort commander was punching out the cartridge's spent primer with a special tool and then running a brass bristle brush into the casing to remove any powder residue. Neat as always, he had a wood bowl to collect the powder residue and spent primers. Then, after another careful inspection, he set each clean empty cartridge in a large china bowl on the end of the table.

The fort's tabby cat wandered in to the office. It spotted the bowl and jumped on the desk to inspect the contents.

"Your cat looks disappointed. How's the fort's lead supply for casting bullets?" He asked, while examining one of the cleaned brass shells. "Any idea on how many times we can reload one of these?"

"I think that one has been reloaded three times, this will be its fourth," Matt said. "It still looks fine. As to the lead inventory, we're good. Your lady friend was asking if we had any copper or zinc, which we don't. I told her that wrecked sternwheeler at Smithtown had a copper bottom sheeting that she might talk Andy into parting with. So what should I tell John? Start another war, or let them pass?"

"These soldiers will be dangerous to approach if their orders are to storm the fort in the middle of the night." Matt's shoulder shrug irritated Rex. "Let me explain why it's so dangerous. The clandestine Prussian force is hardly in a position to take prisoners. As a result, the Prussians will likely kill any witnesses they encounter on their approach, in order to keep their presence secret. So someone, say John Baler, just confronting them, might trigger a firefight. I don't want some egotistic admiral looking for glory to wreck our chance for a territory by precipitating a bloodbath between Wapitis and Prussian troopers. Just send a few men who are very good at not being discovered, and have them report on who lands and where they head."

"So you have a plan?" Matt asked, putting the cartridge cleaning to the side so he could check the contents of Wu's wallet. Gold coins spilled out on the desk. "My, my, twenty gold coins."

"Starting tomorrow, enforce the 'no weapons inside the fort' rule. Have a couple of young women set up a weapon checkpoint at the main gate and reinforce the front gate's guard force. Also, load the front cannons. The gold belongs to Wu, your prisoner."

"Solid ball or canister?"

196

"Some of each, and have Herr Crouch available to aim those four cannons above the wharf. Are you okay with using Crouch?" Rex asked. He knew Matt and the Prussian didn't get along, but then no one got along with the crotchety old bastard. But Crouch was their best ordnance man.

Today would be fun. Billy Walker's teacher had cancelled school so everyone could watch the arrival of the Prussian warship at noon. Billy liked his new life. He and his mother had been among the slaves freed by the Wapitis from Purnell's saline works at Bone Valley. She worked in the fort's kitchen and had a small hut among the dozen workers' huts near the southeast corner of the fort's massive rock wall. He did odd jobs for the soldiers when not in school and sold bags of nuts, earning a few pfennigs to help his mother put food on their table. His father was dead. He had been one of Donnelly's slavers and had raped his mother when they captured her near Hopkins River.

Billy's other source of income was fish. The fort cooks, being Wapitis, were partial to fresh fish, and would buy walleye pike, yellow perch, and channel cats from the local fishermen. His most reliable catch was yellow perch from off the wharf using his five-meter-long cane pole. Herr Knight had given him six priceless hard brass fish hooks, four small ones for trout and perch, and two larger hooks for carp and walleyes, along with twenty-five meters of thin, strong, waxed silk fishing line as a gift for helping him locate all the missing Wapiti women at Bone Valley .

The cooks paid two pfennigs for any perch bigger than thirty-five centimeters. Well, they didn't really pay in coin. Instead, they credited an account that he could redeem for camp scrip that the local traders would take in trade.

This morning Billy had decided to check out the barge of firewood before fishing. He discovered the barge's load consisted mostly of new whiskey barrels, which surprised him. The firewood appeared to be an afterthought to finish loading the barge. So what was in the barrels?

Being curious, the boy moved several pieces of the split oak firewood to better inspect the barrels. The young entrepreneur knew that brand new barrels were expensive and only used for valuable cargo, things like whiskey, tobacco, and gunpowder, cargo that wasn't normally left unattended in a poorly secured barge. He got on his hands and knees and sniffed along the barrel's top joints trying to identify the contents. The barrels had a faint smell that reminded him of stale urine. Could the cargo be saltpeter, he wondered? The barge moved, causing Billy to look up and see a large man, lifting his sword to take a killing swing. He leaped back just in time to avoid losing his head.

The wild man had one of those long curved swords that the Ichneumon troopers used. To Billy's good luck, the sword had wedged in the barrel. That required the man, who looked just like those soldiers who had guarded the Bone Valley fort, to put his foot on the barrel in order to pull the sword free. The man said nothing.

"I wasn't hurting anything," his voice a high whine, then realized the trooper's intent was murder.

As the sword came free and the trooper turned to take another swing, Billy jumped in the river. The water was cold, but not freezing. He was a good swimmer and in among the wharf piling in a flash, hoping the Ichneumons' reputation for being poor swimmers was true. At least the killer hadn't followed him into the river. Instead, the man had pulled a revolver and was working his way along the barge, searching the river for him.

The tie-off rope holding the barge was only half dozen meters and two pilings away from the piling he hid behind. Ninety-nine percent of Wapitis carried knives, and young Billy was no exception. If he cut the rope, the current would sweep the barge out into the Erie and take the crazy man with it. Quietly paddled over to the rope, he cut it, and dived back under the wharf just as the killer spotted him. The killer was fast, and he was off the barge before it swung clear of the wharf. The man then leaned over the edge of the dock and looked back under the wharf. Billy concentrated on keeping the piling between him and the killer silhouetted by the breaking dawn.

Chopra didn't want to believe his eyes. The barge was floating down the river, while that brainless trooper was looking under the wharf for a damn kid. Then the trooper fired. If he could hear the shot, Wapiti guards in the fort could too. The barge was picking up speed and in a few minutes would be in the Erie River, headed toward Hickory Ridge. As he feared, two guards ran out of the fort toward the wharf to investigate.

The emperor's beautiful plan fell apart in front of him as his trooper panicked and shot the two Wapitis running onto the wharf. The surprised guards on the fort wall recovered quickly and shot down the Ichneumon trooper in a hail of bullets before he could reach the riverbank. By then the firewood barge had swung into the Erie River, and several more Wapitis were running toward the wharf.

"Get down, you can't help that fool. We'll stay out of sight until the garrison settles down, then we'll head for Hickory Ridge." There was still hope that he could salvage the emperor's plot, if he could catch the barge before the Prussian warship passed it on the Erie.

Rex and Matt had been walking across the fort's common area, toward the jail for an early visit with Cinnabar, when the firing and yelling from the guards started.

"Who the hell is shooting at this hour?"

"It was from the wharf," Matt said. "I'll sound the general alarm."

Rex ran to investigate, and in moments, Wapitis were rushing to their assigned battle stations. No one knew what had happened, but he could see three men were sprawled on the wharf. As he ran onto the wharf, he spotted the blue blood seeping out of the stranger's body and then realized the man was the Ichneumon guard from the firewood barge.

"The barge of firewood is missing. Surely, no one would get in a gunfight over a barge of firewood," Matt said as he caught up with him. "What a mess. And the Prussian envoy and warship will arrive in less than four hours."

"Look at this," Rex said, holding up the cut barge rope. "Someone cut it. The bastard who shot our men is the man who was guarding the barge. It doesn't make any sense. Who freed the barge? Was someone trying to steal the gin?"

Two Wapiti soldiers dragged a wounded and soaked Walker boy from under the wharf. A bullet had cut off the kid's left index finger, a wound that Rex figured was extremely painful, but not life threatening. Obtaining Billy's information required multiple assurances that he wouldn't send the sobbing boy back to Bone Valley. Why the kid was so nervous wasn't clear. No one cared if he fished off a barge. The mysterious Ichneumon had no call to attack with a sword.

The Mischief was maneuvering to dock. Tara and Fritz scrutinized the dead bodies from the boat's bow and waved to Rex who waited with Billy at the wharf's entrance. The wharf looked like a war zone with the bodies, scattered firearms, and pools of blood. The runaway barge was in the Erie and would soon be out of sight

"Matt, we have to clean this up before the admiral arrives. He already thinks we're savages, and this mess won't help our image."

Rex gave Billy his shirt. The wet kid was shivering and turning blue as they waited for his mother, who had been at work in the fort's kitchen making biscuits.

"I have several guards looking for the next of kin. I don't understand why the man started shooting over a damn load of firewood," Matt said. "At least the gunfire wasn't the start of an assault on the fort. Billy, you're damn lucky."

The boy's mother, Frau Walker, arrived. She told them that first she'd take the scared boy home for dry clothes and then to the fort's infirmary.

"He'll be there if you needed to ask him additional questions."

After the boy left, Tara, Fritz, and Captain Malik arrived with questions. Rex told them Billy's tale, which required only a minute. The questions in everyone's mind were why had the Ichneumon trooper shot our men and what was in those barrels. The boy said they smelled like urine.

Wu arrived at the wharf. Matt had thought he might know why the dead Ichneumon had shot the two Wapiti troopers. If the guard was after a trespasser, why didn't he asked the Wapitis to help him? Wu professed to have no idea.

"I bought two of the barrels and had them unloaded at Salt Furnace," Wu said. "I'd planned to buy two more barrels of gin here, until you acted up and threw me in jail. So where's the barge?"

"Must be good stuff if it smells like piss," the Prussian officer said who was examining the bloody revolver. He appeared to be endeavoring to avoid contact with the blue blood on the firearm.

"Those savages who cut firewood probably piss wherever the urge strikes," Wu said. "Maybe one of them pissed on the barrel. Regardless, a man gathering winter-sloe nuts doesn't quite have the refined taste of a Prussian aristocrat."

He silently cursed those idiotic Chopra gang members for calling attention to the barge by attacking a boy who was just fishing. The kid had probably smelled dirty saltpeter, which meant that Ruffner's finest Prussian military gunpowder was actually some of Purnell's low grade blasting powder.

"Did the barge float off?"

He hoped the damn thing had sunk, vanished. For sure, he needed to be gone before word of the explosion at Salt Furnace arrived, though he wasn't even sure if it had happened. Now, he hoped the timers had failed and the barrels hadn't exploded.

Wu couldn't catch a break. The Wapiti fort commander had his bags and wallet with the remaining gold D-marks, and Tara Smith was unharmed. Chief Cinnabar, who knew where he was, and the Wapitis were voting to join the Prussian empire. His mission so far was a complete failure.

"Captain Malik, does the boat have enough coal to run down the Erie and retrieve the firewood barge?" Rex asked. Wu hoped not. Maybe the Prussian warship would hit it and blow both of them to kingdom come. The turncoat captain and that Wapiti with the shotgun conferred.

"We have enough coal to catch it. Anyone mind if we use part of the firewood in the barge to return up the river?" The captain's audience shook their heads. "I should go now, before that Prussian warship manages to collide with the runaway barge, not take time to load coal."

"Yeah, use the wood," Rex said. "Matt can replace it from the fort's stores. Don't let Kyle get in the gin." The group laughed.

Two young boys wanted a ride and asked the captain if they could come along. Wu was surprised to hear the captain okay it. Then again, both boys were strapping teenagers and seemed well behaved. Even Knight nodded okay.

The bad news continued. Wu then learned the Mischief's crew hadn't blown down the steam coils and the boiler still had good pressure. The boat pulled away from the dock within a couple of minutes. Knight told the guards to take him to the cell. Other Wapitis started gathering the bodies and washing away the bloodstains.

David C. Brown

Chapter 10

The sandbar at the confluence of Panther Creek and the Erie River had narrowed the main channel and increased the river current. Captain Wolfgang required all his piloting skills to avoid scraping one side or the other of the large sternwheeler as he threaded his way up the channel. The broad, deep river above Panther Creek was a welcome sight and he ordered more speed.

A couple of hours later Admiral Scheer joined him in the pilothouse. The captain figured they were about an hour below River Point when he spotted the small steamboat beside a barge of firewood that had grounded in a small cove. The boat flew the gold and white flag with a large green star. The captain had never seen such a flag.

"Do the Wapitis have a navy?" The admiral asked, while studying the small boat with his brass telescope. The captain admitted he had never heard of such a navy. "That boat has a cannon mounted on its bow. Could they be pirates? Block them in and we'll check their papers."

The captain thought the admiral was forgetting where he was. Native boat captains in this wilderness frontier were very unlikely to carry registration and travel permits similar to the documents required on vessels operating on Prussian rivers. To his surprise, the tugboat crew was friendly and waved as they pulled alongside. The half dozen armed marines who jumped on their small boat eliminated their smiles. One of the marines' officers escorted the surprised captain to the pilothouse where the admiral waited. Bishop Bingen arrived just behind the tugboat captain.

"I'm not clear on what papers you are requesting."

The tug's captain was clearly an Ichneumon, and Captain Wolfgang wondered how he came to be operating a Wapiti flagged vessel. He thought the groups were bitter adversaries, and apparently so did the admiral and the bishop.

"If you're just recovering a runaway barge, why do you have a cannon mounted on the boat?" the admiral asked, while motioning for the steward to refill his cup of tea. The admiral failed to offer the Ichneumon any refreshments, which was a serious breach of good manners. "Who owns that boat? My men said they found an Ichneumon flag in the pilothouse. Are you a pirate?"

"Admiral Scheer, I work for Herr Knight, and the boat is owned by the Wapiti Council of Chiefs. The cannon is on the boat because the Wapitis used it during the recent hostilities with slavers and haven't removed it. I'm on private, peaceful business for Herr Knight and having answered your questions. I request permission to return to my boat and finish securing the barge."

"Herr Knight? I've heard his name. Apparently, he is cozy with the Ichneumons. Okay, until I verify who owns the boat, you will operate the vessel under the Prussian navy's instructions. Finish securing the barge and then return it and the boat to River Point, where I will sort out fact from fiction. The royal marines will ensure your crew's compliance."

"Just a moment," Bishop Bingen said. "Captain, what business is Herr Knight in?" The admiral appeared to be a bit irritated that the bishop had injected himself into the issue.

"He brokers coal along the river, and has branched into the winter-sloe nut."

"What kind of man is this Herr Knight?" The bishop asked. He apparently noticed the admiral sipping tea, for he added, "Do you have any extra cups? I'd like a cup of that tea and I'm sure Captain Malik would also." The admiral looked embarrassed and ordered a sailor to serve tea.

"Thank you, a cup of tea would be good," Captain Malik said. "Herr Knight looks like one of Emperor Schnabel's Imperial Guards. He's the son of a Wapiti slave and a cod fisherman. Hates slavery, he thinks the Wapitis' future is in becoming a Prussian territory."

"Well that's all very interesting, but it doesn't explain an armed river boat or those different flags. Bishop Bingen, I'll have to insist that we proceed to River Point. You'll have plenty of time for your questions then. Lieutenant Caprivi, escort the captain to his vessel."

The Ichneumon captain wisely refrained from parting remarks, gulped his cup of tea, and left peacefully with the marine officer and guard.

"Captain, bring the boat up to speed and just prior to the fort, go to a hundred and forty percent military power," Admiral Scheer said. "The savages need to see the might of the Prussian Navy. It will also allow you to make the drop and still beat the tug to the River Point wharf."

Bishop Bingen appeared startled by the admiral's order, started to say something, and then stopped. Instead, the bishop finished his tea, put his empty cup on the chart table, and left the pilothouse.

Captain Malik and Kyle were thankful that they had taken Rex's advice. He had told them before the earlier trip to Bone Valley to find a simple way to disable the Mischief and thus prevent pirates from stealing the boat. They would need some obvious problem that they could quickly fix, but no one else could promptly repair. The disabling event had to be of such a nature that a person ignorant of machines would believe the problem to be irreparable with a glance.

They chose the eccentric rod that opened and closed the engine's steam valve. The heavy brass rod, three centimeters in diameter, had yoke ends connected to the eccentric and steam valve with pins easily remove. They carried an extra eccentric rod that Rex had had Imus cast out of poor quality cast iron with a pocket of slag that would allow a man easily to snap it in two pieces. He explained that the break had to look fresh, so they shouldn't break the rod ahead of time.

Makil made the gesture as he boarded with the lieutenant. Kyle yanked the pins out of the rod's yolks and hid the brass rod in the oil sump under the steam cylinders. The cast iron rod he snapped and attached the dangling broken iron rod pieces on the eccentric and steam valve yolks. The slight would explain the immobility of the boat to the boarding Prussians.

The Belcher boys, busy gawking at the warship and asking the Prussian marines questions, helped the captain delay the boarding party. The Prussian warship had left as soon as the three troopers boarded the Mischief.

"Make yourself comfortable, I need to supervise the barge recovery," Malik said. He then climbed onto the firewood barge to supervise. He told the two Belcher boys to help Kyle wrestle the barge around so they could tie it off to the Mischief's bow.

Lieutenant Caprivi watched from the pilothouse, still unaware the boat was disabled. The activity had attracted an audience of a dozen Clovis men and women from the nearby farm community. The Mischief's crew knew several of the men in the group of curious farmers who had gathered to watch the barge recovery operation. The farmers also were curious about the armed Prussians and the large warship. The Belcher brothers bantered about with the spectators who offered friendly and useless advice on freeing the grounded barge, until the lieutenant yelled at them to stop.

Malik knew their spectators were members of the Beaver tribe and intended no harm. The tribe inhabited both sides of the Erie River from Panther Creek to thirty kilometers above River Point. They and their neighbors, the Wapitis, got on fine and lived together in peace. They had even started sending the tribe's children to the River Point School. Of course, as seemed to be the Wapitis nature, they charged for the service, asking for a fresh buffalo every other week.

Unfortunately, the Prussian marines didn't know peaceful tribes from the belligerent ones and became noticeably nervous when they realized that a number of armed Clovis warriors had arrived to learn what the attraction was. Malik, until recently equally ignorant of the tribes, could appreciate the marines' concern, but he also understood how important it was for the Prussians in their ignorance not to precipitate a tragic fight that could alienate the Clovis and Wapiti people. He needed to disarm the troopers without killing anyone.

As if there wasn't enough going on, a canoe with several men approached the boat from upriver. It finally got close enough for Malik to recognize that the man in front was the Ichneumon trader, Chopra. He reckoned the trader was looking for the barge and his cargo of firewood and barrels. They could use his help, but to everyone's surprise, when the lieutenant hailed them, they turned away, and started paddling vigorously down the Erie.

A concerned Captain Wolfgang knew he had no choice. A captain in the Prussian Navy did not refuse an admiral's direct order. An order for the HMS Hendrick to proceed past the fort at River Point at eighteen kilometers per hour was an invitation for disaster in the narrowing Erie River about the confluence with the Southern River.

This was especially true considering that attaining that speed against the river current required operating the boilers at one hundred and forty percent of their maximum allowable pressure. Then there were the unknown river obstacles, like sandbars and submerged trees that could rip the bottom out of the boat.

The admiral was correct about one point. At that speed, the boat with the large Imperial flag streaming in the wind, the foaming trail of water from the paddles, columns of smoke, and large waves from the wake would present an impressive spectacle. Whether it was worth risking the boat was another matter, but at least the savages watching from the fort and along the riverbanks should be awed. He rang the engine room, and ordered maximum power. The engineer could worry about the safety of the Focke-Wulf boiler and its massive steam engine. Keeping the boat in a clear channel would require his full concentration as he felt the sternwheeler's paddles pick up speed.

Captain Wolfgang knew the admiral had come of age when all ships still depended on wind and sails. He also suspected steam engines and their boilers were a mystery to the admiral, though the vain man would never admit it. Hendrick's chief engineer had attempted to explain his concern about the boat's power plant. The admiral had been dismissive of the engineer's concerns.

"I know what a boiler is, it's a tea kettle on a grate over a fire and the hotter you make it, the more steam and pressure comes out of it," the admiral said. "If the Ichneumon can run their boilers at two million pascals, I don't understand why we can't run our new boiler at one million."

The old engineer had explained the Ichneumon boilers that ran at two million pascals pressure were unlicensed copies of the Caroom water tube boilers, not fire tube boilers. The man tried using the admiral's teakettle metaphor to explain why they shouldn't run their fire tube boiler at high pressure.

"A fire tube boiler is like a tea kettle with fabricated tubes throughout the kettle that the hot gases can pass through to provide additional heated surfaces within the vessel instead of just the bottom of it. The reason for the lower allowed pressure is the size of pressure tank. Remember, each of our boilers are three meters in diameter and ten meters long, whereas water tubes are only a tenth of a meter in diameter and much stronger. . . ."

"Enough! Spare me that engineering nonsense. Focke-Wulf makes the best boilers in the world. If they say operate at some pressure, you know the boiler is good for twice that pressure."

"Sir," the engineer said, as he tried again. "The Hendrick pressure tanks hold thousands of kilograms of pressurized boiling water. The walls of the boiler tanks holding the superheated water are subject to the same pressure as the steam driving the engine that runs the paddlewheel. Focke-Wulf instructions are to never, and I repeat, never exceed a pressure of two-thirds of a million pascals."

The engineer had looked to him for support. "Captain Wolfgang, a million pascals would risk rupturing the boiler, releasing a massive amount of superheated steam and boiling water, destroy the boat."

"I'm tired of arguing. When we approach River Point, go to one million. I want to demonstrate Prussian maritime might." The admiral finally noticed the engineer's trepidation and added, "Hell, it's less than half of what the damn Ichneumons use every day. It's only for a short time. Now go make the arrangements."

The Hendrick's captain had known the engineer for several years and knew that by nature the man tended to be overly cautious. Besides, the admiral was right, there'd be a safety factor. The recommended maximum steam pressure was probably only a half or less of the ultimate design pressure. His more serious qualm was the admiral's other order. Once the boat was out of sight of the fort, the exact spot the admiral would pick, the boat would stop. In the process

211

of reversing the boat, Wolfgang would accidentally bump against the east river bank long enough for twenty Imperial marines to disembark.

Amy joined Rex on the fort's wall facing the Erie as he watched the Prussian warship race by with dense gray smoke pouring out the twin stacks and the large imperial flag flying in the breeze.

"My goodness, they have to be going at least sixteen or eighteen kilometers per hour against the current. They're pushing those boilers. I've seen the engine room, and those boilers are massive. I'll bet those firemen are busy."

"I need them for a coal customer," Rex said. "Look at the size of the wake, those waves will stir the banks. Those boys had better be careful."

From the laughing and shouts, the boys appeared to think the waves from the boat's passage great fun.

"The Prussians must feel frisky," Amy said. "Hendrick's captain had better hope there's no partially submerged tree in the river."

"I agree, too reckless for my taste."

The Prussians had an impressive boat, but Rex had just seen that it was not very efficient in transmitting the engine's power into thrust. Most of the paddlewheel's effort appeared to be going to flinging water up in the air and stirring the river sediments. The Erie was brown in the wake of the boat's passage. Clearly using a stern wheel paddle wasn't that efficient.

"Amy, I've been meaning to ask, have you ever seen a propeller? I think they're called water screws on a boat?"

"Like a windmill? Never heard of using one on a boat, but I'll look into it when I get a chance." She then launched into a discussion of a battery she had started fabricating. He listened with half his attention, while wondering what was delaying the Mischief.

A number of the neighboring Beaver tribe members had decided to enjoy the feast the Wapitis were providing to honor the arrival of the Prussian Navy. Then apprehension as Rex realized several canoes full of Beaver families were crossing the Erie River. What if the big boat came storming back down the river like it had gone by the fort? Coming back, it would be running with the current, flying. Those canoes would be in the way, and in danger.

A sweaty, grimy Hans Melas rushed into the fort with Fritz, who was yelling at Rex and Amy to wait. The men jogged up the stone stairs to the top of the west wall, and told them about the failed attempt to assassinate Slim and the explosion at Salt Furnace. He was thankful he had left Slim a revolver.

"Has the cause of the explosion been determined?" Rex asked while glancing up the river valley for the telltale smoke. There it was and moving fast. "Fritz, does the captain know to watch out for small boats?"

Fritz looked up the river, saw the crowed river, and ran back down the steps and to the riverbank, yelling and pointing.

The Prussian stern wheeler tore around the last bend on the Erie River above the confluence of the Southern River. It looked like some smoke-belching prehistoric monster, hell-bent on devouring the canoes. It pushed a large bow wave that would swamp every canoe in the river. With an audible bang, the huge stern-mounted paddle wheel went into reverse.

"Oh my, oh my. . ." Amy said. "If only it holds. . . ."

A moment later the center of the boat exploded with a rolling boom, creating a momentary crater in the river flow that sent out a wave, which swamped all the Beaver canoes and rolled them over. Bodies and pieces of the boat rained down as an enormous cloud of steam and smoke filled the valley. A large piece of one of the boat's smoke stacks crashed onto the riverbank near Fritz. Most of the rest of the debris fell back into the river adding to the terror of the Clovis and surviving Prussian sailors trying to reach shore.

The rear part of the boat not submerged was burning. Rex wondered if the gunpowder for the rear turret was secure, or if there would be another explosion. The bow of the boat had capsized and snagged on the west bank of the river, the heavy front gun turret serving as an anchor.

Pandemonium reigned. Rex screamed over the noise to attract the gate guard's attention. "Close the gate! Allow no one in the fort."

"The boiler exploded," Amy said as she brushed by him to go help at the river, and he jogged to the commander's office.

Matt had just finished a bath, to be clean for greeting the various visiting dignitaries. He had heard a muffled boom, and in order to investigate, had rushed his toiletry. Rex interrupted his effort by beating on the apartment door.

"Hendrick's boiler exploded."

"So that's what I heard," Matt said. "What happened?"

"Regardless of what caused it, a lot of injured people need help. The other concern is that we don't know if Prussian marines landed. Protection of the fort has to be your first concern. I'll help with the survivors, you secure the fort."

"I'll seal the fort," Matt said. He ran shirtless to the main gate to check on the men.

Fritz Caprivi had organized several canoes to pull people from the wreckage and the river. Amy, Tara, and several of the younger Wapiti and Clovis students were organizing a medical station on the Erie dock used for small boats. It had survived the waves from the explosion. The location made a convenient place to sort the living from the dead. Most of the injuries were from shock, steam inhalation, and burns. Rex was surprised at the number of uninjured sailors and Clovis who had managed to reach shore unassisted.

Next Fritz and Hans organized the recovery of the floating bodies before the river current carried them away and established a temporary morgue by the west fort wall. After collecting all the dead and administrating first aid to survivors, Rex asked Lily to start a list of their names. Later, someone in authority would need to question the crew survivors to determine what had occurred, though he suspected Amy had it right: a boiler explosion. Whatever the cause, the disaster would have reverberations across the Prussian Empire, and Rex wanted their conduct above reproach.

Hans's crew found Admiral Scheer in the shallow water along the west riverbank with a broken leg and burns across his arms and face. Rex helped lift the admiral from the canoe.

"He's hallucinating that the fort had fired on the boat," Hans said. "Shock has him confused."

Rex didn't want that nonsense spreading among the Prussian survivors and looked for Tara. She was by the dock checking the injured.

"Hans, take the admiral directly to the infirmary."

"Tara, we have a problem. He's claiming we fired on the boat. Can you calm the man? Crazy accusations will serve no one's purpose," Rex said.

The blood-splattered woman gave him an exasperated look. "First the fool blows up his boat. Now he'll blow up our peace."

"Would you see to his treatment, please?"

"He's not the only one. Captain Wolfgang is in terrible shape. A rivet from the boiler ripped through his left leg and penetrated his right knee, causing massive bleeding. Freda managed to stop that for the moment, but he needs to go to the infirmary."

The amount of blood on Tara's smock was frightful, if it was from the captain, than his prognosis was indeed grave.

"Handle him with care, we may need his testimony," Rex said.

"I'll go ahead and get the medicine and beds ready for both of them. You get them there." She then walked back to the dock, said something to Dr. Freda Hopkins, and they then hurried into the fort.

"The men just brought a man dressed like a priest to the dock," Fritz said. "He's alive, but unconscious."

Rex had just instructed the two Wapiti warriors with the injured priest to carry him to the infirmary and Tara, when John arrived. He looked a bit like a brush pile in his camouflage outfit.

"I saw twenty Imperial marines, heavily armed I might add. They headed inland. I figure they're headed to those trees off the northeast corner of the fort." He drank some water and then finished his report. "Zoe and his brother will track them and report where they bedded down. I think we all agree they won't try to seize the fort before dark."

"Son of a bitch," Fritz said. "That foolish windbag did intend to seize the fort. It'll screw everything up."

"There's a badly injured marine lieutenant on the south wharf. Would he know the names of the officers commanding the assault force? If we knew their names, they might listen." Rex said. Fritz went to talk with the survivors.

"John, you did good, now I'd like you find Matt. The last I saw him was in the warehouse, rounding up several of those large tents. He's loaning the tents to the surviving Prussian troopers for a temporary camp near the wharf."

"Those old tents we acquired after defeating Donnelly's forces at Hinton?"

"Yes. His plan also has the advantage of keeping the Prussians outside the fort's walls. Now, go find Matt, tell him what you found, then tell him to meet me in the infirmary and then help with the tents."

Fritz had learned that Captain Beck was the name of the officer in charge of the marines who were lurking near the fort. In the hallway to the admiral's room, Tara, Fritz and Rex decided on their ploy.

"I gather you have a plan?" Fritz said.

"How about I'm a Prussian feldwebel who Captain Beck sent to check on whether their orders had changed because of the boiler explosion," Rex said.

"You're hoping he'll tell you what those orders were?"

"The admiral has never met me, and dressed as I am, in a set of the Prussian marines' camouflage fatigues, I look the part. You are a Prussian army officer trying to help the navy after a terrible accident. You need to know Captain Beck's orders in order to help. Tara, before we go in the admiral's room, how's that priest?"

"The priest is still unconscious. Freda fears he may have inhaled live steam. If he did, there's nothing we can do." Rex shrugged his shoulders and Tara added, "I gave the admiral a dose of the cannabis tincture for the pain. He's still in a lot of pain, but also intoxicated."

"Think he should have more of the drug before we go in?" Rex's hope was that the drug would make the haughty admiral a bit more agreeable to a mild interrogation from his subordinates.

The drug given the admiral was a concoction that the Wapiti made from a tincture of grain alcohol and cannabis. The other use of the tincture was in spiritual rites. Rex reckoned that anyone who drank much of that concoction would likely see spirits.

"No. If I give him any more, he may pass out," Tara said. "Ask your questions. I'll wait in the hall by the room's door, case you need me." With the blood washed off and changed into a clean white doctor's smock, she looked like an angel. Rex and Fritz marched into the admiral's room and snapped to attention.

"Sir, Captain Beck sent the feldwebel to ask if he should proceed," Fritz said.

"Who are you, major? How did you get here?" the admiral asked in a slightly slurred voice.

"Sir, General von Moltke sent me to oversee the Wapiti vote. I arrived after the explosion, and finding all the commission officers incapacitated by injuries, I took command of the survivors. I've been organizing the relief effort, and will do so until you can appoint someone to relieve me."

"Major, watch your back. Don't trust the Wapitis. Those cowardly savages ambushed the Hendrick." The admiral then looked around the room to verify that only Fritz and Rex were present. "Now they've lost their nerve and will pretend to be helping, which means they'll try denying ever firing on us."

The admiral then addressed Rex directly. "Feldwebel, tell your commander his orders remain unchanged. He is to avenge the Hendrick and us."

"Will he need a code or password to prove the order came from you?"

Rex's friend appeared shocked to learn the admiral's disdain for the Wapiti people, and to discover that their concerns were well founded.

"Iron Fist, Feldwebel," the admiral said. "Tell him my orders are still to attack tonight, not to wait. Major, you need to organize the survivors and have them ready to assist Captain Beck." A coughing fit caused the admiral to pause. Red faced he added, "These lawless savages need a lesson in Prussian might. I want them taught their place. I want the fort commander hung for sinking us."

The admiral glared at Fritz, before adding, "I don't want any mercy shown to those cowardly bastards. Are you up to the duty?"

Fritz snapped out a, "Yes, sir." Rex wondered why the admiral was so determined to blame the disaster on the Wapitis.

"Also, Lieutenant Caprivi should soon arrive with the pirate vessel that I had seized," the admiral said. "Use it to get word to the Schlesien. It's anchored off Port Delta with the rest of the fleet."

The admiral was clear-headed enough to remember Fritz's name and he asked, "Are you and the lieutenant related?"

"We're first cousins, sir."

"I want a salvage crew here before these thieving savages can strip the boat of valuables. Now, do your duty for the emperor. Major, on your way out, tell that pretty nurse to bring something for this burn."

Both men saluted and left the admiral's room. Rex, wondering what pirate vessel the admiral was referring to, noticed that Tara gave Fritz a questioning look as they passed in the hallway outside the admiral's room. His Prussian friend had nodded in response to her unasked question.

The Prussian lieutenant, Adolf Caprivi was a young, wiry man and a head taller than Captain Malik was. Getting control of the Mischief would require overpowering the lieutenant. The other two Prussians appeared less intent on the boat crew and more focused on the thirty or so warriors now lining the bank. Malik figured the opportune time to strike at the lieutenant was when he learned of the broken control rod. With the barge fastened to the Mischief's bow, it was time to leave.

The Belcher boys winched in the anchor, and Kyle yelled from the boiler room that the steam pressure was over a million pascals, enough to engage the paddle drive. He ordered Kyle to flip the steam valve, to allow reversing the paddle rotation, and he opened the boiler's steam valve to the engine. Nothing happened. The lieutenant looked alarmed as the current swung the boat against the bank.

"Captain, that damn rod broke again. Drop the anchor."

The Belcher boys struggled with the pawl to get it to release the winch drum and allow the anchor chain to unwind. The lieutenant yelled for the two Prussian marines to help with the winch, while he checked the boiler room. The Clovis farmers on the riverbank thought it was great entertainment. They yelled more unhelpful advice and jeered as the current swung the boat and barge into the river.

The two guards bent over the troublesome winch, laying their rifles on the deck. Captain Malik was pleased to see that the Belcher boys had remembered his instructions. They each tackled a surprised guard, knocking them off the deck and falling into the river with them.

Running down the stairs from the pilothouse, he grabbed one of the rifles, taking a moment to hit the bigger guard on his head with the rifle butt and knock him loose from the boat. Unfortunately, the other guard was paddling in the river and screaming for help. The boys were swimming hard towards the west bank and cover. If Kyle hadn't disarmed the lieutenant, they were in trouble. The boat was out of control and picking up speed in the river.

The cursing and thumping from the boiler room suggested that Kyle had his hands full with the lieutenant. Letting the boat pick its own path, the captain hurried down to the boiler. The two men had each other's throats in a death grip, and if he didn't do something to stop them, one of them was bound to crush the other's larynx. He fired the rifle through the rear wall and kicked the lieutenant, who at that moment happened to be on top, in the ribs.

"Stop, you fools."

The lieutenant let go of Kyle's neck, but the Wapiti was unyielding and the captain kicked him in his ribs while yelling for him to stop choking the Prussian. The moment that Kyle let go of the lieutenant's neck, the lieutenant lashed out at Malik's leg. He was expecting some reaction, and so he withstood the Prussian's blow. The choking had weakened the officer, but still he tried again to grab the captain's leg and upend him.

"Stop, you idiot, or I'll pull the trigger," he screamed, jamming his rifle's muzzle in the lieutenant's chest.

Kyle had difficulty standing, but finally stumbled back in the boiler room and retrieved a set of leftover slave manacles and secured the furious lieutenant.

"The admiral will deal you, scum. The admiral has you trapped between him and Hickory Ridge. There'll be no escaping justice." He jerked and rattled the manacles. "You'll hang," the lieutenant added in a rasping voice.

"Maybe so, but that pompous ass had no legal right to seize our boat. Kyle, use his revolver to guard him, while I fix the boat and retrieve the crew."

First, the captain ran back outside to check that none of the Prussians had boarded the Mischief. He was surprised to discover how far the boat had drifted without colliding with something or grounding. The two guards were splashing towards the west bank a couple of hundred meters upriver. The Belcher boys were not in sight. The only threat was the drifting boat ramming a bank or sandbar. Satisfied, he went and replaced the rod. It'd be dark soon and he wanted to find the boys before night.

Rex, Hans, and Fritz gathered at the wharf with the uninjured sailors who had finished erecting the tents.

"I just came from Admiral Scheer. The explosion badly burned him and broke numerous bones. He's not expected to survive the night and he asked I get word to Captain Beck that his orders have changed," Fritz said.

The bastard didn't look that ill, Rex thought, nor did the men standing around the group look that upset on receiving word about their admiral's critical condition.

"Captain Beck doesn't know us, so I need a few volunteers whom he knows to travel with us and prevent his men from shooting first and asking questions later."

"Major, are you the Volga River Caprivi?" Asked one of the older troopers, a feldwebel Rex figured. Fritz nodded.

"Your cousin is bringing that Ichneumon pirate boat back. He's the one you need. He's the captain's friend. But he's not here, and if Captain Beck attacks this hornet's nest, he'll get all of us killed. So I'll help," the feldwebel said. He pointed at three of the troopers listening. "Gather your rifles; we're going with the Major."

Rex watched Fritz, Hans Melas, several Prussian troopers, and the feldwebel head into the night. They carried torches and each had a rifle. Either Captain Beck would be sensible, or he had just gained several more fighters, if Fritz failed to convince him.

The torches were pinpricks of yellow at the far edge of the clearing east of the fort when word came that the admiral had died. Rex didn't believe that and was going to return to the infirmary to check, but he heard a steamboat approaching the wharf.

The dozen or so Prussian sailors had also heard it, and they walked out on the wharf with him to watch the Mischief, with the firewood barge approach and dock. The torches, which the two Wapiti laborers had placed on the last two pilings to guide the captain in his approach to the wharf, lit a strange scene. The Belcher boys stood ready with the ropes needed to secure the boat and the barge. The boisterous boys were subdued, not their normal demeanor.

The sight of two Prussian sailors sitting on the firewood with hands bound behind their backs caused the crowd on the wharf to go silent. Maneuvering the Mischief against the dock had Captain Malik occupied, so Rex asked the older Belcher boy, Art, the question he knew was on the sailors' minds.

"Why are those men prisoners?"

Art remained mute. Worse for wear, Kyle walked to the bow of the steamboat holding a rifle and said. "The Prussian admiral thought we were pirates and seized our boat."

The remark started murmurs in the crowd as Rex asked why the man would think that.

"I don't know, maybe because Captain Malik is an Ichneumon."

The Wapiti guards at the fort must have sensed a problem, because six armed Wapiti warriors jogged to the wharf to stand by Rex, as the captain finished docking. About a dozen unarmed Prussian sailors gathered around the main wharf entrance.

"Everyone on the wharf where you can hear the captain," Rex yelled. He waved them onto the wharf.

Captain Malik joined him on the wharf and finished the story. He told how they seized back control of the boat. He ended by telling of the Clovis warriors on the Erie's west bank rounding up the Belcher boys and two Prussian sailors at the river shore. The Clovis warriors had turned them over to him.

"They thought it was a drunken brawl. The Clovis hunter, a sub-chief, told me the warship had gone up the river and had passed them at an insane speed. The chief thought maybe the Prussian captain had drunk too much schnapps."

"Where is the warship?" Captain Malik asked.

"It's over in the river, sunk. The boiler blew up." That comment didn't sit well with a few of the sailors and comments about cannon fire were audible. He feared to hear the answer to the next question. "Where is the boarding party's officer, Lieutenant Caprivi?"

"That asshole is in the pen," Kyle answered.

"Sergeant, release those two sailors," Rex told the fort guards' sergeant. "Post guards on the wharf and bring the Prussian lieutenant to the infirmary."

Next, Rex addressed the crowd. "We need to work together, so finish setting up your camp. Thankfully, no one was injured. Lieutenant Caprivi and I are going to talk with the admiral."

"Didn't someone just say the admiral died?" A voice yelled.

"If the lieutenant was following the admiral's orders, that's the end of it, as far as the Wapitis are concerned, a misunderstanding. If he wasn't following the admiral's orders, then I'll arrest him for piracy."

Fritz's cousin had his size, but not his attractive looks, though the lieutenant wasn't ugly. However, the man was still seething from his treatment by the Mischief's crew. Rex thought he should be thankful Malik hadn't shot him dead. The lieutenant probably owed that good fortune to the fact the captain liked Major Caprivi and he didn't want to endanger that friendship by killing a troublesome cousin of Fritz's.

"Admiral Scheer will have that captain and savage hung for their treachery," Lieutenant Caprivi said as they crossed the common area inside the fort, headed to the infirmary. Rex wondered if the rumor was correct, that the pompous ass was dead. He hoped so.

Tara and Freda were in the admiral's room, pulling the sheet over his head.

"Is Major Caprivi available?" Tara asked. "The admiral was asking for him just before he had his seizure. I think the brave man's heart gave out."

The guards released the lieutenant, who rushed to the bed and pulled back the sheet. The burns and frozen look of agony caused the lieutenant to gasp and step back from the bed, dropping the sheet back in place.

"How many men died?" The shaken lieutenant asked.

"Counting the missing engineer, twenty-two sailors and marines, and three Clovis children run over by the boat," Rex said.

"I only counted thirteen men at the wharf. Where are the rest of them?"

"That's a good question," Rex said. "Major Caprivi has five Prussians with him looking for Captain Beck and a force of marines. The admiral had the force put ashore above the fort in case the garrison proved hostile."

Lieutenant seemed unsurprised by that information. Rex figured the lieutenant would have been with those marines, except for the admiral's spur-of-the-moment assignment of him to the Mischief impoundment.

"Once the admiral realized his fears were unfounded, he dispatched the major to tell Captain Beck of the explosion and of the need to secure the wreckage. I hope to hear from them soon."

Freda Hopkins was one of those cute, willowy, young Wapiti women that Rex found attractive. The Hopkins tribe seemed blessed with a large number of such women. The Jesuits had trained her to be a doctor and she normally worked out of Clay and served the upper Hopkins River area. She had been in Salt Furnace for supplies when Tara told her about the Prussian warship's visit to River Point, and she had decided to tag along to see the warship. Freda was taking the admiral's death hard. She looked close to tears.

"A heart attack is a better way of dying than from gangrene in those massive infected burns," the lieutenant rationalized.

Rex wasn't sure what to think. The admiral's burns were serious, would have been frightening, but he didn't think they were infected or that they would have killed him.

"What do you use to treat the pain associated with serious injuries, such as those the admiral suffered?" The lieutenant asked Freda.

"For pain, I use a tincture made from grain alcohol and cannabis, and on burns an ointment with extract of wolf's bane."

"Wolf's bane, is that the same as monkshood?"

Freda and Tara both responded in the affirmative.

"That's a deadly poison that is used on bear hunting arrows."

After giving the two doctors a hard look, he turned and pulled the sheet off the admiral's face and lifted his right eyelid to study the pupil.

The three Wapitis in the room exchanged glances while the lieutenant studied the admiral's eye. Tara's look reminded Rex that under the beautiful exterior there was a hard, no-nonsense woman who was determined to do right for her people.

"If you're finished, Lieutenant Caprivi, we have other patients that require our attention," Tara said. He pulled the sheet back in place, and started to leave the room.

"Just a moment, lieutenant, until I'm sure you're here to promote peace, not start a war, I'm placing you under arrest for piracy."

The guards seized the lieutenant's arm before he could swing and marched the cursing officer off.

"Fritz can deal with him. I think a funeral pyre first thing in the morning for the admiral would be best." Tara nodded, and Rex thought he detected a hint of relief.

The two women left to check on Captain Wolfgang. The lieutenant commander of the Hendrick had died shortly after entering the infirmary, which, with the admiral's death left Captain Wolfgang as the lone surviving naval officer. The priest was still alive, but unresponsive.

Captain Beck and his marines intercepted Fritz and his five men just inside the edge of the forest-clearing line.

"You are aware, Major Caprivi, that those cannons on the fort are zeroed on your torches," the captain said. "You trust those Wapitis not to fire and get rid of a bunch of troublesome Prussians?"

Unlike his group, Fritz could see that the marines weren't exposed. The captain had scattered his men along the upper slope of a shallow ravine formed by a small creek crossing the flood plain. The ravine would have offered good protection from any cannon fire.

"If they did, it'd be understandable, but no, I believe we're safe. How did you know my name?" Fritz felt a great relief. Some officers, especially in the marines, were more interested in fighting than thinking. This captain appeared to be one of the sensible ones.

"I was in the marine battalion unit that reinforced the Royal 77th Division on the Volga beachhead. That was something else, the piles of dead horses and riders . . . Well, anyway, to business. What happened to the Hendrick?" Captain Beck asked.

"The consensus is that the boiler exploded. The admiral's orders have changed. You're to secure the wreckage site until navy engineers can salvage and inspect the Hendrick."

"I gather that getting blown into the river put some sense in the xenophobic windbag, because assaulting that place would be tough. I had Feldwebel Schwinger reconnoiter the fort's defenses during the uproar following the explosion. The Wapitis never dropped their guard. In fact, Schwinger was sure they knew about us and expected an attack. The fact that you were able to walk straight to our location tonight would seem to verify my feldwebel's information."

"Those Clovis hunters are like ghosts. I figure there's one lurking nearby and eavesdropping. So, are you ready to come in?"

"There's not going to be any nonsense about giving up our arms?" Captain Beck asked.

"Only if you want to enter the fort," Fritz said. "Then it's no arms allowed."

"Hah, sensible folks, they're worried we'll do to them what they did to the Ichneumons. Let's go."

Word that the barge with the firewood also contained numerous barrels of trade gin was common knowledge throughout the River Point community, within a few minutes of the Belcher boys telling the troopers at the fort's gate about the barge's cargo. The news had Seaman Himmler's full attention. His thirst for gin was intense after a forced abstinence on the HMS Hendrick's voyage up the Erie River from Port Delta. The alcoholic seaman had earlier made acquaintances with the lone Wapiti trooper who guarded the wharf, barge, and the Mischief. The guard had an equal thirst for gin.

The arrival of the marines had the Prussian camp by the wharf in turmoil until late into the evening. However, the camp had settled down and the men were asleep, with several hours of night remaining before sunrise, when the seaman crept over to the barge. A few minutes later, the seaman was trying to pry the bung out of the top keg while the nervous Wapiti guard hovered nearby with a metal pail.

"Don't smell like no gin, smells like piss. Okay, I've found the bung's edge." After a few indistinct mutters, "Well, hell, someone threaded the damn thing. Who ever heard of threaded bungs . . . its turning, get the pail ready." The Wapiti guard took a last check of the camp, saw no one, and jumped on the barge to hand his partner the pail.

"Damn, it's salt."

He twisted the bung back in the hole, hugely disappointed, and scooped up a handful of the powder that had spilled. "Smells off, I can't tell what it is," he said and walked across the firewood to the guard for a better look.

The guard struck a match to inspect the powder. A bright flash followed by a crack, and Seaman Himmler's screams woke the camp and startled the guards on the fort's wall. The wharf guard, temporary blinded by the flash, fell in the river, followed shortly by the seaman jumping in to extinguish his burning hand, hair, and shirt.

Loud pounding on the door shattered Rex's dream that he had just gotten Amy's leggings off. The guard captain yelled that there had been an explosion on the wharf. Two minutes later, Rex was jogging out of the fort's gate shirtless. He met Hans Melas, who was also shirtless, though both men had their revolvers drawn. They ran to the crowd by the river's shore above the wharf, arriving to hear one of the seamen say the kegs contained gunpowder. He yelled for the guards going onto the barge with lanterns to inspect the barrels to stop, and told them to get away from the barge. Amy and Hokee arrived.

Within an hour, the Wapitis had the twenty-three barrels of gunpowder in the fort's magazine, and Rex, Hans, Amy, and Matt had Captain Malik and Herr Wu in the commander's office. Then Fritz and Tara arrived at Matt's office to learn what had everyone up at such an early hour.

"Herr Ruffner contacted me to ship twenty-five kegs of trade gin for Herr Wu and a partial load of firewood to River Point for Herr Chopra," Captain Malik said.

"I'll bet that's what exploded in the warehouse. The surviving guard said it was the barrels of gin, but at the time it made no sense," Hans Melas said.

It made sense to Rex, a castaway from twenty-first century Earth. Those whiskey barrels full of gunpowder were this world's version of IEDs and their purpose was to kill and terrorize.

"It's pretty obvious that Chopra, Ruffner, Wu, and Hickman were in cahoots to eliminate Chief Cinnabar as a witness," Amy said. "When I told Hickman that Wright was dead, he went to Wu, who supplied the distraction with a couple barrels of gun powder."

"That's nonsense, I don't know any Hickman, and those barrels had gin in them. I use gin to help get a better price for winter-sloe nuts. Gun powder would be of no use." The trader finally looked concerned as he sat in the chair with his hands tied.

"Knowing Len Ruffner, I wouldn't be surprised the gin and gunpowder business was a way for the trader to ship stolen Prussian gunpowder to Hickory Ridge for the Ichneumons to use," Tara said. She pointed at Wu and added, "That worm probably nicked a couple of Ruffner's barrels to help Purnell's assassin get by the guards. If it killed a bunch of us savages in the process, he would figure all the better. Herr Wu deserves to hang for that alone."

Wu bitterly denied any knowledge that the barrels contained anything other than gin as the guard hauled out of the chair and marched him back to his cell.

"Where are the Haggards when you need them?" Tara said in a loud voice to ensure that Wu heard her. "They'd get the truth out of him."

"For sure they'd get a story. Whether it was the truth would be anyone's guess," Rex said after Wu was out of hearing range.

"There's another player, the mysterious Herr Chopra. He ordered the firewood and was at River Falls with Wu when Kyle arrived to pick up the barge," Malik said. "In fact, he paid for the barge to be delivered to River Point but never showed up to claim the load. He passed us in a canoe while I was busy with the lieutenant, so I figure he's long gone."

"Ah, the lieutenant, Fritz, has your cousin settled down?" He asked, while Matt told the captain that he was free to leave.

"Adolf is a bit of a hothead, but he's a loyal marine. He'll do fine under Captain Beck who is his brother-in-law."

"I hope you're right," Rex said and told the young Wapiti at Matt's office door to go and release Lieutenant Caprivi. "Tell him that his cousin Fritz wants a word."

"Just bring him here," Fritz said, before continuing. "Well, since the admiral managed to kill himself, what do you suggest for delivering Cinnabar's testimony on Purnell's involvement in the illegal cocaine trade?"

"Take him to Herr Hansen and the IRS in Roanoke?" Rex asked, while wondering why the admiral couldn't have been a sensible man. "My greater concern is that someone in authority needs to get word to the Prussian fleet off Port Delta that a boiler explosion sank the Hendrick, and that Admiral Scheer is dead. Rumors that the Wapitis sank the sternwheeler will serve no one's purpose, except the Ichneumons. Is Captain Wolfgang conscious?"

"Freda said he's now awake, but very weak. He lost his right leg above the knee," Tara said. "Bishop Bingen has also regained consciousness. He seems the sensible sort, Fritz. Why don't you ask him about what happened? While you two are deciding on who does what, remember the voting will be finished today. So far, about eighty percent of the eight thousand votes are to join the Prussian Empire. I need to take the ballots and inventory sheets to Berlin and finish the petition for a territory."

Captain Wolfgang was a bitter man. "He destroyed my boat. The engineer told him repeatedly not to exceed the rated pressure, but he wouldn't listen."

Rex, Amy, Fritz, and his cousin, Adolf, had crowded around the captain's bunk with Freda hovering nervously at the tiny room's door. She had just scolded them for tiring her patient with their questions. They learned that a suspicious Lieutenant Adolf Caprivi had questioned the Hendrick survivors earlier.

"That agrees with what I learned," Adolf said. "The sailors' opinion is the boiler exploded because the engineer operated it at too high a pressure. Several of the survivors heard the captain tell the engineer to run a higher pressure. But in his defense, two men heard

231

Admiral Scheer order Captain Wolfgang to exceed safe pressures. Several of the seamen claimed the engineer had strongly disagreed with those orders, but the captain still told him to proceed. Unfortunately, the man who knew, the ship's engineer, had died in the explosion."

"Your information is correct," Captain Wolfgang said. "I did tell the engineer, over his objections, to run the boiler up to one and half million pascals." Amy gasped when she heard that number. After a quick glance at her, the captain added, "I, in turn was relaying Admiral Scheer's direct order to run the boat at the higher pressure. He wanted speed. The boat might have held together if the admiral hadn't panicked and ordered the paddles reversed. The resulting pressure spike ruptured the boiler vessel."

If I heard right, the bastard would have run over those Beaver families, Rex thought. He knew peace and that the Wapiti nation needed Captain Wolfgang's testimony, and so he refrained from commenting on the captain and admiral's disgraceful conduct.

"The Clovis Belle should arrive in the morning," Rex said. "Captain Wolfgang, I'll arrange your passage to Port Delta along with any other Prussian who wants to leave. I think it's important for peace that you arrive at Port Delta before any rumors about the sinking of the Hendrick."

Bishop Bingen greeted Rex and Fritz from a chair by his bed. "Herr Knight, I was hoping to meet you," the bishop said in a weak voice. "The Ichneumon commander of Hickory Ridge said I should talk with you. I understand you support Emperor Schnabel's efforts to end slavery."

The grandfatherly man, in a gray robe, appeared friendly, but he remembered Franciscka's caution.

"Slavery is an evil business. Emperor Schnabel's efforts deserve all of our support. We just spoke with Captain Wolfgang, and he said the admiral ordered the boiler run at an unsafe pressure. Do you know what occurred?"

"The captain is correct," the churchman said. "Where are you from, Herr Knight? You look like one of the imperial guards."

"So I've been told, Father. I'm from another world, one of endless ice and cold, and fish." He could see the flash of interest in the old man's eyes. Maybe the man was one of those alien hunters. "I'm a mutt from the northern ice floes. My mother was a Wapiti slave named Ruth Lowdermilk, raped by Prussian slavers and then sold to a cod fisherman."

Remembering Chief Smith's advice, he added, "Twice a year we went to Mercia for salt and supplies. Those were the only times my mother wasn't cold. I came here a year ago to look for my mother's family, and I liked the climate."

"Did you find your mother's family?"

"I did. Chief Smith said she was the only child of Ray Lowdermilk. Raiders swept through the valley twenty-seven years ago, one of the valley's periodic slave raids, and seized her. She was sixteen at the time. Chief Smith told me that my grandparents died years ago, probably from a broken heart."

"Can I catch a ride to Smithtown? I have an old friend there, Mazie Keeney, whom I'd like to visit."

"Father, I'm headed to Salt Furnace in the morning. You're welcome to ride along."

The previous two days had been wild. Rex needed to sleep for a whole day, but he only managed four hours in the hay pile by Zack's stall on the Mischief. The boat whistle woke him. On the second whistle blast, Rex got up and staggered to the handrail to join Amy and Hokee. They were watching Salt Furnace slide into view. The wharf had survived the blast; the warehouse hadn't, and the new council office appeared seriously damaged. That the costly glass windows were gone was no great surprise, but the caved-in wall suggested structural issues repairable only by replacing the structure. Several piles of rubble still smoldered where the warehouse had been.

Slim, the faux Cinnabar, and Chief Smith greeted them at the wharf.

"I've closed the voting," the chief said. "It was a success. Nine thousand, seven hundred votes with over eighty-four hundred of them in favor of the territory. That information needs to be delivered to Berlin, and I was hoping Fritz would escort Tara there with the voter rolls and our petition."

"Berlin will not view favorably any petition for a Wapiti territory until it's proven that the illegal cocaine source wasn't Wapiti bootleggers. Cinnabar's testimony would accomplish that. Someone needs to deliver him to Roanoke so that the IRS can confirm his confession. It would also substantiate Amy's earlier testimony."

"We'll send him with Tara and Fritz."

"The other potential snag is the investigation into what happened to the Prussian warship," Rex said. "So far, everyone involved in the explosion blames the admiral for ordering the captain to exceed the boiler's safe pressure. The danger is that a board of inquiry staffed with naval officers will be reluctant to blame the loss of a warship on a fellow admiral's recklessness. The board might leave open the possibility that cannon fire from the Wapiti fort caused the ship to explode. They could withhold a finding of cause until they salvage the boat and have the boiler inspected. It could holdup a decision on our request."

"Good point," Fritz said. "Berlin is not likely to grant a territory to savages who attack their naval vessels without warning. I wish Bishop Bingen had gone with Captain Wolfgang. His testimony in support of the captain's would have ended the matter. However if I'm in Berlin I can verify that no cannon fired on the HMS Hendrick. No one will know for sure what happened until the naval investigators reassemble the boiler's pieces, and inspect the magazines. Captain Beck will ensure that the site isn't disturbed until the investigators arrive."

"Herr Wu is being held at River Point," Rex said. "He's the same man I think was stalking Amy in Roanoke. His two barrels appear to be the ones that exploded here. Then there's the matter of the other barrels found on a barge docked at River Point. Instead of gin, they contained gunpowder. Wu claims he thought the barrels contained gin and he planned to trade it for nuts. I think he's one of Purnell's assassins, but I have no proof. The question is what do we do with him?"

"Hang him," both the chief and Tara said simultaneously.

"Our friend here, who has killed dozens of enemies, doesn't believe circumstantial evidence alone is sufficient to justify capital punishment." The Smiths shook their heads in wonder at such foolishness.

"The warehouse explosion killed two of Larry Hopkins' nephews, along with thirteen other people. Whoever did it deserves to die," Tara said. "And I believe Wu was involved." Rex agreed.

"Did the bagger survive?"

They learned that Suzie Sweetwater hadn't liked the tent arrangement and had moved the contraption and bagging operation into the old salt drying shed beside the furnace the morning of the warehouse explosion. She had started roasting and bagging nuts again yesterday. It also reminded Rex that he needed to check with Tom on the new lab building.

"Suzie is promising the farmers that you'll pay two D-marks per kilo for their unshelled nuts. They have delivered a large pile of winter-sloe nuts, so I hope you have some money," Chief Smith said. "Suzie has several women working with her, which means there's another payroll. You might want to touch base with her."

No kidding, Rex thought, and wondered what Eva and Lou Jarrell had committed him to buy in Panther Creek. He asked the chief for a moment in private.

"One more item to consider," Rex said, after he was along with the chief. "The Wapitis need at least one more steamboat running on the river. Amy says the boiler on the Mischief needs to be descaled. The operation takes several days."

"We're broke, no way can we pay for a boat," Chief Smith said. "That raises another issue that the council is concerned about, the Mischief. Currently, everybody wants to use it, but no one is responsible for the maintenance. You have had use of the boat for months. Now Chief Moyer wants it to move firewood barges before the river freezes and the council voted to let him use it."

"I'm willing to pay the council for the use of the Mischief. Without that boat, I can't finish the harvest. None of the big Erie River steamboats can go past Smithtown and reach Salt Furnace."

The truth of the matter was Rex had started to consider the Mischief his boat and had made his plans based on having the boat. He needed to convince the chief that taking the Mischief away from his control would hurt the Wapitis.

"Moving the roasting and bagging operation this late in the season would be terribly disruptive. It would probably cut our finished bagged product in half. And Moyers is right. The ice will be forming and blocking the river in a month. If that happens before I can ship the crop to Port Delta, there'll be no payday. Be a lot of unhappy nut gathers and workers."

"I get the picture," Chief Smith said. He appeared a bit out of sorts. Rex knew his blatant maneuvering of the chief would irritate the man, but the use of Mischief was critical to his plans.

"My son wants to buy the Mischief," Chief Smith said. "But he doesn't have near enough money. The council wants a hundred thousand D-marks for the boat."

Rex knew he and Andy Smith had worked well together in the past, and he would be a

good partner.

"Ask the council if they'll grant your son and me a month to come up with the money," Rex said. If he could actually deliver the full nut crop to Port Delta, he'd have enough profit to pay for the boat. "And during that period I can use the boat to haul the winter-sloe harvest."

"The price we discussed?" Rex nodded. "If my son's agreeable, I'm sure the council will be okay with that arrangement. Oh, I forgot, there's a fellow named Al Leslie due in tonight with Herr Simpson. They both want to meet with you."

Indira had wanted to see the Prussian warship during its visit to River Point, but the death of a goat had delayed her. A troublesome panther with a taste for goats had moved into the Hopkins neighborhood. It had killed her mother's prized Toggenburg dairy goat and she feared the big cat might snatch one of the neighborhood children.

Since Indira's father was at Salt Furnace, she volunteered to deal with the predator. Two nights had been required to lure the panther into her rifle sights. Its pelt was now salt curing in the Hopkins' barn.

Since the Prussian warship wasn't going anywhere, Indira had stopped in Smithtown to visit with her Aunt Mazie before traveling on down the river to view the wreckage. They both wanted to meet the Caroom woman, who rumor had as Rex's girlfriend. The knock on the door stopped their gossiping. An elderly man in a black cassock was at the front door, and he asked to speak with her aunt.

The priest was Bishop Bingen, a friend of Mazie's husband since the Berlin theological college. Her aunt asked about the HMS Hendrick explosion after introducing Indira.

"As you can tell, my voice and lungs haven't fully recovered from the whiff of live steam I inhaled."

The man's voice did sound weak to Indira, as he described the events leading up to the boiler explosion and its aftermath. Indira eavesdropped on their conversation from the kitchen and while serving tea and small cakes. Her aunt and the bishop chatted for a while about past friends and the need for more priests west of the mountains, before the bishop broached his concern.

"One of the church's concerns with the Wapiti's territory request is to avoid a repeat of the York rebellion." He had Indira's full attention with that comment. "The church needs to know that there is not another Joseph Warren involved in the Wapitis' sudden military success. Jesuit Wilhelm was supposed to check this out, but he vanished in Panther Creek a month ago."

"The church is worried about a false prophet?" Mazie asked. "I thought the church would have outgrown those old myths of witches and aliens. There's no secret about the Wapitis success, Krupp rifles. Indira, would you refresh the Father's tea?"

"Do you know Rex Knight? He is not your typical Wapiti," the bishop said.

"I just recently had the pleasure of meeting Herr Knight. I knew his mother, Ruth Lowdermilk, before those evil slavers carried her off. Years ago, she wrote that she had a baby boy who her husband had named Rex."

Indira wondered if that was true, or was that her grandmother's payback to Rex for saving her daughter and granddaughter at Hinton.

"But you can't say for certain he's Ruth son?"

"No, but really, who else could he be? How would anyone else even know about a missing Ruth Lowdermilk from nearly thirty years ago, other than her own son?"

"All excellent points, can you think of anyone who might try to turn the Wapitis away from the Prussian Empire?"

"Pete Chin had been pushing for the Wapitis to vote for an independent country aligned with the Ichneumon Empire. But he's no alien or false prophet. Pete's just a greedy traitorous fool."

That evening Herr Simpson and Rex had dinner in the rooming house kitchen and discussed the financing of Al Leslie's dot-dash line. The distiller had just gone up the stairs to get a bottle of his brown whiskey when Amy and Al walked into the kitchen.

"My battery works," Amy said, glowing. Al nodded in agreement with her assessment. "Tara said she'd help me file the patent request, and her brother wants to build them for Al, if he ever gets his wire up and running."

Herr Simpson returned with a bottle of his aged-in-oak whiskey and greeted the newcomers with an offer of whiskey.

Amy still wore part of her ugly woman disguise, the unsightly black hat and dark gray coveralls. Even though by now it was common knowledge, she hadn't perished in Panther Creek. In Rex's opinion, it should be a crime for a beautiful woman to dress in such baggy, drab clothes. The young engineer needed Jenny Jarrell as her fashion adviser. Amy would look beautiful in one of those pink, frock-style dresses, or the shirt and denims outfits like young women worn in Roanoke. Her acquiescence to Herr Simpson pouring a generous shot of whiskey in her teacup surprised him. After she had taken a small taste of the whiskey, she placed a mangled piece of brass about the size of a barrel bung on the table.

"The warehouse blast was no accident. This is what killed Terry Hopkins, Larry's nephew. It is part of an Ichneumon detonator, with a timer."

The item was a threaded brass bushing with a short brass nipple welded in the center. The broken weld at the end of the bent nipple indicated something else was missing from the device.

"Amy, how do you know about Ichneumon timers?" Rex asked for the rest of the men sitting at the table that were passing the brass item between them and inspecting it.

"That's a long story, trust me on this. That bushing is part of a very expensive timing device used by the Ichneumons to explode their barrel mines. Its advantage is the time can be set for up to twenty-four hours. The detonator's disadvantage is not being very safe or waterproof."

Chapter 11

The Mischief left Salt Furnace as the dawn was breaking on a frosty autumn morning. Amy, still sleepy, had wrapped herself in a blanket and snuggled in among the rolls of burlap that had arrived from Roanoke the previous day. She had stayed up late and wanted to catch more sleep. Hokee joined her as Rex watched the white-coated fields below the wharf pass by. It had been over a year since he'd mysteriously landed in this alien world, this twin of Earth. Every day it felt more like home.

Monogamy and marriage formed the foundation of Wapiti family life. That fidelity was all proper and good, but Rex feared it made any causal relationship with a Wapiti woman ripe for misunderstandings. For that reason, he had followed the "look, but don't touch" approach with women in this new world. Until he was ready to settle down with a wife, he planned to avoid any entanglements with Wapiti women, but Amy Caroom definitely had him thinking about changing that strategy. He just wasn't sure about her feelings toward him, and he feared damaging the alliance that was developing between them.

Then there was the winter-sloe nut gamble. Failure to complete the harvest, processing, and delivery of the roasted nuts to the tobacco company in Port Delta would be financially devastating to him and hundreds of Wapitis who had put their faith in him. He

241

didn't need any new problems nor obligations until he settled that matter.

The Clovis Belle was loading at the River Point wharf when the Mischief arrived mid-afternoon. Grease-smeared, Amy joined Rex at the bow's handrail by the cannon. She had been helping Kyle repair the spare condensate-boiler feed pump packing after her earlier snooze.

"The whole Mischief boiler system needs a thorough cleaning," Amy said. "You need to buy a boat so we have a spare."

"I don't know anything about boats." Rex didn't bring up his discussion with Chief Smith. First, he needed to feel out Andy Smith on forming a partnership to buy the Mischief.

"Well, I do, and I know where there's another one of these tough little river boats in Orleans. No one wants it. The captains consider it too small for carrying cargo, and they think barges an annoyance, even dangerous on rivers. You could steal it." She sounded serious.

"Purnell would hang you if he caught you in his boatyard." He knew one way to get her prolific mind off piracy. "You smell, what is that, grease?"

"It's not the grease, it's the bilge water, and besides, it's very rude to tell a young lady she smells." Amy gave him a quizzical look, and then suddenly smiled. "What a sneaky way to distract your business partner. That boat is not one of Purnell's boats. It belongs to an old crabber, Herr Lafayette, and he'll sell it cheap for whiskey money, probably for less than a hundred thousand D-marks."

If she was correct, and she knew vastly more about steamboats than he, then the Mischief at a hundred thousand D-marks was a bargain. Hearing Amy considered him her business partner, pleased him. Maybe she'd consider joining them in buying the Mischief. He also wondered if Jacobs had managed to sell Cinnabar's stash of gems.

"How do you know the boiler isn't rusted out, or that the thing even runs?"

"I helped with an overhaul on Lafayette's boat in the spring, when he thought a crabber out of Port Delta might buy it. It has a funky condenser. We'd have to replace the old boiler with one similar to the type the Mischief has, or at least add a superheater. But other than that, it's an efficient setup with a compound engine. The paddlewheels are rugged and designed for shallow rivers."

Captain Dalporto greeted them on the dock. "Thanks for the business. I'll have the Hendrick survivors in Port Delta within a week. Hi, Amy, I'm glad those reports were wrong. You'll have to tell me the tale someday."

She asked him if Crabber Lafayette still had that little twin side-wheeler for sale.

"The Princess? Yeah, he did a month ago when I was there. Why do you ask?" He looked about the wharf. "What's that smell?"

"Me, and mind your manners. The reason I asked is that the Wapitis need a backup boat on the river and I thought it would make a good one."

Captain Malik, satisfied the boat was properly secure, joined them on the wharf along with Kyle. A sudden commotion in the river at the stern of the Mischief caused them to look just in time to see a cloud of feathers. Hokee had caught one of the wild mallards that lived under the wharf.

"His boat would be a good choice, but don't you dare go near Orleans," Captain Dalporto cautioned. "Purnell has posters at every dock on the Erie below Hickory Ridge offering a ten thousand D-mark reward for you or your head." Seeing her stunned look, he explained further. "To those downriver folks you're a runaway slave, Amy. Please don't get careless. That monster means you harm. Don't end up like that duck."

"I suspect the manumission offer is dead," Amy whispered. She then walked over to where Hokee had emerged from the river with his prize.

"She had to be told," Captain Dalporto said. He appeared troubled and looked to Malik and Rex for support. They both nodded.

Rex felt sorry for her. Amy was by nature a cheerful upbeat person. Not that it wouldn't be a shock to anyone to learn your father despised you and wanted you dead. That Purnell had listed her name on the boiler patent had raised Amy's hopes that perhaps her father didn't hate her. Learning about his dead-or-alive wanted poster had shattered that illusion. Rex had always thought Purnell's manumission offer unlikely. She knew too much about her father's illegal activities.

"Captain Dalporto, don't disembark yet, I have a matter to resolve in the fort that might require an hour, and depending on the outcome, might also require your involvement." He walked over to where Amy was watching Hokee rip the mallard apart. "Please get that brass fragment and meet me in Matt's office."

The River Point commander was just exiting the fort's main gate when Rex intercepted him. "Is your wolf terrorizing our ducks?" he asked.

"It was a river mallard, one of the wild ones. If anyone complains, I'll pay for it, but let's return to your office. I want to inspect Edward Wu's bags."

Wu's leather saddlebags had three changes of clothes and toiletry items, razor, and other essentials. The large duffle bag had a beautiful rolling block rifle with a powerful scope, a bag of hand tools, a bag of gold coins, socks, gloves, heavy coat, and winter-style leather knee boots that were too heavy. Stuffed in each boot was a brass contraption. Other property found on Herr Wu consisted of that leather wallet with twenty gold coins, two 9 x 19 mm-chambered revolvers, a hunting knife, a pocketknife, and a dagger.

Breathless, Amy arrived with the fragment.

"Are those Ichneumon detonators?" Rex asked. After a glance at the device, she nodded. "Matt, have Wu brought here." After Matt left, he asked her, "Just how rare are these detonators?"

"Very, at Heidelberg University, the Prussian military had only obtained one for study. Purnell had two that I know of, and one of them was broken. He wanted me to use it to make copies, but I told him the Prussian acid-wire timers were cheaper, safer and better. Of course, he never listened and told me to make a dozen for him. I never had a chance to work on them before he sent me to Cinnabar's operation. He did tell me the Ichneumon rarely sold them and even then at a five-six hundred D-marks a pop."

"So the chance of the detonator used at Salt Furnace not being one of Wu's is remote?"

"And it was his two barrels of gin that exploded. He had to be involved and I'll bet he planned to use the other timers on the barrels of gun powder in the barge to wreck River Point."

"I suspect you're right. He didn't expect us to be on the Mischief that morning and or to arrest him. Wu took a chance and lost."

Matt and two of the fort's burly Wapiti guards marched Wu into the office. The prisoner visibly faltered when he saw the unwrapped detonators on Matt's desk. Rex pulled his revolver.

"Any last words, assassin?"

"I'll testify if you spare my life. I can help put Purnell away, the Guderian governor, Ruffner, and back up Cinnabar's testimony about the illegal cocaine."

"No one would believe the assassin," Amy said. "He killed those boys. Shoot him and we can put his head in a barrel of salt and send a message that his boss understands."

Matt and Rex both looked at her. She was not joking. Wu apparently agreed, because he started pleading.

"My testimony would guarantee the emperor's approval of the Wapitis' territory request," the desperate man said. "You know I'm correct." Matt and the guards looked amazed by the sudden change in the previously defiant prisoner and by his offer, which amounted to a confession.

"Is he responsible for the explosion that killed all those people at Salt Furnace?" Matt asked. Rex hesitated before nodding.

"Yes, he is," Amy, added. "Cut off his head." Matt appeared seriously conflicted as he looked from the infuriated woman to the frightened prisoner.

Rex hoped Matt realized that Wu's testimony, if presented properly, would help the Wapitis' cause. The assassin's information added to Cinnabar's testimony offered a chance to unravel Purnell's vast web of corruption in the Prussian territories. He was disappointed that Amy seemed to have forgotten how critical Wu's testimony was. Then again, she had just learned her father wanted her murdered. The desire for vengeance was the immediate threat to making use of the prisoner's testimony. If Matt Brewer didn't support his request to keep Wu alive until Prussian investigators could interview the man, then a great opportunity to deal their nemesis a serious setback would be lost.

"Matt, have your men return the prisoner to his cell. We need to discuss Herr Wu's offer." He held his breath as the Wapitis exchanged looks and Amy quivered with indignation. After a moment, Matt told the guards to return Wu to his cell to await justice. To Rex's relief, the men obeyed and they left. Wu had enough sense to keep a poker face and stay silent.

"Amy, send a pigeon to Salt Furnace telling Fritz not to leave yet with Cinnabar," Rex said. Seeing her rebellious attitude, he added, "If you're not willing to use that fine brain of yours, just leave. Matt can send the pigeon and Freda will help me prepare Wu's confession."

Boilermaker

"Freda left this morning for Johnson Village. Frau Walker has beautiful penmanship. I'm sure she'll help," Matt said.

Amy Caroom had recovered from her anger over Rex's refusal to behead Wu. She still wasn't as warm toward him as before learning about the reward for her capture and about Wu's murderous business, but she had tagged along on the trip up Panther Creek to deliver the burlap. He figured her desire to see firsthand how her nutcracker and shelling device had worked over came her disgust with him. The two of them, along with four Wapiti soldiers from River Point and ten packhorses, made the trip into Cinnabar's old stockade without encountering any hostile parties.

Rex had brought eleven thousand D-marks in small denomination paper bills. He had a payroll to meet. Thankfully, the Panther Creek Clovis families only expected one D-mark for a kilo of unshelled nuts, not the two D-mark rate that Suzie had promised at Salt Furnace without his approval. No one seemed to know how many kilos of winter-sloe nuts might be harvestable in Panther Creek. He hoped the seven thousand D-marks he left with Lou and the eleven thousand D-marks in his saddlebags would cover the harvest.

The windrows of empty nutshells outside the warehouse were an encouraging sight. Lou Jarrell and Eva Benes had processed a small mountain of winter-sloe nuts using the water wheel for power. A cheerful crowd of people greeted them and under the supervision of Frau Benes, the rolls of burlap disappeared into the back room of the warehouse. Amy was still inspecting the nutcracker when Lou found Rex standing in front of the huge pile of winter-sloe nuts in the warehouse. The room had a smell that reminded him of peanuts.

"I figure there are about twelve thousand kilos of clean nuts in that pile."

Rex agreed; it appeared to be a reasonable estimate.

247

"We still have a lot of nuts to shell, but need to get the shelled ones bagged and safely stored. You may need thirty thousand D-marks to pay everyone, by the time we're finished."

"I brought another eleven thousand D-marks to add to the seven thousand I left with you. Will the loose nuts attract rats?"

"There're no rats, they were ate long ago," Lou said. "I don't want any trouble with the nut gatherers who are uneducated and whom Cinnabar had much abused in the past. They still half expect to be cheated."

"Then I suggest paying the nut gatherers now, and I'll pay for the processing when I load the nuts at the Erie River wharf," Rex said. "Are there any more nuts out there to pick?"

He hoped not. The winter-sloe harvest threatened to spiral out of control and beggar him. Any income was at least a month and a thousand kilometers away. He was frightfully in debt and weary of unexpected expenses.

"They have pretty well cleaned out the area around here. The other problem is that when the pickers get paid, they'll be drunk in short order," Lou said.

"Who sells them the whiskey? Moonshiners," Rex asked. Lou gave him a knowing look. "You?"

Amy ran up to him. ."Come look," she said, grabbing his hand to tug Rex to the warehouse door that opened by the creek. Hokee and another smaller, very dark wolf were sniffing each other in the field across the creek and down from the water wheel dam.

"The nut gatherers talked about seeing a female wolf several times around the northern ridges," Lou said. "It's probably responsible for the several devastating henhouse raids that have occurred in the last month. There's been talk of forming a posse to hunt for it."

Amy's attention was on Hokee and the black wolf. Hokee resolved the stranger's sexual identity as they mated.

"It's a female," she said, clasping her hands together in delight. "Lou, you have to tame her! Many people would want one of the puppies, including me. Tell the folks that we'll pay for the chickens, if they don't kill the black wolf."

Rex figured he knew whom Amy's "we" was that would pay. His snarky thought embarrassed him. Without her ingenious nut sheller, he would never have had a chance of processing the Panther Creek harvest. He owed that woman a great deal. Besides after all the other outlays, what could a few chickens cost.

The hundred fifty-kilo bags of clean and shelled winter-sloe nuts that Rex delivered to Salt Furnace thrilled Suzie Sweetwater's gang of baggers. Manual cracking and shelling of the raw nuts that the Wapitis were harvesting in the ridges around Salt Furnace was proving to be labor intensive and a real production bottleneck. The obvious solution was to duplicate Amy's arrangement at Panther Creek, but the absence of a water wheel to power the device blocked that approach.

Amy suggested that Rex buy a small steam engine and boiler. It was a good suggestion, he agreed, but other than the cost, the time to locate and have an engine shipped to Salt Furnace barred the idea from being a solution for processing this year's nut crop. He told Suzie to do her best, protect the winter-sloe nuts until they could process them, and expect another several hundred bags of shelled nuts in the next load from Panther Creek.

Next, Rex learned that Chief Smith and the council had agreed with several of his suggestions. He suspected that Tara had convinced her father who in turn had convinced the council to turn Wu and Cinnabar over to the Prussian IRS head, Joe Hansen, who was investigating the source of illegal cocaine sold in the territories. A strong guard force under the command of Larry Hopkins would escort the prisoners to Roanoke. Bishop Bingen would travel with them to Roanoke.

The council, aware of Wu's confession, had seized his hundred thousand D-marks, which they planned to use to fund the council and police until the property taxes started rolling in after the first of the year.

Rex needed to find another source for the thirty-five thousand D-marks to pay for the nuts Sally had collected and to cover the balance owed at Panther Creek. Jacobs was holding his and Amy's gold coins in Roanoke and part of it was committed to help finance Leslie's venture.

"Chief, would the council loan me forty thousand D-marks for six months?" Rex asked. Chief Smith had just finished telling him about instructing Larry Hopkins to kill both prisoners if there appeared any chance that Purnell's gang might rescue them. "It's to pay for the local harvest and Suzie's crew."

"It'd be awkward. Paul Moyer would vote against any help to you after the nut bagger embarrassment. He already regrets agreeing to transfer the nut harvest to you," The chief said while opening a package of the winter-sloe nuts. "The Orcel family is starting a bank, the Crawford Trust. I figured they'd be interested in your business."

"Is that Brian's family? Pete's dead son-in-law," he asked. Pete Chin was a former Wapiti chief, a traitor, and completely untrustworthy. "Is Pete involved?"

"Not officially, but Chin's daughter runs the bank. Also the rumor is that Ichneumon money backs the operation." Hokee came over to investigate what the chief was eating. "I would find a certain poetic justice in Ichneumon money financing a Wapiti business that will hurt their cocaine sales," He slipped Hokee a piece of buttered toast.

250

"Well then, if the other deal I'm working on falls through, I'll stop and talk to her," Rex said. "The other problem is the amount of bagged nuts promised to Atlantic Tobacco. If everything falls in place, we might process thirty thousand kilos of nuts. About a million bags, way less than the five million promised to Atlantic."

"I'd hoped we could do better. The Wapitis depend on the winter-sloe nut income."

"Correct me if I'm wrong, but last year's crop amounted to about a tenth of that amount."

"Yeah, it wasn't much," the chief said. "The buyers bitching about Pete Chin's dirty nuts didn't help."

"This year's gross should be around two million D-marks. An improvement on last year's gross sales, you would agree?" Rex paused to toss the ever-hungry wolf a bread crust that was in his coat pocket from the egg sandwich Helen had given him earlier. "Did you have any basis for that five million bag promise?"

The chief appeared irritated by the mild rebuke, but after a moment laughed. "I'm a politician, so I'm expected to exaggerate, and I needed an amount big enough to interest the tobacco company in a deal. Besides, I'm not good at numbers and sums. Blame the weather, or the squirrels, if anyone complains about the smaller amount. Just remember, you promised the council ten D-marks per kilo of bagged nuts, so we can expect three hundred thousand D-marks from this year's crop?"

For a man who claimed to find math difficult, the chief had no trouble determining his share, Rex thought. "Sure, if the tobacco company pays. You have any problem with selling the nuts to other dealers along the river. I know Captain Dalporto wanted to buy ten cases." The chief asked what the price would be. "For him, I planned to charge twelve hundred and fifty D-marks for a case."

251

"A case? You're referring to those neat wooden boxes Simpson delivered the other day?" Chief Smith asked, after yelling for more hot tea.

"Have any coffee?" The chief amended his order to include coffee.

"Yes, that's a case," Rex continued, "Each box holds five hundred bags. Since the Erie Valley is still outside the Prussian jurisdiction, no one has to pay the emperor's excise tax. Dalporto thinks he can sell all the bags down the river. Of course the attraction of the deal to me is the captain will pay for the ten cases on delivery, which helps my cash problem."

"I don't care who buys the crop. As long as the nuts are roasted first and can't be used for cocaine."

The chief then jotted down some numbers. "You're paying one or two D-marks for the raw nut, a couple of D-marks to shell them, a couple of D-marks per kilo to roast and bag them, or around six D-marks per kilo and selling them for a hundred per kilo, is that fair?"

"Fair? The deal with the captain is the same as your deal with the tobacco gang. Those neat wooden boxes you were admiring cost a hundred and fifty D-marks each. I have to pay for the bagger and the bags. Then there is the cost of shipping along with the loss from shelling, rotten nuts, theft, spills, cargo lost, and nonpayment. Hell, I'll be lucky to clear as much as the council when everything is paid."

The chief smiled. "You remind me of Jacobs justifying his outrageous prices. Well, it's your business. As long as the gatherers and workers receive what you promised for the nuts and their work, and pay the fee, the council wishes your venture well. Go to it, we need the taxes."

Suzie Sweetwater's crew had completed filling twenty-five cases with the individual-serving-size wax-paper bags of roasted, salted winter-sloe nuts. Earlier that morning, Rex had loaded and stacked the wax-sealed, pine boxes on the Mischief. The distiller's craftsmen had made a branding iron to burn the name "Panther Creek Nut Company" on the long sides and top lids of the wooden boxes. The cooperage crew had also made another branding iron to burn an outline of a panther in the center of each box's end panel.

The watertight cases were works of art, with the neat cursive writing, dovetail corner joints, and tongue and groove joints between the pieces forming the panels in the box's walls. Small brass screws with rounded, slotted heads fastened the top cover to the box.

Amy was sitting on one of the boxes studying him while petting Hokee. "What deal did you make with Suzie to get her to work so hard?"

"Besides her hourly pay, she gets a hundred D-marks for each completed case of bagged nuts that she can split as she sees fit among her crew." Rex wondered what would happen if he kissed her, but instead asked, "You ready for another lesson on using a revolver?"

"I can shoot it just fine," the lissome engineer said, standing up. "My problem is hitting the target."

Rex had gotten in the habit of working with Kyle, Larry, and Amy on their marksmanship. The moving boat turned rocks and logs on the riverbanks into moving targets for their practice. Amy's marksmanship showed great promise. The young woman was a natural with a rifle and at judging the distance to a stationary target. With the revolver, she still needed practice to hit consistently a moving man-sized target. A pumpkin bobbing in the backwater of a small cove provided an interesting target for her. However, she missed it five times from a distance of thirty through fifty meters. Though in fairness, all the bullets did land close to the orange flotsam.

"The gun isn't shooting straight," Amy said, unable to avoid smiling at her pitiful excuse. She ejected the brass, deftly catching the spent shells in her left hand. She then loaded one cartridge in the revolver and handed it to Rex. "Here, you hit it."

"That's hardly fair. It's a hundred meters away now."

With the distance rapidly increasing, he stepped to the rail, aimed up the river at the barely visible pumpkin, and fired. A spray of orange showed the bullet had hit its mark. She just shook her head.

"Nothing wrong with the revolver, it must be the shooter."

The afternoon on the river passed peacefully with Amy shooting several more times along the unsettled sections of the river valley. The black powder made a mess in the revolver, and she cleaned the pistol while Rex knocked the fired primers out of the shell casings and then ran a brush through each shell to remove powder residue. The Wapitis and Rex reloaded every rifle and pistol cartridge, often numerous times. They never threw away or left fired brass behind.

"The Prussians need to invent a cleaner gunpowder."

As he knew it would, any talk about chemistry had her interest. She told him about the university's experiments with nitration of various organic materials like cotton, phenol, and toluene.

"Why couldn't guncotton be used to replace black powder? It burns clean and sounds reasonably simple to make."

"It's called nitrocellulose, and it is easy to make if you have concentrated nitric and sulfuric acids. Try locating nitric acid in the territories. It's not available. Even in Prussia, nitric acid is scarce. The other problem is guncotton's tendency to spontaneously ignite and explode," Amy said while putting away the cleaning kit.

"Ah, I can see where that would tend to dampen enthusiasm for the product." He wished he had paid more attention in the chemistry classes at WVU. "Still, a safe, clean-burning gunpowder would have a large market. You need to invent smokeless powder. You'd be a wealthy woman."

He finished inspecting and cleaning the spent brass shells that he would exchange at River Point for loaded cartridges. He handed Amy the little brass brush and punch he'd been using. "Put those in the cleaning kit."

"What's your goal, make a few D-marks and return to Newfoundland?" She asked, after she finished loading her revolver and putting it in her shoulder bag lying on the deck.

"No, I have no plans to return to that life. I like this area, and I have that block of land in Jarrell River to develop. How about you, what's your goal?"

"I'd like a machine shop and enough money to turn my ideas into reality. And I want a daughter, which I suppose means I'll have to find a husband." She laughed and looked a bit embarrassed.

"Lord, a woman who looks like you should have her choice of husbands," Rex said, surprised by the sudden turn in their conversation. Sitting on the boat deck, Amy was studying him. *Kiss her, now, don't let the moment escape,* he thought. And he did, pulling the willing woman to her feet, and kissing her. Her body language removed any doubt about her willingness as she snuggled into his arms for some serious kissing. She smelled wonderful.

"We have visitors," Captain Malik said, ruining the moment. He pointed down river.

As River Point came into view, they were surprised and concerned to discover the Orleans Queen; Benjamin Purnell's only surviving large riverboat, docked at the wharf.

"I can't believe Purnell would risk walking into Wapiti territory. And those are Wapiti guards on the wharf, so Matt's on top of it, but do keep your revolver handy and stay out of sight. Malik, Kyle, keep your shotguns close."

Captain Hube, of the Orleans Queen was in Matt's office with his first mate, Herr Saad. The latter man reminded Rex of a hard-bodied Bill Jacobs. A florid-faced Prussian, Colonel Maxim, along with Captain Beck, and John Baler joined Rex in the office. The Orleans Queen's captain was angrily waving a sheet of parchment in Matt's face. The first mate was studying the office bookcase, as the Colonel finished putting forth his grievance.

"The colonel claims the document gives him the authority to salvage the sunken Hendrick," Matt said. "Captain Beck doesn't know Colonel Maxim, though that is understandable, given the number of colonels in the Prussian military. I have no way to verify the order is valid. Fritz was clear that the wreckage wasn't to be disturbed until a naval board could investigate the cause."

"Where did you pass the Clovis Belle, Captain Hube?" Rex asked to gain a moment to think. Why would the Prussian navy with several ships and a thousand sailors and officers at Port Delta send one army colonel to supervise a major naval salvage operation? Because they didn't know about it, he realized.

"Below the Great Western River," the captain answered.

"Shame you didn't connect. The Hendrick survivors were on that boat and headed to Port Delta and the HMS Schlesien. They will report to the naval board. Until we hear back from the naval authorities, we'll have to ignore this order."

"This is outrageous. Captain Beck, are you going to take orders from a foreign national, an uneducated savage, instead of your superior officer?" Colonel Maxim asked.

"No sir," Captain Beck said. "I'm honoring orders from my commanding officer, Major Caprivi. He was quite clear on where my next orders would come from: the naval board, not some trader out of Orleans."

"You're throwing away your career, captain," the colonel said. "Berlin will hear of your insubordination and that you helped the Wapitis hide their sabotage."

"Captain Hube, let me see that order," Rex said. Startled by the request, the captain hesitated for a moment before handing it over.

"Thank you, I'll make sure the naval board receives this document."

"Wait a minute, that an official Prussian military document and not to be let out of our control," the colonel said. "Hand that over, young man."

Rex shook his head.

"Captain Beck, seize that order," the colonel demanded.

Rex figured the marine captain might follow the direct command. He pulled his revolver. "Guards, escort the colonel, Herr Saad, and Captain Beck out of the fort. Captain Hube, I wish a word in private." Matt had his pistol aimed at the colonel and the three guards had their rifles aimed at Captain Beck, who had pulled his revolver partially out of its holster before stopping when he heard the rifle safeties clicking off.

"Is this worth dying over," a grim Captain Beck asked.

"No, no, forget my order. Berlin will hear about this vicious behavior."

Rex figured that Berlin would never hear about this nonsense. He wondered if the Orleans Queen's captain knew and would tell them what Purnell was after in the wreckage. After the officers had left, he asked.

"The colonel wants proof that the Wapitis shot a cannon ball into the Hendrick's boiler. I'm looking for Herr Hickman and Herr Wu. Their families asked that I try to locate them."

"They both died in an explosion at the Salt Furnace," Rex lied. "The best the council could determine is that two barrels of black powder blew up in the main warehouse. The barrels that exploded supposedly contained trade gin according to Herr Wu's manifest. Since he's dead, we have no way of knowing how the barrels came to be full of gunpowder or why they exploded."

The captain looked doubtful, and Rex added, "Eighteen people died, including three young boys playing in a nearby sand pile. If you have any knowledge on the matter, I'd like to hear it."

"Was it Ichneumon sabotage? They probably have little love for Wapitis." When no one offered a comment, the captain added. "The other matter Herr Purnell asked me to look into is his missing slave, Fraulein Caroom. She stole several valuable documents that he wants returned."

"I'm surprised at your insensitivity," Rex said. "You have to be aware that all Prussian territories, including the Wapiti territory, have outlawed slavery. In fact, the council considers trafficking in slaves to be a hanging offence."

"If the Wapitis were to search the Orleans Queen and find slaves and learn that you knew about them," Matt added. "We'd hang you along with the slaves' owner."

"Surely you jest," Hube said, looking apprehensive. After a moment, he added, "Just down the Erie, slavery is legal."

"Matt, as soon as we finish on the personnel matter, I want you to organize a search of the Orleans Queen. If she's gone, well then, don't worry about it."

An agitated, Captain Hube bid a brief farewell to Matt, and left. "You certainly know how to end a meeting," They both laughed at Hube's alarm. Suddenly grave, Matt asked, "Could he have slaves on board?"

"Surely not . . . they couldn't be that stupid." They looked at each other, and then Rex added, "Maybe you'd better check. I'll go find Amy."

Frau Walker and her son had boarded the Mischief to get another full case of the bagged, salted winter-sloe nuts for her inventory. After Billy had carried the case of nuts home for his mother, he returned to the Mischief for twenty more bags of nuts.

Amy knew Rex had hired the boy to pass out free samples in the wharf and market area to visiting river men. She got a screwdriver and opened a new case. The brass lid screws went into her vest pocket.

"Billy, when you're finished with handing out the free samples, tell me, and I'll reattach the lid."

Amy then jumped down on the wharf and walked out to inspect the Orleans Queen, before she headed over to Lily's apartment. She sighed, remembering her fears the day she had disembarked from that riverboat at Panther Creek with Herr Wright. Instead of perishing, she had had one adventure after another.

One thing hadn't changed, though: the Orleans Queen still had that evil aura. Purnell's steamboat did look in good repair and she wondered how her superheater was holding up. The boat's weakness was the undersized Focke-Wulf condenser and inadequate boiler-feed pump from the condenser. Being an engineer at heart, she couldn't help wondering how the crew was managing that problem.

Amy recognized the elderly man who was leaning on the stern rail smoking a small, clay pipe. He was Herr Nickels, father of the Orleans Boatyard's engineer, John Nickels. He must be running the boiler and engine room. They had known each other since she was an annoying five-year-old running around the boat yard.

"Amy, is that you? I'm glad the reports of your death were nonsense," a smiling Herr Nickels yelled.

That Herr Nickels had recognized her surprised Amy. She had disguised her appearance a bit. The large black hat hid her raven locks and the blanket she'd wrapped around her waist made her look pudgy. She put her finger to her lip in the universal gesture for quiet and walked over to stand on the wharf directly below the engine room operator.

"Please, Herr Nickels, no shouting. I'm supposed to be incognito. How's your grandson doing, is he working on a boat?"

Amy and Herr Nickels talked for several minutes about family and friends they knew. She was pleased to learn her mother and sister were fine.

"She never believed those reports. I'll let your Mom know you're alive and well." He then talked about the boat. "That condensate pump is giving us fits, just as you predicted."

"It just too small for the volume of steam the condenser has to handle at full power. So what are you doing in order to move that volume of water?" Amy said. She rechecked the wharf area and relaxed when she saw none of Purnell's men had returned. Hokee had wandered off with Billy.

"I cobbled together a dump valve, and yeah, also run it way too fast to last."

"You're wasting the clean hot condensate water?" she asked.

"Well it's not clean water anymore," he said. "Don't give me that look. It's been a mad rush from Orleans. To maintain the power the captain demands, I've been forced to use muddy river water, even salt water."

"Well, you'd better take time to clean the superheater tubes before they're hopelessly plugged, or weakened by corrosion." Then, on second thought, why should she care if her nemesis's boat was ruined. "How long are they here for?"

"I figure several days. You want a tour of the engine and see the pump and valve I rigged up? There's no one around."

Rex went looking for Amy while Matt organized a search party to check the Orleans Queen for slaves. He needed to run to Panther Creek, pick up the rest of the burlap bags of raw nuts, and take them back to Suzie's crew for roasting and bagging. He figured Amy would want to go with him. He was surprised to see the Orleans Queen backing away from the dock.

"Where's Amy?" Rex shouted from the wharf to Captain Malik, who was in the Mischief's pilothouse working on the steam valve linkage.

"Last I saw her, she was talking to Orleans Queen's engine room chief. I thought she was with you."

Rex spied Billy at the end of the wharf and asked him.

"She was on the Orleans Queen. Why'd she leave? I need more bags of nuts," the boy said. Rex learned Amy had been talking to an old man about pumps and had entered the steamboat to see the pump. "She told me to wait, she'd be right back."

"How could such a smart person do such a . . . thing? Bring the pressure up while I tell Matt what happened," Rex ordered the Mischief's crew.

Matt, as was his wont, listened without interruption until Rex finished. "If only I'd been quicker," he said, as they watching the Orleans Queen disappear down the Erie. "Boss, don't be stupid, or you'll get Amy killed." He added, "Take John Baler and a half dozen of his men with the bolt-action rifles. They'll match anything you're likely to encounter on the Orleans Queen."

Rex wished Has Melas and Larry were here, instead of with the Cinnabar-Wu prisoner escort headed to Roanoke. Tom Jarrell had been delivering a barge of coal, and Rex yelled for him to grab his rifle and come. To his surprise, Captain Beck called to him as he headed to the Mischief.

"I heard what happened. Can I come along to observe and be a witness?" the Prussian officer asked.

"If you bring a rifle," he said. The Prussian Captain endeavored to explain his offer to help the Wapitis.

"I wanted to thank you for your quick thinking. It saved my career. If you hadn't pulled that revolver, I'd have had to try enforcing the colonel's ridiculous order, or face a court martial when I returned to Berlin. Also my men tell me the Orleans Queen has bounty hunter teams scattered down the Erie looking for escaped slaves."

"So it would be best to confront Purnell's gang before they can pick up any of those teams for reinforcement." Rex said. Beck nodded in agreement, as they jogged to the wharf.

"What happened in there? Captain Hube seemed to be in a panic," Malik said. "He told that Prussian Colonel to shut up and get aboard or find his own way to Delta."

"I was stupid," Rex said. "I threatened to have their vessel searched for slaves and didn't follow through."

"Obviously, they had some aboard."

And now they have Amy, Rex thought as he heard the captain yell at Kyle to bring up the steam pressure.

"The boat won't go far without stopping for fuel," Malik said. "According to the first mate, he had planned to run up to the Smithtown Coal Dock and fill the coal bunkers, while the captain and Prussians worked at salvaging whatever they were after from the Hendrick's wreckage. I don't think they have nearly enough fuel to reach Hickory Ridge."

Chapter 12

Amy was feeling that satisfaction one gets on seeing proof she was right and the experts were wrong. The Focke Wulf engineer had mocked her warning that their pump for moving the condensate water from the condenser outlet to the boiler was inadequate. The volume of condensate water at full power was twice the volume that the pump could move.

"You were right," Nickels said. "At half power, the condenser starts accumulating excessive liquid and increasing back pressure."

"The real threat is condensate water collecting in the low-pressure side piston cylinder. We all know water is incompressible." She looked about the empty engine room, and then added, "Show me your valve. I don't want to be here very long. Never know when one of Purnell's thugs might return."

"I understand. Stand over here, by the condenser and you can see how I rigged up that trip valve in place of the drain port plug?"

The old man got painfully on his knees beside Amy who was looking under the condenser. He pointed out a small brass contraption of two levers, springs and a dashpot-cylinder.

"It allows running the boiler at full power by wasting the clean boiler feed water that the pump can't return," he said, and with a groan got back on his feet, before adding, "Higher back pressure

263

activates the dashpot and it opens a ball valve to dump the excess condensate."

"That's a fragile looking arrangement to survive the shaking and vibrations," Amy commented. She couldn't resist testing it and she lay down on her belly to crawl further under the machinery to reach the lever. She gently moved the upper lever with her finger, and a small spurt of steam and hot water spit out of the ball valve port.

"Ouch," Amy said, holding her bleeding finger to her mouth. "That brace has a jagged edge." She backed out from under the condenser, nursing her finger.

"Sorry, I used a chisel to cut the brace from a scrap piece of plate. I haven't had a chance to grind off the edges. I was afraid to chance the pump being unsupported. It vibrates, along with being noisy. Otherwise the pump and valve works fine."

"Why didn't your son replace it with the correct size pump?" It's plain as day, it's too small. It can't be easy to keep those flows synchronized."

"Not enough time. Everyone was in a hurry to beat the Prussian navy to the wreck. And you're right. At full power, I'm constantly adjusting the makeup water to prevent overfilling the boiler." Seeing Amy's dubious look as she stood up, the engine room foreman added, "I know, but I have to do something when the captain is yelling for more steam. I use that pump by the ash pit for the makeup water to replace the dumped condensate. I can't let the boiler go dry."

They both heard people shouting and running on the deck. A man yelled for Nickels to fire up the boiler. Several laborers rushed into the boiler room and started shoveling coal into the firebox. Unfortunately, for Amy, the first mate was Herr Saad, one of those experienced, no-nonsense Phoenician men upon whom ship owners and captains depend to control crews.

Amy had encountered the wiry black-haired man around the Orleans boatyard several times over the years and knew his oldest daughter. It was no secret that he thought a young woman working in a machine shop and on boats was disreputable conduct. However, the man had always been polite toward Amy and her mother. Still, she didn't really know him and the fact that he was working for a gang of slavers stopped her from greeting him.

"Hunker down behind the condenser," Nickels whispered, as they watched Saad, whose attention was on the firemen feeding the boiler. She decided to hide until the doorway was clear. The first mate yelled something to someone on the exterior walkway, and then, to her disappointment, he stayed in the only exit from the engine room to watch. The man obviously wanted to be sure that the crew was responding with sufficient dispatch to his orders for steam. The condenser hid her from the first mate's view as long as he stayed at the door.

"Wait for him to leave," Nickels whispered. "Pretend you're working on the pump. I have to organize the crew, open dampers and fire up the boiler. You escape the moment the door is clear."

The boiler still had some pressure and a bed of hot embers in the firebox. Amy knew that in a few minutes it would reach sufficient pressure to power the paddle wheel. The hiss of steam and clank of the paddle wheel linkage moving alerted her that the captain was going to chance the river current at low steam pressure, and she felt the boat move backward.

Still, the first mate blocked Amy's escape and he shouted at Nickels, wanting to know why one laborer wasn't shoveling coal from the rear bunker, and he pointed toward the condenser.

"He's working on that damn piece of junk Focke-Wulf calls a pump so we can get full power," Nickels said. "Tell the captain we're low on coal, we need more coal."

"He knows that, old man. You worry about getting him enough power to make the turn into the Erie, and I'll worry about the coal."

The first mate walked over for a better look at the pump. Amy tripped open the drain port, which hissed as it spit a bit of hot water and steam into the drain, causing him to back away from the condenser.

"Hurry up, pal, and get that leak stopped, or we'll all hang as slavers."

Amy chanced a deep "Yes, sir." Satisfied, the first mate turned back and went to the coal bunkers where Amy could hear him confer with Nickels on the dismal state of their coal inventory.

Saad's comment about hanging as slavers puzzled her, as she realized her hat was too big and out of place for the confined spaces in the engine room. Sure enough, the wide-brimmed black hat had attracted the attention of one of the laborers shoveling coal into the boiler's firebox. He was the youngest one, a thin Clovis man wearing a bead-decorated headband and not much else. Amy figured he was likely looking for an excuse to quit shoveling coal. He walked toward her as she stood to bolt for the door.

"Why aren't you shoveling? What are you working on?" he asked. She ignored him and shoved her way past him. He grabbed her hat and her hair fell down. After a moment of silence, the laborer shouted, "There's a girl in here!"

It attracted everyone's attention, including the first mate, who was in the far coalbunker. Amy grabbed the small, pointed spud bar lying by the condenser, and whacked the inquisitive laborer in his leg with the iron bar, knocking him out of her way. She bolted for the exit and ran straight into a fat Prussian colonel, who grabbed her arm before she could clear the railing to jump into the river. She had left her revolver on the Mischief. The Colonel was hollering for help and had grabbed her hair for a better grip.

"Let go, you fool," Amy yelled. After a moment, when he hadn't, she jabbed the pointed end of the spud bar into his ample belly and felt the point penetrate. A moment later, the Prussian screamed in pain and flung her against the wall of the engine room. Dazed, she stumbled and fell back through the open engine room door just as two of the coal-shoveling laborers arrived ahead of the first mate to grab her.

The blood, moans, profanities and threats from the fat Prussian flopping on the walkway added to the confusion. Someone in the pilothouse was yelling down at them for more steam, while the colonel was struggling to pull his revolver from its holster, presumably to shoot her. The uproar distracted the first mate from recognizing her as he turned his attention to preventing the Prussian colonel from shooting up the boat.

"Throw the damn prostitute in the slave holding pen. Tell those Jackson brothers to behave," the first mate said as he disarmed the colonel.

The holding pen, two horse stalls enclosed with a heavy iron mesh, contained two rough-looking, rawboned Prussian men and three Clovis women huddled in the corner.

"Saad said not to mess with her," the older laborer told the two thugs.

"Don't do it," Amy said. "I'm an engineer, ask Herr Nickels. You think those two are going to listen to you. They'll rape me." The laborers ignored her plea and shoved her into the pen, threw the door bolt, and rushed away.

"Take your pants off and we won't hurt you," said the ugly man with the nasty green-streaked teeth. Amy, thankful that in the confusion no one thought to search her, grabbed her boot knife.

The older man, missing most of his teeth, laughed at her. "Isn't that just like a whore, threatening her betters."

The two rapists approached her, forcing her back against the door. Amy knew she was doomed unless she managed to hurt the monsters enough to make them lose interest. The man with the missing front teeth grabbed for her knife while shoving her against the door.

Expecting the move, Amy managed to jerk her knife below his reaching hand and stab at his lower abdomen. Her knife sliced into the man, stopping him, but before she could recover, his cohort, the man with green teeth, smashed his fist into the side of her head. Instinct made her hold onto the knife handle as her world went dark. An ungodly scream was the last thing she heard.

The pain and the Clovis women screaming for help brought her awareness back. She was face down in a warm puddle of squishy stuff and she had to turn her head to the side to breathe. The foul odor and the jerking on her coveralls confused her for a moment. Then Amy realized one of the men was trying to tear her coveralls off.

Opening her eyes, she searched for the knife and saw her face had been against a loop of intestines that had spilled out of the man with missing teeth. He lay on the floor in front of her, curled up in a fetal position whimpering while feebly trying to gather up his entrails and stuff them back into his belly. The knife was within reach.

The rapist had spotted her movement and grabbed Amy's neck with both his hands, abandoning her coveralls for the moment. He started choking her while shoving her face back in the loop of intestines.

"Die, you bitch!" the man screamed. He jerked Amy's head back and slammed it hard against the intestines to emphasize her fate while thrusting his knee hard into her pelvic area. She was blacking out again and felt her grip on the knife weakening. She couldn't turn to strike at the beast. All the while, the man screamed in her ear. "Damn miserable whore . . ."

The gunshot was deafening.

The sound of a gunshot and several women screaming startled a curse out of Saad who, as a rule, avoided blasphemy. The sounds of savagery from the holding pen reminded him that he should have listened to his wife. She had said that agreeing to be the Orleans Queen's first mate on the trip to River Point with that gang of criminals would prove a mistake, might even get him murdered. And his wife wasn't aware the trip was a cover for a slave raid.

He had learned this fact at Bone Valley saline works when the Orleans Queen had taken aboard fifteen men. They were rough, heavily armed thugs who worked for Apophis, a notorious Prussian slave catcher out of Delta. Saad had been surprised to see Apophis board with his men. Normally the man stayed at his plantation above Port Delta. The ten thousand D-mark reward for Purnell's escaped engineer probably accounted for the monster leaving his lair. The captain told him they were to recover property stolen from the Bone Valley saline works.

A good ship captain needed to be diplomatic, respectful of local cultures, and set an example of propriety and integrity for the crew. Saad had known when he agreed to the trip that those were not qualities usually associated with Captain Hube. The captain's acquiescence to Apophis's brutes seizing three Clovis women at Hickory Point market made him realize he was involved with an illegal, evil operation. He was disgusted that the residents of Hickory Point and the Ichneumon soldiers hadn't protest the seizure. He was no better, for he had just stood by, even though he suspected Apophis had no proof those women were escaped slaves from Bone Valley. The ogre had just picked out three women for his thugs' entertainment.

Curiosity about meeting the Wapitis had been Saad's excuse to his wife for agreeing to make the trip. He wanted to learn how a bunch of farmers had managed to boot the Ichneumon army out of their fort at River Point. That, along with the captain offering him twelve thousand D-marks to supervise the Orleans Queen's crew for a twenty-day commitment, had sold him on the job. The pay was about double the normal first mate rate on ocean voyages. The gunshot and screaming meant he was about to earn that extra pay.

"I thought you had disarmed that fat fool," the captain said. His concentration was on lining up the boat to enter the narrow band of deep water between an island and the Erie's east river bank. The low steam pressure wasn't turning the paddle wheel fast enough, and the boat was drifting with the faster current, instead of powering through the narrow chute.

"Go find out what's happening. And tell Nickels I want more steam pressure."

The one crewmember he thought acted as an adult, Herr Nickels, the engine room manager, had brought a whore into the engine room. That moron colonel, instead of just letting the woman jump off the ship and be rid of her, had grabbed her and gotten stabbed for his troubles. Now, from the sounds, the slave pen was in an uproar. And worse, someone had a gun.

Pulling his revolver, Saad checked that all the cylinders were loaded, and then jogged to the lower deck and horse stalls. Several crewmembers had beaten him to the slave pen, where he found the door open. The Clovis women huddled in the corner, and a crying Herr Nickels helping the blood splattered whore to her feet. She was holding one of those wicked double edge daggers that witches seemed to favor. One of the Jackson brothers lay whimpering on the cell floor disemboweled. Her handiwork he wondered.

Saad walked over and shot the man in the head. The shot stilled the room, and he checked the other brother who was spread-eagled face down on the floor in a pool of blood. He was dead, the top of his skull ripped open.

"Get back to your posts." In a moment, between the gunshot and his order, the hallway cleared of onlookers. As the last of the spectators hurried away, he asked what had happened.

"What do you think happened? How could you throw her in with these rapists?" The engine room manager looked distraught and flustered. "We're all evil, deserve to die. We allowed those men to terrorize and rape the women for the last three days and did nothing. We're as evil as those animals."

Nickels kicked the brother with the shattered skull for emphasis. The agitated man held an old-style cap and ball revolver. It had Saad nervous as the old man glared at him. "How could you throw your daughter's friend in here?"

"She tried to kill the colonel. Wait. What do you mean?"

The engine room manager was right about the Clovis women; he shouldn't have allowed that. He was as bad as Hube in treating the women like sub-humans, and he hoped his family never learned of his involvement. He looked again at the prostitute. Her swollen nose appeared broken. Under the blood and dirt, she might be pretty, but he didn't recognize her.

"Who is she?"

"Amy Caroom. I swear I'll kill you if you turn her over to Hube," Nickels said. The engine room manager now had the revolver pointed at him. The girl still seemed a bit dazed, standing there bare footed in tattered blood smeared coveralls.

"Amy, across the hall in that room is a sink and bath. Go clean the blood off. I'll find something for you to wear."

Saad kept quiet. The engine room manager appeared to be daring him to counter the order.

The woman skirted around him as he studied her. She picked up her boots and then moved quickly across the hallway to the room and closed the door. The girl could be the one whom Purnell was after. For sure, Nickels thought she was the Caroom girl. Regardless, he needed the man back in the engine room and this mess cleaned up.

"I promise she'll be released unharmed. Now quit saying that name before one of the crew hears you. If you had told me who she was from the beginning, we wouldn't be in this mess. Now make us some steam."

"Apophis's gang is working the west bank above Panther Creek. If those bounty hunters spot her onboard, she's doomed." The engine room manager looked worriedly around the hallway. "She needs to be gone before that, and we're not that far from the pickup point."

Saad nodded and then ordered the youngest woman to help the Caroom woman and the other two women to drag the Jackson brothers to the rail and shove them overboard. He returned to the pilothouse.

"What was that all about? Remember, I hired you to maintain order, among other duties."

"Apophis's drunks, the Jackson brothers, got in a fight over that whore." At least that was somewhat true. Now, thanks to Nickels and that foolish woman, he had to lie. "One of them went crazy and knifed his brother. He then assaulted the whore who will probably be dead before sunset. The guard shot him before he could kill the Clovis women."

"They're no loss. Where'd they get a knife?"

"From the whore, the fools didn't search her."

"Thankfully, Apophis and his men are just a few kilometers down river. I'll feel better stopping for firewood when they're aboard with their firepower."

Amy couldn't believe how fear had affected her judgment as she looked at the bloody, bedraggled stranger staring back from the tiny looking glass above the hand basin. She had blindly panicked when the laborer discovered she was a female, and she had bolted for the exit like a scared deer. She would have made it except for that damn Prussian colonel, though reflecting on it now, the icy cold water or early eels might have gotten her.

Her mind was still having difficulty catching up with the disastrous turn of events. To think, less than an hour ago she had kissed a man she liked and respected. Silly her, she'd even thought she had accomplished her goal of finally being free from Purnell. How fate could mock a person.

If she had had any inkling that Herr Nickels was involved with a slave operation, she would have had nothing to do with him and would not have set foot on the Orleans Queen. He or that first mate had prevented that terrifying man from raping her. For that belated bit of decency, she felt some gratitude, though the truth be known, maybe they feared those thugs would try to claim the reward. She wouldn't put any depravity past this crew.

The thought that she had at least killed one of her assailants gave her some comfort as she assessed her future. Possibly, she had no future if the captain beheaded her for the reward.

Everything hurt, her painful battered neck was a throbbing mass of bruises, and her nose was broken or at least seriously traumatized. Her menstrual bleeding had started yesterday, adding to the mess. She had been on her way to find Lily Hopkins for some clean clothes when she made the dreadful decision to inspect Herr Nickels' condenser fix.

Amy was lost in contemplation, staring at her woebegone image in the tiny encrusted mirror, when the opening of the room door roused her. "Who are you?"

"The first mate sent me," the young Clovis maiden said. The girl's painful hobble and the blood dripping on the floor alarmed Amy.

"You're hurt, let me help you."

The girl's name was Sparrow, a member of Redfox's tribe. Sparrow's tale drove home the absolute evilness of this crew.

"Several of Apophis gang caught us at the market two days ago. No one would listen or help as they dragged us to the boat. They've done awful things to us."

"Who were those men?"

"Those were the Jackson brothers. Apophis will kill all of us now. The Jackson brothers were members of his gang from Port Delta. There're about a dozen of them. The brothers got drunk and Apophis left them behind. Both of them raped my aunts and me. I fear another assault will kill me."

She silently agreed with the girl's distressing assessment.

The door banging open startled them. Herr Nickels, looking uneasy, had kicked the door open. After handing her a bundle of clothes, he closed the door without speaking a word.

The bundle consisted of her boot knife, a clean, dark gray coverall, a long-sleeved pull-on shirt, and several clean cotton rags that the engine room workers used for cleaning parts and towels. Amy knew the normal procedure used on steamboats for cleaning oily rags was to soak the rags in hot lye soap water, rinse in hot water from the condenser drain, than hang the rags in the boiler room until dry.

The cotton rags had that well-used look acquired after a dozen washings and were likely the cleanest material she'd find for a bandage. Sparrow fashion a small plug of cotton rag to stop her bleeding. Amy cleaned herself and then helped the girl.

Shouting and the slowing of the boat alerted them that something had upset the crew's routine. Dare she hope it was Rex and the Mischief's crew? Or were her friends still unaware of what had happened?

Her boots were still wet from washing off the gore, but she pulled them on anyway, to finish her switch to clean attire. The men were on the starboard side of the boat, which meant whatever had the crew's attention was on the west bank of the Erie River. She opened the door and checked the hallway. There were no guards. Encouraged, she walked to the nearest starboard exit to see what had everyone's attention. The vibrations told her that the captain had reversed the paddlewheel to hold the boat against the river's current. Three men hanged from a large sycamore growing near the riverbank. Whoever had done the deed had gone to the trouble to make sure any boat passing by on the river would see the dead men.

A crewmember recognized one of the hanging men. "That's Lee," he said.

Like dogs that had killed their owner's chickens, the Orleans Queen's crew went quiet, sudden apprehensive. The lark of watching and even participating in the rape of defenseless women had lost its amusement. Retribution was now a real threat.

The captain resumed the voyage down the river. Most of the men ignored her, standing on the walkway, but not the two guards outside the pilothouse. The older one, the Ichneumon-looking man, nonchalantly pointed his rifle at her, silently daring her to try reaching the shore. Amy went back to the washroom. She wasn't going to abandon Sparrow and her aunts. Surely, Rex would come after her. There had to be some way to stop the boat and allow the Wapitis time to catch them.

Toward dusk, the first mate opened the door to the small room with the hand basin and told Sparrow to return to the cell across the hallway. After he had the Clovis woman locked up, he returned to the room and closed the door.

"Are you this woman?" the first mate asked, handing Amy a wrinkled reward poster.

"Yes," she figured he knew anyway. "We've met. I helped your daughter Heidi with her math a couple of years ago." She was tempted to ask him if his daughter knew he worked for slavers, but decided against it.

275

"I won't ask why a smart girl would voluntarily board a boat owned and operated by the man who put a ten thousand D-mark reward on her head. Instead, I'm asking for your cooperation. In about thirty minutes the captain is going to stop at an island for firewood and to pick up Apophis and his gang, or at least those who are still alive."

"Those men were part of this Apophis gang?"

"Apparently they were, but there are plenty of them left. There are about half dozen bounty hunters in the group we are stopping for, and another half dozen of them across from Panther Creek. The point is Apophis will board at the island when we stop for the hunters and firewood. If they find you, first they'll rape you, and then behead you."

"The captain can't control them? Sparrow will die if she's raped again."

"It's the way our world is. The strong survive, and the weak are consumed."

What a jerk, Amy thought, *does he have no sense of right and wrong?*

"Now come, Nickels thinks he can hide you from Apophis until we reach Hickory Ridge where he can sneak you over to the Wapitis' coal dock." The first mate reached for her arm while opening the door to check the hallway.

"No, protect all of us or none. Sparrow deserves better than this."

"Apophis will kill you for the reward after his gang has satisfied themselves."

"Maybe so, but Rex will avenge us," Amy said. The first mate studied her for a moment, and then, without warning, his hand grabbed her neck. As she struggled to reach her boot knife, her world went dark.

The turbulence from black eels feeding had attracted John Baler's attention, and he quickly realized there were two bodies floating in the river. John's shout brought Rex to the boat's rail to investigate.

The bullet wounds in the men's skulls meant they had died violently. The fact that sufficient flesh remained on their skeletons to float suggested the bodies hadn't been long in the river. For sure, the eels were in a feeding frenzy and in another few minutes, there would be nothing left of the bodies. The scene reinforced Rex's phobia about swimming in Erden's rivers.

"They had to have been from the Orleans Queen, as no other boats had passed the Mischief since River Point." John and the Mischief crew nodded. Rex ran up the stairs to the pilothouse.

"Kick it in the ass, captain. Back to full steam while there's still light to spot debris in the river. The bastards aren't far ahead and they're killing each other."

The little boat was fast. The river banks were racing by, the shadows lengthening as night approached. Rex stared into the dim surroundings wondering if he had any hope of saving Amy. Wait, he suddenly realized, those were bodies hanging from the sycamore tree on the west riverbank.

"Whoa, stop the boat," Rex yelled. "Those are men."

Captain Malik gave him an aggravated look, but complied by exercising care in stopping and reversing the paddles. Several minutes were lost backing up against the current to allow an inspection of the sycamore's ghastly decorations. The crows had discovered the bodies but had not yet rendered the faces unrecognizable. Still, none of the people aboard the boat knew the three hanged men.

"More slavers, I reckon," Rex said. The men gathered at the railing agreed. The hanging men had the same rawboned build and marauder appearance as the two dead men discovered earlier floating in the river. "Be nice to know who else is hunting the bastards."

Not knowing who was killing their enemy added to his apprehension for Amy's safe recovery. He had little faith in the belief that the enemy of your enemy is an ally. They could be another band of outlaws after the reward. And though he could care less if someone killed all of Purnell's men, he didn't want Amy shot by accident. The wooden walls of a steamboat would offered her little protection from gunfire if two gangs got in a gun battle.

"You want to put ashore?"

"No, back to full steam, rescuing Amy is our business. The crows can have the bastards."

Though Malik grumbled about all the unnecessary starting and stopping, the Mischief quickly resumed its pursuit of the Orleans Queen.

The western sky had been dark for an hour when the Mischief suddenly stopped, causing Rex to rush to the pilothouse. Ahead about five hundred meters, parked against the upper end of a three-island chain in the middle of the Erie, was the Orleans Queen. The distance and darkness interfered with determining why the Purnell boat had stopped, but obtaining firewood for the boiler was Malik's guess. Rex feared the slavers would spot the Mischief any moment and end his hope of surprising them.

"Captain, reverse and back it into that cove. I don't think the gang has spotted us."

Malik nodded and expertly backed the paddle wheeler into the cove. The Orleans Queen's crew had started several small fires on the island, to help the firewood crew see. A foolish move, for the fires would mess up their night vision and make them lit targets.

"Captain Hube's only stopped to get enough firewood to reach Panther Creek and buy, or more likely steal some coal. He'll not be there for long," the captain cautioned.

"What about Amy?" Tom asked the question on everyone's mind.

"I pray she's unharmed, but you know as well as I that if you were on the second deck with a Mauser rifle, you and a couple of men could kill all of us before we could close the gap. Their crew saw those hanged men and will be jumpy and on guard. Then there's the question of where on that boat Amy might be. Those upper walls won't stop a bullet, so we might kill her while we're trying to save her."

"Don't forget Colonel Maxim," Captain Beck said.

"Good point, that's another reason we need to be careful, same with using the cannon. With one shot, we could take out their boiler, but that might cause an explosion. Instead, I want several of us to jog down the riverbank until we're across from the boat. From there, we can take out the firewood crew in a few seconds. Just be careful not to shoot anyone on the walkways where the bullet could pass into a room."

"I'll bet the captain will run on the first shot," Captain Malik said. "He'll forget firewood, and chance not running out of steam before Panther Creek."

"Maybe he will, but he'll run with a hell of a lot fewer crew members. John, you need to stay with the Mischief. Make sure whoever hanged those men doesn't ambush the boat while we're down the river making Hube's life miserable. Malik, wait for the Orleans Queen to get underway before coming to pick us up off the river bank."

Once ashore, Rex reminded the men of what they needed to do. No talking, no smoking, maintaining their spacing between the man in front and the man behind, no bunching up. The area they had to traverse was the river's floodplain. It offered endless opportunities for any hostile bounty hunters in the area to hide and ambush them.

Rex was counting on Hokee, the ruggedness of the area, and surprise to protect them.

Snarls of driftwood wedged against trees interlaced with enormous grape vines prevented them from traveling in a straight line, though a few reasonably brush-cleared sandbars helped them make up for lost time. Still, a pinched off section of river channel formed a daunting moat, and crossing it in the dark delayed them.

Twenty minutes later, the soaked and muddy Wapiti force arrived across from the area where half a dozen men were sawing and splitting driftwood. Three small fires illuminated the work site. The Orleans Queen bow-ramp was down and two more men were carrying firewood on to the boat.

"Those two men with rifles silhouetted on the roof above the pilothouse are easy targets," Captain Beck said.

"The operation appears in the process of wrapping up," Tom said. "It's a long distance, at least two hundred meters; shouldn't we try to get closer?"

"Don't have time. Distance isn't the problem. It's the darkness. The rifle flash will blind us. At best, we'll be fortunate to make two aimed shots before the gang members find cover. Beck, Tom, assign each of your men a target. I don't want them shooting at the same man."

"Mind if I put a couple of shots into the pilot house?" Captain Beck asked.

"I doubt Amy's in there, but your colonel might be, so it's your call. But your first shot should be the front guard on the roof." Rex then verified each of the men had a target. As his target, he picked the man on the bow who was shouting at the woodcutters to wrap it up.

The blow nearly knocked the first mate off the gangway and into the water. His butt felt ripped apart. The sound of gunfire reverberating across the water answered his question of what had hit him, a sniper's bullet. He needed to get out of the gunman's sight and desperately crawled to the edge of the gangway where he dropped onto the Orleans Queen's deck. The pain nearly knocked him out as splinters ripped from the gangway planks by another bullet rained down on him.

The gangway offered him limited protection from the sniper on the opposite shore. The pain was intense, but thankfully, his legs worked. Trying to resolve where to find protection, Saad looked down the deck on the starboard side of the boat. One of Apophis's men was poking at the body of one of the Ichneumon guards he'd posted on top of the pilothouse, probably searching the body for valuables, rather than offering aid. None of the five woodcutters on the island had run back to the boat, and the two he could see appeared to be dead.

The gunfire from the opposite shore had stopped. Gun smoke and darkness was probably interfering with the snipers' vision. They needed to take advantage of the very brief lull. Instead, the boat remained stationary, though a few of Apophis's men were firing blindly at the opposite shore.

Saad crawled along the starboard side of the boat where its superstructure offered some shelter from the snipers on the east bank. He could hear Apophis in the engine room yelling at Nickels to get the boat moving.

Where was Hube? The first mate crawled to the stairway to the pilothouse, then dragged himself up the stairs, and found the answer. The captain was dead. Several bullets had hit him in the back and head.

Steeling himself against the pain, the first mate stood up to read the steam pressure gauge. The pressure was in the red. The gauge was obviously broken. Saad's legs threaten to give out before he finally managed to force the reverse drive linkage to engage the paddlewheel. He felt the satisfying thump of the linkage engage and saw the boat creep away from the island. A frantic Apophis busted into the pilothouse.

"Who are those bastards? Where's that worthless Hube?" The slaver saw the captain's bloody body and broken glass. "Damn those sons of bitches. Do you know how to run this? We have to get out of here."

The monster studied the corpse for a moment before reaching down and turning the skull to expose the wound.

"Why waste good food," Apophis said, pinching off a piece of brain matter exposed in the shattered skull and tasted it.

"You're not . . ." Saad started. He'd heard Apophis wasn't right in the head. Anyone who ate human flesh, raw brain matter, no less, as if it was a piece of jerky, had to be insane. Then he remembered the ogre's question. Not wanting further to upset an insane killer, he said.

"I know how to run it. You need to raise the gangway, or when the boat starts down river, it'll drag. If it breaks off, it might jam the paddlewheel. Then we're really sitting targets come dawn."

Apophis appeared ready to argue, but then three more bullets tore through the pilothouse. The slugs of lead missed them, showering them with pieces of the pilothouse wall, and galvanizing them into action. The freak raced back down the steps to the gangway winch and started to turn the crank rapidly while he disengaged the paddlewheel linkage to give him time to lift the walkway.

The slaver might be insane, but he was strong. The moment the tip of the gangway structure cleared the ground, he reengaged the reverse paddle linkage, opened the boiler steam valve to the engines, and backed away from the island. Another bullet tearing through the pilothouse reminded him that they had a ways to go before they were safe.

The engine room engineer and crew needed no motivation, judging from the sparks and smoke pouring out of the twin stacks. He chanced rising up to check the steam gage and saw the pressure was past the red. The boat had backed away from the island far enough to allow him to turn it into the river. Saad slammed shut the steam valve to stop the engines, so he could switch the paddle rotation to forward and escape.

Disoriented, Amy required a moment to remember the first mate grabbing her throat and then to realize that he had tied her hands and legs together. She was lying in the engine room, near the condenser. Strange men were coming and going with piles of firewood. The boat was stationary. Amy could hear Nickels telling the two firemen to feed the boiler's firebox. He said they would be leaving in a few minutes and the captain wanted at least a half million pascals of pressure.

Her hands were in front of her and she used her teeth to try loosening the knot on the leather strip binding her hands. She bit and pulled at the unyielding rawhide strip before remembering the boot knife. It wasn't there. Then Amy remembered the jagged pump brace. She flopped and wormed her way under the condenser to reach the pump used to recycle the condensate water. The condenser shell was now hot enough to burn. Avoiding contact with it added to her difficulties in reaching the sharp edge on the pump support brace.

The first gunshots and the noise of something heavy slamming onto the boat's deck by the engine room exit caused pandemonium among the men carrying firewood and feeding the boiler. Dare she hope it was Rex?

"Old man, get that fire going, the captain needs steam," one of the slavers yelled from the doorway. Two shots rang out. "If I see another one of you bastards not feeding the firebox, I'll kill you."

"The fire is hot enough. Tell the captain he has steam."

"You can tell him." The man talking, and Nickels, left the engine room.

Adding to Amy's misery, the heat from the condenser had her sweating. Salt was getting in her eyes. Half-blind, she shoved her bound arms ahead to find the brace. Several painful nicks and burns later, Amy managed to align the leather strap with the sharp edge and she started sawing.

The distant gunfire had stopped, replaced by shots from the upper deck. The moment the leather strap parted and her hands were free, she heard a clank. Someone was trying to engage the drive linkage. The distant gunfire started again as she finished freeing her legs. Whoever was doing the shooting, they apparently wanted to stop the Orleans Queen from escaping.

She eyed Nickels' trip valve. If she could jam that upper lever up, the valve would stay open regardless of the steam pressure. The open valve would dump all the water condensed from the steam-engine exhaust, not return it to the boiler for reheating into more steam. If the crew didn't discover the leaking valve before the boiler went dry, the operator would have to let the red-hot boiler cool before refilling with river water to prevent cracking the superheater tubes and a ruptured boiler.

There was nothing to tie the lever to, short of looping a string clear around the condenser shell. Even tying all the pieces of her leather bindings together wouldn't make a string near long enough for the job. A small screw in the lever's slot where the dashpot-cylinder cam pushed the lever would jam the trip valve.

When she had shed her filthy coveralls, she had remembered to clean out the pockets, so she still had the half dozen brass screws from the wood box, along with the tiny screwdriver. In a moment, she had one of the screws jammed into the slot, holding the drain valve about halfway open. Splashes from the hot water pouring out the valve scalded Amy's hand, but she made sure the screw was wedged tightly.

The faster the captain ran the steam engine, the quicker the boiler would run out of water. When the steam stopped, several angry killers would arrive to investigate the cause. Amy wanted to be gone before that. From the sounds, most of the crew was on the stern of the boat trading shots with the snipers. Her best chance for escaping was to jump in the river. No one was near the boiler, nor in the coalbunker. Nickels or one of the laborers had closed the dampers in the firebox to avoid over heating the boiler while there was no demand for steam.

She stole over to the ash pit and turned the valve on the boiler feed pump suction line to off. The pump would quickly self-destruct with no water. A quick glance through the firebox door's port showed her a massive hot coal bed ready to flare up when supplied with oxygen. Amy realized if she opened the dampers with the steam valve closed there was possibly enough fuel in the bed of coals to explode the boiler. That would be far more destructive to the boat, and happen faster, than waiting for the boiler to run out of water. In a moment, she had the dampers full open.

Amy then crept to the engine room door to check if the way was clear. With the only illumination from a quarter-moon and the crew's preoccupation with the snipers, no one should notice her in the river. A short jump and she'd be in the water, and then she remembered Sparrow.

A large man was at the bow struggling with the walkway winch. The paddlewheel started to turn as Amy studied the body on the walkway by the door into the slave cell. Time to act, she had to travel several meters toward the bow and cursing man at the winch to reach the hallway to the cell. A scream from above her preceded a body landing in front of her. The laborer who had discovered her and sounded the alarm lay twitching and bleeding on the walkway in front of the engine room door.

His Krupp rifle had landed beside him along with a small leather shoulder bag. Amy grabbed the rifle and worked the action, ejecting a fired shell. Hell, she thought, an empty rifle wasn't of much use, and she snatched up the leather bag, searching for a cartridge to load the rifle. A dozen cartridges were in the bag and she loaded the rifle and slung the bag's strap over her shoulder. She could hear the firebox roaring and knew she had only a little time left before the boiler exploded. The man on the bow had vanished, and she dashed to the cell.

"Sparrow, I'm going to shoot the lock," Amy said. The old brass padlock wasn't much, but whether the bullet would break it or just ricochet, she didn't know. Hoping for the best, she pulled the trigger. She looked up. The lock was gone, and with her ears ringing, she reloaded the rifle and opened the cell door.

"Let's move it; the boiler may explode at any moment," Amy yelled. The Clovis women seemed stunned, and Amy went in the cell to help them stand. "Go up the stairs and jump in the river, the bank is nearby. Sparrow, lead the way! Go!"

"What the hell is going on?" a man yelled from the door before Sparrow could reach it. He had a revolver. "Who opened the cell?"

Rex waited patiently for the Mischief to maneuver close enough to the riverbank to allow his men to board. Everyone was silent. Little of the Orleans Queen remained above water, except the paddlewheel assembly. Debris from the explosion had even landed among the Wapitis. The odds that anyone had survived were slim and among the prisoners in the holding pen, zero. If Amy had perished, he would hunt down every man involved in her death, including Benjamin Purnell.

The water was cold, but getting soaked while boarding would be unavoidable. Then Malik unexpectedly jammed the bow of the Mischief in the riverbank and everyone leaped aboard.

"Bless you, captain. Can you see any survivors?" Captain Malik shook his head. "Beck, I want you on the roof of the pilot house, watching for survivors. Shoot any that act hostile."

Maybe ten minutes had elapsed since the boiler explosion when the Mischief arrived at the wreckage site. The dark east horizon was lightening, dawn and a new day would soon be on them. The Mischief eased against the upper end of the island at the same sandy beach the Orleans Queen had just backed away from before the explosion. They made a quick search. Three bodies floated in the backwater by the island and six dead men lay among the abandoned tools and piles of firewood on the island. Thankfully, Amy Caroon wasn't one of the bodies.

"Watch out for the eels," Captain Beck cautioned.

Rex watched the bodies floating in the backwater and saw one disappear, and then resurface. The black eels were feeding, and that probably explained the lack of bodies floating around the wreckage site, though a lot of the boat debris had landed along the west riverbank.

"If there were any survivors, they'll be there."

Amy had chanced a shot by Sparrow's head and killed the man blocking their escape. Sparrow had frozen and Amy had to yelled, "Run Sparrow!"

In a moment, they were off the boat. Amy paused to look back for the man at the bow. He wasn't there, nor in sight, though the bow ramp was up and the boat was moving slowly backward up the river. The water was cold and went just over her head. The rifle made for awkward swimming, but within a few strokes, her feet felt the bottom. A moment later, she collided with one of the Clovis women, floating dead.

She looked back at the now-moving sternwheeler. There was a man on the upper walkway aiming a rifle at them, and he fired as she looked. His shot missed her, but whether it hit one of the other women, she didn't know. However, she now had a solid footing that allowed her to bring her rifle up and reload it. The man fired again and Amy heard the bullet hit near her. Had her firearm been a muzzleloader, it would have been useless, but the Krupp rifle used a waterproof metallic cartridge. She shot before he could reload.

"Hurry, the eels are here," Sparrow screamed. Then the boat had exploded.

The wave from the boiler explosion had thrown Amy and the black eel attached to her right boot onto the riverbank. Parts of the boat's structure and bodies rained down on them. The body nearest to her was Nickels who appeared intact, but dead. Something extremely heavy had crashed into the sandy shore spraying water and sand on her. Sparrow was sprawled on her back in a grapevine tangle, moaning. Leaves were falling from the shrapnel-ridden trees.

Amy still had the rifle and no broken bones. Cries and wailing in the darkness meant some of the crew and Apophis's gang might have survived. She got carefully to her knees, ejected the fired case, looked through the barrel toward the east horizon to verify the barrel was unobstructed, and reloaded the rifle. The black eel from her boot was wiggling toward the river. She thought about smashing its head, but thought *why bother*, what difference will one less eel make in that river.

Sparrow was in terrible pain with a broken arm. The surviving Clovis woman guarded her. "Who is shooting at the boat?" the woman asked.

"I hope they're Wapitis, but we'll know shortly. There's a steamboat out on the river. No talking, the slavers may have survived."

It was still too dark to see far, and she sat down with a tree to her back where she could see Sparrow and the river. A few minutes passed, and then she heard voices. Men, they had to be slavers, speaking quietly.

"We need to run before those bastards get here," one unseen man said. They had heard the steamboat.

"I want to check, see if the safe fell out of the water," a different slaver said. "Look, here's Nickels." Now Amy could see the Mischief about a hundred meters down the Erie River, but not the men she heard speaking.

"Damn, they're putting out boats. I'd hoped they would jump in with the eels. Wait, there's someone over there," the first slaver said. He was fast and on the Clovis women in a flash. "Get up, bitch."

Amy, remembering her experience with the slink, fished out another cartridge to have ready for a fast reload of her rifle. She had an easy shot, but there were two men. The man did something that made Sparrow scream in pain. Amy shot the man in the back.

Her shot precipitated a volley of rifle fire from the Mischief at her. Bark and pieces of rocks were flying about. The hefty sycamore saved her. The girl just stood out in the open while Amy crawled tighter down against the ground and tree. She realized the marksmen on the Mischief could apparently see well enough to tell Sparrow from the slavers and knew not to shoot her.

That left the partner of the man that Amy had just shot lurking nearby. Where had he disappeared?

"Stop shooting!" Rex yelled. "Tom, when you reach the bank, I want you to go inland about hundred meters, before sweeping up river. I'll row up river to where most of the debris landed and inspect the area along the riverbank. I don't want them escaping."

All the eel activity around the wreckage chilled Rex. He wondered if he'd ever discover what happened to Amy. Hokee was anxious to reach land, but with the swirling eels around the boat, he kept a tight grip on the wolf's collar.

"Beach the boat, John," A moment later, he and Hokee were on the river shore. The wolf vanished into the underbrush and Rex with his revolver, cautiously walked into the woods.

"Be careful, there's a slaver in front of you," Amy yelled. *She'd survived*, he thought. He nearly threw caution to the wind, but years of training kicked in.

"Is Hokee with you?" He asked, taking shelter by a willow tree. A snarl, a shot, and scream from a jam of flood debris against several trees about thirty meters upriver from his willow tree answered his question. He arrived as a man was slashing at Hokee with a knife. The wolf had ahold of the man's arm with the knife. Rex shot the man.

John arrived, and Amy a moment later. "Take over, John." He garbed Amy and hugged her as other Wapitis arrived to help.

"Oh God, I thought I'd lost you for sure when the boat exploded." Those words were inadequate to express what he really felt for this woman. Amy appeared equally at a loss for words, she just hugged him as the sunlight spilled into the valley.

Epilog

Daylight allowed the Wapitis to conduct a thorough search of the riverbank, island, and Orleans Queen's wreckage. They found several bodies, and those of Herr Nickels and Colonel Maxim. Only the first mate, Herr Saad had survived, though dreadfully wounded. Bodies that had fallen in the river, the eels had reduced to raw skeletons and were unidentifiable, which made determining who had died, and who had escaped, impossible. Tracks indicated three men had fled to the west, but whether one of them was Apophis, couldn't be determined. Their trail was lost within a kilometer.

The men wanted to organize a posse to hunt the survivors of Apophis's slave hunting gang, but Rex vetoed the idea. Amy and the rescued Clovis women needed medical help and winter was about on the area. If the Mischief didn't leave in the next week or two, the Erie River might freeze and block river travel until spring. Financial ruin, or worst, threatened Rex and a large number of Wapiti families, if he failed to deliver this year's winter-sloe nut crop to Port Delta.

During the return trip to River Point, Rex learned Amy wanted his help in obtaining the metal working equipment that Purnell had promised her. Rex told her to forget the idea. No way was he risking her, the Wapiti's money from the winter-sloe sale, or their only steamboat to make a perilous attempt to abscond with junk machinery and pieces of rusty iron. Making the unavoidable and hazardous trip to the Ichneumon's Port Delta to deliver the winter-sloe order was risky enough. To then venture another five hundred kilometer across the unfriendly and storm tossed Gulf waters to Orleans and into Purnell's stronghold was suicidal. Besides, he reminded Amy, there was the not trivial matter of the ten thousand D-mark reward for her, dead or alive.

Fine, Amy had grumbled. She would find another partner.

Rex's adventures continue in <u>THE ORLEANS RAID</u>.